I WANTED TO FEEL HIS MOUTH UPON MINE...

I had no thought of tomorrow, only of here and now as my hands, fingers tensed and spread wide, slid up to my Gypsy cousin's face and wantonly, impetuously, I drew him to me, heedless of the consequences of my brazen actions. I had just brushed his lips with mine when he dragged his mouth away and caught my wrists so roughly that I felt certain I would have bruises upon them in the morning. His breath came raggedly, and his eyes were dark and opaque as he gazed at me with sudden, naked hunger, so I knew my desire for him was plain upon my face.

"I'll not be teased, Maggie—not by you," he warned me, his voice low and harsh. "So be sure—be very sure—that this is what you want."

"It is. Oh, yes, it is! Hold me, Draco! Love me! Please," I begged. "Please, I need you so."

Draco groaned low in his throat as his lips swooped down to capture mine again and again, as though he could not get enough of me. His teeth grazed the tender flesh of my lower lip so I tasted blood upon it, and a thrill of pleasure and pain I had never before felt shot through me, arousing and exciting me, filling me with violent longing...

To my everlasting shame, I allowed him to spread his greatcoat beneath us and to press me down upon its purple folds.

* * * * *

"ONE OF THE TEN BEST AUTHORS IN HISTORICAL ROMANCE FICTION."
—*Barbra Critiques*

Also by Rebecca Brandewyne

And Gold Was Ours
Desire in Disguise
Forever My Love
Love, Cherish Me
No Gentle Love
The Outlaw Hearts
Rose of Rapture

Published by
WARNER BOOKS

UPON A MOON-DARK MOOR

Rebecca Brandewyne

WARNER BOOKS

A Warner Communications Company

For Lisa, Rob, Jessica, and Trey.
With love.

The Family Tree

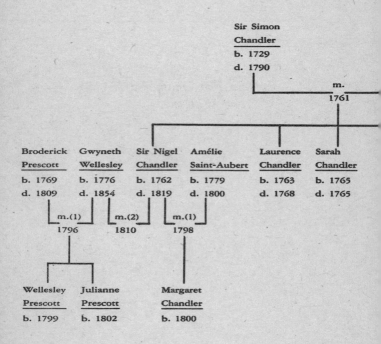

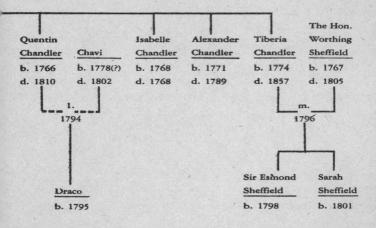

Margaret
Darnley
b. 1743
d. 1798

Quentin
Chandler
b. 1766
d. 1810

Chavi
b. 1778(?)
d. 1802

Isabelle
Chandler
b. 1768
d. 1768

Alexander
Chandler
b. 1771
d. 1789

Tiberia
Chandler
b. 1774
d. 1857

The Hon.
Worthing
Sheffield
b. 1767
d. 1805

l.
1794

m.
1796

Draco
b. 1795

Sir Esmond
Sheffield
b. 1798

Sarah
Sheffield
b. 1801

Contents

Upon a Moon-Dark Moor

Age doth bring wisdom
And regrets, they say,
And memories, pale, unbidden;
Yet how wondrous sharp and clear,
I see those shadows of my past,
Those images that once were dear—
In twilight dim, I think . . .

And I remember that certain summer
And then a spring so bittersweet,
When the way of it had gone awry
And blind kismet, I ran to meet.

Ah, the follies of youth!
I can but weep—and wonder
What perverse little imp of portent
Kept sleep from me that night?
Set my feet upon a moon-dark moor
Bathed in pale starlight?
I swear I do not know.

'Twas some fairy bent on mischief
Did entice me from my bed,
Or mayhap a piquant, changeling child,
My hushed footsteps led.

Oh, spiteful creature!
Heartless rogue!
Had you no regard for innocence,
No pity for my plight,
That you pierced me with your
        wretched barbs

That wicked, wild spring night?
And still were not content;

For I had no chance to flee, had I?
To escape the fate you planned with
            glee?
To elude that rakish nemesis
You had waiting there for me?

Oh, ill-gotten sprite of jest!
You vile and hateful thing!
You loosed him on me in cruel delight—
That bold cohort of your deed.
Like a raging storm, you swept our lives
To the winds and, without heed,
Scattered hopes and hearts like ashes. . . .

'Twas madness! Madness, wild and
            savage,
Which sought me in that place,
Foul witness to my wanton fall,
Mocking bringer of disgrace.

And yet how glorious!
How splendid was my shame!
I cannot lie. Such brazen passion . . .
Oh, I blush when I recall
How eager my surrender
When love demanded all.
I've none but myself to blame.

Daring robber of my maidenhood,
Carnal thief of purity and youth,
Who stripped away my childishness
To expose a woman's naked truth—

Be damned to you!
You, who trod upon my dreams
And trampled all I e'er did cherish
Years ago; I've not forgotten,
For I'm haunted by sweet torment
Born of us, the misbegotten.
Still long have I loved you now.

Shadows of My Past
1898

Our acts our angels are, or good or ill,
Our fatal shadows that walk by us still.

—*An Honest Man's Fortune*
John Fletcher

Stormswept Heights, England, 1898

It is late—and yet I cannot sleep.

My thoughts, as always, keep slumber at bay, and
tonight they seem especially turbulent, though why this is
so, I cannot say. Perhaps it is the way the wind blows, high
and wild, as though to sweep all before it from its path, and
the manner in which the sea crashes against the massive
rocks of the crumbling cliffs along the shore, as though to
batter them to shards, that make me clutch my wrapper
more tightly about me and pace the floor, as I am often wont
to do. But I do not think so.

I am old, older than my years, too old to be frightened
by the ominous shrieking of the wind, the violent crack of
the lightning and thunder, the brutal slash of the rain upon
the moors—and still I am afraid. But it is not the storm I
fear. It is the madding memories that set my body trembling. With each rasping breath the tempest takes, they
come rushing to engulf me.

How they do haunt me even now, those shadows of my

past. I will them to be silent, but still they crowd in upon me, unbidden, unwelcome.

My solitary candle flutters in the draft, small and helpless before the gust that would extinguish it.

How like that flame I was once, I think.

And yet . . . was not much of what I suffered my own doing? In my heart, I know it is so, for I have none but myself to blame for the choices I made, the road I set my feet firmly upon in my youth and so was forced to travel, though there were many times when I would have retraced my steps—if only I could have done so.

Still, though there are those who would give much to be young again, I am not one of them. To be young is to be filled with passion and to run headlong toward folly—as I did once. Now my days are one much like another. But they are safe and comfortable, and that is what I long for as the close of my life draws nigh. How ironic it is, I think, that in the end, I should have, after all, what Julianne wanted above all else. Only the memories, with their sharp teeth and claws, tear at the edges of my security, and they come only in the darkness, like all wicked things. Tomorrow I will banish them. But tonight they prey upon my soul.

I am frozen now, listening, as though I can hear their muffled footsteps, their whispering voices—the hushed sounds of those long dead and buried, ghosts that live only in my mind.

On Sunday, I will go to the cemetery, as usual, and lay flowers upon the graves of those who were once so much a part of my life, who sleep now, as I do not. And I will think of the pattern we wove together, ill made and much mended, as life often is, fashioned by rough tailors and poor seamstresses with little enough light to guide their eyes and hands. But I do not complain. My stitches were as ragged as the rest, and if sometimes I lamented my lack of a sharper needle or stronger thread, in the end, the fault lay in the fabric that was mine. I was what I was, what we all were, and perhaps it was not within us to be other than that. I do not know.

I know only that the memories will not be silenced, not until I, too, lie among the rest. I am the last. When I am gone, there shall be none to speak of those days long past, those days that now, like a winter fire, have burned and died and are but ashes scattered upon a cold, empty hearth.

Well, then, I will speak of them—and be honest in the telling. But more than this, dear reader, I will not do, for I, who am so much a part of this story, am not fit to judge the right or the wrong of it. That is only for God to decide, and now, more than ever, as my bones grow brittle with age, do I pray He is indeed merciful and forgiving, for if He is not, I shall surely be damned for my sins, which are many.

Yet I do not fear death. I have seen too much in my time for that.

Let me go back to the beginning, then, back to that certain summer so long ago, for though I was born ten years earlier it was that certain summer when those whose lives were to intermingle so intricately, so irrevocably with my own came into my world.

BOOK ONE

That Certain Summer
1810–1815

Chapter One

My Father Takes a Wife

So sweet a face, such angel grace,
    In all that land had never been:
Cophetua sware a royal oath:
    'This beggar maid shall be my queen!'

—*The Beggar Maid*
    Alfred, Lord Tennyson

Highclyffe Hall, England, 1810

I shall never forget that certain summer, for it was then that my father, Sir Nigel Chandler, Bt., remarried—and that Draco came to live at Highclyffe Hall.

I remember it quite well, for I was ten years old at the time, old enough, certainly, to have made my own observations, so I do not now confuse my recollections with stories of my childhood that were told to me by Nanna, and others, and that I can not truly recall. But even had I been younger then, I should not have forgotten that certain summer, for it was to change my life drastically and must therefore be forever impressed upon my memory in sharp detail.

I was, too, an only child, and as such children often are, I was both precocious and curious. Early on, I had learned I must know all there was to know about what went on in our house. My father's moods were determined accordingly, and though all of us at the Hall were subject to

9

Sir Nigel's displeasure when things did not go well, I had to bear the brunt of his anger more often than anyone else. For this reason, I had become adept over the years at cleverly ferreting out every scrap of information possessed by those in our household, so I might know Sir Nigel's whereabouts and disposition every minute of each day.

It might seem unnatural to you that I, his only child, had such a fear of him that I would spy upon him like a skulking beast, when even in a rage, he had never struck me and, indeed, treated me far better than many of the rough men who worked our farms and mines behaved toward their own offspring. Nevertheless I had cause to be afraid, as you shall learn, and so I went to great lengths to keep out of his way.

In this, I was aided by the rest of our household, who felt sorry for me and thought me strange, though I often heard them mumble that naught else might be expected of me, I had been reared in so peculiar a fashion. Under the circumstances, the staff had decided among themselves, I ought to have been sent away to a boarding school, where my mind, which was bright, might have been properly channeled in those accomplishments best suited to a girl of my station. After all, our butler had once snidely remarked to our housekeeper after I had particularly annoyed him, the Bow Street Runners did not employ females, something I deemed scornfully a great stupidity, for I was certain they might have made good use of my detective talents.

It was just as well I was intelligent, for I was not a pretty girl—or so the staff commented pityingly when they thought I was not listening. I was tall for my age, and slender, with a wild mane of black hair that refused to be tamed, no matter how often Nanna brushed and plaited it. My black eyes were too large for my dark, thin face; my nose was not quite classic; my mouth was far too generous. My bones seemed to stick out so sharply all over my body that I appeared to be all angles, lacking the gentle curves that would come to me later in life.

Because of this, my clothes fitted me poorly, hanging on my frame, making me resemble, I thought, a scarecrow.

Miserably aware of the fact that I was a gawky girl, I tried to make myself as inconspicuous as possible by slouching and drawing my gangling limbs in as close to me as I could instead of standing up straight and proud as I should have done, and so my posture only accentuated my gracelessness.

Consequently I was a constant source of irritation to Sir Nigel. He could not once look at me except to find me painfully inadequate, and he often cursed my birth, which had taken my beautiful mother from him, with a fury that made my knees knock together uncontrollably. I—and I alone—was to blame for my mother's death, for if I had not been born, she would still be alive.

"Why couldn't it have been you who died?" my father would ask me sourly during his brandy-soaked stupors, as though I somehow knew the answer to this and he did not. "She was worth ten of you."

He would mumble this last over and over, as though trying to convince himself of it, though I thought it was only because he was drunk. Certainly I did not need to hear the words, for I would have been the first to proclaim their truth. Though I had never known her, still I loved my mother with all my heart, and I cherished the memory of her that had been given to me by others. Amélie Saint-Aubert Chandler had been her name, and she had been as fragile and ethereal as the pale mist that sometimes hangs low over the moors. Sir Nigel had met and married her in Paris and brought her home to Cornwall, to a place of greyness and dampness so different from the sunny French plains where she had lived most of her life.

Had my mother missed her own country? I often wondered. In all the portraits I have ever seen of her, her gentle smile is tinged with wistfulness and her luminous eyes are sad. I do not think she can have been a happy woman. But a woman of inner strength and quiet dignity, a woman of great value . . . yes, she had been that. My father would not have loved her otherwise; he would not have so despised me for taking her from him.

How terrible I felt, knowing my birth had been the cause of her death. I did not blame Sir Nigel for feeling as he did toward me, and I suffered his abuse as best I could, understanding, I thought, what prompted it. I was a constant, painful reminder to him of my mother, so the grievous wound his heart had been dealt at her death could never fully heal; and because he loved her so deeply, I, who loved her also, endured him for her sake.

Still it did not make me any less afraid of him, for often, especially when deep in his cups, he would stare at me fiercely, as though by sheer willpower alone, he could blot out my very existence. Thus, in his befuddled mind, he eradicated me and so somehow brought my mother to life again—or so I believed and wished only that he did not hate me quite so much.

How they terrified me, those occasions late at night when Nanna would rouse me from my bedchamber and I, dazed with sleep and frightened, shivering in my thin nightgown, my bare feet cold, would be ushered into my father's presence so he could torture us both with my being.

No wonder I eluded him whenever I could!

The only other times I saw him were on Friday afternoons, if he were home. Then he would call me into his study to pay out my allowance. He always made quite a ritual of this, taking the key from the gold chain hanging at his vest pocket and unlocking his top desk drawer to remove the small iron strongbox inside. From this, he counted out five shillings—no more, no less. After that, trying hard not to glance at my dead mother's portrait above the fireplace or to dwell on the nights when I quailed before his drunken wrath in this room, I would carefully sign my name in his receipt book to show that he had paid me.

Other than this, my father ignored me.

He was a very busy man, for Highclyffe Hall and the rest of his holdings composed a relatively large estate, and he took great pride in his inheritance.

The house was set in northern Cornwall, upon the wild, savage moors that stretched to the sea, cutting a stark, brutal line against the horizon, for the heaths here were barren of trees, although alders, birches, oaks, and ashes could be found in the deep, sheltered combes. A wood consisting in the main of ancient Cornish elms surrounded the manor itself. But their branches were sparse and pointed steeply upward before spreading into narrow crowns, so the elms seemed a part of the fierce sweep of the land as well, though other, less austere trees had been planted over the ages and helped to soften the harsh effect.

The Hall itself was old and fashioned in the shape of an E, for it had been built during the reign of Queen Elizabeth. It was constructed of Pentewan rock hewn from the cliffs near Mevagissey at Chapel Point and brought by wagons to the site where the house stood. Over the ages, the rough stone had weathered to a pale silver grey that reflected every nuance of light and shadow, giving the manor a forbidding appearance, especially at dusk, I thought.

It was three stories high, counting the attic. The main portion was topped by a flat, battlemented roof; the wings were capped with steep hip-and-valley roofs from which rose distinctive Tudor chimneys. Flanking the short, square, crenellated portico that jutted from the center at the front were two slender, hexagonal watchtowers that soared above the house itself. Ivy grew up the front wall, around the arch framing the massive oak doors, and halfway up the sides of the towers, making the Hall seem less stern and grim than it really was. Long, narrow casement windows with leaded, lozenge panes of fine Venetian glass overlooked a portion of the wood that, along with the beautiful multicolored gardens and sprawling verdant lawns surrounding the manor, formed the park. The gardens and lawns especially were all constantly and diligently cared for, lest the untamed moors beyond reclaim the stolen terrain, as I often fancied they wished to do.

Sometimes late at night, when I lay huddled in my bed with the covers pulled up close around me, the wind blowing in from the coast a few miles away would carry to my ears the sound of the roaring seas breaking against the distant cliffs—the long, gnarled, aged black fingers of rock that stretched like claws into the ocean—and I would imagine the earth crumbling before the onslaught of the waves, the Hall falling down into the sea, as some said the ancient lands of Lyonnesse and Ys, which had once lain beyond Cornwall, had tumbled into the ocean's depths. I would listen fearfully as the old house shuddered about me, straining and creaking as the wind whipped and whined and snarled its way around the manor, prying at the tightly shuttered windows, howling ominously when it could not get in; and I would wonder how the walls that encompassed me continued to withstand the ruthless, relentless elements.

The Hall was very much a place of isolation, for we had only one near neighbor. This was a farm, Pembroke Grange, some few miles to the northeast of us, which one of my ancestors, Sir John, had bought to increase the Chandler holdings. There my father's sole surviving sister, a widow, Tiberia Chandler Sheffield, lived with her two children, my cousins, Esmond and Sarah. To the southwest of us, there was another estate, Stormswept Heights, whose lighthouse had once prevented ships from wrecking upon the dangerous boulders below it. But the place had been deserted for many years now and had fallen into ruin. So I had few friends and little social life.

When my father was not occupied with the management of the estate, he went most often to London, leaving me behind. I did not mind this in the least; indeed I looked forward to his long absences, for no one except Nanna and Hugh, our head groom, paid any attention to me then, and I was free to come and go as I pleased.

I spent many a solitary hour upon the commons, with only my pony, Clothilde, in attendance, and I grew as wild and tempestuous as the land itself. Only Hugh and Nanna ever saw this side of me, however, for upon my reluctant return to the house, my nurse would make haste to change my grass-stained frock and replait my wind-tangled hair into two thick braids. From her ministrations and admonitions, I would emerge once again as the quiet and composed daughter of Sir Nigel Chandler, Bt., master of Highclyffe Hall.

Sometimes my cousin Sarah would accompany me on these expeditions, but this was not often. The Sheffields, being dependents, were poor as church mice, and Sarah must help in the house and with the sewing my aunt Tibby took in to help make ends meet, for my father was not overly generous with the funds he allotted the Grange. But sometimes Aunt Tibby would say, ''There, Sarah, you've done more than your share. I'll finish up the last of the lot this evening.'' Then, mounted upon Clothilde, Sarah and I would gallop over the moors, she hanging on tightly to my waist.

She was a year younger than I, smaller of frame and not so angular, taking after her father's side of the family, the Sheffields, with her dusky-brown curls, sparkling hazel eyes, retroussé nose, and rosebud mouth. She was as gentle and cheerful as a wren, laughing and chirping quietly as she fluttered from flower to flower upon the heaths, gathering sweet bouquets with which to brighten the Grange upon her return. Anyone who knew her must love her, for she was as pure and good as a saint.

Once in a great while, when he could get away from his studies, Sarah's brother, Esmond, would go with us. Like his sister, Esmond had soft brown hair and fine hazel eyes; his other features were handsome and regular. I often envied him his classically sculpted profile, so different from mine, I thought. He was a solemn, reserved boy with a maturity that belied his twelve years, for his father had been killed in a carriage accident some years before, and it had fallen to Esmond to undertake the responsibilities of the man of the family, Aunt Tibby not having remarried.

Indeed I often wondered how she had come to be wed in the first place; she was as meek and unassuming as a rabbit—and thus a sore trial to my father. Still she was harmless and meant well; and Sir Nigel, never being one to shirk his duties, had grudgingly allowed her, after the death of her husband, to move into the Grange, there being no money remaining in what little estate the Honorable Worthing Sheffield, who had never quite been able to manage, had left behind.

Aunt Tibby was always very kind to me, treating me like one of her own children; and when I was not upon the moors, I could be found most often in the drawing room at the Grange, chatting with her over a cup of tea or helping

Sarah with her chores. Except for Nanna, there, in that house, was the only love I knew.

It was not this alone that brought me there, however, for even had I not been welcome, I should have gone just the same. It was Esmond who drew me. I loved him even then.

How often I lingered in those four walls, hoping Mr. Trahern, Esmond's tutor, would release him early from his lessons that day so my cousin could be free to come to the drawing room to sit beside me. There, giving me his slow, thoughtful smile that always warmed me with its tender glow, he would ruffle my hair in his gentle, teasing fashion and say, "Ah, Maggie, what a scolding you shall get from Nanna, I fear, when you return home." And I . . . I would toss my wild mane of hair and laugh and boast that I did not care.

These occasions were infrequent, however, for Esmond studied hard in preparation for the time when he must go to school for the education that properly befitted a gentleman, Sir Nigel having presciently set aside a sum for this purpose.

Oh, how just the thought of Esmond's leaving tore at my heart! I did not know how I would bear our parting and was glad my father had insisted Esmond be older before entering school, his education having been shockingly neglected before he'd come to us, so he was far behind other boys his age.

When the thought of his future absence grew too painful for me to endure, I would slip quietly into the library, where he took his lessons. There I would sit silently in a corner, watching him as he applied himself to his studies, his brown locks curling softly over his forehead. Sometimes he would chance to look up and see me sitting there. Then old Mr. Trahern would gruffly clear his throat and, with his handkerchief, soberly wipe his silver-rimmed spectacles.

"Very well, Esmond," he would say. "That will be all for today."

Oh, what joy I knew upon hearing those words! For if

Sarah were still occupied, Esmond would be mine alone for the remainder of the afternoon.

We would go to the moors to talk and dream of the day when we would marry, for our betrothal had been arranged since my birth, I being Sir Nigel's only child and Esmond his heir. My father's only remaining brother, Quentin, a ne'er-do-well who was the black sheep of the family, had disappeared several years ago and had long been presumed dead.

I believe those were the only innocently happy days of my life. I was filled with immeasurable gladness at the expectation that I would someday be Lady Sheffield, mistress of Highclyffe Hall, and that Esmond would be my husband. With eager anticipation, I would listen to his plans for us and dare to hope he loved me as passionately as I, with all the fervor of a child's heart and mind, loved him.

"Perhaps I shall go into law or politics, Maggie," he would say, "and stand for Parliament—though I do so love life in the country. And when we are not in London for the Season, we shall retire to the Hall. Sarah will come to live with us, and we shall be always as we are now. Would you like that?"

"Oh, yes, Esmond, yes!" I would cry and clap my hands together like any silly child enraptured by a fairy tale—for what could a girl of ten truly know of love and life?

At my obvious delight, Esmond would smile and tell me more of his dreams, which gradually became my own.

And so my life passed until that certain summer when Sir Nigel came home from London, a bride on his arm and he himself looking ten years younger than when he'd gone away.

How strange to think that as a tiny pebble tossed into a pond causes ripples that reach to the water's farthest limits, so does a single instance in one's life change its entire course—as mine was to be irrevocably altered that day. I had no inkling of this then, however, for in the beginning, things were as usual. But I have since discovered that dreadful events often have their roots in ordinary beginnings, so what follows is made all the more terrible by contrast; and what was to come ultimately from that day was to bring me the greatest unhappiness I ever knew, as you shall learn.

But I get ahead of myself.

As I said, it was a day like any other. The weeks of rain had ceased; the sun shone, glorious in its radiance, upon the moors, and the wind whispered across the grass to the sea, where the gulls called raspingly to one another and soared like white arrows against the sweep of the azure sky.

Earlier Clothilde had plodded steadily through the heather and bracken that bloomed upon the commons and she had skirted without guidance the gorse that grew in thick clusters here and there. Thus, lost in thought, even I, the household detective, was totally unprepared for the sight that greeted me upon my return home.

How like my father, it was, not to send word to us that his days as a widower had ended, so we knew nothing at all of the matter until he stepped down from his carriage in front of the Hall, then turned to assist his bride from the coach. As she descended the carriage steps, I glimpsed a woman of average height and a well-proportioned figure attired in a smart traveling costume topped off by a plumed hat. Then, her feet planted firmly on the ground, my new stepmother glanced up for a moment, and I saw her clearly.

She was a beautiful woman, was Gwyneth Wellesley Prescott Chandler, with upswept blond hair and crystal blue eyes, a haughtily chiseled nose and thin, expertly painted lips. But there was no warmth to her beauty, only the cold, lofty arrogance of a marble statue. How different she was from my dead mother, who, even from her portraits, radiated warmth and life.

Swiftly Lady Chandler's glittering eyes took the measure of our house. An almost imperceptible nod of her exquisitely coiffed head and a quick, smug half-smile marked her approval, her triumph in seeing she had done very well for herself.

Although I did not then know it, Sir Nigel's bride was a fortune hunter. She had been married once before—to a sea captain and moderately successful merchant, Broderick

Prescott, who had gone down with one of his two ships just off the coast of India.

Captain Brodie, as I would soon learn Lady Chandler always called him, had had several years in which to apprise himself of his wife's true nature, and perceiving that she was both a spendthrift and a coveter, he had, before his last voyage, wisely tied up his limited estate in a trust fund for his two children. The bulk of these monies was to be his son's inheritance, the smaller portion his daughter's dowry. To Lady Chandler herself, Captain Brodie had allotted a monthly allowance to be drawn from the interest paid on the trust fund. As she had an additional source of income from a piece of property left to her by her grandmother, she'd been able to live comfortably, if not to luxurious excess.

Moderation, however, as Captain Brodie had foreseen, was not a word in Lady Chandler's vocabulary. She did not want to live comfortably; she wanted to live as royalty—or, at the very least, as the gentry did. And so, although none knew better than she how to squeeze every shilling from a pound (Captain Brodie having been possessed of an extremely frugal nature), she'd soon outspent her budget and was being dunned by her creditors.

When informed by her late husband's solicitors of her dire circumstances, however, Lady Chandler had not panicked. Instead she'd gone to one of the moneylenders who did business in the shadier streets of London, and for an exorbitant rate of interest, she'd borrowed an amount equal to her yearly income. Then before she could be arrested and thrown into Ludgate Prison for her debts, she'd paid the most pressing of her bills, decked herself out like a queen, and set about catching a rich husband. To her vast relief, her desperate gamble had paid off.

Sir Nigel had not, as Lady Chandler believed, been duped by her widowed-heiress charade. He was not a fool, and after she'd attracted his initial interest, he had had her thoroughly investigated. But instead of scorning her cunning, my father had admired her cleverness. Here was a woman with a backbone of steel and a mind sharp as a sword. She would not cower before him as others did, but would match him word for word and best him if she could. It was a challenge Sir Nigel could not refuse. Recognizing in the then Mrs. Gwyneth Prescott a kindred spirit, he had asked her to marry him.

Now, as I watched them from the window on the second-story landing of our house, he said something to her that I could not hear, but that must have been amusing, for Lady Chandler laughed brightly, a high, trilling sound that floated up like the clear tinkling of a bell to the open sash where I knelt spying on them. Then my father turned back to the coach to help her daughter, Julianne, alight.

Oh, what a vicious stab of jealousy and resentment pierced my heart at the sight of my new stepsister! At eight years of age, she was everything I was not: small and fragile, curved and graceful, with an array of fat blond sausage ringlets and wide blue eyes like saucers in her delicate face. Slyly Sir Nigel tweaked one flaxen curl peeping from beneath her pert, pretty bonnet—handsomer than any I had ever owned—and as she giggled, a childish echo of her mother's laugh, two tiny dimples flashed up at him from her china-doll face.

Then they were sweeping into the manor and my father was introducing them to Mrs. Seyton, our housekeeper.

Upon learning the identities of the two lovely interlopers Sir Nigel had brought to Highclyffe Hall, I saw and heard no more, for hot tears suddenly scalded my eyes, blinding me as I stumbled from the landing to my room. Hate welled up in my breast as I sobbed bitterly upon my pillow.

How could he? How could he? I raged silently, hurt and angry.

I thought with pain of my dead mother. Did she know of this betrayal?

I had not suffered long, however, when Nanna tapped upon my door to say I was wanted below. Hastily I splashed some water upon my face to soothe my red-rimmed eyes. Then slowly I followed my nurse down the dark, narrow corridor to the head of the stairs, which I descended alone, Nanna's quick hug doing little to ease my despair. From the hall, I turned into the short passage that led to the small drawing room. There, before its doors, I paused and drew a deep breath, my hands quivering momentarily on the twin brass oval knobs. Then at last I pushed open the portals and went in.

What a happy little picture they made, that trio that did not include me! Lady Chandler sat to one side of Sir Nigel on the sofa, pouring tea from our sterling-silver teapot into our best porcelain teacups, which were used only on special occasions. The china doll perched upon my father's lap, her blue eyes sparkling as she merrily regaled him with some amusing tale at which his own eyes twinkled appreciatively. It was she who observed me first, abruptly breaking off her lively story and staring at me curiously, as though she were inspecting some oddity at the zoo. Her mouth pouted slightly, and she would have spoken had not her mother flashed her a stern, warning glance that escaped Sir Nigel's notice.

"Ah, Margaret"—he beamed at me jovially, most unlike himself—"come in, come in." I closed the doors carefully, then sidled a little way into the room. "Well, hurry up, miss! Don't dawdle!" he continued on a sharper note. "Where are your manners? I've someone I want you to meet."

"Oh, Nigel, really," Lady Chandler drawled, a glimmer of indulgence softening her hard, selfish face briefly as she glanced at him from beneath half-closed lids. "The poor thing is only a child and probably not used to strangers." She stood and moved swiftly across the room to hug me, a gesture calculated to win my father's approval. "I am your new stepmama, dear." She enveloped me in her arms and a crush of heavy rose scent. "And this is your new stepsister, Julianne."

The china doll dropped me a very proper curtsy, then returned to sit upon Sir Nigel's knee, gazing at me with pretended, wide-eyed innocence as she snuggled again into the crook of his arm and gave me a sweetly condescending smile.

As it had earlier, shock washed over me, stark and unreal.

No! It's not true! Father, say it's not true! I wanted to scream.

But of course I did nothing of the sort. I made a curtsy that was all the more clumsy in light of Julianne's pretty dip and mumbled, "Welcome to Highclyffe Hall, Lady Chandler, Julianne," before seating myself gingerly on the edge of a rather hard, high-backed chair a short distance away from the little group. I felt very much out of place, as though I were an intruder in my own home.

My stepmother surveyed me critically in the somewhat strained silence that soon fell upon us all. She must have known even then that I, so young and so lacking my father's affection, posed no threat to her. Thus she did not fence verbally with me, carefully feeling her way, as she would have been forced to do with a rival. Instead she made her position—and thereby my own now—clear from the outset.

"Well"—she smiled that peculiar half-smile of hers—"so you are Margaret."

"Maggie, my lady," I corrected her politely. Only my father called me Margaret.

"Yes, of course." Lady Chandler nodded. "But you will soon be a young lady, and Margaret is more suited to your station." She smartly dismissed my preference, as though it were of no importance, as she was to do everything concerning me, as you shall learn. "How old are you, child?" she then asked me.

"Ten, my lady."

"My, you're big for your age. I would have guessed you fourteen at least." She raised her quizzing glass to scrutinize me more closely, then dropped the gold-rimmed lorgnette and shuddered ever so slightly, making me feel even more gauche and awkward. "Sit up straight, Margaret. Don't slouch. It's so unbecoming. And those clothes . . . simply dreadful. Really, Nigel, as you said, the girl will never be a beauty like Julianne—or even taking, for she is indeed plain. But surely there's no need for her to be such a ragamuffin either."

How those words pierced my being, as Lady Chandler must have known they would do, for they cruelly informed me that my father had described me to her as an unprepossessing drab sorely in need of the talents of a woman such as she.

"Why, the child looks like a street urchin," she went on ruthlessly, as though my case were even worse than she had been led to believe. "What would our friends say if they saw her? I don't know what you can have been thinking of all these years, darling," she playfully chided Sir Nigel, her lips pursed together with disapproval, "to have allowed Margaret to be seen in those—those . . . garments. However is the girl to make an impression or catch a husband when she looks like such a dowd? Lud!"

"Oh, you must have no fear for me on that account, my lady." I spoke up courteously once more, for I was not without pride and would have died rather than let this spiteful woman see how she had wounded me. "I am to marry my cousin Esmond, Father's heir. It has been arranged these many years past."

My stepmother seemed highly displeased by this remark.

"Don't be impertinent, Margaret," she stated coldly. "You are much too young to be thinking of such matters. Your father and I shall, of course, make an appropriate match for you when the time comes. Until then, you must diligently apply yourself to improving your appearance and manners, lest you mortify us all and repulse your prospective suitors."

"Yes, my lady," I replied, duly chastened but seething inside—and frightened, too.

Of course I was to wed Esmond, my beloved! How dare this woman insinuate that I might not?

"It is just as well your father married me, Margaret, so I may take you in hand as your own mother would have done had she lived," Lady Chandler went on. "Tomorrow morning, I will send for the dressmaker, and you, Margaret, shall have some new clothes. Won't that be nice?"

"If you say so, my lady," I intoned dully, for I wanted

nothing from this horrid creature who had hurt me and who so obviously intended to disrupt my quiet life.

She had no care for me—only for herself. Doubtless she resented my existence and wished to be rid of me. But as I was Sir Nigel's daughter, she must outwardly do her best for me, even if inwardly she despised me. It was not to her advantage to do otherwise, for socially she was beneath my father and must strive to gain acceptance among his peers and acquaintances alike. Shunting aside his only child would not be a mark in her favor, and as I have said, she was clever.

"Really!" Irritated, Lady Chandler started to fan herself vigorously, as though the summer heat had begun to melt her frozen veneer. "What an odd child you are, to be sure, Margaret. Run along now. You, too, Julianne. I'm certain that after you become better acquainted, you two girls will be the best of friends."

With that parting shot, she forgot us both and turned to Sir Nigel. With a slow, seductive smile that led me to believe she was not all marble and ice as I had at first thought (for I was indeed a precocious child, far advanced for my years), Lady Chandler laid her hand upon my father's knee.

Julianne stalked regally from the room, obviously used to her mother's high-handed dismissals. I shuffled along sulkily in her wake, now more than ever convinced I hated them both. Miserable, I closed the door, embarrassed as I caught a glimpse of Sir Nigel fumbling with the buttons on Lady Chandler's bodice.

Supper that evening was held at eight o'clock instead of the usual five, Lady Chandler being quite determined to begin her rise in society immediately and thus adhering to the fashionably late hours kept in London.

It was for me a very strained affair. I was not used to eating in the dining room, preferring to take my meals with

Nanna in the nursery instead. But my stepmother had insisted I come downstairs.

"Nonsense, Margaret." She'd overridden my protests coolly as she'd begun to make the first of the many changes she was to instigate in my life. "You are far too old for Nanna and the nursery. I cannot imagine why your father has not seen fit to engage a governess and an abigail for you. I shall certainly speak with him about the matter presently. In the meantime, when we are *en famille*, you will join us in the dining room for all your meals, starting this evening."

"Yes, my lady." I'd studied the toes of my shoes carefully, afraid of giving way to an outburst of temper if I did not.

Lady Chandler had glanced at me shrewdly.

"From now on, you will also refrain from addressing me as 'my lady' in that snide fashion, Margaret." She'd spoken sharply. "It is plain you are an inordinately rude and unruly child; and while I do not blame you for your want of conduct, since you have had no mother's hand to guide you, I intend to make it clear from the very beginning that I will not tolerate your frightful behavior. As your stepmama, it is my bounden duty to point out the error of your ways and to try to correct them so you will be a credit—rather than a detriment—to the Chandler name. Do you understand me, Margaret?"

"Yes, my... Stepmama."

So now I sat, stiff and uncomfortable beneath Lady Chandler's stern and disapproving eye, picking dejectedly at my food.

At any other time, I would have been delighted by the feast upon my plate, for we had no such scrumptious fâre as this in the nursery. Turtle soup, game hens stuffed with wild rice and mushrooms, roast beef drenched in burgundy, fish smothered with white sauce, steaming potatoes, glazed carrots, French green beans with slivered almonds, hot bread, pies and cakes, fresh fruit and cheese, and garden greens... the array seemed endless as one dish after another was served to us by the footmen or removed by the maids under the watchful eye of Iverleigh, our butler. Had I not been so unhappy and ill at ease, fearful of making a mistake with my silverware or committing some other unpardonable faux pas that would earn me Lady Chandler's displeasure, I believe I might have eaten everything in sight. As it was, I could manage no more than a choked mouthful here and there.

"The meal is excellent, Gwyneth," Sir Nigel commented. "Indeed I do not know how you accomplished it amid your unpacking and settling in."

"It is the obligation of a good wife to be able to manage such things, darling," she cooed in return, preening with satisfaction at my father's compliment. "You are much too important, Nigel, to waste your time bothering about trivial household matters."

"How right you are, my dear," he agreed as he sipped his wine. "In the morning, we must make arrangements to transfer some of those duties to you."

"As you wish," Lady Chandler purred, fairly itching to obtain control of the domestic side of Highclyffe Hall. "There are some other items of business I must discuss with you then as well. Shall we say nine o'clock in your study?"

"I knew we would deal very well together, Gwyneth." Sir Nigel nodded his approval before heartily attacking his burgundy beef. "Very well, indeed."

"Papa"—Julianne spoke up, startling me by addressing my father in the familiar and diminutive fashion I had never been permitted to use—"do you know when Wellesley is to arrive?"

"Why, within the fortnight, I believe. Is that not so, Gwyneth?" He looked to my stepmother for confirmation.

"Yes." She inclined her head in assent. "A week from Tuesday to be exact."

"Who is Wellesley?" I ventured to ask.

"Dear me. In all the excitement, I must have forgotten to mention him." Lady Chandler's laughter tinkled. "How remiss of me! Wellesley is my son, Margaret, your new stepbrother. I know you will be as pleased to welcome him to Highclyffe Hall as we will be."

"Yes, my . . . Stepmama," I dutifully responded.

But inwardly I groaned, angry and anguished at the thought of yet another Prescott invading my once solitary existence, and I cried myself to sleep that night.

The next morning, Lady Chandler met with Sir Nigel in his study. Afterward there followed a flurry of activity. My stepmother was given charge of the entire household, even the accounts, for it appeared, despite her many extravagances, that she had convinced my father of her ability to stretch a pound—and get her money's worth besides.

The first thing she did upon assuming the reins of management was to dismiss Nanna. I am quite ashamed to say I ignominiously wept and pleaded with Lady Chandler over this, to the point of falling upon the floor and groveling at her feet—all to no avail. My stepmother jerked me up impatiently and shook me roughly, giving me the tart side of her tongue in the process. For a moment, I was half afraid she would box my ears as well, but she did not.

Instead I was sent to my room in disgrace; and Nanna, who had been with me since my birth, was packed off within the hour, a month's wages in her pocket in lieu of notice. I could not bear to be parted from her without saying good-bye, however, and braving Lady Chandler's wrath, I dared to creep down the back stairs and slip outside to see my old nurse off.

"Here, lassie," she crooned when she saw me hiding in the shrubbery, her voice still tinged with the soft burr of the Scots, despite her more than twenty years in England, "dinna fash yerself aboot me. 'Tis many a long year since I ha'e seen the Highlands of my gelhood, and I be looking forward to going home. My sister has written me often enough, begging me to come live wie her, and in truth, she can use the help, the puir lass, what wie her husband scarce better than a sot and seven wee bairns a-tugging at her skirts."

"Oh, Nanna!" I cried. "I shall miss you so dreadfully!"

"And I, ye, lassie." She wiped her eyes, which were moist with tears. "Ne'er ye think otherwise. But, there. Ye'll soon be a bonnie young lady, in need of more than I can gi'e ye. Lady Chandler is right. My wee gel is growing up and doesna need her auld Nanna any longer. 'Tis time ye had a governess to teach ye and an abigail to attend ye, as Lady Chandler said. Ye maun write to me now, do ye ken?" she asked as she hugged me close.

"Of course, Nanna! Of course I will!"

"Well, guid-bye, lassie. God be wie ye."

"And you, Nanna."

I watched, grief-stricken, as my nurse's dear, bent figure trudged down the long, winding drive to the wrought-iron gates of Highclyffe Hall, for Lady Chandler had not even had the decency to provide my faithful Nanna with a coach—or even a wagon—and she had a five-mile walk to the nearest post.

After my nurse had gone, my stepmother wrote a notification to be mailed to London for insertion in the *Morning Chronicle*, advertising the position of governess at Highclyffe Hall and listing the qualifications for employment. Following this, much to her delight and astonishment, Linnet, one of the young housemaids, was promoted to serve as my abigail.

These matters thus disposed of, Lady Chandler then sent a note to Launceston, the nearest town of any size, requesting the dressmaker, Mrs. Faversham, to wait upon her that morning if it were convenient.

In due time, Mrs. Faversham arrived, out of breath and all aflutter at having been summoned to Highclyffe Hall. She had never before had the privilege of catering to the manor, for in the past, the bolts of cloth for my garments had been bought twice a year from whatever peddler happened to be present when my father remembered me. My dresses themselves had been cut and sewn by Nanna, whose idea of fashionable had been "plain and serviceable"—God bless her, for it was all she had ever known, and she'd done her best for me.

The likes of Mrs. Faversham's skills were, of course,

beneath Lady Chandler, whose exquisite gowns came from Bond Street and Oxford Street in London (France being at war with England, and dresses from Paris thus being hard to obtain). But the seamstress from Launceston was considered good enough for me—and, indeed, for Julianne as well, who was also to have a few new frocks.

And so, I now being released from the punishing confines of my room, my transgression of sneaking out earlier having gone undiscovered, Julianne and I were summoned to the morning room to be outfitted by Mrs. Faversham.

I would not be honest if I said I felt no twinge of excitement as I pored over the designs in her fashion books and gingerly fingered scraps of material finer than any I had ever known. I was, in truth, elated; and though I had no hope of being allowed any voice in the choosing of fabrics for me, it was nice to dream and helped to take away some of the pain of Nanna's departure.

My dear nurse. How soon I forgot her as the morning wore on, for never had I owned the likes of what was now displayed before me by Mrs. Faversham.

She was a peculiar little woman, to say the least, and, oddly enough, the cause of the first stirrings of much begrudged kinship I felt toward my new stepsister, Julianne, when I chanced to catch her eye and saw she was trying as hard as I to stifle her laughter at the strange sight the dressmaker presented.

Mrs. Faversham was thin as a pin and no taller than the length of a good measuring tape. A white lace cap perched upon her grey-streaked hair like a plump little pincushion; beneath, her withered face was sharp as a seam ripper. Her oval, wire-rimmed spectacles sat firmly upon her beaked nose and resembled nothing so much as a pair of pewter embroidery scissors. She wore a stiffly starched muslin gown that buttoned up to her throat, where it met primly the nicely pressed edges of her round white collar. In one hand, she carried a pair of spotless white gloves; but they were mainly for show, for she never once put them on and, indeed, quite forgot them when she left, so one of the footmen was forced to make a special trip to town to return them.

She was as quick and deft as a tiny bird as she plied her craft upon Julianne and me, measuring, draping, and pinning, taking darts here and tugging hems there.

"For heaven's sake, Margaret! Stand up straight, else how can Mrs. Faversham ever get her figures right?" my stepmother chided me crossly even now. "I know children grow by leaps and bounds—but surely not in a matter of hours. That is the third dress length Mrs. Faversham has recorded for you this morning!"

"Yes, Stepmama."

"Goodness gracious, Julianne! Just look at your waist size! No more bonbons or sweetmeats for you, young lady, else you grow to be a lard bottom. Give me that candy this minute. No, not the piece in your mouth, you naughty child! Whatever is left in that sack behind your back." Lady Chandler held out one hand for the bag of treats Julianne finally surrendered after a brief, somewhat undignified tussle, for which I was certain she would be soundly chastised later. "Now, Mrs. Faversham, if you would show me the rest of your materials. Yes, I think the pink for Julianne—"

"I don't want pink! I'm sick of pink!" my stepsister protested in a most unbecoming manner, her face flushing, her eyes narrowing, and her lower lip pouting so she looked more like a misshapen strawberry than a china doll as she shot her mother a challenging stare—no doubt in retribution for the loss of her candy. "I want that red velvet." She pointed to a length of cloth that earlier had caught my own eye, though I'd had no thought of having it.

"Don't be silly, Julianne," Lady Chandler retorted, her words clipped, her eyes snapping sparks, and her cheeks high with bright spots of color as she struggled to maintain her decorum before the seamstress, who would certainly gossip to the entire village about the morning's events. "Red is for dark girls—like Margaret. You are far too pale to wear such a strong hue. You must stick to pastels, as Mama does. Perhaps a blue or the lavender, if you cannot abide the pink. . . ."

Evidently Julianne decided she had tried Lady Chandler's patience far enough, for she put forth no additional arguments, but flounced off in a huff, sticking her tongue out at her mother's back. After sulking in a corner for all of ten minutes, she rejoined us, urged on, I felt sure, by the thought that I might be given more clothes than she to punish her for her behavior.

Thereafter she danced about impatiently, standing on first one foot and then the other as she peered nosily over Lady Chandler's shoulder to see what else would soon be forthcoming.

"What a fidget you are, Julianne," my stepmother at last remarked, exasperated. "Can you not sit quietly—like Margaret?"

At that, Julianne stamped off once more and proceeded to spend the remainder of the morning alternately making horrid faces at me, and at Lady Chandler's back, and imitating poor Mrs. Faversham when the dressmaker wasn't looking. In light of this, my earlier spark of friendliness toward my stepsister vanished, as did my previous jealousy of her. I saw that for all her beauty, Julianne was little more than a spoiled brat, and I felt a pang of pity for one who had so much—and yet so little. In her own way, she was as pathetic a creature as I.

Matters were not improved when, much to my surprise and delight, Lady Chandler, who was, I must admit, a woman of excellent taste, purchased the red velvet for me. Although I disliked intensely its source, I could not help but be pleased when Mrs. Faversham pulled it about me and I saw myself in the mirror. As my stepmother had foreseen, the red suited me in a way it would never have done Julianne, making my hair and eyes seem blacker than midnight and my dark skin as warm as honey. I would never be pretty, but I saw that with the right accoutrements, I need no longer be drab either; and I marveled at the change wrought in me.

"Well"—Lady Chandler spoke, somewhat rankled by my improved appearance, though she had been the cause of it—"perhaps you may yet be turned to some account after all, Margaret. You see, Julianne, what the proper colors will do for one."

No more was said, and though the rest of my fabrics were chosen from more subdued shades—my stepmother having astutely perceived that I might indeed grow from an ugly duckling to a swan—I had the red velvet, and it was enough.

Finally all was finished, with so many sketches made, spidery notes written along the margins and snips of cloth pinned to the pages, that I soon lost count, my head filled to bursting with the knowledge that half of them were mine alone. Lady Chandler had not won my heart, of course; but I must confess she had at least made a dent in it that morning, for I could not find it within myself to dislike completely someone who had just outfitted me with the most beautiful clothes I had ever owned.

No more must I wear the wretched garments Nanna had made for me so painstakingly and with such love. In a few weeks' time, when my new gowns were delivered, my old ones were to be given to the Church for distribution to the poor and needy.

"Never forget, Margaret," my stepmother admonished me, "that it is your duty to remember those less fortunate than you."

"Yes, Stepmama," I answered quietly, turning away so she would not see the guilty flush that stained my cheeks.

From what had once been my wardrobe, I intended to save the best to give to Sarah. After all, I reasoned, she *was* poor; and though the dresses would be too large for her, she could easily cut them down and make them over, clever with her needle as she was, and perhaps we could dye them, too, so they wouldn't be so dull and horrid.

How quickly I forgot that once they'd been all I'd had. Now, scornfully, I tossed aside my worn brown frock and, with petty triumph, held to my bosom the prize Julianne earlier had so coveted.

Yes, the ship of my life had forever changed its course. Now my bow was turned headlong into the rough waves ahead; my sail was a bright length of red velvet billowing in the wind.

Chapter Two

Pembroke Grange and Julianne

Remember that the most beautiful things in the world
are the most useless; peacocks and lilies for instance.

—*The Stones of Venice*
John Ruskin

Later that afternoon, after I had finally managed to escape
from my stepmother and Julianne, I hurried upstairs and
locked myself in my room. There I carefully sorted through
my wardrobe, choosing as many of my old clothes as I
dared to give to Sarah. These I tied up as best I could in a
worn cape. Then I crept down the back stairs and quietly let
myself outside. Casting several furtive glances over my
shoulder to be certain I was unobserved, I made my way to
the stables as fast as I could while lugging my heavy, bulky
burden.

"Shall I be saddlin' Clothilde fer thee, then, Miss
Maggie?" Hugh, our head groom, asked when he saw me.

"Yes, please," I said, "and, Hugh, do be quick about
it. I want to get away before anyone sees me."

Though he was only in his early thirties, Hugh's skin
was tanned and lined, the result of a hard life lived mostly
out of doors, and he seemed quite old to me. Still he was a
great favorite of mine, for he had always treated me kindly,
and today was no exception.

"Like that, be it, eh, miss?" he inquired, his head cocked a trifle on his tall, wiry frame, his keen grey eyes filled with a wealth of wisdom and compassion. "Well, I did not doubt but what t' new missus would have her own way of doin' things—an' p'rhaps all of 'em not ta yer likin'. Still an' all, Miss Maggie, 'twill do 'ee no good ta be runnin' off now, if that's what thee've set yer mind ta, a-wantin' yer pony an' a-totin' that bundle besides. T' master shall only fetch 'ee back, 'ee know, an' thee'll get nowt but a tongue-lashin' an' a day or two spent in yer room fer yer pains, I daresay."

"So I should imagine," I agreed, "if such were my intent. Dear Hugh. You have ever been a good friend to me! But you need have no fear on my account, I assure you, for no thought of running away has crossed my mind. Indeed the very fact that it has not should cause you to be at ease, for where would I go but the Grange? And that the first place my father would look for me! No." I shook my head. "Perhaps you know that Mrs. Faversham, the dressmaker, was here this morning? I am to have some new garments, mine having found no favor with Lady Chandler. I am but taking some of my old ones to Miss Sarah before her ladyship can give them to the Church."

Hugh smiled then, understanding and sympathy lighting his face, for he was an observant fellow and knew well how matters stood at the Grange.

"Well, then, thee'd best be about yer business, hadn't 'ee?" He led my pony out of the stables. "Up 'ee go now, Miss Maggie."

He assisted me into the saddle and made certain my bundle was securely fastened behind me. Then he gave Clothilde a friendly pat and me a wave as I nudged my pony forward into a brisk trot.

The crunch of Clothilde's hooves on the gravel drive sounded louder than usual to my ears; once more I glanced back fearfully at the manor, worried that someone would hear my leaving and venture forth to prevent it. But nobody did. Still it was only when I had got by the lodge without incident (old Gower, the porter, was no doubt asleep at his post) and had passed through the open gates of the Hall that I breathed a sigh of relief at having made good my escape. After that, I set off across the moors toward Pembroke Grange.

It was a pleasant afternoon, and with as much resolve as I could muster, I determined not to ruin it by brooding about Lady Chandler and Julianne. Still this was easier said than done, and I found I could not put them out of my mind after all. They had invaded my world, and I could see no hope that they could be vanquished. I wished fervently that they had never come to Highclyffe Hall, and the thought of yet another of their ilk arriving was loathsome to me. I did not doubt that Wellesley Prescott would prove as dreadful as his mother and sister.

So caught up was I in the turmoil of my thoughts that I did not once halt my pony, as I normally did, to gather flowers for the Grange in case Sarah had not had time to do so. Nor did I let Clothilde poke and wander, as I was often wont to do, but kept her at a smart pace and on a straight path; so presently the familiar farm came into view. Only then did I allow my pony to slow and finally pause so I might catch my breath.

As always, the sight of Pembroke Grange lifted my spirits, though perhaps some might have wondered at this, for it was not nearly as grand or imposing as Highclyffe Hall. But it was this very lack, I felt, that gave it warmth and charm. Of course the fact that I was welcome there would have imbued it in my eyes with such traits, even had it not possessed them; but I believe even a stranger would have found it a cheerful place.

The Grange was not as old as the Hall, having been built in the late seventeenth century, and it was smaller and of simpler design. It was constructed of some pale yellow rock whose origins I did not know, though I'd heard some say it was Bath stone, brought here by the elderly gentleman to whom the Grange had initially belonged and who had been fond of taking the Bath waters. Over the ages, the rectangular blocks had weathered to a beautiful cream shade that reminded me of fresh buttermilk. When the sun shone upon them, they reflected its rays with a rich, mellow gold that faded gently at dusk.

The house itself was quadrangular in shape, the stark, angular lines of the front softened by a wide porch with pillars that supported a balcony with an ornate stone balustrade above. Long, narrow casement windows with muntined panes of lead glass were set at regular intervals along both the first and second stories. The mansard roof was of black slate, its length broken by a plain pediment rising above the balcony. On either side of the pediment were three dormer windows, so the top floor provided a pleasing contrast to the bottom two. Four tall chimneys rose from the roof's peak.

The Grange had a shabby, seen-better-days air about it, but this was because my father provided no more than was necessary for minimal upkeep of the place. He was more interested in the profits it brought him, for as at the Hall, both cattle and sheep, and a few goats as well, were raised at the Grange, the commons providing plenty of rough grazing.

Sweeping green lawns dotted with the inevitable Cornish elms sloped away from the front and sides of the house; flower beds in full bloom curved prettily about the walls. To the back were the more extensive gardens, a riotous profusion of color and foliage. From these, Sarah cut blossoms to arrange with the heather, bracken, and wildflowers she gathered on the heaths. Neither the gardens nor the lawns were as neat or well tended as those at the Hall, however, since only a single gardener, Dugald, worked at the Grange. Sarah helped the old man when time permitted, but this was not often, a circumstance that grieved her sorely, I knew, for she loved all flora and enjoyed planting and nurturing it. Her herb garden, to which she gave special care, was a living testament to her ability to make things grow.

When I reached the house, I handed Clothilde's reins to Jack, the groom, then made my way to the back door and, without knocking, let myself into the kitchen, for I had no need to stand on ceremony here.

"Why, 'tis Miss Maggie, ta be sure," Mrs. Hopkins, who served as both housekeeper and cook, greeted me as I stepped inside. "Did I not just say that sounded like her pony a-comin' up the drive, Betsy?"—this to one of the two young maids of the household.

"Aye, missus, that 'ee did," Betsy agreed.

"Thee art just in time fer tea, miss," Mrs. Hopkins said to me. "Go along ta t' drawin' room, an' Betsy shall bring t' tray directly."

I did as I was bidden, hearing, before I reached the room, Esmond's low voice and Sarah's gentle laughter. Upon my entering, they looked up and smiled and rose from their chairs, coming forward with outstretched hands and cries of delight to welcome me.

"Dear Maggie!" Sarah said, her face filled with love and quiet concern as she hugged me. "Come in and sit down." She plumped up the cushions on the worn sofa and made certain I was comfortably settled, while Esmond relieved me of my bundle and deposited it on the floor. "We heard the news of Uncle Nigel's remarriage only this morning and did not know whether to expect you today. You must tell us all. But, wait. I shall fetch Mama, for she has been most anxious ever since learning of the matter."

So saying, Sarah moved lightly, gracefully, as was her way, from the room, calling for my aunt Tibby to come and join us.

"You look tired, Maggie," Esmond observed gravely as he sat down beside me and took my hand in his. "Have the past few days been very trying for you, then?"

"Oh, yes, Esmond, yes," I replied fervently, "for Lady Chandler is the most horrid creature! You cannot imagine— But, there. I must wait for Sarah and Aunt Tibby, too, for I know they are longing to hear everything as well— Ah, here they are."

I stood to embrace my aunt, who did indeed appear quite upset, for she was no doubt worried about how my father's remarriage would affect her life at the farm. I sympathized with her, for I remembered the look on Lady Chandler's face early this morning when she'd emerged from Sir Nigel's study, and I thought it was entirely possible she would curtail the household expenses of the Grange, which were already very much reduced.

Nevertheless I said nothing of this, for if such were the case, there was naught I could do about it, and I did not want to add to my aunt's anxiety. Instead I described Lady Chandler and Julianne in great detail and related everything that had occurred since their arrival. Aunt Tibby's apprehension was a good deal lessened by my tale; indeed, much to my surprise, she was actually affronted by the thought of what my father had done, for she was not without pride in the Chandler name and heritage. I had never before seen her truly angry, and for a moment, as her eyes flashed and her cheeks flushed, I had a glimpse of the indulged, pretty girl she must have been in her youth, before heartbreak and poverty had humbled her spirit.

"I do not know what Nigel can have been thinking of," Aunt Tibby sniffed after I had finished speaking. "Even Worthing, whom my brother ever scorned as being painfully inadequate—although it was not true!—," she defended her late husband indignantly, "was from an old and honorable family. Depend upon it! For all her airs and graces, Nigel's new wife is nothing more than a common fortune hunter—and you cannot tell me he did not know it, for he was never one to be taken in by a schemer, no matter how cunning or clever!

"Why, if Papa were alive, no doubt he would have my brother horsewhipped for disgracing the family in such a manner." Her lips tightened briefly, then softened with sadness as, sighing, she added, "Although I daresay it wouldn't have answered after all, for Papa and Nigel were always at each other's throat, each being set on having his own way.

"Well"—Aunt Tibby shook her head, quivering with emotion—"Lady Chandler needn't think she shall interfere with affairs here at the Grange. Though I have borne much from Nigel—for I do so dislike quarreling; it quite shatters my nerves, and he *is* the head of the family after all—I certainly do not intend to be dictated to by the widow of a mere merchant, and so I shall inform my brother when next I see him!''

"Now, Mama, there is no need to work yourself into such a state," Sarah stated firmly, taking Aunt Tibby's hand in hers and patting it soothingly. "I'm sure Uncle Nigel does not mean to neglect his duties toward us—Esmond is his heir after all—and from what Maggie has told us, Lady Chandler seems much disposed toward making her mark in society. I do not see how casting off her new husband's family can win the favor of those whom she would impress."

"No, indeed," I said. "In fact, if such were her intent, she would surely have allowed me to be shunted aside, as I was before, rather than making such a fuss over me— though I *do* wish she had not been so hateful to Nanna!"

After that, Betsy appeared with the tea tray, and while Aunt Tibby poured, I opened my bundle to show Sarah the clothes I had brought her. Though now, knowing what I was to receive in their place, I felt embarrassed by my plain, threadbare former garments, Sarah was genuinely glad and grateful to have them. She exclaimed over each and every one, observing how a bit of frayed lace might be mended or a spotted cuff turned so as not to show the stain, and she would have fetched her sewing basket at once had not Aunt Tibby smiled and bade her wait at least until we had finished tea.

Shortly thereafter, noticing by the light streaming in through the windows how late the afternoon had grown, I reluctantly stood and said I must take my leave, for no longer did I have an indulgent Nanna to turn a blind eye to my caprices and to cover for my long absences from the Hall. I was certain to have been missed by now, and Esmond feared I would receive a dreadful scolding upon my return to the manor.

"I hope they will not be too harsh with you, Maggie," he said.

"I don't care," I declared bravely, tossing my head. "Like as not, 'twill not be the last time I am punished."

"Nevertheless you must say we delayed you," Esmond insisted, "for 'twas only natural that we should be curious and wish to be fully apprised of any change in Uncle Nigel's circumstances; and you know 'twould not be appropriate for us to call when Lady Chandler has only just arrived, though I'm sure Mama will pay her respects at the first opportunity.''

"Yes, I suppose so," I agreed. "Then you may decide for yourself what sort of woman Lady Chandler is. It may be that I have misjudged her, though I think not."

I said my good-byes, retrieved my pony from the stables, and set off toward home, pushing Clothilde as fast as her short legs would carry her, for despite all my boasting, deep down inside, I cringed at the thought of a scathing lecture from my father and secretly hoped to sneak up the back stairs to my room before my absence from the house was discovered.

It was not to be, however, for my pony had no sooner rounded the last bend in the drive than I spied Julianne, a basket of flowers upon one arm as she strolled through the gardens—and in such a proprietary manner that one would have thought they belonged to her instead of Sir Nigel. In the process of pointing out to one of the gardeners a particular bloom she wished to have cut, she broke off her demands abruptly upon seeing me and strode toward me, a smug smile of triumph much like her mother's upon her face.

"Where have you been, Maggie?" she asked with the excited air of one who is about to deliver a coup de grace. "Mama has been looking for you ever so long. You're not to go off without permission again, she said, and you're to be punished as well."

"So?" I shrugged coolly, though inwardly I trembled a little.

Still, Julianne could not see that, and some of her mean delight at being the bearer of bad tidings lessened when she saw she was not going to upset me. Her smile disappeared to be replaced by a pout, and a small frown knitted her brow.

"Don't you care if you're to receive a beating?" she queried, disappointed but curious, too.

"My father has never struck me, and I doubt that he'll permit your mother to do so either, no matter what she may have said," I replied loftily. "Besides, I've done nothing but ride over to Pembroke Grange to visit my aunt and cousins, the Sheffields, as I often do."

"Well, you might have invited me to accompany you," Julianne pointed out. " 'Twas quite rude of you not to have done so. Mama was most provoked by it. I've had no one to play with all afternoon, and though Papa promised to take me to buy a pony, he was too busy to do so after all."

Poor Julianne, I thought, though not without a small measure of gloating.

Sir Nigel was not very fond of children, and it was now obvious to me that since Lady Chandler had been won and wed, my father no longer deemed her offspring of any real importance. His daily affairs had once more claimed his attention, and Julianne had been relegated, as I had been, to the farthest corner of his mind. I, of course, was accustomed to Sir Nigel's lack of regard. But Julianne, who had been spoiled and petted all her life, was not. Further, I sensed she had yet to grasp the fact that she would not in the future occupy a prominent place in my father's heart, and I suspected that when she finally did learn it, the blow would be quite devastating. Still I could not help but feel some satisfaction that she was not, after all, to prove the recipient of the love Sir Nigel had denied me.

"Is this your pony?" she asked, changing the subject and eyeing Clothilde in much the same manner as she had done the gardens earlier.

"Yes," I admitted reluctantly, guessing her intent at once. Then, thinking to put an end to the idea before it took root in her mind, I continued, "No one has ever ridden her except me."

"Nevertheless you are my sister now, and 'tis only right that you share your possessions with me," she insisted firmly, undeterred. "If you don't, I shall be forced to tell Mama and Papa how mean you are being to me."

"I might have known you would prove a spiteful little tattler!" I retorted, unable to curb my unruly tongue. "Do as you please, but do not think to bully me, for I do not scare easily, I promise you!''

With that parting shot, I kicked Clothilde into a trot and, shaking with emotion, continued on toward the stables. I had no doubt that Julianne would run immediately to her mother to report my behavior, and once I got inside, I discovered this was indeed the case. Lady Chandler reprimanded me quite severely; but it soon became quite evident to me that the primary cause of her anger was not that I had left the house without permission, or even the rude words I had exchanged with Julianne, but the fact that I had not taken my stepsister with me to the Grange. Julianne, it appeared, had made a thorough pest of herself in my absence. She had whined about being bored to tears until her mother had smartly boxed her ears. Then, unbeknown to Lady Chandler, she had slipped into the study to annoy my father with her constant demands for a pony, her own having been sold after Captain Brodie's death.

I escaped further punishment by the simple expediency of promising I would show Julianne about the Hall tomorrow and, in addition, by grudgingly agreeing she might ride Clothilde. Then I hurried to my room and stoutly bolted the door behind me, venting my rage upon a hapless feather pillow.

The following morning, I gave Julianne a tour of the manor from top to bottom; and though she tried very hard to adopt a disdainful, supercilious air, I could tell she was most impressed, for the Hall was far grander, I was sure, than her mother's London town house had been. This had been sold after Captain Brodie's death, and thereafter the Prescotts had moved frequently, each new residence, I suspected, proving worse than the last.

I must admit I played my role to the hilt as well, for Mrs. Seyton, our housekeeper, had given me her chatelaine, and at each door, I jangled the keys upon the huge ring in a nonchalant manner, as though I were already the lady of the manor and quite accustomed to having their care and authority entrusted to me.

"This is the chamber where Queen Elizabeth slept

when once she visited Sir Geoffrey, the knight who built Highclyffe Hall," I announced casually in one room. (Though I did not know whether the tale about the queen was true, the Chandlers had always claimed it was so, and I saw no reason to inform Julianne otherwise.) "That was, of course, before King James the First instituted the baronetage," I explained as we walked on, "and Sir Francis, Sir Geoffrey's son, was created the first baronet of the Hall."

In the long gallery, I pointed out the portraits of the Chandlers through the ages. Then we went downstairs, where, in the library, I showed her an ornate snuffbox upon an occasional table.

"That is the snuffbox King Charles the Second gave my ancestor Sir Richard. 'Twas but a small token of the esteem and appreciation he received for helping His Majesty to ascend the throne of England."

In a curio cabinet in the dining room was a silver goblet from which George Villiers, the then Earl of Buckingham and a favorite of King James I, had drunk. Next I took Julianne to the grand ballroom, where Sarah Jennings Churchill, the Duchess of Marlborough, who, with her husband, John Churchill, had proved the power behind Queen Anne's throne, had danced. And then, most thrilling of all, there was the secret room beneath the cellars. . . .

"This crypt, as we call it, was dug at the instruction of my ancestor Sir William during the time of King Charles the First, when Oliver Cromwell, the Roundhead leader, crushed all England in his puritanical grip," I told Julianne. "Here Sir William concealed the family jewels, plate, and so forth during the Civil War, when such riches were seized by the traitors who beheaded the king.

"As you can see, the crypt is not used for much of anything nowadays," I went on as we gazed about the dank, dusty room, our lamps casting eerie, flickering shadows on the walls. "But since it saved the Chandler fortune, no one has ever had it filled in."

At that, my stepsister could no longer maintain her lofty pose.

"How exciting!" she exclaimed, her eyes wide. "Do you suppose they ever kept prisoners down here, too?"

"I don't know," I confessed. "I imagine they might have. I *do* know that several Royal sympathizers were hidden here until they could be smuggled into France. Cornwall has often proved a haven for such illegal activities." Then, driven by some wicked imp of mischief, I said, "Who knows? Perhaps people were actually tortured to death here in this crypt and buried beneath these very stones upon which we are standing."

Julianne shivered and, glancing down with horror at the floor, began to sidle nervously toward the steep, narrow stone stairs that led to the cellars.

"Let's go upstairs," she suggested hastily. "It's dirty down here, and I don't want to muss my dress."

Suppressing my strong desire to laugh at the stricken expression on her countenance, I followed her up the steps to the cellars, from where we continued on to the kitchen. There one of the scullery maids told us luncheon was almost ready, and after tidying our appearance, we hurried to the dining room to take our places at the table.

Once the meal had been served and eaten, Julianne and I were excused. Having spent the entire morning exploring the house, I hoped she would now leave me alone, for though in reviewing my old and respected lineage, I had thoroughly enjoyed deflating her high opinion of herself, she had tried my patience to the utmost. I yawned hugely and said I was tired, thinking she would take the hint and go away. But instead she persisted in following me, peevishly reminding me of my promise to allow her to ride Clothilde. I still did not care for the thought of sharing my pony with my stepsister; but as I saw she was determined not to relent until she had got her way, I decided that the sooner I acceded to her demands, the sooner I would be rid of her. So we made our way to the stables, where, whistling between his teeth and winking at me surreptitiously to let me know he understood how cross I was, Hugh led Clothilde out and saddled her.

"I shall manage the reins, Maggie," Julianne declared firmly. "You can ride pillion."

"Why, I'll do no such thing!" I cried. "Clothilde is *my* pony!"

"Yes, but you know what Mama said: I am your sister now, and you must be nice to me. Besides, if you let *me* manage the reins, I'll let *you* play with my dolls later."

I knew this was not true, for I had seen Julianne's dolls last evening and been consumed by envy at her collection. Captain Brodie had brought them to her from all over the world: beautiful china dolls dressed in elegant silk costumes; simple stuffed dolls clothed in gingham; strange, carved wooden dolls; dolls with heads of dried fruit or nuts; tiny dolls created of pebbles and shells; and plain dolls woven of straw and grass. They were Julianne's most prized possessions; she would not allow even her mother—much less me—to touch them.

"You're not only a tattler, but a liar as well, Julianne!" I accused.

But she just smiled that hateful smile so like her mother's and tapped her foot impatiently, eager to be off. To avoid further delay, I finally consented to ride pillion; and presently, mounted upon Clothilde, we were trotting past the lodge through the open gates of the Hall.

"In which direction does Pembroke Grange lie?" my stepsister asked once we had turned onto the road.

"That way, across the moors"—I pointed. "Why?"

"I should like to visit my new aunt and cousins, the Sheffields."

"They're not really your relations," I said stiffly, "any more than I am your true sister, so there is no point in our going there."

I did not want Julianne at the Grange. I felt that somehow she would spoil it for me, as she had disrupted my life at the Hall.

"Nevertheless we shall go there anyway, Maggie," she announced.

Since it was she who held my pony's reins, there was little I could do to stop her as she reined Clothilde off the road and set out determinedly across the commons. I frowned with irritation at her back, contemplating whether it would be worth the punishment I was sure to receive if I suddenly pushed her off my pony. Deciding at last that it would not, I reluctantly thrust the idea—along with that of giving her a sharp pinch—from my mind. I did, however, rebuke her sternly when she hit my pony smartly with her riding crop.

"Stop that, Julianne!" I ordered. "Clothilde's not accustomed to rough treatment, and you're scaring her."

"Well, she's slow as a turtle—and too fat besides! Can't she go any faster?" my stepsister asked, kicking my pony hard in the ribs several times.

"No. She's not used to carrying two people—especially when one of them is as heavy as you are." I spoke snidely, angered by her insulting remarks about Clothilde and remembering Lady Chandler's comments about Julianne growing to be a lard bottom. "She's doing the best she can."

"Well, when Papa buys *my* pony, I promise you it shan't be a slow, fat one!" she shot back over her shoulder, miffed. Then, addressing my earlier statement, she sniffed and said, "Besides, 'tis far better to be rounded than to resemble a scarecrow like you, Maggie. Mama says you shall most likely never catch a husband!"

"That's not true!" I retorted, stung. "I am to marry my cousin Esmond, as well your mother knows."

Fortunately the Grange came into sight just then, for which I was profoundly grateful; otherwise I fear I should have lost my temper entirely and given in to my urge to push Julianne out of the saddle.

"Why, 'tis not nearly as grand as the Hall," she scoffed as she gazed at the farm, inadvertently revealing how greatly she had been impressed by the manor. "And 'tis very run down, too. Why isn't it kept up better?"

"I'm afraid you'll have to ask Father that question," I said, "for the Grange belongs to him."

"But I thought you said your aunt and cousins, the Sheffields, live here."

"They do, but only because my aunt Tibby, who is

Father's sister, is a widow and her son, my cousin Esmond, is Father's heir. 'Tis Father's duty to care for them.''

"What you really mean is that the Sheffields are nothing more than poor dependents living off Papa's charity and Esmond's expectations!" she cried. "Why, had I known that, I should not have come!"

"Well, no one asked you to, so if that's the way you feel about it, we may as well return home!"

Scowling, Julianne nevertheless propelled Clothilde forward; and soon I found myself sitting in the drawing room at the Grange, while Aunt Tibby made polite, stilted conversation with my stepsister. Sarah had taken her sewing and retreated to the far corner of the room, and Esmond was still hard at work at his lessons, a circumstance about which for once I could not help but be glad; the thought of my beloved cousin being subjected to Julianne's scorn and ridicule was more than I could bear.

While she had not overtly said or done anything that could be considered in the least disrespectful, she had made it quite plain by her imperious manner that she considered the Sheffields beneath her. Aunt Tibby was stiff and curt with disapproval, and Sarah, who was normally so gay, had withdrawn into an unnatural shell of silence, her eyes downcast as she bent her head over her sewing, her mouth set almost grimly. Now more than ever did I regret the fact that I had brought Julianne to the farm.

Just then, the drawing-room door opened, and Alice, Betsy's older sister, appeared with the tea tray. When we'd first entered the Grange through the kitchen, I had observed Mrs. Hopkins's keen eyes assessing my stepsister shrewdly. As a result, Aunt Tibby's second-best china had been carefully arranged on the tray and the tea she poured from the sterling-silver teapot into the delicate porcelain cups was the kind the family saved for special occasions. Julianne should have no cause to sneer at the Sheffields' hospitality at least, I thought.

As she had not expected a visitor, Mrs. Hopkins had prepared nothing fancy; but her hot, buttered scones were, as always, delicious, and there were crumpets with brambleberry jam, too. I was not surprised when Julianne accepted a generously filled plate and, after cleaning it, made no demur to Aunt Tibby's offer of a second helping. My stepsister, I reflected, would soon be plump as a little partridge. With a good deal of relish, I imagined her growing fatter and fatter until she burst.

However, before she was halfway through eating, the door again opened, and Esmond came in. To my amazement, at the sight of him, Julianne at once set aside her fork and plate and, with her napkin, dabbed daintily at her lips.

"The scones are excellent, Mrs. Sheffield," she remarked, "but I vow I simply can't eat another bite. Mama says I have the appetite of a bird, you know." Then, while I was biting my tongue to keep from snorting aloud at this obvious untruth, she glanced through her demurely downcast lashes at Esmond and, as though just noticing him, said, "Oh, hullo."

For a moment, Esmond made no reply but merely stared at her in a manner that reminded me, oddly enough, of a poleaxed steer I had seen once during the butchering season. I shivered a little, as though a sudden draft had chilled me, though the air was still. Then, remembering his manners, Esmond stepped forward and took my stepsister's proffered hand in his; and I thought I must have imagined the look on his face after all.

"Hullo," he responded courteously. "You must be Julianne."

"Why, yes," she confirmed, her dimples flashing, "and you must be Cousin Esmond, although perhaps I shouldn't call you that, since we really aren't related after all."

"But of course you may," he declared, smiling shyly, "for you are one of the family now that Uncle Nigel has married your mother. Isn't that right, Maggie?" he asked, turning to me as he sat down in a chair beside Julianne.

"Yes, of course," I agreed coolly, somewhat hurt that he had not chosen to sit by me. But, then, he was a gentleman and must be polite, I told myself. I put my cup and saucer down and stood. " 'Tis a pity you were so long at your lessons, Esmond, for we were just leaving, so I'm afraid you and Julianne won't have much time to become acquainted.''

''Oh, I doubt that Mama will mind if we stay a while longer,'' my stepsister insisted airily. ''She was all sixes and sevens with her settling in, so I daresay she will be glad to have us out of her way.'' Her laughter tinkled. ''In fact, she was most annoyed to learn I didn't accompany Maggie here yesterday.''

''There. You see,'' Esmond said to me. ''There's no need for you to rush off after all, Maggie.''

Indeed, since it appeared Julianne did not intend to budge, I saw little choice but to remain. Somewhat crossly, I resumed my seat, thinking Esmond would not be so eager for us to stay once he realized what sort of person my stepsister was. But much to my vast annoyance, instead of snubbing Esmond, as she had Aunt Tibby and Sarah, Julianne went out of her way to captivate him. Her blue eyes sparkled engagingly as she chatted with him; her laughter rang out so often that I thought it was a wonder her dimples did not become permanent dents in her cheeks. Her eyelashes and hands fluttered like a tiny bird's wings as she related one anecdote after another and giggled appreciatively at Esmond's own stories, making him blush and stammer with delight at his cleverness in amusing her. I hated her for secretly laughing at him—for I felt certain she was—and I wished Esmond were not so kind and honest, taking her at face value instead of looking beneath her enchanting countenance and affected demeanor to see her as she truly was. Now, though I had not wanted him to suffer her derision, I was sorry he had not, for I could not bear to see him making such a cake of himself.

Neither Aunt Tibby nor Sarah was more relieved than I when Julianne finally said we must take our leave. My stepsister preceded me out the door, bent on reaching the stables before me, I felt sure, in order to mount my pony first and thus ensure her position of being the one to handle the reins on the way home. I did not care. I lingered behind anyway, hoping somehow to lessen the sting of the cruel barbs she had delivered to Aunt Tibby and Sarah.

"Never you mind, Maggie," my aunt said kindly, guessing my intent. "It is not your fault the girl is so common; and in truth, even she cannot be held to blame for her manner. Depend upon it: The brazen little hussy learned those hoity-toity airs from her mother and so knows no better. Imagine! A mere child behaving so coquettishly! It isn't decent, I tell you!"

"Why, Mama!" Esmond exclaimed, his words like a knife in my heart. "I'm surprised at you. It is not like you to judge someone so harshly. I thought Julianne was charming. Oh, perhaps she is a bit more forward than is becoming; but she is, after all, very young, and allowances must be made for that, surely. It is only because you are wroth with Uncle Nigel for remarrying that you dislike her, and Julianne certainly cannot be held accountable for that."

"That is true," Sarah chimed in gently, biting her lip. "Perhaps we *are* being too hard on her. After all, she, too, has been thrust into a situation over which she has no control. Not only that, but she has been uprooted from her home as well. Even if her circumstances *are* much improved, it must have been very upsetting to her to leave London and all her friends behind to come to Cornwall, a place that is strange to her and where she knows no one."

"Yes," I agreed slowly, feeling slightly guilty now over my churlish behavior to my stepsister. "I'm sure that's true."

I said my good-byes and walked on toward the stables, Sarah's words still ringing in my ears. *Had* I let my own tumultuous emotions cloud my understanding of those Julianne must be feeling? Yes, I must admit I had. What if it had been I, forced to leave Highclyffe Hall, to journey from Cornwall to London, a city unknown—and therefore frightening—to me, to unfamiliar people, who resented my coming? How would I have felt? Terrible, I thought. Worse than terrible. I resolved to be kinder to Julianne, for perhaps it was only her own feeling of insecurity that drove her to attempt to instill a like emotion in others.

On the way home, filled with my newfound sympathy for her, I bit my tongue to keep from protesting when she haughtily pronounced Aunt Tibby an old fidget and Sarah a mousy drab. Somehow I even managed to remain quiet when she said Esmond was a boring clod but that having no other prospects, I no doubt considered myself fortunate to be betrothed to him. Nevertheless, even knowing, I thought, what prompted her snide remarks, I could not like her any better; and I was relieved when we reached the Hall at last and I could escape to my own room and lock the door behind me. There, at least, Julianne could not intrude, as she had at the manor and the farm.

Still, after that day, she did not go soon again to Pembroke Grange, as you shall learn.

Chapter Three

The Arrival of Wellesley and Miss Poole

Says he, 'I am a handsome man,
but I'm a gay deceiver.'

—*Love Laughs at Locksmiths*
George Colman the Younger

Though afterward she tried to blame Clothilde for it, the mishap with my pony was all Julianne's fault.

A few days after our visit to the Grange, she decided to ride Clothilde herself—without my knowledge or permission—and though Hugh tried to dissuade her, Julianne, who considered servants her inferiors and therefore unneedful of civility, rudely dismissed his protests, claiming Lady Chandler had given her leave to explore the park. She insisted Hugh saddle my pony, and at last he reluctantly did so. My stepsister set off down the drive; but as before, Clothilde's ambling pace was too slow to suit her, and this time, I was not there to curb her temper. With her riding crop, she struck my pony hard upon the rump several times; and then when Clothilde, confused by the rough treatment, did not respond as she wished, she pulled a long, sharp pin from her feathered riding hat and jabbed my pony with it.

Clothilde jumped, then bolted, pounding down the drive and sending gravel flying. Julianne, despite imagining herself otherwise, was not really a very good horsewoman, being accustomed to sedate rides in one of London's public parks, and she was unable to control my poor runaway pony. She screamed and screamed, dropping the reins in her panic and frantically clutching the underside of the pommel's curve. Hugh and two of the other grooms, hearing her cries, came racing from the stables to see what was amiss; but there was little anyone could do to help her. Nevertheless, shouting, the men set up a chase, and Clothilde, white-eyed with fear and hearing the commotion behind her, veered off the drive into the wood. There my pony wove in and out of the trees until finally the low-hanging branch of a spreading yew caught Julianne squarely cross the chest, knocking her from the saddle. Riderless, Clothilde galloped on, leaving my stepsister sprawled upon the ground, moaning weakly for assistance.

One of the grooms carried her into the Hall, where an immediate uproar ensued as Lady Chandler took one look at her daughter's crumpled figure and began to issue orders right and left, bidding someone to turn down the bed in Julianne's chamber, someone else to fetch clean cloths and a basin of water, and someone else to summon the physician.

In due time, Dr. Ashford appeared and, after examining her, announced that my stepsister had suffered no worse injury than a sprained ankle, but that she was fortunate not to have broken her neck. At that, Lady Chandler declared indignantly that it was a crime to keep such a violent pony in the stables and that Clothilde must be got rid of at once.

Luckily Hugh had found Julianne's hatpin lying on the drive and was even at that moment in my father's study, explaining his quite accurate suspicions about what had been done to my pony to make her behave as she had. Sir Nigel was aware that Clothilde was possessed of a normally sweet temper, and he did not suffer fools gladly besides. Though I doubted that he cared that my stepsister had been so stupid and cruel as to prod my pony with a pin, the idea that she could not cope with the result of her deliberately provocative action did not sit well with him at all; and though, fearing the consequences when my father, glowering, entered her room to question her about the matter, Julianne attempted to deny any wrongdoing on her part, Sir Nigel's merciless interrogation soon pried the truth from her.

As punishment for her ineptitude, and for lying as well, she was confined to her room for a fortnight and forbidden to ride Clothilde again. She further bore the brunt of her mother's displeasure, for afterward my father made it quite clear to Lady Chandler that he would not tolerate such upsets in his house and that even if I were not "all the crack," as he put it, I certainly knew better than to stick a horse with a hatpin. It was the first time I could ever remember Sir Nigel finding anything to my credit, and I was as pleased by the remark as Lady Chandler was annoyed.

For the next few days, knowing how angry my step-mother was that Julianne's foolishness had caused me to garner my father's approval, however briefly, I took care to keep out of her way whenever I could.

Having been refused permission to ride over to the Grange, since Lady Chandler curtly insisted I spent far too much time there, I took to haunting the park, reading to while away the hours. So it was that book in hand and perched comfortably in a tree whose leaf-laden branches shielded me from all unwelcome eyes, I got my first glimpse of Wellesley Prescott.

Truth to tell, initially I thought he was some homeless urchin come a-begging, for from head to toe, he was covered with dust; one button dangled by a thread from his jacket, and his socks had come free of their garters to slip down baggily around his ankles. A battered cap was cocked jauntily on his tousled blond head; he had his hands jammed into the pockets of his torn knee breeches, and he was whistling tunelessly through his teeth as he strolled up the drive, looking, for all his disheveled appearance, as though he had a perfect right to be there.

Curious, I closed my book and carefully tossed it down onto the grass. Then, hanging from one of the tree's limbs, I dropped to the ground and brushed the loose bark from my hands.

"Hullo," I said.

"Hullo," he greeted me, his blue eyes sparkling and his friendly, impish grin revealing even white teeth. "Who are you?"

"I might ask you the same question," I replied, "though it seems fairly obvious you're some pauper brat in need of a meal and work. Well, if you go around to the kitchen, Mrs. Merrick, the cook, will no doubt give you something to eat, and perhaps Nathan, the head caretaker, will have some odd jobs you might do for a few shillings."

To my surprise, the boy threw back his head and laughed.

" 'Pauper brat,' is it? By heaven, that's rich! I haven't tried that one before, though I daresay it probably wouldn't prove half as much fun as riding on top of the stagecoach. I mean, after all, if one were to go about pretending to be a pauper brat, one might be caught and put in the workhouse before one's true identity was made known. And just think what a tangle that would be!" With that, the boy swept off his cap and bowed with a flourish. "Wellesley Prescott, miss," he said by way of introducing himself, "at your service. I believe I am expected, though not until Tuesday, to be sure. And who do I have the pleasure of addressing?"

"Maggie. Maggie Chandler," I answered, momentarily nonplussed, for he was such a ragamuffin and so engaging that it hardly seemed possible he was Julianne's brother. For a minute, I thought he was teasing me.

"Ah. My new stepsister, of course. Well, and 'tis no wonder you mistook me for some pauper brat; I daresay I'm not in the least what you expected." He glanced down at himself ruefully, then grinned and ran one hand through his ragged hair, which was parted on the side. Then he flung back his head so the sheaf that now fell over his forehead into his eyes flew back into place. "The sad state of my appearance is due entirely to a grand lark, which if the Captain were alive, I'm certain he should have found a great joke. However, I have no doubt that I shall be thoroughly reprimanded for it by Mama. She has absolutely no sense of humor, you know."

"Yes, I know," I agreed. Then, blushing, I nearly bit off my tongue at my rudeness.

Wellesley only laughed.

"Don't worry, Maggie," he said gaily. "I'm not such a tattler as Julianne. A proper cat, she is—even if she *is* my sister. Tell you what, dear girl: I can see already that you're a regular good 'un, and if you could find it in your heart to sneak me into the house so I can get cleaned up a bit before facing the mater and Sir Nigel, I'd be forever grateful."

Of course I knew I should do no such thing; but he was so charming, so different from his mother and sister that I couldn't resist.

"All right," I consented, smiling, finally convinced this winsome boy was indeed my new stepbrother. I was both intrigued and delighted by the idea, for somehow I felt that despite all my previous fears to the contrary, Wellesley would prove a ray of sunshine to brighten the gloomy Hall. "But you're not to tell anyone I helped you."

"Not a word of it," he promised. "Cross my heart, and hope to die; stick a needle in my eye. I've never yet implicated a friend in one of my plots, even when the headmaster took a cane to my backside!"

As Esmond would have done, Wellesley courteously offered to carry my book for me, earning him another mark in his favor; and we started up the drive to the manor, talking all the while. I soon learned he had been sent down a few days early by the headmaster of the prep school he attended. A small matter of a cockfight, which he had secretly staged on the grounds and which had got a trifle out of hand and so had been discovered, had proven his downfall. Then, instead of traveling inside the stagecoach as he ought to have done, ample funds for this having been mailed to him by his mother, Wellesley had persuaded the driver to let him ride on top and so had saved a good portion of the fare and used it for assorted purposes, the last of which had been to see some novelty in Exeter. Knowing he was not expected until Tuesday, he had left his baggage at the post in Camelford and, after asking directions to Highclyffe Hall, had set out on foot for the manor. Halfway here, he had been fortunate enough to get a lift in a passing farmer's wagon and so had finished the remainder of his journey lodged atop a pile of vegetables.

I was astounded by his tale, for I had never known anyone who so blithely embarked upon such adventures, and I thought him quite dashing, though, no matter how handsome or taking, he could not compare to Esmond, of course. Still, by the time I had led Welles, as he asked me to call him, up the back stairs of the house, he and I were fast friends, and I marveled that I had ever been filled with dismay at the prospect of his coming.

"Be quiet," I whispered, putting one finger to my lips, "for Julianne is just across the hall, and like as not, if she hears us, she'll hobble out to investigate."

"Hobble?" Welles inquired, lifting one eyebrow and grinning. "Has she had a mishap, then?"

"Yes, indeed." I nodded, tiptoeing to my chamber and ushering him inside, after which I closed the door softly behind us. "She was riding my pony, and Clothilde wasn't going fast enough to suit her, so Julianne stabbed her in the rump with a hatpin. Naturally Clothilde, who is unused to being treated so, bolted and ran into the wood. Your sister was knocked from the saddle by a tree branch and twisted her ankle in the process. She is confined to her room for a fortnight as punishment."

"Well, I should think so," Welles drawled, disgusted. "Of all the dumb things I've ever heard, that must be the dumbest. Imagine! Poking a horse with a pin!"

"Yes, that's what *I* thought," I said. "Wait here, Welles, while I fetch a needle and thread. Then I'll sew on that button and mend the rip in your knee breeches. In the meantime, there's a pitcher of water and some towels on the washstand, so you can tidy up."

"Thanks, Maggie, dear girl. I really appreciate it. I'll pay you back somehow, I swear it!"

I smiled and blushed and shook my head, then hurried from the room, unable to put my abruptly overwhelming emotions into words. Welles was so friendly and cheerful that he had made me realize suddenly how terribly lonely I was at the Hall. It was enough that he liked me; I needed no other repayment.

After he had finished washing, I fixed his button and knee breeches and brushed the dirt from his clothes. Then, Welles looking much more presentable than when he had come, we crept back downstairs to the outside, where I brought him in properly through the front door, both of us behaving as though he had only just arrived.

Lady Chandler was happy to see him, though she wondered at his early appearance, something Welles attributed to a "small scrape of no importance, since it was the end of the term anyway," and when my stepmother would have pursued the subject further, Sir Nigel put an end to the matter, saying, "Now, Gwyneth, I'm certain that if it had been anything serious, the headmaster would have contacted us." After that, Lady Chandler gave instructions for Welles's baggage to be fetched from Camelford and said that since it seemed he and I were already on the best of terms, I might take him up to greet his sister and show him his chamber.

This I did, amused to see how cavalierly he treated Julianne, dismissing her airs as silly and her threats as childish.

"I'll tell you what, Julie," he said, frowning, "if you don't sweeten that tongue and temper of yours, you shall grow up to be an old maid for sure. No man wants to be shackled to a shrew, and that's the truth! Why, Freddie Houghton-Smythe's brother is married to such a virago that I'm surprised he hasn't drowned her in the Thames! Which is surely what shall become of you, dear girl, if you don't mend your wicked ways."

"Well, that's all very well and good for *you* to say, Welles," Julianne shot back, offended, "for *you* are not stuck here in this horrid old house in the middle of nowhere. Why, do you know there are actually *bodies* buried beneath the cellars here?"

"What? You don't say?" Welles exclaimed, his eyes gleaming with sudden interest and excitement. "Is that so, Maggie?"

"No. I mean . . . I don't know," I replied truthfully. "I

suppose 'tis possible; but really I only said it to frighten Julianne because she was being so awful to me.''

"Oh! How mean!" she cried. "I shall tell Mama at once, Maggie!''

"You'll do no such thing, Julie," Welles insisted sternly, "for 'tis more than likely what you deserved for being such a twit! No, don't pull that long face with me, dear girl; 'twill do you no good in the least, I assure you. I'm wise to your tricks, Julie, and will have none of your stuff and nonsense!''

"Oh, Welles, you sound just like the Captain," she declared, pouting.

"Yes, and what's wrong with that, I'd like to know? Our father was the best of men; he didn't hold with hoity-toity behavior—and neither, I'll wager, does Sir Nigel. Look, Julie, I know you haven't had an easy time of it since the Captain died, but that's no reason to mistreat other people—or a poor dumb beast either—and so far as I can see, it hasn't done you any good at all."

At that, much to my consternation, since I had come to think of her as having no feelings at all, Julianne puckered up piteously, then burst into tears.

"Oh—oh, Welles," she sobbed, "it's just that—that nothing's been the same since the—the Captain died! And it was so—so dreadful being poor, with—with Mama running up bills, and—and creditors dunning us, and having to—to move from place to place, and poor Tinker, my—my pony, having to be sold! I couldn't bear it! I just couldn't bear it! I shall never be poor again! *Never!*''

"Of course you shan't, Julie," Welles assured her kindly, patting her hand. "There, there. I didn't mean to make you cry, poppet. Dry your tears now, and if Maggie has a board, she and I will play a game of ludo with you. I know it can't be much fun for you—being stuck in here all by yourself and your ankle no doubt paining you like the dickens.''

I did indeed have a board, and though Welles proved as good a player as I, by tacit agreement, we allowed Julianne to win three games in a row, after which she was much cheered. As we left her chamber, having been summoned for supper, Welles dropped a careless kiss on her forehead, and I saw that for all his earlier impatience with her, he loved Julianne and wanted her to be happy.

That night, as I lay in bed, I thought about her tearful outburst, and I realized my stepsister, as Lady Chandler did, aspired to the finer things in life because she had tasted poverty and found it bitter. I felt sorry for Julianne, of course, but I could not help comparing her to Sarah, whose own wretched means were borne with quiet dignity and who enriched the lives of all she touched. How different from Julianne, Sarah was, I thought—and how ironic that I, who had so much, should long to trade places with either of them, who were so beloved by those they held dear.

A few weeks after Welles's arrival, Miss Poole, the governess, came to the Hall. Both Julianne and I, who were watching from the window on the second-story landing as she alighted from the landaulet, groaned when we saw her, for she was the embodiment of our worst fears. She was in her late thirties, we judged, tall and thin, her dark brown hair streaked with grey and scraped back into a severe bun from which not a single strand escaped. She was dressed in a plain brown traveling costume and a small, prim hat adorned with a simple half-veil. Even from a distance, we could see that her mouth was lined on either side with deep grooves borne of a serious and austere nature.

"Oh, Maggie, she's terrible!" Julianne whispered. "Just the sort of woman Mama *would* engage to drum French and art and deportment—and heaven only knows what else!—into our heads!"

"Well, perhaps she is not as bad as she looks," I suggested halfheartedly, hoping I were right but certain I was not. "At any rate, there is nothing we can do about her. She has already been hired. I saw the letter before your mother mailed it, you know. It was lying on her desk in the morning room."

"Uh-huh. What a pry you are, Maggie!" Julianne accused, making me flush guiltily, for when I'd found the missive, I had indeed been nosing into things that did not concern me. "Still 'tis just as well, else we should not have known about Miss Poole until Mama sprang her on us. Well, perhaps we shan't be stuck with her after all," my stepsister asserted, her eyes narrowing. "No doubt we can think of something to speed her on her way."

"Julianne!" I exclaimed, remembering poor Clothilde.

"Hush, Maggie! Do you want someone to hear us?" She glanced over her shoulder nervously, as though expecting to discover not only her mother, but the entire staff spying on us. "Don't be such a goose! I wasn't planning to jab *her* with a hatpin, if that's what you're thinking! I only meant that if she finds we are difficult charges, she might take a dislike to us and refuse to stay."

"I could put a toad in her bed," Welles offered, almost startling us out of our skins, for we had not heard him come up the stairs.

"Welles!" Julianne cried. "What do you mean by sneaking up on us like that?"

He grinned and tossed his head, flinging back the sheaf of blond hair that was forever falling forward into his eyes.

"I merely wanted to see what you two were conspiring about up here. I say, Miss Poole does seem like a regular tartar, doesn't she?" he commented as he peered through the window at the governess, who, bag in hand, was now ascending the steps of the manor. "She looks as bad as the old beak at school."

"What's a beak?" I asked.

"The headmaster," Julianne explained, frowning. "You know Mama doesn't approve of slang, Welles," she chided.

"Mama doesn't approve of a lot of things—more's the pity," he replied, "but that's never stopped me from doing 'em. If you'd like me to give you a few pointers on how to get rid of the governess, let me know. I've learned quite a few neat tricks at school, you know."

"I'll bet," Julianne drawled sarcastically. "Take yourself off someplace, Welles. Your pranks are always far worse than any *I* ever dream up—and they always get me into more trouble, too!''

"That's only because you always get scared and blab everything afterward,'' he rejoined, disgusted. "Now Maggie, on the other hand, knows how to keep her tongue in her head. Take a hint from me, Julie, and learn how to do so yourself before you embark on any wild scheme to drive off Miss Poole, else you shall surely wind up imprisoned in your room again!''

Whistling, Welles bounded on around the landing, thereby missing seeing the tongue Julianne stuck out at his retreating figure.

"Bothersome boy!" she muttered. "No doubt now *he'll* do some dreadful thing to Miss Poole—just to spite us—and *we'll* get the blame for it! Come on, Maggie. Mama's bringing her upstairs. Let's be off before they catch us!''

After the coming of Welles and Miss Poole, Julianne and I got along much better than we had before. The reasons for this were many. Having Sarah point out to me that Julianne must be experiencing as much difficulty as I in adjusting to our unwelcome relationship had given me my first inkling of what drove my stepsister to behave as she did. After witnessing her tearful outburst the afternoon of her brother's arrival, I now had an even clearer grasp of her character.

The hurly-burly days following her father's death, when the Prescotts' income had been abruptly and sharply reduced, had left Julianne with an abiding horror of being poor. When her mother wasn't there to curb her appetite, she ate ravenously because there had been times in London when she had gone hungry. She coveted things because Lady Chandler, in her desperate bid to stave off her creditors, had either pawned or sold outright so many of the Prescotts' possessions. Julianne resented Welles, even while she adored him, because despite all her other failings, Lady Chandler had managed somehow to obtain the funds to keep him in school, permitting him to escape much of what his sister had suffered and sacrificed.

Welles was a male, Lady Chandler had explained to her daughter, and it was a man's world; a woman was nothing if she had no man to support her. Only witness what had become of them upon Captain Brodie's death! No matter how they must scrimp, Welles must get ahead so he could drag them out of the mire into which they were slowly sinking—and Lady Chandler must do what she could in the meantime to prevent them from going under.

Sir Nigel's arrival on the scene had been a propitious event indeed! Small wonder that Julianne made every effort to win my father's favor. He was security personified: food on the table, clothes on one's back, the wolf gone from one's door.

So, while my stepsister often tried my patience sorely, I attempted to make allowances for her, though, in truth, I did not always succeed at this. Still, on those occasions when I did not, Welles was there to smooth things over, to bully and cajole us both; and so we managed, for his sake, to rub along together tolerably well.

We had also, much to my surprise, developed a strong common bond: We were united in our dislike of the ubiquitous, redoubtable Miss Poole. She was all we had surmised—and more. We had lessons with her each morning and again each afternoon until three; and it was clear to us from the outset that no matter how much she might come to despise us, Miss Poole would not be driven away. She knew both her place and her duty; and because the Hall was so isolated, she received a handsome salary that more than compensated her for any additional discomforts she might suffer.

Our mornings were taken up with the usual studies: languages (primarily French and Italian, though we learned a smattering of German as well), reading, writing, speech, deportment, and the barest fundamentals of arithmetic, history, and geography. It was not, after all, considered necessary or desirable for a woman to know too much about these last three. Our afternoons were devoted to skills. Miss Poole both sang and played the piano creditably; her watercolors were commendable (though I thought they lacked life), and her needlework was even finer than Sarah's. In addition to this, once a week, the dancing master, Mr. Rutledge, came, and Julianne and I learned everything from country dances to the scandalous waltz.

Occasionally, under our governess's watchful eye, we were given over to Mrs. Merrick, the cook, who taught us the basics of food preparation. Miss Poole was of the firm opinion that even though it was extremely unlikely we would ever be called upon to produce a meal, we should be capable of recognizing whether our cooks were substituting lesser cuts of meat for those we had approved and whether our butlers were watering the wine.

Our governess also devoutly believed in keeping fit, so we took long walks in the park, during which we were told more about trees, flowers, and plants than we ever needed or wanted to know.

Welles, who disliked Miss Poole as much as we did, made up a wicked limerick about her, and whenever she said or did something that particularly annoyed him, he recited it to us, making fun of how she had come to be a governess in the first place. It went like this:

> There once was a woman named Poole
> Who attended an exemplary school,
> From books, she was taught,
> But, alas, all for naught,
> For Poole was a very dull fool.

One night, much to our dismay—for by now, Julianne and I had taken Miss Poole's full measure—Welles made good on his offer to put a toad in her bed. Though we knew it to be futile, still we hoped that our governess would scream or swoon and that we would soon be rid of her. But instead she captured the creature in a box; and the following morning, Julianne and I spent a thoroughly dreary hour learning all about amphibians before Miss Poole gave us leave to release her small, warty prisoner in the gardens.

After that, we begged Welles to cease his pranks, fearful that next we should find ourselves examining a snake. Upon being reported by the astute Miss Poole to Sir Nigel for his behavior, Welles himself was summoned to the study, where he was swiftly and smartly paddled by my father, who considered corporal punishment quite proper for a boy.

Even Sarah did not elude our formidable governess, for when Aunt Tibby at last called on Sir Nigel and Lady Chandler, my father was reminded of his niece, and he declared he would be neglecting his duty if he did not see that Sarah, too, was properly educated as befitted a young lady of good breeding. Even if the Honorable "Worthless" Sheffield, as Sir Nigel always referred to Sarah's father, had never amounted to anything, he had been the younger son of an earl; and if, after his death, the Sheffields (whose estates were grossly encumbered, the line being prone to produce drunkards and gamblers) had cast off his family, it was not Sarah's fault.

Thereafter she walked over every day to join Julianne and me at our lessons. Much to my surprise, a heart did indeed beat beneath Miss Poole's flat bosom, for she liked my cousin and was always much nicer to her than to Julianne and me. Because of this, though she despised our governess, Julianne was extremely jealous of Sarah, for my stepsister hated not being the center of attention. To be a woman scorned or overlooked was to be a woman who was nothing, and a woman who was nothing could not be assured of security in a man's world. Only witness Miss Poole, who must work for a living and might at any moment be turned off without a reference! And so Julianne tormented Sarah spitefully until Welles staunchly put a stop to it.

I think he must have loved Sarah even then, for he was always very kind to her, never teasing her in the careless, though affectionate, manner he did Julianne and me. He talked to my cousin often, for hours on end, as Esmond and I had used to talk, though after Miss Poole's coming, we had little time together. Thus what we did have was all the more precious to me.

None was happier than I, therefore, when Sir Nigel,

who had discovered too late that the addition of two more children to his household would result in a very large and most annoying increase in both his responsibilities and expenses, announced that all of us, including my aunt and cousins, would attend a forthcoming fair in Launceston. There, he said, he would purchase ponies for Welles, Esmond, and Sarah. He included my cousins, I knew, because he could hardly refuse his nephew and niece what he gave to his stepchildren, lest he be thought to be avoiding his obligations to his heir.

There would, in addition, be a pony for Julianne, my father continued, provided, he reminded her severely, that she intended to treat it in a responsible fashion. This, Julianne agreed to do, ignoring his stern visage to climb up in his lap and hug him, smiling at him so sweetly as she apologized again for the incident with Clothilde that for a moment, Sir Nigel was quite taken aback. He harrumphed and frowned and grumbled under his breath; but in the end, he tweaked her saucy curls and called her a naughty puss, and all was forgiven and forgotten.

He was by then in such a rare good humor that he even went so far as to promise me a present as well. I smiled and thanked him quietly, wishing I dared to embrace him as Julianne had. But despite the fact that since his remarriage, my father had not once got drunk and verbally abused me, still I sensed I had yet to find any real favor in his eyes; and so I hung back, as always, on the fringes of his notice.

Chapter Four

The Horse and the Letter

The horse,
Who stood at hand, utter'd a dreadful cry: . . .

—*Sohrab and Rustum*
Matthew Arnold

It was a beautiful morning when we set out on the road toward Launceston. The sun had burned away the early mist and dew. Now the sky was a vast expanse of cerulean across which white mare's tails flew, and the moors were an endless sweep of green, dotted with purple and gold where heather and bracken grew. The wind stirred faintly, its breath tinged with the cool, salty kiss of the sea lapping against the rocky beach in the distance; and the mournful cries of the gulls along the shore broke the stillness of the day.

My father cut a handsome figure astride his big bay gelding. For a moment, it was as though the portrait of him as a young man, which hung in the long gallery of the Hall, had come to life; and I saw how reckless and dashing he must have been once, before the full weight of his many responsibilities had settled upon his broad shoulders and he had been forced to curtail the caprices of his youth. Truly it was no wonder that he had swept my mother off her feet and that his courtship of Lady Chandler had proved such a whirlwind affair as well. He was fit as a man in his twenties, and there was about him still a devilish air that attracted women like moths to a flame.

Lady Chandler herself was a breathtaking vision in a swirl of sprig muslin and a flowered hat scrumptious as a confection. The ruffles of her sheer, open parasol fluttered delicately in the breeze, framing her face like a picture and casting Aunt Tibby and Miss Poole, who sat also in my father's barouche, into the shade. I was reminded of the peacocks strutting upon the lawns at the manor, causing the poor little sparrows to pale into insignificance beside them.

The rest of us rode in Aunt Tibby's ancient landau. I sat by Julianne on one seat, for she had adamantly insisted she would not have her gown crushed by her unruly brother piling in beside her. Welles and Esmond were opposite us, with Sarah placed comfortably between them, for she scarcely took up any space at all. To pass the time, we played Twenty Questions and then, when that palled, I Love My Love, during which Julianne set us all to laughing because all her answers had to do with means: She loved her love because he had a country estate, a house in London, money to make the mare go, and so forth. Welles drawled dryly that it was a good thing she hadn't got the letter *z*, to which she promptly replied that she loved her love because he had a Zedland farm, sending us all off into fresh gales of laughter. Thus we were in high spirits when we finally arrived at Launceston, the gateway to Cornwall, as it was sometimes called.

It was a very old town, I explained to Welles and Julianne, who had previously passed through it but briefly and so knew little of it. It had been settled even before the Norman Conqueror's half brother, Robert of Mortain, had built on the site Dunheved Castle, as the fortress had originally been named, though it had been called Launceston Castle from the time of the Tudors. The ancient keep towering above us in the distance dominated the village, which, for the most part, had grown up around it.

The fortress was a ruin now, standing on a high, steep

motte in a park that had once been the bailey; for though the Royalists had tried valiantly to defend it, most of the castle had been destroyed during the Civil War. It was still possible, however, to climb a flight of narrow stone stairs to the plateau at the top of the motte and to go up a winding staircase inside the old stone donjon, as I had done once, from where, on a clear day, one could see out over the surrounding countryside for miles in every direction. Small wonder, then, that in ages past, the keep had been so important to the Dukes of Cornwall.

Near the center of town, on Castle Street, I pointed out Lawrence House and then, farther on, the ancient parish church, St. Mary Magdalene, which had been built in 1524 and overlooked the large market square to which people came from miles around to sell their products. Here vendors hawked their wares, and as we passed, I heard the old, familiar cry of "Cockles and mussels, alive, alive-o" and smelled the tangy, enticing odor of the shellfish fresh from the sea.

The hooves of Sir Nigel's gelding and the wheels of our vehicles clattered noisily upon the cobblestones amid the hustle and bustle of the market, which was even more crowded than usual because of the fair. The square and the adjacent streets were filled to overflowing, and the resulting cacophony was deafening. Men stood in groups on corners, some heatedly discussing politics, others exchanging the latest news and calling hearty greetings to passing friends. Women gossiped and laughed as they moved from stall to stall, the bags and baskets they carried crammed to bursting with their purchases. Determined buyers bargained loudly with equally determined sellers. Doors on thatch-roofed cottages banged as children ran in and out, adding to the general hubbub.

We reached the fair at last, though it took some time to find a place where we could wedge my father's gelding and our barouche and landau in among the rest of the horses and vehicles that littered the plain on the outskirts of the village. Then, shepherded along by Lady Chandler and Miss Poole, we made our way toward the gaily striped tents, carts, and caravans at the far edge of town.

As we joined the raucous, milling crowd that had flocked to the fair, we caught glimpses of jugglers and acrobats, ropewalkers and even more skillful ropedancers, a strong man and a fat lady; and once, we watched a man stride by on a pair of stilts. He doffed his hat as he passed us, and for the rest of the day, Miss Poole preened like a parrot who had got an almond, no doubt thinking his gesture had been meant for her alone. There were mimes and mummers, a man who swallowed swords, and a family who did tricks with dogs and barebacked horses. Bold, sloe-eyed Gypsy wenches, their zils ringing or tambourines shaking, danced to the music of ouds, flutes, and doumbeks, while others of their dark-skinned ilk read palms and told fortunes. Farther on, a group of children howled with glee at a puppet show in which a little humpbacked husband quarreled comically with his tart-tongued wife and exchanged violent blows with her. At a high-wheeled, brightly painted caravan, one side of which had been opened down and laid upon two stout barrels to form a platform, a troupe of players was performing a melodrama, much to the delight of the audience, who hissed and booed enthusiastically whenever the villain appeared.

There was as much to buy as there was to see, for farmers, craftsmen, and merchants alike had come from distant places in the hope of making a profit. Horses whinnied, cattle mooed, pigs oinked, and goats and sheep bleated, adding to the uproar of excited babble and laughter. Mongrel dogs barked as they chased dirty urchins who, with sticks, batted hoops and balls along the ground. I saw one lad shove another into a cart, sending a crate of apples and pears tumbling, and the peddler shouted and boxed both boys' ears soundly before he scurried to gather the fruit being snatched up by the pauper brats who had descended upon it like flies. At another stand, an old woman screeched while she caned away a rascal attempting to filch one of her trinkets.

At Lady Chandler's insistence, for the crisp morning

air and the drive had quickened our appetites, Sir Nigel stopped at a pastry booth, and we all had strawberry tarts topped with clotted cream (this last was a Cornish specialty), before continuing on our way.

A short time later, Lady Chandler bought some buttons and trim from a weaver; Aunt Tibby silently laid some lace upon the counter, too, shooting my father an indignant glance, as though daring him not to pay for it. But he did so without so much as a frown, resigned, I suppose, to the fact that having foisted an unsuitable wife on his family, he must now suffer the consequences if he were to have any peace. Miss Poole, however, handed over her own hard-earned money for a bolt of coarse grey wool, from which I was sure she intended to make a winter cloak; devoutly I prayed she would be gone from the Hall before she had a chance to wear the cape.

Long before we had made a complete tour of the fair, Sir Nigel became impatient with our gaping and exclaiming, our dilly-dallying and constant halts; and finally he suggested we go our separate ways, as he had no desire (as Welles clamored to do) to view the anomalies the barkers claimed were inside the pavilions or (as Julianne kept lagging behind to do) to ogle the dolls displayed at various stalls. He gave each of us children a crown, and after bidding us all to meet him at three o'clock at the livestock pens, he strolled away, Lady Chandler hanging on his arm—like a leech, I thought.

Once my father and stepmother had been safely swallowed up by the throng, Welles, grinning mischievously, declared he'd see us all later and, dragging a startled and protesting Esmond behind him, hastily disappeared into the crowd, pretending not to hear Aunt Tibby calling anxiously and Miss Poole sharply after him.

I could not help but smile, certain my dear, unsuspecting Esmond was about to embark on the most adventurous day of his life; and the neatly foiled Miss Poole, discerning my thoughts and having reached a like conclusion, glared at me repressively for finding such a notion so entertaining. But even she could not dampen my high spirits this day. I envied my stepbrother and cousin's escape, and I longed to slip away, as they had done, to do as I pleased. But having once been deftly eluded, Aunt Tibby and Miss Poole were not to be taken unaware again; clucking like hens, they gathered Sarah, Julianne, and me under their wings and shooed us before them as though we were hatchling chicks in need of protection.

Still Aunt Tibby proved an indulgent chaperon, and even Miss Poole unbent slightly, for it was seldom that one in her position had an opportunity to enjoy herself as she did today. Thus she was as apt to stop and gawk at oddities and enticements alike as we were, though when she spied Julianne smirking at her slyly and jabbing me covertly in the ribs with an elbow, she tried to disguise her obvious interest in the freaks and wares by sniffing and hurrying us on.

The day seemed to fly by in a whirlwind of laughter and activity. We saw wondrous sights: a three-legged sheep, a two-headed cow, contortionists whose bodies seemed to be made of rubber and who twisted themselves into unbeliev-able positions, even a man who ate fire. We spent our money recklessly on the shows, and trinkets and games, too. Julianne bought a doll; Sarah, more practical, pur-chased ribands for her hair. At one of the barkers' stands, I threw darts and, much to my delight, won a wooden monkey that danced when I shook the stick from which it dangled. We sampled so many delicious tidbits that I thought I should soon grow to be a lard bottom myself, if I were not sick first, for my stomach groaned from so many unaccus-tomed treats: Bath buns and currant bread, pasties and toad-in-the-holes, prawns and winkles, and banbury cakes and rock cakes. I ate nearly as much as Julianne, who was clutching her own stomach and moaning by the time we reached the livestock pens to meet Sir Nigel and Lady Chandler.

Nevertheless my stepsister forgot her stomachache soon enough when she saw the ponies being trotted out for her inspection: sleek Connemaras and rugged Dales, little Exmoors and shaggy Highlands, fat Shetlands and beautiful Welsh ponies, like my own Clothilde. Welles, his cap gone and his jacket torn, for he had got into a fight with some of the local youths, chose a splendid Welsh cob, the largest and strongest of the Welsh breeds. Esmond, who had unwillingly been dragged into the fray with my stepbrother and looked the worse for wear, having received a black eye and cut lip, picked a handsome New Forest. Sarah, speechless with delight, pointed to a gentle, sure-footed Dartmoor; and Julianne, having taken her time deciding, finally selected a pretty Fell and, with winsome smiles, persuaded Sir Nigel to buy her, as well, a small, yellow-wheeled red cart for the pony to pull.

To my utter surprise and pleasure, I learned my father had not forgotten his promise to me either, for after the others were done with their choosing, he handed me a basket, saying gruffly that he hoped I were pleased with its contents. When I opened the lid, I discovered a furry black kitten nestled inside, a huge scarlet bow about its neck. It was a most unexpected present, the only real gesture of kindness I had ever known from Sir Nigel. For a moment, my eyes brimmed with tears as I stroked the soft, mewing creature. Gravely I thanked my father for the fairing, and I saw in his eyes a strange, fleeting expression, as though he had suddenly realized I was of some account, after all, and he regretted our past. For an instant, it seemed as though he would speak. Then the dealer, having taken Sir Nigel's measure and recognized he was a man of excellent taste— and, more important, had the means to indulge it—led out a fine colt to catch his eye; and my father turned his attention from me to the horse.

Later I was to think how different all our lives might have been had it not been for that fierce, magnificent animal, for it was to prove a fateful beast, as you shall learn. But once more I get ahead of myself. I must tell you now about the horse as it was when first I saw it, before it became Sir Nigel's, though in the end, it was only to Draco that it ever truly belonged. . . .

The colt was young yet, not above three or four years of age at the most; but it promised someday to be a stallion beyond compare. It stood well over seventeen hands high and was massively muscled. Its chest was deep; its legs were graceful but strong. Power seemed to ooze from every pore of its coat, black and shiny as a raven's wing glistening in the rain, without a single trace of white. Its mane and tail were long, thick, and shaggy, streaming away from its well-proportioned body as it cantered spiritedly about the roped-off plain, arching its neck and tossing its beautifully shaped head. I inhaled sharply at the sight, for never had I seen a horse at once so lovely and so barbaric.

I sensed even then that it was a dangerous animal, for its ears were laid back warningly and its proud nostrils flared as it snorted and pawed the earth; and the dealer, though he had it on a long lead, warily kept his distance from the beast.

"I'll be honest with 'ee, sir," he said to my father, "t' colt's hardly used ta t' halter, much less green broke, despite his age, fer I've nivver yet managed ta get a saddle on him. He's a vicious divvil—an' no mistake. He's already crippled two good men an' killed a third; an' no doubt he ought ta be destroyed—an' rightfully so. Still an' all, I've not been able ta bring meself ta do it, sir, fer I've nivver laid eyes on a grander horse. I thought ta put him ta stud, fer he'll throw some fine get, ta be sure. But I've not got t' heart fer it since he murdered poor Tom; an' what with me missus bein' afeered fer me own self ... well ... I thought 'twas best just ta sell him. If thee've men enough with t' time an' t' experience ta do so, p'rhaps 'ee can tame the colt, sir, though I don't rightly know. He's a proud 'un, not like ta bend ta just anyone. He's fit fer a king, that 'un is!"

I never knew what Sir Nigel saw in the horse that day to draw him so powerfully to it; but from that moment on, it was as though some demon had seized him as far as the animal was concerned, for he became utterly obsessed by it and behaved toward it with an irrationality that bordered, I think, on madness. His desire to possess the beast was so strong as to be almost tangible; his eyes glittered with greed and lust and a strange, fervid light when he examined the colt. At the look of unnatural craving on my father's face, an odd chill prickled the hairs on my nape, so I shivered beneath the hot sun and suddenly wished we had never come to the fair.

"How much do you want for him?" Sir Nigel asked the dealer.

After some minutes of haggling, the bargain was struck, and my father made arrangements for the horse to be delivered, along with the ponies and the cart, to the Hall the following day.

Then he glanced again at the animal and, as though speaking to himself, declared, "I'll break you to the bit, or I'll break your proud neck! But one way or the other, you'll soon learn who's master between us, for I'm more than a match for you, my fierce beauty!"

At that, almost as though it had understood the words, the beast flung back its head and whinnied a challenge of its own in return, looking so wild and defiant that for a moment, I feared it would race across the roped-off plain and attack its new owner. But Sir Nigel, his eyes narrowed, did not flinch from the colt, but smiled grimly and nodded to it, as though acknowledging the gauntlet that had been thrown down between them; and once more I shuddered uneasily, stricken by a peculiar sense of foreboding.

After that, as the afternoon had grown quite late, we started for the manor. Following the excitement of the fair, the conversation on the drive home seemed unnaturally subdued, with only Julianne chatting brightly about the day's events. Earlier Welles and Esmond had exchanged harsh words over the fracas in which my stepbrother had involved them; now they were not speaking. Pointedly they ignored each other, Welles's demeanor scornful, Esmond's frigid. Sarah, upset by the breach between them, attempted to serve as peacemaker; but she quickly desisted when Welles referred to Esmond as a "poor-spirited pig-wigeon," and Esmond retaliated by calling Welles "harebrained" and saying he was like as not "headed for a horse's nightcap." Naturally Esmond was angered by the thought of being labeled a cowardly fool, and Welles resented being told he was an idiot destined for a hangman's noose. I don't think either one ever much cared for the other after that day, a circumstance that saddened me, for I should have liked my cousin and my stepbrother to be friends. I could not help but be torn between them, for I loved Esmond, and I had come to love Welles, too, as though he were my own brother.

Even Julianne had little to say after that, and I was glad when we finally reached the Hall and I could retire to my own room to play with my new kitten, which I named Grimalkin. I had never before had a cat—or, indeed, any pet—and I found him a delightful creature, both intelligent and curious. He explored my chamber thoroughly, mewing and nosing into everything and feistily defying me when I sought to rebuke him. Then, much to my mortification, before I realized what he was about, he proceeded to christen my rug. I scolded him even more crossly after that; but in truth, I was more frightened than wroth, for I feared that if the damp spot were discovered, Grimalkin would be banished to the stables or, worse, taken from me entirely and given away. Hurriedly I began to clean the carpet. Linnet, my abigail, came in while I was at the task, and she saw at once what I was trying to do. Shaking her head and wrinkling her nose, she helped me finish the job. Then, having had more experience than I with animals, she ran down to the stables to fetch a little box of dirt, and we fixed a place in the corner of my dressing room and showed it to the kitten.

For all that he was tiny, Grimalkin seemed to grasp the purpose of the box right away; at least I found no evidence of further accidents when I returned from supper, though he had got into my knitting basket and strewn yarn all over the place.

"Naughty little imp!" I said accusingly, but Grimalkin only stared at me and switched his tail. Then he sprang at me and batted my hand when I bent to pick up the mess.

I had brought a dish of scraps, which Mrs. Merrick had saved for me, and a saucer of cream, and these I now placed on the floor in the hope of distracting him. The kitten ran to the food and ate hungrily. Then, his stomach bulging, he curled up beside me on my chaise longue, purring as sweetly and contentedly as though he had never misbehaved.

I reading a book, we sat together comfortably for some time; and not until Linnet returned to help me undress for bed did Grimalkin once more exercise lamentable conduct. Hearing the sound of the doorknob rattling, he rose, his green eyes wide, his pointed ears pricked forward alertly. Then, before I realized what he intended, he jumped down from the chaise longue, and as Linnet opened the door, he scampered out into the corridor. Crying out, I ran after him, but the kitten eluded me, bounding down the hall toward the south wing, his fluffy tail waving like a gay banner as he rounded the corner.

"Here, Grimalkin. Here, puss," I called softly as I followed him. "Here, Grimalkin. Here, puss."

I spied him at last, sitting in the middle of the floor, licking his fur. I could have sworn he was grinning when he ceased his preening and glanced up at me lazily, for he looked as cocky and pleased with himself as though he had swallowed a canary. Quickly, before he could escape again, I pounced upon him, grabbing hold of the ribbon tied about his neck. Then I snatched him up and reproached him quietly, for this wing was where my father's and stepmother's rooms were located. I knew that Sir Nigel and Lady Chandler had already retired for the evening, and I did not want them to hear me. With the kitten held fast in my arms, I tiptoed back whence I had come, pausing only when my stepmother's voice, sounding unnaturally shrill, reached my ears from her chamber.

"Your brother Quentin . . . *alive,* Nigel!" she exclaimed.

At first I thought I must have misunderstood her, and frowning, I drew near to her door and slowly, stealthily, pressed my ear against it, my heart thumping with fear that if she suddenly ripped open the portal, I would tumble headlong into her room.

"But I—I thought you said he was dead, darling," I heard her murmur, obviously flustered and confused.

I must admit I was somewhat bewildered myself, for as far as I knew, Uncle Quentin had indeed been cold in his grave for several years now. Now it seemed clear from Lady

Chandler's words that he had not, as we had all thought, been slowly moldering to dust after all.

Imagine that! I thought, wondering what it all meant.

"Yes, I did," my father replied, his voice low and harassed, as I had seldom heard it. "But for God's sake, Gwyneth! I thought he *was!* Everyone did. He disappeared over twenty years ago, and no one has heard from him since! Of course we assumed he was dead. Who wouldn't have?"

"Yes, of course. Who wouldn't have?" Lady Chandler echoed faintly. "But, then, how do you explain the letter, Nigel?"

The letter? What letter? I wondered curiously. Then I remembered the plain, dirty, creased envelope Iverleigh had disdainfully handed upon a silver salver to my father after our return home from the fair. At first Sir Nigel, frowning, had merely glanced at the missive cursorily. But then, his eyes narrowing, he had suddenly plucked it from the tray and stridden to his study to read it. Afterward he had emerged looking like a thundercloud, his face dark and scowling, his mouth set in a thin, tight line of rage. He had snapped at us all so fiercely during supper that we had grown silent and been grateful when the meal had ended.

Now he spoke again.

"My dear," he said dryly to my stepmother, "I fear my news has addled your wits, for you are thinking like my sister Tiberia—or, rather, *not* thinking like her, as I'm certain she so very seldom *does* think! It's quite obvious, isn't it, that everyone was mistaken and that Quentin is not dead after all, else how could he have written me the letter?"

"Are you—are you quite sure he *did* write it, Nigel?" Lady Chandler asked sharply.

"But of course. Had it been a fraud, I would simply have pitched it into the dustbin, Gwyneth, and we would not now be having this conversation, would we? No, much as I hate to admit it, Quentin, my brother, is alive, for though it has been over twenty years, I would recognize his dreadful scrawl anywhere. He never could write legibly, you know."

"Well ... what is to be done, then?" Lady Chandler inquired. Then suddenly she cried, "Oh Nigel! Do you realize what this means? *Quentin is your lawful heir!* If anything should befall you, everything would go to him instead of your nephew, Esmond, who's dull and spineless and thus would be easily managed. But Quentin Chandler ... my God, he's a—a scoundrel! A—a blackguard! What would become of us?" Her voice broke off abruptly, catching on a sob.

I hoped she would burst into tears, for I hated her fervently for the mean things she had said about Esmond, which were not at all true, I thought adamantly. But moments later, like a fox who senses the hounds have its scent, my stepmother pulled herself together. I could well imagine the wary, guilty look that must have come into her eyes at my father's next words. I could actually visualize the way she must have lowered her lids to conceal it, then opened them wide with pretended innocence.

"My dear," Sir Nigel drawled to her, "I'm quite sure that in such an unfortunate event, you would rise to the occasion magnificently, as you did upon the late Captain Prescott's demise." He paused for a moment, then laughed wryly. "Oh, come now, Gwyneth!" he chided her. "Did you really think me such a fool as to be taken in by your widowed-heiress charade? No, do not bother to answer, for I can see you did. *Tsk, tsk.* Really, my dear! Surely you know me better than that! I had you investigated most thoroughly before asking you to marry me. I was well aware of your ... er ... shall we say *desperate*? ... circumstances before our marriage."

"Then ... I'm—I'm afraid I don't understand. Why did you wed me, then?"

"Why, I admired your cleverness, of course, my dear. It has long been my experience that women with both daring and brains are very few and far between indeed. Besides, I needed someone to take in hand that poor little misbegotten waif of mine, and at that, you have succeeded splendidly, as I knew you would. Margaret's appearance and manners *are* much improved. I make you my compliments on that, too, Gwyneth.''

Since I did not know what the word ''misbegotten'' meant, I resolved to look it up in the dictionary. But still I was hurt by my father's referring to me as a waif, as though I were naught but a miserable stray he had found on his doorstep. Nevertheless I did not sneak away, but continued to listen, despite the fact that Grimalkin had grown impatient and had begun to squirm in my grasp. Fearing he would set up a howl otherwise, I released him, telling myself I could catch him later, after I had learned all there was to know about Uncle Quentin and his letter; for I had realized at once what it would mean to Esmond, and to Aunt Tibby and Sarah, too, if my cousin were not Sir Nigel's heir after all.

''Be at ease, my dear,'' my father was saying, ''for though Quentin is all you have surmised—and more—I see little likelihood of his inheriting, since he made it clear in his letter that he is dying.''

''Dying? Well, thank God for that!'' Lady Chandler uttered uncharitably. ''But . . . if that is the case, why has he written to you? What does he want if not to press his claim to the estate?''

''He wants to be accorded a proper burial in the family crypt,'' Sir Nigel answered. He paused, then went on. ''Further, he has a child, a son, fifteen years old, the product of his union with a Gypsy wench whose family cast her off upon learning of the liaison. Apparently gypsies have some morals after all. At any rate, the mother died some years ago, Quentin wrote, and soon the boy will have no one. My brother wishes me to come to London to fetch both him, if he is still alive by then, and the child. He wants, before his death, to be assured of his son's welfare, else he fears the boy will be put in a workhouse—or worse.''

''The child is illegitimate, then?''

''Yes, as misbegotten in his own way as poor Margaret. I don't know what Quentin can have been thinking of, taking up with a Gypsy wench—and no doubt a pox-ridden whore at that! Father is probably turning in his grave at the very thought! But what my brother means me to do with his Gypsy bastard, I haven't any notion. God knows, the Hall is overrun by too damned many bloody brats already! With Margaret and your own children and Tiberia's two, one would think I were running a foundling home!" Sir Nigel snapped. "Still, blood is blood, and the boy's not the first of his ilk to blot the family Bible—and like as not, he won't be the last either. I can't let him starve. I guess 'twould do no harm to put him to work on the farms or in the mines."

"Well, surely Quentin can't expect you to do any more than that anyway, darling," Lady Chandler remarked, her voice calmer now. "It isn't as though the child is your heir—or even a proper Chandler. He was born on the wrong side of the blanket after all."

"Yes, that's true; and too, I've no doubt that in the end, he'll prove to be little more than gallow's bait anyway, no matter what I do, for Quentin was always a hotheaded ne'er-do-well. Frankly I'm surprised he didn't wind up on a gibbet himself. I'm certain from my brother's description of him that the boy has inherited his father's disposition—and no doubt his mother's as well—and God knows, those Gypsies are naught but tramps and thieves! Well, I suppose if the wretched little bastard can't be turned to some account, I can always put him off the place later, when he's more able to fend for himself."

"Of course you can, darling," my stepmother agreed. "Now, hadn't we better turn in? 'Tis getting late, and if you intend to leave for London tomorrow, you'll need your rest."

"Yes, I will, won't I? See that my bags are packed first thing in the morning, Gwyneth, and instruct Mrs. Seyton to prepare a room for Quentin, just in case he *is* still alive when I arrive and survives the journey here. I suppose we'll have to have the child here, too, until my brother's dead and we can make the necessary arrangements for... damn it! What did Quentin say the boy was called? Some accursed, heathenish, Gypsy-sounding name, as I recall. Ah, yes. Now I remember. Draco. That was it. Draco."

And so it was that I, with my ear pressed against Lady

Chandler's door like any common eavesdropper, first heard of my uncle's illegitimate son. There was irony in that somewhere, I was to think later, though not until eight long years after Draco's coming. But the thought was only fleeting then, swiftly driven from my mind by the cousin who was to play such a crucial role in my life, as you shall learn.

Thoughtfully I returned to my chamber. Linnet, I saw, had laid out my night rail and then had fallen asleep on the chaise longue, waiting for me. I shook her gently, and when she started awake and began to mumble some excuse, I told her to be at ease and sent her to bed, saying I wished to read a while longer. After she had gone, my mind drifted back over Sir Nigel and Lady Chandler's conversation, and I was reminded of the word I wanted to look up. Hoping I would not wake Julianne or, worse, Miss Poole, I lit a candle and slipped into the dark schoolroom, where I took the dictionary from the bookshelf and, laying it upon a table, riffled its pages until I found the entry for which I searched.

"Misbegotten," I read, meant illegitimate or ill conceived. Since I knew I was Sir Nigel's lawful daughter and not a bastard like the unknown Draco, I realized my father thought of me in terms of the latter explanation; and though it had been many a long night since I had been roused from my bed in response to his drunken summons, I felt sure he still blamed me for my mother's death.

He wishes I had never been conceived or born, I thought, *just as he wishes poor Draco didn't exist.*

I felt a sudden kinship with this unwanted cousin I had yet to meet, this Gypsy bastard. I remembered the Gypsies at the fair. Would he be like them? I wondered. Strange and foreign and faintly disturbing? "Gallow's bait," Sir Nigel had predicted. I shivered, feeling as though a goose had just walked over my grave. Then hurriedly I crept back to my chamber and, after undressing and pulling on my nightgown, slid into bed and drew the covers up close around me.

It was not until the next morning, when I was awakened by a scream, followed by the loud crash of a breakfast tray and Nora, one of the housemaids, shrieking, "Lud save us! There's a mad beastie loose in the house!" that I realized I had forgotten all about retrieving Grimalkin.

As punishment for not looking after him properly, I was confined to my room for the rest of the day; and thereafter I made certain the roguish kitten was safely tucked in his basket each night before I went to bed— although I was tempted by Welles's malicious suggestion that we set him on Miss Poole instead.

Chapter Five

The Night of the Gypsy and the Black Sheep

Has he not a rogue's face?...a hanging-look to me...has a damn'd Tyburn-face, without benefit o' the Clergy...

—*Love for Love*
William Congreve

On a night dark and wild as my Gypsy cousin himself, Draco arrived at the Hall. Earlier the day had turned cool and grey, and there had been in the air that peculiar stillness that presages a summer storm. A moonless blackness had fallen swiftly after dusk. Then suddenly the wind had risen with an ominous shriek, as though a legion of ghosts had descended upon the moors, and the roiling thunderheads massed in the dark, sullen sky had abruptly opened up to disgorge their contents violently upon the earth.

Now, in the distance, I could hear the roar of the sea, turned angry and brutal with the onslaught of the tempest, crashing against the scarred black cliffs that edged the jagged coast; above this rang the savage crack of the lightning and thunder that accompanied the pelting rain. Fancifully I thought it must have been just such a night as this when Taliesin the Merlin, disguised as Brithael, had brought Uther Pendragon, he who was to become a king, across the dangerous, narrow causeway that led to Tintagel Castle, whose ruins stood not far from the Hall.

I lay huddled in my bed with my covers drawn up comfortingly about me, shivering as I felt the old house creak and groan around me, as though it were on the verge of collapse, as though the all-powerful elements had triumphed over it at last. Somewhere a shutter had come loose; with each gust of the howling wind, it banged eerily against one wall of the manor. It sounded as though some horrible, unworldly thing were thudding against the door like a battering ram, demanding to be let in. I shuddered at the thought, my vivid imagination running wild as the storm, filling my head with one awful scene after another, so I could not sleep, but lay wide-awake and trembling from my dreadful whimsies. Thankfully I did not then know that what I was to see this night would prove even more monstrous than anything my mind might ever have conjured.

At last, after what seemed like hours, though it was only just after midnight, I heard the faint but distinct pounding of horses galloping up the drive and, in their wake, the clatter of coach wheels turning far too rapidly. The sounds were punctuated by the repeated lashing of a whip and shouted curses, caught and carried away by the gale; and I thought the coachman must either be mad or fleeing the devil himself to be traveling at such a reckless speed and on such a bad night.

Something has happened, I thought, *perhaps an accident. . . .*

I quivered at the notion, glad I was safe in my bed. But still, besieged by curiosity, I did not sleep, but strained my ears, listening, wondering what was amiss.

Presently, from the attic above, there came the murmur of servants' voices and the tread of hurried footsteps, and I knew that Iverleigh and Mrs. Seyton had awakened and were even now issuing orders to sleepy footmen and maids, roused from their warm, snug beds. Then, through the thin space beneath my door, I spied the flicker of a lamp or candle as someone passed hastily through the corridor outside. Some demon suddenly seizing me in its fist, I rose silently and drew on my white cotton wrapper, determined to discover for myself what was wrong.

Like a wraith, I slipped from my chamber, taking care that none should see me as I sneaked down the hall to the landing, where I knelt and pressed my face against the cold, rattling glass panes of the window that overlooked the front lawn below. Through the pouring rain, I could glimpse the glow of the lanterns that hung from the carriage and that now swung to and fro crazily with the jolting coach, so the light seemed to flash like fireflies among the branches of the trees.

A sudden, chilling draft swirled up the stairs as, in the hall beneath me, Iverleigh opened one of the massive oak front doors to light the lamps on either side of the portico. I heard him curse under his breath to Mrs. Seyton when the wind blew out his torch and he was forced to ask her to fetch another. Then came her muttered reply, terse and sharp, for she alone of the staff was unafraid of him. I shivered as the cold air swept up beneath my nightgown, brushing like ice against my bare skin, and I pulled my wrapper more tightly about me, aware that I was behaving foolishly, that I ought to go back to bed. But still I made no move to do so, compelled into remaining where I was by my desire to know what was happening.

The carriage had finally come to a halt before the doors of the manor. Now I could see that the coach bore Sir Nigel's crest upon the panels, and I knew something terrible must have taken place, else old Phillip, my father's coachman, would not have been pushing the horses so hard on a night like this. I shuddered as I watched the scene below me unfold as in a drama, for it seemed to have a theatrical quality, as though I viewed it through an ebony vignette and everything moved slowly, as though by design.

Now Iverleigh and two of the footmen appeared. Before they had even finished letting down the steps of the carriage, Sir Nigel flung open its door so violently that I thought it must have shattered the side of the coach when it slammed against it. Impatiently my father alighted, scowling blackly, his face even fiercer than usual in the wavering flames of the lamps as he began to snarl orders right and left. With the many capes of his greatcoat flapping about him wildly in the wind, he appeared like an ominous bird hovering upon the drive before without a backward glance, he abruptly swooped into the Hall. I heard the slap of his leather gloves against his thigh and the thud of his boots as he strode rapidly across the floor. Still I made no move, but stayed crouched by the window, my eyes fastened fixedly on the carriage. I could not tear them away, for I knew there was more to come.

After a time, my diligence was rewarded, for slowly, reluctantly, my cousin Draco emerged. Unwittingly my breath caught in my throat as he paused to gaze up at the house and I saw him for the first time—all too quickly, but clearly nevertheless—wet with the sheeting rain and eerily illuminated by the lamps and the serrated lightning that slashed across the maddened black sky.

He was big for his age, tall and painfully thin, as though he were no stranger to need or want and had suffered much in his short life. Still I could tell that the body beneath his ragged black garments (for he wore no cloak) was lithe as a whipcord and massively muscled, evidence that he was accustomed to grueling manual labor. His soaked shirt clung to strong, bulging arms and a broad back and chest that tapered to a firm, flat belly; his breeches hugged powerful thighs and calves that looked hard as iron. His long, shaggy hair, plastered to his head, was black as the night sky and gleamed like jet where the pale, fitful light touched the sodden strands and stray locks the savage wind caught and lifted. His skin was dark, much darker even than mine, which was born of the blood of Irish and Spanish, as well as French, Cornish, and English, ancestors, so that even had I not known he was a Gypsy, I should have guessed it at once.

But most of all, it was his hollow, upturned face as it appeared at that moment that I shall never forget: wild and brutish and ugly, I thought, like that of some cruel, hungry predator, and naked with such hatred that involuntarily I gasped and drew back from the windowpanes as though I had been struck a stunning blow. The rain streamed unchecked down his dark visage; the light danced across it erratically, one moment revealing it, the next casting it in shadow. I shuddered at the sight, feeling a sudden, strange foreboding, as though the devilish effect were somehow a reflection of Draco himself. Fierce, thick brows swooped over eyes blacker than any I had ever before seen, hard eyes that glittered as they stared with bitter mockery and contempt at the manor. I had a fleeting impression of a broken, aquiline nose and full, carnal lips twisted in a jeering caricature of a smile before at last the boy turned away, leaving that scornful, defiant expression stamped indelibly upon my mind.

I had seen that look somewhere before, I thought; but like mist, the memory eluded me, and I could not place it.

Now I observed that Tim, one of the footmen, had climbed up on top of the coach to assist old Phillip and David, the escort, with the unloading; and to my utter horror, as they untied the straps that held the baggage in place and, with difficulty, threw off the blanket, heavy with rain and snapping in the wind, that covered the whole, I saw my uncle Quentin for the first time. A scream and bile together rose sickeningly in my throat, for his grim countenance, dripping with rain and looking, despite its deep, harsh lines of pain and dissipation, so similar to my father's, was cold and white as the belly of a fish. His black eyes stared up at me glassily, unblinkingly, and his body, stretched haphazardly over the portmanteaus, was so stiff and still that I knew he had been dead for some time.

Slowly, carefully, the men began to lift his corpse in order to hand it down from the carriage to several of the other male servants who had gathered outside to assist them under the direction of Iverleigh. Although he had been quite ill before his death, Uncle Quentin was still big and heavy, and Tim, the youngest of the footmen, was not very strong. He missed his footing on the wet, bulky baggage and lost his balance, nearly toppling over the side of the coach. In the process, he lost his grip on my uncle's body as well, and the corpse slipped free of Phillip's and David's grasp, too, and rolled off the top of the carriage. The others tried to catch it as it fell, but they were taken unaware and so were slow to react; and my uncle's body hit the muddy drive, his head smashing horribly against one wheel of the vehicle before his corpse lay rigid and flat once more, toes up, eyes open and fixed in an accusing glare upon me.

Choking, one hand clapped to my mouth to hold back the vomit in my throat, I turned and ran blindly from the landing down the corridor to my room, now wishing I had never thought to spy on the scene outside. I slammed the door shut behind me, stumbled to my chamber pot, cast aside the lid, and retched into the bowl until there was nothing left to come up. Then, trembling with shock and the aftermath of my heaving, I crept into my bed and snatched the covers up about me.

I had never seen anyone dead before. Nothing had prepared me for the terrible emptiness and ugliness of it, as though the soul's exit from the body took its dignity as well, leaving it graceless and pathetic, an awkward, untidy thing to be hidden from view, lest it embarrass the living with the knowledge that they, too, would someday lie just as helplessly and mortifyingly exposed. Shaken, I prayed that when my own demise came, I should have someone who loved me there to shut my eyes and compose my appearance so my every blemish would not be revealed to all who looked upon me. For a long time, I could not put the hideous picture of Uncle Quentin from my mind; over and over, I saw his corpse fall, his head hit the wheel, his sightless eyes stare into mine. But at last, to my vast relief, I managed to force my thoughts back to my cousin Draco, and Uncle Quentin's macabre, dead image paled beside the wild, quick one of his Gypsy bastard.

As though it were all happening again, I could see Draco's dark face, filled with rebellion and repudiation, stare up at the manor. Once more I wondered where I had seen such an expression previously, why it had seemed so familiar to me, why it haunted me now. I did not know. At last I closed my eyes and made myself breathe deeply and evenly in the hope that sleep would come.

I dreamed that night—strange, disjointed dreams in which I watched my cousin Draco slip into the paddock like any other common Gypsy to steal that demoniac colt that Sir Nigel had bought at the fair; and when I awakened in the morning and remembered what I had dreamed, I realized where I had seen before that look upon my cousin's face last night: It was the same look the fierce black horse had worn when my father had vowed to master it or see it dead.

Chapter Six

Draco

> I look where he lies white-faced and still
> in the coffin—I draw near, . . .
>
> —*Reconciliation*
> Walt Whitman

"I tell you, Linnet, it was enough to turn your hair grey, Mr. Quentin a-lyin' there still and silent as the grave, with the rain a-pourin' down on him and his black eyes a-starin' up at me like he knew I was the one who lost hold of his body in the first place and started it on its way off the coach into the mud! Why, it makes gooseflesh prickle my arms even now just to think about it!" Tim said, making a shivering sound.

"And as if that weren't enough, that stiff-rump Iverleigh was present, and he gave me a dressing-down I shan't soon forget—and that's the God's honest truth! Still 'twas better than the master findin' out, for I shudder to think what *he* would have said if he'd known. Even if he never liked him, black sheep or not, Mr. Quentin was still his brother, and a Chandler to boot, not like that dashed Gypsy bastard, born at Hogs Norton and a-sittin' this very minute in the drawin' room, lookin' like he were a bloody nob or something! Aye, no doubt the master would have seen me flogged or turned off without a reference or both if he'd been there, for he's as cold as Mr. Quentin is now—may the poor devil rest in peace—and no mistake!

"Why, David said as how Mr. Quentin was still alive when they left London, and he up and died long about Dartmoor, and Sir Nigel rapped on the box and told Phillip to pull over, that Mr. Quentin was dead and that he— meaning the master—wasn't aimin' to ride on to the Hall with a worthless blackguard's corpse a-stinkin' and a-starin' him in the face all the while. At that, David said, the mutton-fisted Gypsy bugger got all wrought up, and all of a sudden, he went for Sir Nigel's throat—liked to choked the master half to death!"

"Nay, you don't say!" Linnet exclaimed; and I knew her eyes were sparkling with appreciation at the morbid tale that had already set the entire household agog.

My abigail was a bold, brassy piece, a few years older than I. She had, I suspected, a good deal more knowledge of those things about which all ladies profess to know nothing. I knew I ought to continue on down the back stairs—before she got herself in trouble—and put a stop to her cosy little tête-à-tête with Tim, which was taking place around the corner, halfway down the steps; but I made no move to do so. After all, my sole purpose in being on the back stairs in the first place was to glean what gossip I could from the kitchen just beyond.

"Aye, that was the way of it, all right," the young footman went on. "David said as how it took him and Phillip both to yank the peery clod-skull off, and even then, the noddy brat liked to darkened their daylights before they managed to get him under control—wild as a mad dog, he was.

"David said that after that, Sir Nigel looked pert near angry enough to spit in a pew, with his cravat all askew and him also havin' been poked in the chest with his bloomin' tiepin durin' the fracas. He gave the rum little urchin the sharp side of his tongue, and then, with that cane he always carries, he cracked the cull over the head hard enough to send 'em both reelin'. Then the master himself dragged Mr. Quentin's body out of the carriage, pushed the Gypsy bastard back in, and told Phillip and David to load the corpse on top of the coach and get on home. So they hauled the body up and strapped it down and drove on like the hounds of hell were after 'em!''

"As they shall certainly be after you, Mr. Jensby," I heard Iverleigh's voice drawl dryly, "if you and Miss Tyrrell don't get on with your work!"

Stammering their excuses, the two startled servants escaped from the fish-eyed butler as quickly as possible. I heard Linnet coming up the stairs and knew she would guess I had been spying on her, so I turned and made my way back to my chamber as swiftly and noiselessly as I could. Between what I had seen last night from the window overlooking the front lawn, the tantalizing tidbits I had garnered this morning with my ear pressed to the kitchen door, and the conversation I had just overheard between Tim and Linnet on the back stairs, I was certain I had got the gist anyway. No wonder Sir Nigel had looked so irate! My cousin Draco had actually attempted to strangle him!

This piece of news intrigued me most of all, for I had never before known anyone to lay violent hands on my father—and live. He was an expert with both pistols and swords; and on at least three occasions of which I was aware, he had bested unfortunate opponents in duels, all of which had taken place at the crack of dawn and had been over in time for Sir Nigel to consume a hearty breakfast afterward. But, then, he could hardly challenge a fifteen-year-old boy and one who, even if he *were* illegitimate, was still his nephew.

Yet I could not imagine Esmond or Welles—or, indeed, anybody on the estate—attacking my father. I was fascinated by the thought that Draco had done so. As Linnet, bursting with her tale, came in to help me dress, I tingled with a strange, nervous excitement, for I knew that Draco was below in the drawing room, and I thought that if I hurried, I might catch him alone and speak with him before anyone prevented me from doing so.

At last, clothed in a subdued grey gown Linnet had hastily trimmed with some black ribbon, I descended the

stairs to the hall. Here I saw that despite their many duties
to the living, the servants had somehow found time for the
dead, for the windows were already hung with black crepe,
and I supposed there must be funeral wreaths, as well, on
the front doors. Though I could hear the murmur of voices
in the dining room and the kitchen beyond as the footmen
and maids moved to and fro, setting on the sideboard the
steaming dishes that had been prepared for breakfast, the
hall itself was still—like a tomb, I thought; and I shivered,
for despite the servants' usual morning noises, it seemed to
me as though Uncle Quentin's death had cast an unnatural
pall upon the manor. A trifle uneasily, I wondered what
other changes would be wrought with his demise.

After making certain no one was about, I tiptoed to the
drawing-room doors and opened them a crack. Then, just as
quickly, I pulled them shut, hesitant now to enter, for my
brief glimpse of the chamber had shown me that upon a
large table in the middle of the room lay my uncle's body.
Still I had seen, sitting in a chair nearby, my cousin Draco,
too; and finally, my curiosity proving stronger than my fear,
I once more pushed open the doors and went in.

Though I tried hard not to look at Uncle Quentin, my
eyes were drawn to his corpse, for this was my first close
view of death. He did not appear nearly so ghastly or
frightening as he had last night. Someone had closed his
eyes, and now, if not for the stern, grim set of his mouth
and the deep lines of pain that engraved his face, I might
have supposed he was only sleeping. His sodden clothes had
been changed, too; now he was dressed in an old white shirt
and a black jacket, waistcoat, and breeches that belonged to
my father. The garments fitted my uncle poorly, but I
guessed he had not expected to survive the journey and so
had brought no others. Or perhaps he had possessed none.
Earlier this morning, I had heard old Phillip tell Mrs.
Merrick that Uncle Quentin had been living in a dreadful
part of London—in a hovel "mean as a cutpurse an' just as
dirty," the coachman had said. Candles in tall brass sconces
stood all around the table upon which my uncle's body
reposed, and these were burning brightly, dispelling some of

the gloomy shadows in the drawing room, where the heavy red velvet curtains had been closed to shut out the overcast day.

To one side of his dead father, Draco sat stiffly on one of a pair of elegant Hepplewhite chairs upholstered in red-and-white-striped satin. Apparently in all the commotion last night, no one had thought to see to his needs; he still wore the same black shirt and breeches he'd arrived in, dry now, though the stains of his travels had not been brushed from the clothes. They were very wrinkled, too, and I wondered if he had slept in them. He looked terribly out of place, as though he had wandered in by mistake from the stables—and without so much as even scraping his boots at that! It seemed quite likely he had indeed been "born at Hogs Norton," as Tim had declared, meaning my cousin was both ill mannered and uncouth. Yet despite all this, Draco did not seem in the least ill at ease, and I realized why the young footman had accused him of behaving like "a bloody nob." My cousin's hard, dark countenance bore such an expression of arrogance and disdain that I believe it would have cowed even Julianne. I was at once both attracted and repelled by him. I thought I should leave him; yet I could not seem to stop myself from approaching him and sitting down on the edge of his chair's twin.

He did not speak. Indeed, even though he must have been aware of my presence, he did not even so much as glance in my direction, but continued to stare broodingly at his father's corpse. I wondered what he was thinking and wished fervently that I could see into his mind, as the Gypsy fortune-tellers claimed they could see into the future, for his face revealed nothing of his thoughts.

After an extremely long, uncomfortable minute of silence, it became plain to me that my cousin did not intend to acknowledge me, and anger that he should snub me, especially when I had done naught to provoke him, rose within me. I cleared my throat pointedly, to no avail; and at last I realized that if I desired to have any conversation at all with him, I would have to speak first.

"Hullo," I said. Draco made no reply. He did not even

look at me. Both irritated and embarrassed by his rudeness, I stumbled on anyway, determined to make him talk to me. "I'm Maggie, Maggie Chandler, your cousin."

His hooded black eyes flicked to my face then; he looked me up and down just once, coolly and insultingly, making it obvious he found me lacking. Then he returned to contemplating his father's body. My hands itched to box his ears for his impertinence, but remembering that he had laid brutal hands upon Sir Nigel, I restrained myself. If he would set upon my father, a powerful and an important man, he would certainly have no compunction whatsoever about attacking me, a mere girl. The thought of this fierce Gypsy boy unleashing his temper upon me was unnerving, and I swallowed hard, forcing myself to breathe calmly so he should not see he had upset me. Then I tried a different tack.

"Is it true you attempted to strangle Sir Nigel?" I asked, awe and something akin to admiration creeping into my voice, despite myself. As before, I received no answer. "That was quite reckless of you, you know," I pointed out. "My father is a baronet and master of Highclyffe Hall. No one here has ever before dared to do such a thing, and I shudder to think what would happen if someone did. Sir Nigel's rages are infamous; all of us at the manor have at one time or another borne the brunt of his anger when we displeased him. He shall not soon forgive you, I'm sure. I should take care in the future, if I were you, not to risk his ire again. He is certain to beat you, as he did Welles, my stepbrother—and that for nothing more than putting a toad in my governess Miss Poole's bed as a lark. Welles is Sir Nigel's ward, as I expect you are, too, now that Uncle Quentin is dead."

In response to my recital, my cousin cast at me such a vicious look of loathing that it was unmistakable. Involuntarily I drew back, expecting him to spring upon me at any moment like some dangerous beast. But he only glanced away to resume his silent vigil over his father's corpse.

"Well, you aren't very friendly, are you?" I accused hotly, rising and warily sidling away, suddenly deciding I wanted nothing to do with this boorish boy after all. "I'm sorry, now, that I intruded on your privacy. I thought that you might stand in need of a friend and that we might have something in common, you being my cousin, after all, and as misbegotten as I—or so my father said. However, I see I have misjudged the situation, and so I shall take my leave of you!"

"Wait!" The word was low and sharp, causing my heart to beat fast with both fright and excitement, for Draco's voice had a faint foreign accent that must have come from his Gypsy mother. It made him seem all the more alien, and it occurred to me that I was totally alone with him—this strange, violent, unpredictable cousin of mine. Perhaps he would grab me and choke me so I could not scream for help! My imagination fueled my fear like peat a fire. "Wait," he said again, more softly. "Don't go."

"Why should I stay when you've been so hateful?" I retorted with a bravery I did not feel; and though I turned back to face him, I remained poised for flight in case he should assault me. "And when I was only trying to be kind, too?"

"Yes, I know. I can see that now," he confessed reluctantly, and I sensed the words were as close to an apology as I would get from him. "Sit down. I mean you no harm, and even if I did, there must be at least a dozen servants within earshot whom you could summon for aid."

"Yes, that's true," I agreed; and seeing no sign that he meant to harm me, I gingerly retook my scat, prudently making no mention of my notion that he might easily render me unable to call for assistance.

Having bidden me to stay, Draco now grew silent, as though he did not know how to go on. For all that he had been born and bred in the crowded city of London, he seemed unused to people, I thought. Perhaps the haughty air of indifference he feigned was but a facade, like Julianne's, to hide his inner feelings of loneliness and insecurity. He had known a poverty far meaner and crueler than any to which my stepsister had ever been exposed, I suspected, based on what I had overheard in the kitchen; and I realized it must gall him bitterly to know that if not for an accident of birth, he, not Esmond, would be Sir Nigel's heir, master someday of the Chandler estate.

For a moment, stirred by pity, I almost wished Draco *were* my father's heir. Then, stricken by my disloyalty to Esmond, I dismissed the idea, for the thought of this graceless Gypsy boy in my beloved cousin's place was both ludicrous and appalling. Of course Draco, reared by Uncle Quentin, the black sheep of the family, could have no sense of pride in the Chandler name and legacy. He would not care that Queen Elizabeth had once slept in a chamber upstairs or that the Duchess of Marlborough had, on occasion, danced in the grand ballroom. The portraits that hung in the long gallery would be just pictures to Draco, not the unbroken chain of years, lives, and history they represented to Esmond and me.

No, I thought, it was as Sir Nigel had said: Draco had inherited his father's disposition—and no doubt his mother's as well. Uncle Quentin, I knew, had cared nothing for the estate, only for the money it had provided for his drinking, gambling, and wenching, until finally he had got into one scrape too many and the Chandlers had disowned him. After that, the funds had stopped and his name had been stricken from the family Bible by my grandfather Sir Simon, who, it was said, had never mentioned him again.

About Draco's unknown mother, I knew little. But the one time, unbeknown to my father, that Gypsies had camped on our land, they had allowed their horses to trample the grass and wildflowers and had chopped down trees indiscriminately for firewood. In addition, they had poached animals in the wood, caught fish in the streams, and shamelessly strewn the grounds with debris from their feast before Sir Nigel's gamekeeper had spied them and hanged those few who had not managed to escape.

Scoundrels and Gypsies, they were . . . Draco's kind. It was no wonder Sir Nigel had said my cousin would wind up as gallow's bait!

I shuddered as I recalled the words. Draco was certainly not the sort I wanted to inherit the estate I loved. I must have been mad to imagine him in Esmond's place, Draco, who would not care, I thought, as Esmond did, for everything the Chandlers had built over the centuries. Even my father, who was so unmindful of the shabbiness of the Grange, took great pride in the Hall.

"What did your father mean—that you are as misbegotten as I?" my cousin asked suddenly, startling me from my reverie, for indeed, lost in thought, I had nearly forgotten he sat beside me, still and silent as his dead father.

"Why, that I was as ill conceived as you," I replied, now glad I had looked up the word in the dictionary and so need not appear a fool before him, "for though I am Sir Nigel's lawful daughter, he wishes I had never been born. My mother died the night of my birth, you see, and my father blames me for her death, though I could not help being born, of course. He despises me, I think."

"Does he?"

"Yes, but I try not to mind very much," I admitted, wondering why I should reveal my innermost feelings to this strange, uncaring boy. "I believe he cannot help it, you see. He is a hard, cold man and not overly fond of children. Perhaps if I had been a son, he would have felt differently toward me. I don't know." I paused, pondering this.

Yes, I mused, *perhaps Sir Nigel would have loved me had I been a boy.*

But, then, he did not really care for Esmond, who was his sister's child and thus his own flesh and blood as much as I; and so no doubt it wouldn't have mattered, after all, had I been other than what I was. I stifled a sigh and shook off the depressing notion, telling myself that I hated my father and that it was therefore of no importance to me that he did not love me. Then, lifting my chin, I directed my attention to my uncle's body.

He looked as cold and ruthless as my father, I reflected, though there was, too, upon his face an expression of utter disillusionment and world-weariness that Sir Nigel lacked. I did not think my uncle had been a happy man; and like any child who sees only black and white, I decided it must be because he had already paid here on earth for his many sins and would continue to pay in the next world, for I was positive his wicked soul had been condemned to hell. I had a horrible, morbid desire to touch his corpse, to see what it felt like, if it was as hard and rigid as it looked and already burning with the devil's fire. But I did not, fearing that my cousin would misinterpret the gesture and end our conversation.

"Was Uncle Quentin kind to you?" I asked.

"He drank heavily, and when he was in his cups, he often beat me," Draco responded in that low, accented voice that so intrigued me. "But he kept me out of the workhouse."

He said no more, and I supposed he felt he had answered my question well enough. He had, though his reply had chilled my bones, for I had never before known anyone who considered it a kindness to have been abused by a drunken father rather than sent to a workhouse. I had heard terrible stories about the workhouses; but somehow, deep down inside, I had always suspected the grisly tales were far worse than the actual places themselves. Now Draco's dread of them convinced me their reputation must be deserved.

Someone ought to improve the workhouses—or close them down entirely, I thought; but that was because I was young and naive, and I did not then know that politicians cared more for their own bellies and purses than for the well-being of the working class and the poor.

I had, in truth, led a relatively sheltered life at the Hall, wrapped up in the secure cocoon of Sir Nigel's title and riches, if not his love; and the vast, lonely green moors of Cornwall bore little resemblance to the close, overpopulated, sooty cities of England. I had been no farther from Highclyffe Hall than the town of Launceston. What could I, then, know of the world? Not a ha'p'orth, I felt sure, when compared to Draco, whose eyes, despite their defiance, were too old and careworn for his years.

Poor, miserable boy! I found myself longing to comfort him, to stretch out my hand and smooth back the black, unkempt locks from his face, to run my finger lightly over the ugly gash, bruised and swollen and encrusted with blood, upon his forehead, where my father's cane had struck him. But I made no move to do so, certain my overtures would be rejected as scornfully as I myself had been earlier before Draco had changed his mind and bade me stay and, in doing so, paved the way for the odd, wary friendship we were to develop.

Long afterward, I was to remember this morning, when I, alone of all others at the manor, kept watch with my cousin over his father's corpse; and I would think how strange it was that we sat there side by side, two lonely children, scarcely even acquainted, hardly speaking, with my uncle's body lying stiffly before us and the candles flickering all around us in the shadowed room. It is an anomalous memory, yet even now, it seems to me to sum up the whole of my childhood—that thought of Draco and I struggling to find some measure of light and softness in the face of such darkness and harshness that morning. And yet . . . I like to think that I offered him some meager solace then and that, however grudgingly, he accepted it. Sometimes in later years, I was to fancy I saw in his eyes a peculiar gentleness when he looked at me, and I would think he, too, recalled our solitary vigil and thought of me more kindly than he might otherwise have done.

Now we spoke no more, for the sounds beyond the drawing room warned us that the rest of the family had risen and come downstairs for breakfast and that presently our quiet interlude must end. Yet I took my leave of Draco reluctantly, drawn to him now more strongly than ever before. He was someone beyond the realm of my experience; I wanted to know more of him.

I stood and smoothed my gown, suddenly conscious of its greyness and of its black ribbon, hastily tacked on and now seeming somehow disrespectful of my cousin's grief, for I did not doubt that in his own way, he sorrowed for his father, who had loved him after a fashion. I wanted to apologize for my lack of proper mourning garb but could think of nothing that would not sound contrived and thus give offense, and so I said naught, but made my way across the chamber, expecting Draco to follow.

At the doors, realizing he was not behind me, I turned back to him and saw he was still sitting in his chair.

"Are you not coming?" I inquired. Then, as his lashes shuttered his eyes and his lip curled jeeringly, I could have bitten off my tongue, for of course I should have realized, as Draco did, that Sir Nigel would not countenance a Gypsy bastard at his table. "Forgive me," I murmured, stricken. "That was quite stupid and thoughtless of me. Of course you are not joining us, though it does not seem right somehow. . . ." My voice trailed away as I recognized that I had blundered again. Silently I cursed my lack of social grace and wondered if I ought to apologize once more. At last, feeling that if I did, I would only make matters worse, I merely said, "Mrs. Merrick, our cook, is very kind. She will give you something to eat if you are hungry."

Then I passed swiftly out of the room, closing the doors softly behind me.

Chapter Seven

My Uncle's Funeral

Even such is Time, which takes in trust
Our youth, our joys, and all we have,
And pays us but with age and dust;
Who in the dark and silent grave,
When we have wandered all our ways,
Shuts up the story of our days: . . .

—*Written by Sir Walter Ralegh the night
before his death; found in his Bible
in the gatehouse at Westminster.*

I did not see Draco again until the morning of my uncle's
funeral two days later, though I learned from Linnet, who
was as curious as I about my cousin, that he had been given
a place in the stables, for like all Gypsies, he seemed to
have a knack with horses. I was glad of this, as I knew that
Hugh was a fair man, not like the exacting Mr. Lowry, my
father's agent, who managed the estate, or that vicious
young brute, Mick Dyson, who was the head foreman at my
father's two china-clay mines, Wheal Anant and Wheal
Penforth, and who sent shivers down my spine whenever I
saw him. With men such as Mick Dyson and Mr. Heapes, the
mines' weaselly manager, in charge of them, I thought it
was no wonder the politician Edmund Burke railed against
the entire mining industry. I had seen the sick, wasted men

and the gaunt, crippled children who haunted the miners' rows, ravaged by too many long hours of hard labor in cold, wet pits under, at best, unsafe conditions; and I steered clear of the close huddle of tiny, run-down houses whenever I could. I could not bear to see their inhabitants, especially the children, and know there was naught I could do to improve their miserable lot.

At least in the stables, Draco would be able to breathe fresh air untainted by kaolin dust, the chalky residue of the soft white clay wrested from the earth by the poor miners and used to manufacture fine, delicate china and porcelain for the gentry, who never soiled their hands. At least my cousin would work above ground, not deep in a pit that might at any moment cave in on him. Still I felt sure it was small consolation to one who if not for his bastardy would someday have been master of Highclyffe Hall. I thought that knowledge must stick like a fish bone in Draco's proud craw. If it did, however, he gave no sign of it, but, according to the gossip in the kitchen, went sullenly about his work, pitching hay, hauling feed sacks, and mucking out stalls, with little or nothing to say to anyone.

Yet when next I saw him, at his father's funeral, I recognized that life at the Hall had already benefitted him, for his features had lost their sharp, pinched expression, and I could foresee that like the great black colt Sir Nigel had bought at the fair, Draco would someday be a fine figure of a man, though I did not think he would ever be handsome. His face was too coarse and ugly for that, I thought, his broken nose and full-lipped mouth marring what might otherwise have been a pleasing countenance. I was too young, then, to see that they gave his dark visage strength and character and were evidence of a physical nature that would someday prove appealing to women. His eyes, too, which I thought hard and fiery as coal, glinted with intelligence and could flash as boldly and invitingly as any other Gypsy's when he so desired.

Someone had given him a change of garments, too, for when we gathered outside the ancient village church where the funeral services for countless generations of Chandlers had been held, my cousin wore an ill-fitting black suit, and a neckerchief was tied clumsily about his throat, though he had on his own leather boots, worn thin and so badly scarred from constant use that even the blacking that had been applied to them could not disguise their deep pits and gouges.

The morning was damp and grey, as it had rained off and on since the night of the storm and had been drizzling earlier, though now the shower had ceased. The ground was wet and muddy; the cool air was filled with the fresh, rich smells of sodden earth and of grass washed clean. In the silence could be heard the steady dripping of water as it slipped from the leaves of the trees, and all around, sparkling droplets lay like prisms upon the ground.

I watched for some sign that Draco had seen me; but he did not meet my eyes or join the family as we started toward the church, the vicar, Mr. Earnhart, going before us and chanting melodically.

"I am the resurrection and the life, saith the Lord: he that believeth in me, though he were dead, yet shall he live: and whosoever liveth and believeth in me, shall never die," the vicar intoned solemnly, his voice rising and falling in the morning quiet.

"I know that my redeemer liveth, and that he shall stand at the latter day upon the earth: and though this body be destroyed, yet shall I see God: whom I shall see for myself, and mine eyes shall behold, and not as a stranger.

"We brought nothing into this world, and it is certain we can carry nothing out. The Lord gave, and the Lord hath taken away; blessed be the name of the Lord."

The procession entered the church and, after genuflecting to the old wooden Celtic cross with the carved lamb at its center, which was fixed above the altar, we took our places in the Chandler pew but remained standing. Draco waited until most all the retainers and villagers who had come to pay their last respects to Uncle Quentin were inside before he slipped in to stand alone at the back of the church, his eyes veiled so none could tell what he was thinking.

The pallbearers had carried my uncle's flower-draped coffin up the aisle and set it down before the altar. Now I observed that already a few petals had broken off from the blossoms and lay like tiny stars scattered upon the floor; and as I looked at the dying blooms, I thought how fleeting life was indeed. I was glad the lid of the casket was closed, for after the undertaker had embalmed my uncle's body, the fluid had smoothed the lines from his face, so that when next I had seen his corpse, I had gasped, thinking at first that it was my father lying there.

Lost in my thoughts, I did not realize the service had already begun until I became aware of those around me giving the responses to Mr. Earnhart's words. Tardily I opened my prayer book to the place I had marked earlier, *The Order for The Burial of the Dead,* so I might make the proper answers, for this was a rite I did not know by heart, as I did the Mass.

"For when thou art angry all our days are gone," the vicar was saying.

"We bring our years to an end, as it were a tale that is told," the congregation rejoined as one.

The morning seemed to take on an unreal quality after that, hushed and still except for the droning of the voices and the soft clink of the brass censer as Mr. Earnhart swung it out on its chain toward the congregation and over my uncle's coffin at the appropriate times during the ceremony. When he was not using it, the vicar handed it to one of the acolytes, and the pungent aroma of the fragrant incense and acrid smoke wafting from the censer drifted throughout the church. Half dazed and sleepy from the solemnity and smoke, I watched Mr. Earnhart as though through a shifting veil of diaphanous grey mist. He was resplendent in his mourning chasuble and, with the candles burning all around him, crowned by a halo of fire bright as the roses and lilies arranged upon the altar and lying on my uncle's casket. The sweet, cloying scent of the blossoms seemed suffocating in the close, sultry air. Ever since, those two flowers have reminded me of death, so I do not care for them. Heather was my favorite once, though that, too, came to have painful memories for me, as you shall learn.

"Thomas saith unto him, Lord, we know not whither thou goest; and how can we know the way? Jesus saith unto him, I am the way, the truth, and the life: no man cometh unto the Father, but by me."

A hymn was sung; I do not remember which one, for by then, I felt as though I were but dreaming, that presently I would awaken in my bed at the Hall and discover that Uncle Quentin and Draco were only figments of my imagination. Only Esmond, at my side, seemed solid and real, his beautiful tenor voice ringing out through the church, joined by a lovely, throbbing baritone I should have known anywhere was Draco's. It rose liltingly to the rafters, its faint accent making it sound all the more haunting and ghostlike, so it did not seem strange at all when the clouds suddenly chose that moment to release a small portion of their contents and the light, rhythmic shatter of rain upon the roof added its own poignant harmony to the rest.

"The Lord be with you."

"And with thy spirit."

"Let us pray."

I knelt upon the hard kneeling board before me and, after crossing myself, bent my head between my arms until my forehead touched my clasped palms and the benchless oak back in front of the Chandler pew. That way, by craning my neck awkwardly, I could see, from beneath one elbow, Draco far behind me. He did not kneel, but remained standing, and I supposed he was not an Anglican—or had no religion at all. Were Gypsies pagans, then? I wondered. Yet his head was bowed, so perhaps he worshiped God in his own fashion, as he did all else, bound by no rules save his own; for that was ever Draco's way, as I was to learn in the years to come. His face beneath his dark skin was pale, and his thick black lashes looked like smudges against his cheeks. Once—just once—I thought I saw a single tear slip from his eye like a glistening raindrop; but perhaps it was only a trick of the light after all.

"Unto God's gracious mercy and protection we commit you. The Lord bless you and keep you. The Lord make his face to shine upon you, and be gracious unto you. The Lord lift up his countenance upon you, and give you peace, both now and evermore. Amen."

"Amen."

We stood then, and the pallbearers stepped forward to carry my uncle's coffin slowly from the church; the rest of us filed out silently behind. Once outside, the six men loaded the casket into the glossy black, glass-paned hearse drawn by six black horses, which waited without. The black plumes fastened to the tops of the animals' halters drooped forlornly in the rain; the beasts themselves seemed sadly bedraggled as they stamped and shivered in the wet. I thought how typical it was that even this, his own funeral, my ne'er-do-well uncle had not managed to get right.

The cemetery lay not far from the church and the village itself, so the procession followed on foot as the sphinx-like, black-clothed driver brought the reins of the harness down upon the horses' backs and the hearse jolted slowly forward through the mud, wheels churning. The rain drizzled upon us as we trudged along in the vehicle's wake, and I was glad of the light, hooded black cape I wore, though poor Mrs. Faversham and her assistants had been forced to work around the clock in order to finish in time both it and my mourning gown, as well as Julianne's garments. But now, shivering and pulling my cloak more closely about me as the soughing wind brushed my skin with chilly fingers, I did not care. The dressmaker had been handsomely paid for her efforts, I felt sure.

Overhead, the sky was a leaden shade of pale and thunderclouds roiled in the firmament, so I knew it was just a matter of time before it began truly to pour; and like all the living, whose own needs are placed always above those of the dead, I hoped the funeral would come to an end before I got drenched. Already my stockings were soaked through, and my shoes were splattered with mud.

At last I saw the headstones of the cemetery rising like obelisks before me; the grey granite of which most were fashioned was aged and weathered, making it difficult to read upon some the names and dates chiseled thereon. Here and there, a few of the markers had fallen over. Straggling weeds and wildflowers grew upon those graves that were not tended by loved ones or that were part of the section that was the potter's field, where paupers and criminals and those whose names were unknown were buried.

In the midst of the cemetery stood a great stone vault, and in this, the Chandlers down through the ages had been entombed. My mother lay here and rested peacefully, I hoped. I felt saddened, as always, by the thought that I had never known her, though I visited her here sometimes and spoke to her and fancied that she listened and whispered back, though doubtless it was only my imagination and the sighing of the wind that made it seem so.

Their rusty hinges creaking and groaning in protest, the wrought-iron gates and the heavy oak door that sealed the crypt were unlocked and opened by the caretaker; and the vicar began to chant once more.

"Man, that is born of a woman, hath but a short time to live, and is full of misery. He cometh up, and is cut down, like a flower. . . ."

I shuddered as I heard from inside the vault the grating of the massive stone block as it was slowly dragged from the long, narrow cavity that would be my uncle's final resting place. Here, someday, I, too, would lie. Yet the thought had little reality for me then, for at ten years of age, it is difficult to believe one is eventually going to die and be shut away in a cold, dark, solitary chamber for all time. It is only when each year seems to fly by more swiftly than the last that one becomes aware of one's own mortality and how fleeting the moments of one's life truly are.

The pallbearers lifted my uncle's coffin to their shoulders. Then, bending and maneuvering their way awkwardly through the low, arched entrance, they carried the casket down the steep, narrow stone steps into the dark, shadowed crypt. After that, there came the scrape of wood against granite as the coffin was slid into place, in macabre counter-point, it seemed, to the intoning of Mr. Earnhart.

"Unto Almighty God we commend the soul of our brother departed, and we commit his body to the ground; earth to earth, ashes to ashes, dust to dust. . . ."

Several of the older retainers, remembering "Mr. Quentin," as they had called him, from his youth, were crying now; but Draco's eyes, when finally I found his face in the crowd, were dry and distant, as though he stood not upon the rainswept moors, but someplace far away, in a memory or dream in his mind. He did not weep for the father who had been kind to him after a fashion, nor did Sir Nigel shed a tear for his dead brother, the rapscallion who had disgraced the Chandlers and been cruelly disowned for it.

"Lord, have mercy upon us."

"Christ, have mercy upon us."

"Lord, have mercy upon us."

For a strange, eerie moment, I felt as though I stood apart from the rest, watching as my family huddled together among the old headstones beneath the misty shower, my father's face looking as though it had been carved from granite, Lady Chandler's countenance cool and beautiful and bored beneath her umbrella. Welles, scowling, and Julianne, pouting, were slyly poking each other and whispering covertly behind their hands, while Miss Poole, a dutifully grave and pious expression on her face, chided them and hissed at them to hush. Esmond and Sarah, pale and solemn, were on either side of Aunt Tibby, supporting her as she sniffled and sobbed into her handkerchief—for Uncle Quentin had been her brother, too—while I, in my dripping cape and muddy shoes, stood just behind and to the right of Esmond, as though his nearness offered me comfort. Some distance away, alone with his grief, was Draco.

I saw him flinch as the harsh sound of the stone block being shoved back into place, sealing the tomb, reached our ears; and for a moment, he swayed on his feet, and I thought he would be ill. Then he steadied himself, and I knew that whatever his emotions, he would not break down before those who were strangers to him and who already referred to him as "Mr. Quentin's Gypsy bastard."

Finally the pallbearers emerged from the crypt, drawing the solid oak door shut with an ominous bang behind them. Then came the loud clang of the gates and the jingle-jangle of the caretaker's huge ring of keys as he searched for the appropriate one and turned it in the lock.

"O Lord Jesus Christ, who by thy death didst take away the sting of death; grant unto us thy servants so to follow in faith where thou hast led the way, that we may at length fall asleep peacefully in thee, and awake up after thy likeness; through thy mercy, who livest with the Father and the Holy Ghost, one God, world without end. Amen."

"Amen."

The vicar closed his prayer book at last then, just as the heavens, as though to mock us for daring to presume to enter their most precious realm, opened up to unleash their full fury upon us.

Chapter Eight

The Seeds of Fate

For each seem'd either; black it stood as night,
Fierce as ten furies, terrible as hell, . . .

—*Paradise Lost*
John Milton

It was several days after my uncle's funeral that Sir Nigel remembered the colt he had purchased at the fair.

Hugh had been attempting, to no avail, to work with the horse, which my father had named Black Magic. For all our head groom's kindness to and patience with it, the animal remained a wary, clever, vicious brute, all too willing to use teeth and hooves to defend itself. Hugh had not yet been able to get a saddle on it, much less a bit between its teeth. In just the few weeks it had been at the Hall, it had already broken one groom's leg and nearly trampled to death a poor stableboy who had not been nimble enough to leap over the paddock fence before the beast had attacked him. It was Hugh's opinion that the colt was untrainable, and he declared that if it could not be gentled enough to handle, it ought to be destroyed.

On the day Sir Nigel decided to check on Black Magic's progress, he strode down to the stables before breakfast, dressed for riding and carrying his crop in one hand. I, who had thought to have an early morning canter without Julianne, who was a late sleeper, tagging along, encountered my father on the way; and as he voiced no objection to my presence, I stayed to watch the proceedings, curious to see what would happen.

Sir Nigel talked with Hugh at some length, frowning when he discovered our head groom had made scant headway in taming the animal.

"For God's sake, Hugh!" my father expostulated impatiently. " 'Tis only a horse! Back it into a stall and put a bridle and saddle on it! I've a mind to try it out this morning."

"Beggin' yer pardon, sir, but it just ain't that simple. We've tried. T' beast's a divvil, as t' dealer at t' fair told 'ee; an' he don't take kindly e'en ta bein' put on a lead. T' last time we tried ta get him inta a stall, he broke Sam's leg an' damned near killed poor young Billy; an' I swear he done it a-purpose—the peery brute!"

"Nonsense," Sir Nigel drawled dryly. "If I didn't know better, I'd think you've been hitting the bottle on the sly, Hugh. The animal is merely a dumb, intractable horse who must learn to submit to his master."

Then, ignoring our head groom's respectfully delivered advice and warnings, my father began to rap out commands to the others waiting mutely to see what would occur; and the stables came alive with activity, men and lads running to and fro, muttering uneasily to one another and cursing under their breath.

I saw Draco standing to one side, his dark head poised alertly, his black eyes gleaming, his nostrils flared, and his body quivering with nervous tension and excitement; and as I watched, he flung back his head, so his long, shaggy black hair, still damp from his morning ablutions and glistening like jet in the sun that had pierced the clouds at last, rippled like a mane in the cool breeze that stirred faintly. For a moment, oddly enough, it seemed to me as though my Gypsy cousin and the skittishly prancing colt were one and the same: proud, defiant, brought to the Hall against their will and determined not to be mastered; and suddenly I knew that it would be a crime to attempt to break them, that they were not meant to be other than what they were: wild, spirited creatures who must give of themselves freely, if at all, forever resisting those who did not understand their nature and would try forcibly to break their will.

I wanted to cry out in protest, to demand that Sir Nigel rescind his orders; but of course I did nothing of the sort, for my father, after he had got over the shock of my rebellious behavior, would certainly have punished me—and ignored my pleas in any event. Still I bit my lip so hard that I drew blood, trying to stifle the emotional outburst that rose in my throat.

Black Magic, hearing the commotion and sensing danger, was running furiously about the paddock now, as he did whenever anyone approached him. Snorting and whinnying and tossing his head, he galloped this way and that, rushing the fence here and there, only to turn aside at the last moment. I realized he was testing it, judging its height and strength. My breath caught in my throat, for I knew with certainty that sooner or later, he intended to jump the barrier. I marveled that he had not done so before now; but, then, perhaps he recognized that Sir Nigel posed a greater threat to him than the others had done, and no doubt all the noise had frightened him, too.

He will clear the fence, I thought. *It is not high enough or strong enough to hold him. . . .*

Sir Nigel and the rest realized this also, for my father began shouting angrily and gesturing curtly at the grooms, insisting they get on with their work. Now, prudently keeping their distance from the horse, two of the men entered the enclosure, ropes in hand. They had fashioned running nooses in the stout hemp, and after slowly twirling them above their heads, they let the loops fly. Black Magic was too fast for them, however, and he deftly eluded the nooses, ducking his head so they slid along his back to fall ineffectively upon the ground. My father swore, and the two men, sensing his temper was mounting, began hurriedly to coil up their ropes in order to try again to capture the animal. Nearly half a dozen times, they cast the loops; but Black Magic was smart and wary, and each time, he proved too quick to be caught. Finally, however, the two men grew wise to his tricks, and the nooses settled about the beast's neck just as, recognizing at last that he could indeed clear the fence, he suddenly made his bid for freedom.

The hemp jerked and snapped sickeningly, yanking him back in the midst of his leap, so he reared and writhed and, shrieking with fear and rage, fell forward, crashing down on top of the white rails. They shattered with a horrible, loud crack, sending shards of wood flying; and Black Magic hit the earth with a thud, hooves kicking and thrashing as he attempted to disentangle himself from the splintered boards.

The two men could not hold him. Yelling and cursing, others raced into the paddock to help them. It took six of them to drag the colt free of the broken fence; but finally they got him back into the paddock, where he bucked and reared like a wild thing, lashing out at them with his bared teeth and deadly hooves whenever they came too close to him. I thought he might wrench loose from them, for the ropes that held him were strained taut like thong, and when he ran at the grooms, the hemp slackened, then abruptly drew tight, burning the men's palms as it slid across them.

But at last, slowly, with Black Magic fighting the grooms savagely every step of the way, they hauled him toward the stables. Inch by inch, they managed to pull him inside; but it took them nearly half an hour to get him backed into one of the narrow stalls. During the terrible struggle, two men and a young stableboy were injured, and a feedbox, some barrels, and other assorted odds and ends were severely damaged. By this time, tempers were sort, nerves were frayed, and the grooms were exhausted. With a good deal of relief, they slammed the stall door shut and bolted it. But still the horse refused to be subdued. In fact, it soon became evident that the stall would not hold him, that he would kick it down rather than submit to its confines. Even now, the stables rang with each jarring whack of the animal's hooves against the wooden walls of the stall; the stall door itself shook and rattled violently on its hinges as Black Magic vented his fury upon it.

The men would be lucky to get a lead snapped on his halter, I thought, much less a bridle or saddle on him. Still they tried, managing to drop a blanket on his back before the beast drove them away with his teeth. Then he snatched off the blanket and stamped it into the straw that covered the floor of the stall. After that, he resumed his brutal assault upon the door, finally punching a hole in it with one hoof and causing those gathered in the stables to fall back hastily, for fear that he should trample them if he escaped.

At that, Sir Nigel lost patience with the entire ordeal, and to the ire and disbelief of the grooms who had risked their lives to imprison the colt in the stall, he ordered the horse taken back out to the paddock. Then he gave instructions to Hugh to repeat the entire process the following morning—and every day thereafter—until Black Magic grew accustomed to being handled, to having his freedom curtailed by the stall, and a bridle and saddle could be put on him. I could tell that Hugh was angered by my father's demands, but our head groom merely nodded, a muscle working visibly in his set jaw, and said he would take care of the matter. After that, Sir Nigel strode from the stables, paying no heed whatsoever to the havoc that had been wreaked as a result of his unreasoning determination to master the horse— regardless of the cost.

Like everyone else present, I breathed a sigh of relief after my father had gone, for until then, I think we had all been afraid someone would be killed before he would desist in his resolve to ride Black Magic that morning; and I was certain Sir Nigel himself would have been injured had he attempted to mount the savage animal.

I went outside, where I saw that while the men in the stables had been striving to cope with Black Magic, others had been busy temporarily repairing the damage done to the downed section of fence. They had already begun working, as well, to add more rails and posts to the paddock to heighten and strengthen it so the beast could not escape; and as Black Magic was driven into the enclosure, I overheard Hugh telling the blacksmith to forge some iron panels as reinforcement for the stall.

Sir Nigel shall never tame Black Magic—at least, not like this, I thought, dismayed, *for the colt will die rather than be compelled to bend to Father's will. I know it!*

"The show's over, *Miss* Maggie," a voice hissed sarcastically in my ear, causing me to jump and setting my heart to pounding hard. "You can go back to the house now."

"Oh, Draco!" I gasped, one hand going to my throat as I whirled to face him. "You startled me! I didn't know you were there."

"No, I'll wager you didn't," he sneered. "No doubt you were too busy worrying about your father's stiff neck. I hope Black Magic kills him! He deserves to be shot, you know," he muttered fiercely, and I knew he did not mean the horse.

My cousin was wroth, I realized, over Sir Nigel's cruel treatment of Black Magic, and he was taking it out on me because he had no one else to talk to. But still his hateful tone and manner hurt me, for I was not the one who had terrorized the animal.

"It's not my fault—what my father did, I mean. I've done naught, so why should you hold me to blame?" I asked.

Draco had the grace to flush guiltily at that.

"I don't, really, I guess," he admitted, his voice lower and gentler now. "It's just that I was angry. . . . Damn him! He'll never break Black Magic like that—the bloody fool! —and he'll destroy a magnificent creature in the attempt."

"Yes, I know. But my father has little regard for my opinion, and there is no reasoning with him anyway once he makes up his mind about something." I paused, then suggested, "Perhaps when he discovers he cannot tame the beast, he will leave off trying."

"And perhaps he will not! Christ! How I despise him! He is so puffed up with his power and pelf that he thinks he is lord and master of us all. The old baronet, our grandfather, Sir Simon, was just the same, or so my father said! 'Tis no wonder he had so little care for the Chandlers!''

"Yet he wished to be buried in the family vault," I mused aloud. "How very strange."

Draco laughed at that, a harsh, scornful sound.

"No, not in the least, my girl, for 'twas either that or a pauper's grave in London—and me left out on the streets to wind up in a workhouse, like as not. But what would you know of that, *Miss* Maggie?"

"Nothing," I said softly. "Nothing." Then, anguished, I cried out against him. "Oh, Draco! I'm not my father! Why are you being so mean to me? I thought we were friends!"

"Friends?" He spoke bitterly. "Why? Because you feel sorry for me? Well, don't, my girl, for I don't want your pity. If my father had married my mother, *I'd* be heir to all this—not your precious, puling Esmond!—and I'd manage it a damned sight better than he ever shall, I assure you. But just because a bend sinister deprived me of my birthright doesn't mean it deprived me of my pride as well. No." He shook his head. "We'll never be friends, Maggie— not as long as you live in the manor and I'm naught but a stableboy who must doff his cap to you whenever we meet!"

"I haven't asked that of you, Draco," I pointed out quietly, squaring my shoulders against the cruel sting of his words, "and I've not expected it either. You are my cousin after all." That shamed him, I could tell, for he could not meet my eyes after that, but looked away into the distance, swallowing hard. Still he didn't apologize, and after a moment, I sighed and queried curiously, "If you hate us all so much, why do you stay here? Why don't you run away?"

He turned back to me then, his expression wry.

"Because for the first time in my life, I'm clean and dry and warm," he said, "and when I go to bed at night, it's with a full belly and knowing I don't have to sleep with one eye open, lest someone try to rob me or stab me in the dark. I figure the Chandlers owe me that at least."

There was nothing I could say to that, for I didn't know what it was like to be dirty or wet or cold, really, or to be hungry or afraid someone would attack me while I slept.

"Go on back to the house, Maggie," Draco insisted

again abruptly, though more kindly. "You've already missed breakfast, and you'll be late for your lessons with that old harridan, Miss Poole."

The remark about my governess was his way of telling me he was sorry, I knew, so I smiled a little, albeit tremulously, and nodded. Then slowly I turned and headed toward the manor, pondering, as I walked along, how much my cousin, since his coming, had learned of our lives at the Hall. It was odd, I thought, that he should despise us so—and yet take the trouble to find out everything he could about us, as he obviously did. It was as though, against his will, he were somehow as fascinated by us as I was by him.

I saw him quite often as the summer flew by, for now that Julianne had got her own pony and so had no need to be mounted upon mine, I was allowed once more to ride over to the Grange; and since Lady Chandler, who insisted on adhering to the rules of propriety, had forbidden both my stepsister and me to jaunt about the countryside without a groom in attendance, it sometimes fell to Draco to escort us when there was no one else available. Then, mounted upon a rough, hardy black Dale, he rode watchfully behind us, though I did not think he kept his distance out of respect.

Our outings were quite frequent, for we had at last discovered a serious chink in Miss Poole's armor: She was terrified of horses. We took full advantage of this fact to escape from her whenever we could, knowing she would find some plausible, though mendacious, excuse not to join us. We were free then to do as we pleased; and when we were not at the Grange, we sought the sweeping moors, sometimes taking an alfresco luncheon if it were a pleasant day and we did not have lessons.

Though Julianne usually ignored whatever groom trailed along in our wake, she loathed Draco and went to great lengths to torment him. She had, strangely enough, been attracted to him initially, for he was a Gypsy and therefore different. His broodiness and bastardy made him seem somehow mysterious and sinister as well; and as though he were forbidden fruit, he had tempted her so she had fluttered her eyelashes at him in a silly mimicry of her mother and tried to draw him out, as she had Esmond. But Draco had grown up on the mean streets of London, and he had not been fooled by her facade. He had let her know he was not deceived by her attempts to flatter him and, in doing so, to mock him; and she, mortified at having her true self so jeeringly unmasked and flung in her face, had hated him ever after.

Now she taunted him mercilessly, ordering him about as though he were a lackey and calling him "boy" whenever she addressed him. Draco's mouth tightened perceptibly with anger whenever he saw her, and he treated her with an exaggerated courtesy that made it obvious he considered her an object of both ridicule and contempt. Petulantly Julianne complained about him to Sir Nigel and Lady Chandler; but as my cousin had actually said or done nothing untoward to her, she was unable to provide them with specific examples of any misconduct, and so my father merely harrumphed and said that if she could not handle the servants, she ought not order them about. So the battle she waged with Draco continued unchecked, though I could not understand why she did not give it up, for she always came off the loser in their encounters and afterward would flounce around in a huff, planning, with a great deal of relish, how she would even the score between them.

Often Julianne would grow so enraged at Draco that she would gallop on ahead, leaving the two of us to follow. Those were the times I liked best, for then I would pursue my fragile friendship with my prickly cousin. He grudgingly opened up to me a little in response, so I began to believe he had some feelings for me after all, however detached or reluctant. Sometimes Welles, who liked Draco, too, despite all Julianne's attempts to persuade him otherwise, would accompany us and set us all, even my Gypsy cousin, to laughing at his tales and antics. How I loved to hear Draco laugh then, naturally, easily, not the harsh, bitter sound he more often made; and I would think how different he might have been had life been kinder to him.

Esmond and Sarah joined us also when they could; but

I am forced to admit that despite my adored Esmond's presence, those were not happy occasions for me, for he and Draco despised each other from the start. Draco, I felt sure, viewed Esmond as an usurper who had taken what, under other circumstances, would rightfully have been my Gypsy cousin's. Esmond's enmity toward Draco, however, was less comprehensible. I could not understand it, and when I questioned Esmond about it, he said only that Draco was "not a gentleman, but a scapegrace like his father" and that I "should have nothing to do with him." Yet oddly enough, I sensed that for reasons I could not grasp, deep down inside, Esmond was jealous of him.

To my dismay, we quarreled over my Gypsy cousin, the first argument we had ever had; and matters were not improved between us when Esmond coldly informed me I would do well to copy Julianne's behavior toward Draco.

"Esmond!" I cried. "I can't believe you mean that! Draco is our cousin after all, and Julianne treats him as though he were dirt under her feet! Surely you're not blind to that!"

"Maggie, I'm surprised at you! I don't think she acts any differently toward him than she does the rest of the servants," he said stiffly. " 'Tis only that you have never got over your dislike of her that makes you think otherwise; and honestly I find that quite spiteful of you, especially when Julie has done her best to be your friend. That isn't like you, Maggie. You were never before one to hold a grudge."

I could not credit what my ears had heard, and I gaped at him, hurt and stunned.

"I don't know what you're talking about, Esmond," I rejoined snippily. "In fact, I don't think you do either. Your wits must be addled! My stepsister has hardly ever been nice to me—and you know it! Indeed 'twas only yesterday that she told Miss Poole it was I who spilled ink upon our governess's lesson book—when, in fact, 'twas Julianne herself who did so."

"Yes, Julie told me what happened, and I don't understand how you can blame her for it, Maggie, when 'twas due solely to your snatching the pen from her grasp that the inkwell was overturned, thus blotting Miss Poole's lesson book.''

I was rendered temporarily speechless by this remark, and before I could name it the lie it was, Esmond continued his tirade.

"You've always been wild, Maggie, a failing I've scarcely paid any attention to before, since you haven't had, in the past, any mother's hand to gentle you. But now it seems that though Lady Chandler herself has tried her best to show you the error of your ways, you refuse to see it and are bent on becoming a madcap like Welles, who doesn't have a brain in his head! I can't believe you—and Sarah, too—would choose to follow his example!''

He frowned darkly at his sister, who was smiling shyly as my stepbrother leaned over to whisper to her from atop his Welsh cob. Earlier she had also argued with Esmond— though over Welles, not Draco; and now, as aggrieved as I, she was pointedly ignoring her brother to let him know how much she felt he had wronged her.

"Welles may be a devil-may-care young buck, Esmond, but at least he isn't a pompous prig!'' I retorted hotly, angry now. "And I very much fear that is what *you* are becoming! You have never liked him—at least, not since the day of the fair, that is—and for nothing more than because he dragged you into a silly scrape to which no one but you ever gave a second thought!''

"I'm disappointed in you, Maggie,'' my cousin reproached me frostily, "for sniping at me because I believe there are means other than fists for settling a fight. I had not thought that you, having borne the brunt of Uncle Nigel's temper more than once, would be in favor of violence. However, now I see I was mistaken. No doubt that explains your ridiculous fascination with that brutish Gypsy boy and your churlish insensitivity toward Julie's delicate feelings, too!''

Before I could frame an appropriate response to this, Esmond set his heels to his pony's sides and galloped on ahead to ride beside Julianne, who flashed him what I felt was a most revolting, sugary smile when he joined her. I stared hard at his back for a minute, stricken by the harsh words that had passed between us and feeling as though I were poor Cinderella in the French fairy tale, tormented by my wicked stepsister, except that I did not have a fairy godmother and my prince did not seem to know I was the one for whom he searched.

Surely he'll return in a moment to apologize, I thought, tears pricking my eyes and a lump so big in my throat that I feared it would choke me.

But it soon became clear to me that Esmond had no intention of doing so; and at last, my chin held high so he should not see how he had wounded me, I reined Clothilde about and cantered back to join Draco.

"What's the matter?" my Gypsy cousin asked as I drew up alongside him. "Had a tiff with that tut-mouthed young swain of yours?"

"Esmond is *not* tut-mouthed," I ground out through clenched teeth, annoyed, for even though Esmond had infuriated me, I loved him still and took amiss Draco's calling him names.

"No?" My cousin raised one eyebrow skeptically. "You mean he wasn't tut-tutting about something, as usual, then? The stiff-necked noddy!"

"Oh! You are as impossible as he!" I exclaimed; and abruptly wheeling my pony about and galloping away from him, I returned to the Hall alone, my pleasure in the day quite spoiled.

I cursed them all three—Julianne, Esmond, and Draco—and heartily wished them in perdition, and I thought regretfully that nothing was the same anymore since the Prescotts and Draco had intruded at the Hall. How I yearned to turn back the hands of time to the days when there had been only Esmond, Sarah, and I! My hurt and rage were so great that I did not spare even Welles my condemnation, for he was the cause of the breach between Esmond and Sarah, who had been as dear a brother and sister to each other as any could be. What was happening to the three of us? I wondered. We had never used to squabble among ourselves.

Even when Esmond came contritely the following afternoon to apologize for our quarrel, to ardently beg my pardon, and to tell me he had mended the rift between him and Sarah, I could not help feeling as though we three were being wrenched apart in some horrible, inexplicable fashion I could neither halt nor understand. It was as though we were rushing willingly—even eagerly—toward some terrible kismet, I thought; and no matter how hard I tried, I could not shake off the uneasy feeling of doom that assailed me.

"Oh, Esmond!" I cried with all the passion of youth, wringing my hands anxiously, which was most unlike me. "What dreadful words we exchanged yesterday! I hear them ringing still in my ears and in my heart!"

"Shhhhh, Maggie," he murmured, smoothing my hair back from my face, as I had often seen him do to Sarah when consoling her. "Don't cry, dear cousin. 'Twas nothing more than my own crossness—and that due only to my fear that I should lose you and Sarah both. She spends a great deal of time with Welles these days, and you . . . ah, you, Maggie, have a great fondness for Draco, I think."

" 'Tis only that I feel sorry for him, Esmond. He has lived a hard life—far harder than what you and I have known. What harm does it do to show him a little kindness?"

"None, I suppose—and yet sometimes I fear you shall grow to like him better than you do me."

"Oh, Esmond, how silly," I said, smiling now. "I *love* you, and we are to be married someday, are we not? How could you think otherwise? Draco is but a friend—nothing more—just as Welles is, though I will own there are days when I cannot stand his sister."

"Yes, well, Julie's having a difficult time of it, adjusting to her new life, Maggie. You must give her time. She's really very sweet, you know."

Yes, I thought, *about as sweet as a high-toby man robbing a coach at gunpoint!*

But I said nothing of this. Instead I merely nodded, as though in agreement with him; and that strange, disquieting seed of portent I had felt earlier took firm root in my heart—and began to grow.

Chapter Nine

Sir Nigel and Black Magic

Eternal spirit of the chainless mind!
Brightest in dungeons, Liberty! thou art.

—*Sonnet on Chillon*
George Gordon,
Lord Byron

It was near the end of the summer when Hugh at last managed to get a bridle and saddle on Black Magic.

Draco had told me the previous afternoon that Sir Nigel intended to ride the colt the following morning. So bright and early the next day, I rose and dressed without waiting for Linnet to come and assist me, and before breakfast, I went down to the stables to see for myself whether my father would prove successful in mastering the horse.

The men had completed their work on the paddock fence, and since it was now higher than it used to be, I was forced to climb a section of it in order to get a clear view of the enclosed yard; otherwise I would have had either to crouch or to stand on tiptoe to peer through the spaces between the white rails, both of which positions would have grown quite uncomfortable after a while, I felt sure. So, though I feared I would be seen and sent away, I climbed up and gingerly perched myself upon a top board; and although, once or twice, Sir Nigel glanced in my direction, I soon doubted that he even saw me, for his attention was riveted on the recalcitrant animal now being led from the stables.

I saw that Hugh had put a snaffle bit on Black Magic, along with a drop noseband to prevent him from evading the bit and a running martingale to curb upward movement of his head. But still the beast fought against the bridle that had been imposed upon him, and the jingle-jangle of the bit, sounding overly loud in the morning silence, rang out like a bell buoy tolling its warning across the sea. White-eyed with fear and anger, Black Magic snorted and pranced and strained against the lead that held him, so Hugh kept his distance from the colt as he tied him to the post in the center of the paddock.

Whip in hand, my father entered the enclosure and strode toward the horse purposefully, his face set in that grim, forbidding expression that had so often caused me to quail before him, so that even now, I shrank into myself, unable to prevent the sudden racing of my pulse, though I knew it was not I toward whom that look was directed. At Sir Nigel's approach, Black Magic, whinnying, shied away skittishly, his hooves lashing out dangerously as he danced and bucked. But Hugh had fastened the animal's lead to the post so most of the rope lay coiled upon the ground, sharply curtailing Black Magic's freedom of movement, so he was unable to do much damage.

My father was an adept horseman, and deftly avoiding the beast's teeth and hooves, he grabbed hold of the saddle, both hands firmly hooked under the curve of the pommel and cantle. It took him several moments, but at last he managed to set his foot upon the tread of the stirrup and then to fling himself upon the colt's back. But he had scarcely gathered up the reins when Black Magic began trying violently to unseat him. The horse reared and bucked, then twisted his head to snap viciously at Sir Nigel's leg. With his crop, my father struck the animal a sharp blow across the nose, and Black Magic squealed with pain before he intensified his efforts, hampered by the short lead, to pitch Sir Nigel from the saddle.

"I hope he breaks his bloody neck!" Draco growled in

my ear as he climbed up to sit beside me on the fence. "And even so, 'twill be less than he deserves!"

"You ought not wish ill on people, Draco," I murmured, knowing he spoke of my father, not Black Magic. " 'Twill come back to haunt you, you know."

But even I, who had so often been wounded by Sir Nigel's hard, unfeeling manner, hoped he would be thrown off and his pride humbled. Much to my surprise and secret delight, then, even as the thought crossed my mind, he lost his grip on Black Magic and went flying through the air to hit the ground with a thud. The watching grooms and stableboys gasped audibly, and Draco caught his breath with a hiss of satisfaction, though the remote expression upon his face did not change. Only his black eyes, glittering with animosity, narrowed and gleamed with malicious amusement. To my mortification, someone laughed nervously, and I cringed, lest my father should think it was I. Hugh ran to assist him up; but curtly, his face red with fury, Sir Nigel waved him away and, rising and brushing himself off, glared about the paddock so ominously that whoever had snickered quickly smothered any further sound.

I had known, of course, that that would not be the end of my father's attempt to best Black Magic, but still I could not help trembling when he walked toward the beast swiftly and the duel between them resumed.

Now Sir Nigel gave full rein to his temper. That he had been made to look a fool before me and the servants was not something he would take lightly. This time, after he had remounted the colt, he used both his whip and spurs cruelly to try to force the horse into submission. But though Black Magic had been compelled to accept both bridle and saddle, his wild spirit had not been broken. Stubbornly he continued to defy my father, refusing to be mastered. Again Sir Nigel sailed through the air. But this time when he lay sprawled upon the earth, no one laughed. A pall had fallen over us all, for now it was evident the battle between man and animal had turned deadly.

Black Magic's sides were heaving; his chest and flanks were white with foam, the latter dripping with blood, too,

where my father's spurs had roweled the skin and left deep
gashes of bright crimson streaked against the beast's ebony
coat. Black Magic's mouth was flecked with scarlet where
the bit had been yanked hard and relentlessly against his
tender lips and tongue, and his nose was swollen where Sir
Nigel had struck it repeatedly with his crop.

My father looked little better. His hat was gone, his
cravat was askew, and his riding habit was coated with dirt
and torn at the elbow of one sleeve and at one knee. Blood
trickled from a cut on his forehead, and a purplish blue
bruise had formed on one side of his cheek where he had
fallen against it. Now, as he got slowly to his feet, I saw he
was limping as well. But still he hobbled toward Black
Magic, his eyes blazing with rage and resolution.

"The bloody fool!" Draco muttered fiercely at my
side, though now there was a touch of uneasiness in his
voice also. "The colt will kill him yet!"

A cold fist of fear clenched my heart at his words, for
indeed I thought that my cousin was right and that presently
I should see Sir Nigel lying dead upon the ground. Though I
bore him little love, the idea of his dying and being
entombed in the family vault, as Uncle Quentin had been,
chilled me. I must have made some whimper of protest at
the disquieting vision, for Draco rudely and abruptly clapped
one hand over my mouth, nearly knocking me from the
fence. As I swayed backward, he put one arm about my
waist to steady me, and I felt the warmth of his skin through
my light blouse and jacket. Other than to assist me in
mounting Clothilde, it was the first time my Gypsy cousin
had ever touched me.

"Be still, Maggie!" he hissed. "There is nothing you
can do. Your father is bent on his own destruction—and
Black Magic's, too!"

I feared this was the truth, and after Draco had taken
his hand away from my mouth, I bit my knuckles hard to
keep from crying out again, my heart a great lump in my
throat, choking me.

Tiring now, but as yet undefeated, Sir Nigel once more
hauled himself onto Black Magic's saddle, and the grueling

conflict between man and beast dragged on. Exhaustion showed in every line of the colt's body—in the droop of his flowing mane and tail and in the halfhearted tossing of his proud head as well—but still he fought on valiantly against my father, who brutalized him so badly now with whip and spurs that I feared Black Magic would be slashed to ribbons before the desperate struggle was ended.

Then finally, just when I thought the horse was done for at last, he gathered his strength and made one final, frantic attempt to rid himself of Sir Nigel. My father tumbled from the saddle, and this time, he was not flung far enough away to avoid the animal's lethal hooves. Before any of us even realized what was happening, Black Magic reared and whinnied—a tortured wail of triumph—then came down with all his weight upon Sir Nigel's crumpled figure.

Someone screamed and screamed, and it was not until Draco caught me in his arms and crushed my face to his broad young chest that I realized it was my own voice making those terrible, hoarse, shrill cries. I could feel the hardness of my cousin's body against mine, and reality for me in that moment was narrowed suddenly and sharply to that, so I clung to him tightly, sobbing, welcoming the comfort he offered so kindly and unexpectedly.

"Hush, Maggie," he said softly, his lips brushing my hair as he spoke, his hands smoothing the loose strands back from my face. "Hush. He is not dead, but merely bruised and battered, I think. Yes, that is it. Look, Hugh is helping him up even now."

At last, emboldened by Draco's words, for surely, I thought, he would not lie to me under the circumstances, I dared to glance at my father. It was as my cousin had told me. Sir Nigel, one arm about our head groom's shoulders, was slowly limping from the paddock, grimacing with each step. Somehow he had managed to roll aside at the last moment so Black Magic's hooves had only clipped him on one shoulder and side. Still I knew from the lines of pain that engraved his face that he was badly hurt and that his contest with the colt this morning was finished.

The shock that had momentarily held all of us still and speechless was cast off abruptly now as the grooms and stableboys saw that Sir Nigel was not, after all, on his way to meet his Maker. Several of the braver men went hurrying into the enclosure, some intending to assist Hugh with my father, others bent on leading the quivering, bleeding horse back to the stables to care for him if he would let them.

Rudely Sir Nigel waved them all away.

"Leave him—the accursed devil!" he spat weakly, gasping and gripping his side in a way that suggested his ribs must either be cracked or broken. Then to Black Magic, he said, "By God, you'll learn who your master is, or I'll see you rot in hell, you demon brute! But you'll not get the best of me!"

After that, leaning heavily on Hugh, he walked on toward the manor, to which someone was already running to prepare Lady Chandler and the rest of the household for what had occurred. Our head groom, his face looking as though it had been chiseled from stone as he glanced back at us briefly, tersely bade one of the men to summon the physician, then ordered everybody else back to work.

But when Draco would have joined the others, I, laying my hand upon his arm, bade him stay, and soon only he and I remained, gazing silently at Black Magic.

Now that the animal thought himself to be alone, his head hung wearily, and it seemed that even his withers slumped. It was as though he knew that although the battle had been won, the war was not yet over and he did not know how much longer he could hold out against my father. I felt sick inside when I looked at the beast, for it was as though something wild and beautiful—almost godlike—had been desecrated and diminished so it would never again be as it had been before Sir Nigel had damaged it. Tears stung my eyes at the thought, and I swallowed hard and dashed them away, for I did not want to begin weeping again. I felt somehow that if I did, I would never stop.

"I know," Draco said bitterly, seeing my face and guessing my thoughts. "I feel that way, too."

"Next time, either Father or Black Magic will die. I

know it! It mustn't be, Draco," I whispered fervently. "It mustn't be! I've got to stop it before that happens! Somehow I've just got to stop it!"

And then it came to me how I could, and I knew what I must do.

The Hall was still and silent as a grave now, for all had long since retired. I lay motionless in my bed, holding my breath and listening, as a fearful mouse crouches in its hollow, waiting for the shadow of the hawk or owl to pass. My heart thumped deafeningly in my ears, as it always did when my senses were so keenly attuned to the hush of the darkness, when I knew something was about to happen—or, worse, only imagined it was; for the terrors of the mind are amorphous things, not bound by the limits of reality, and for that reason are all the more frightening. What is real can be vanquished; but the shapes and shadows conjured by the mind may rise up again and again to haunt one, even though one has seen them destroyed only moments before.

Yet I did not fear to be attacked in my bed, as Draco had used to be afraid would happen to him in London. I feared only that I would be discovered—by Julianne or Miss Poole—and that a hue and cry would be raised that would bring Lady Chandler scurrying to the north wing and cause Sir Nigel, whose injuries had confined him to bed, to rouse the household by shouting and demanding to know what was amiss.

Nevertheless, certain, now, that all at the manor slept, I rose stealthily and, tossing aside my thin night rail, started to pull on the clothes I had concealed under my pillow from Linnet. I did not bother with my shoes, for my bare feet would make less noise upon the floor; I was surefooted as a pony, too, so I had no worry that the rough ground, hard and uneven beneath my naked soles, would make me stumble.

I did not dare to light a lamp or even a candle, lest the flame flicker too brightly and attract attention as I passed through the hall. But my eyes had adjusted to the darkness now, so it did not matter that I had no light to guide me as I slowly eased open my door and, after peeking out into the corridor to make sure no one was up and about, tiptoed from my chamber to hurry down the back stairs to the side door. There, as quietly as possible, I drew back the bolt and let myself out into the blackness.

I shivered as the cool night air touched my skin and I trod, barefooted, upon the grass damp and chilly with evening dew. For a moment, as I gazed about, I nearly lost my resolve and returned to my room, for the Hall seemed different somehow in the darkness. The old house appeared to loom over me menacingly in the diffuse moonlight and starlight that filtered through the branches of the towering Cornish elms, the spreading yews, and the rustling rowans of the park. The shadowed wood itself looked twisted and forbidding, almost evil, I fancied, as though the limbs of the trees were reaching out to seize me. Somewhere close by, an owl hooted, nearly startling me out of my skin before, gathering my courage and determination, I forced myself to go on, slipping like a wraith through the pale grey, ghostlike wisps of mist that floated on the soughing wind.

At last I reached the paddock; but there I paused, my heart thrumming as I pressed myself against one side of the stables and peered around the corner through the white rails of the fence. Someone was moving silently about the enclosure. I did not know who would dare to enter with Black Magic inside, and further, I could not understand why the colt made no outcry, but merely whickered softly and trembled as a voice murmured soothingly to him in a strange language I had never before heard.

After a moment, my eyes now fully adjusted to the silvery half-light, I could see more clearly who spoke and stroked the horse in gentle reassurance. It was Draco, of course. It could be none other. Only my strange Gypsy cousin, who had such a knack with horses and such a strong affinity for this one, would dare to touch the animal fearlessly, knowing Black Magic would sense they were kindred spirits.

Now, calling out to Draco softly so I should not

frighten him or the beast or wake those few grooms or stableboys who, for one reason or another, might be bedded down in the stables, I crept forward to the fence.

"What are you doing here?" I queried as slowly my cousin walked toward me.

"I might ask you the same question," he whispered back, opening the gate and motioning for me to come inside. I eyed Black Magic warily; but Draco took my hand and drew me into the paddock, shutting the gate behind us and saying, "Don't be afraid. He won't hurt you."

And indeed, though the colt nickered and pranced a trifle nervously as I approached him, he made no threatening moves toward me. To my surprise, I saw that Draco had got the bridle and saddle off him and had put a halter on him instead. To this, my cousin had snapped the lead, but he had loosed the rope and retied it to the post so the horse now had considerable freedom of movement. Still Black Magic stood quietly; and as Draco returned to his work, I saw he had cleansed the animal's wounds and was now applying some sort of healing salve to them. As he ministered to Black Magic's wounds, he began once more to croon to the beast, and as the odd, lilting words washed over me, I wondered again what language they were from.

"What is that you're speaking?" I inquired.

"Romany—the Gypsy tongue," he replied. "My mother taught it to me, and though I was very young when she died, I have not forgotten what I learned."

"What are you saying to Black Magic?"

"Mostly that he is wild and beautiful and courageous, that he must keep his spirit bold and free—like a Gypsy's— and not allow your father to crush it."

"Is that how the Gypsies are, then? I thought as much, but I was not sure. I know so little about them, only what I have heard, though I have often seen them at fairs, and once, they camped upon the grounds. . . ." My voice trailed away as I remembered how Sir Nigel's gamekeeper had caught three of them and hanged them. After a time, I asked, "Will you tell me about them, please?"

"If you like," Draco said. "The Rom are a very old

people who came from India originally, or so it is said.
There are three main tribes: the Kalderash, the Gitanos, and
the Manush or Sinti. My mother was a Kalderash; her name
was Chavi, and she came from a very proud *vitsa*, which
is a large, extended family. She was to marry her cousin
Jal, but she fell in love with my father instead, a *gadje*
—a person who is not Rom.

"For this reason, she was declared *merime*—unclean—
by the *kris*—the elders of her *vitsa*—and she was cast out.
The Rom are very strict and secretive, too; this is the only
way they have managed to survive, for they have always
been persecuted wherever they have gone. Thus to admit a
gadje to gain knowledge of them and their ways is a very
grave crime indeed. Still my mother was happy at first, for
she was young, and in love, and my father was good to her.

"It was only later, when she became ill, that she
longed for her people and for their *drabana*—healer. She
did not trust the English doctors—and there was no money
for one besides—and so she died. But she had consumption,
so I do not think anyone could have helped her anyway."

"How sad. You must have loved her very much."

"Yes, I did. She was like Black Magic—wild and
beautiful. Even poverty and illness never broke her spirit.
She died bravely and bade me always to remember her as
she was before sickness robbed her of her health. I can see
her so clearly even now, Maggie, laughing and dancing . . . and
then—" He broke off abruptly, and there was silence for a
moment before he continued.

"It was after that that Father took to drinking so heavily
and why I never cared when he beat me, for I understood the
demons that drove him. He was angry that she had died and
left him; and I think he fancied he saw her face in mine. . . ."

Now more than ever did I understand why Draco was
so drawn to Black Magic and why he had sneaked into the
paddock to try to heal the colt. Deep in my heart, I knew
what I had come here tonight to do was the right thing, no
matter how much I might suffer for it afterward.

"Come," I said softly to my cousin, "and bring the
horse."

"Why? What are you going to do with him?" Draco asked suspiciously.

"I intend, if I can, to set him free."

"What?" he cried. "Have you gone daft, Maggie?"

"Shhhhh!" I hissed, glancing toward the cottages behind the stables. "Keep your voice down! Do you want to wake Hugh and the rest?"

"No, of course not. But—"

"Hush, Draco. 'Tis the only way to save Black Magic— and you know it. They'll never catch him once he's loose on the moors. He'll be safe then, with others of his ilk to befriend him, wild horses and ponies. Herds of them roam freely in the hills and on the commons. Have you not seen them?"

"Yes, but Sir Nigel will know Black Magic did not escape on his own. Have you thought of that, my girl? How you shall be punished if your father ever finds out 'twas you who helped the colt get away?"

"Yes." I nodded. "And I'm willing to take that risk. Are you?"

Draco did not hesitate.

"Of course," he said. "I thought of it myself earlier, only I didn't know how to get the horse past the gates. They're locked at night—"

"Don't worry about that. Old Gower, the porter, sleeps like the dead, and I know where he keeps the key. I've taken Mrs. Seyton's chatelaine, too, so we can get into the lodge."

As we had kept our quiet vigil together over Uncle Quentin's body, now we were united in this act of revolt against my father. With Draco leading Black Magic, we set off furtively down the drive, both of us afraid somebody would see or hear us and prevent us from carrying out our plan. But to our vast relief, no one did.

We walked quickly, lost in reverie, silenced now by the night and the enormity of the thing we meant to do. Above, the sky was a length of black velvet against which the stars were strewn like glittering diamonds; fixed among them like a lustrous pearl was the moon, round and full and shining with a soft luminescence through the thin veil of mist that swirled about us like a grey mantle. A gentle wind sighed plaintively through the trees so the branches and leaves stirred and whispered. Beneath Draco's booted feet and Black Magic's hooves, the gravel crunched faintly, and from a distant marsh on the moors came the cry of a lone curlew, piercingly sweet and forlorn.

Mrs. Seyton's chatelaine jingled softly in the stillness as we reached the lodge at last. After turning the proper key in the lock, I pushed open the door stealthily, then stepped inside, pausing to listen intently to see if my intrusion had been heard. Old Gower's loud, no doubt drunken, snores reached my ears from his bedchamber; and breathing a sigh of relief, I carefully slipped the key to the gates off its brass hook upon the wall.

After I had unlocked them, Draco swung one side of the gates open, taking care to lift the wrought-iron barrier slightly so it would not drag and scrape upon the gravel. Then, speaking softly to Black Magic, he gingerly removed the halter and lead from the colt. For a moment, the horse stood still, his ears pricked forward, his nostrils quivering with curiosity. Then, as though scenting freedom, he suddenly tossed his head and whinnied—a joyous sound—then galloped through the open gate, his mane and tail flying in the wind, his hooves pounding upon the hard dirt road.

"Godspeed," I murmured, and lifted one hand to wave; but the animal was already leaping the ditch alongside the road to streak across the moors with a power and grace that made my breath catch in my throat at his barbaric beauty.

For a long time, Draco and I stood motionless, watching Black Magic run until he was out of sight. After that, we walked back to the manor, where, at the side door, my cousin did a very strange and unexpected thing: He leaned forward and kissed me hard and swiftly upon the lips. Then wordlessly he raced away toward the stables, looking so strong and lithe in the moonlight that I was reminded of Black Magic—running wild and free into the darkness.

Chapter Ten

Interlude at Highclyffe Hall

We live and learn, but not the wiser grow.

—*Reason*
John Pomfret

Sir Nigel never did find out it was Draco and I who had turned Black Magic loose. I don't believe it ever occurred to him that we were both rebellious and intelligent enough to think of such a scheme and, further, capable of carrying it out. Had he thought about it, he might have suspected us eventually; but during his attempt to ride the colt, my father had indeed broken several ribs and he had severely injured one leg besides. His insistence on walking on it had damaged the limb further, and as a result, Dr. Ashford ordered him confined to bed for nearly a month. This so provoked Sir Nigel that no doubt he was not thinking clearly.

When he was told of the horse's escape, he ranted and raved like a madman and tried to rise from his sickbed; but Lady Chandler, who really did, I believe, care for him in her cold fashion, pressed him back down determinedly, reminding him of the physician's instructions.

"That damned fool quack!" my father roared. "What does he know?"

But to my surprise, he allowed my stepmother to have

her way, although, grumbling heatedly, he demanded she at least send for Hugh so a search for the animal might be instigated. This, Lady Chandler did, and Sir Nigel spent over an hour telling our head groom just what he thought of his management of the stables before ordering him curtly to find the culprits responsible for loosing Black Magic and to assemble a group of men to locate and catch the beast.

Hugh obediently interrogated all the grooms and stable-boys, including Draco, who nonchalantly lied through his teeth when Hugh questioned him about the colt's disappearance. But although I think our head groom suspected my cousin, as well as me, of the deed, he was as relieved as everyone else that Black Magic was gone, so he did not delve into the matter too deeply. All he said to Draco was: "Aye, well, thee've a way with horses, an' 'twould have taken a Gypsy's knack ta handle Black Magic, I'm a-thinkin'; but if 'ee say 'ee were abed, then I reckon there's nowt I can do but take yer word fer it, young Draco, so I'll not be pressin' 'ee further. But, mind: 'Tis a good thing thee art Mr. Quentin's own lad, or I'd not be so quick ta turn a deaf ear ta yer tales!"

Hugh, when he saw me, chided me even more strongly.

"Miss Maggie," he said, eyeing me sternly, "I've me own thoughts about who 'twas what took Black Magic from t' paddock; an' although I'm of a mind ta say nowt ta yer father, I know, too, that young Draco, fer all that he might have set Black Magic loose, could not have been gettin' him through t' gates without t' key, fer t' lock's not been tampered with—I checked. *That* was yer doin', Miss Maggie, a-takin' t' key from t' lodge, an' Lud knows what demon possessed 'ee ta do it! But, there. 'Tis done now, an' truth ta tell, I'm glad of it in a way, so I'll be keepin' me trap shut.

"But, mind: 'Twas wrong . . . what t' two of 'ee did, fer all that yer hearts may say otherwise. Black Magic is a dangerous beast, an' a-runnin' wild on t' moors like that, he might kill someone a-thinkin' ta catch him an' not knowin' his hist'ry. Then where would we be, fer is it not Sir Nigel's mark t' colt be wearin' on his ear fer all ta see?"

Hugh shook his head at me reprovingly. "I should not like ta stand in yer shoes if e'er yer father learns t' truth of t' matter, Miss Maggie!" he declared.

To my vast relief, however, he told Sir Nigel that he did not know who, if anyone, had freed the horse, that all at the Hall were too afraid of Black Magic to enter the paddock alone, and that the gates would have had to be open, besides, for the animal to have escaped from the park. My father grew quite angry at this, and growling to himself about having known that Gower, the porter, was too old to be tending the gates, he pensioned him off and installed a new man in the lodge—one who could be counted on to sleep with one ear cocked at all times.

Hugh and several of the other grooms tried for days to capture Black Magic. But he had taken up, on Bodmin Moor, with a herd of wild horses and ponies that ran for the high hills whenever the men approached; and at last they were forced to abandon the chase, for Bodmin Moor, with its deceptive marshes and steep tors, was treacherous ground, even for those long familiar with its many pitfalls.

The summer drew to a close; autumn came hard on its heels, bringing days cold and grey, and nights that fell swiftly, so dusk seemed to come and go in the blink of an eye.

Lady Chandler wished to journey to London for the Season; but Sir Nigel's leg still pained him (he had always carried a cane for show, but now he must use it to walk with), and he insisted that under the circumstances, he saw no reason to subject himself to an endless round of boring card parties, routs, balls, and evenings whiled away at "that dreary 'Marriage Mart,' " by which he meant Almack's, in the company of "such reprehensible fops and dandies as that young fool Beau Brummell!" So my stepmother was forced to grit her teeth and remain at the Hall, temporarily postponing her grandiose notions of securing a place for herself among the *haut ton*.

Welles returned to prep school, and Sarah, when she

came for our lessons with Miss Poole, seemed quieter and dreamier than ever after his leaving. Though she tried hard to be as cheerful as she had been, she was so often lost in thought that I felt as though I were intruding when I attempted to regain some of our old closeness, so I forebore to disturb her. Julianne missed her brother as well, and she, too, proved a poor companion because of it.

Thus whenever I could, I rode over to the Grange to visit Esmond; but he was studying very hard in preparation for the coming year, when he would take his examinations for entrance to Eton, so we had little time together. What precious few moments we did have were taken up with his fears that he would fail to achieve admittance to the college and so would incur Sir Nigel's wrath, a topic that could not but depress me, since I had so often been subject to my father's disapproval myself.

Oddly enough, I had grown used now to having my many relations about me; and with no one for company, I found myself experiencing a loneliness I was not accustomed to feeling. As a result, I took to spending more and more time with Draco, riding upon the commons, where we would search for Black Magic and sometimes spy him in the distance. Perhaps the colt remembered us and the fact that we had set him free. I don't know. But he never galloped away immediately upon seeing us, but stood and watched us. Sometimes Draco was able to coax him closer, and once or twice, my cousin even managed to stroke Black Magic's silky nose and mane before the horse shied away to rejoin his herd.

Often we dismounted and climbed the green-and-grey tors, where massive slabs of granite, which resembled the megaliths of Stonehenge and other such ancient rings of stone, stood and formed eerie shapes against the stark horizon. There were upon the tors rocks that looked like ruins of temples built by pagans to the old gods. Tall slabs eroded by the ceaseless elements leaned into one another as though pushed over by some giant hand; others, having fallen to the ground or had the earth wrested away to expose their flat tops, lay at the centers of the rest like sacrificial altars waiting for blood to be spilled upon them.

Kilmar Tor, towering over that part of Bodmin Moor that was called East Moor, was a titanic, maimed fist clawing its way up from the ground, knuckles reaching for the heavens. Below the crag, Trewartha Marsh stretched its way across the heaths that now, with the onslaught of winter, were patched like a crazy quilt with blackening heather and bracken and twisted, stunted shrubs of darkening broom with spindly branches grown sideways from the constant lash of the wind, so they looked like a witch's long, straggling hair streaming back wildly in a storm.

Always upon the commons, the wind blew. Sometimes it sang softly and sweetly, rippling the grass and the water of the springs and streams to be found here and there upon the moors. At other times, as it did now in winter, it shouted like a mighty god or moaned like a sorrowful ghost, shrieking through the cracks and crevices of the granite and sending chills up one's spine before its echo faded, only to begin again. Then the grass and gorse would shudder and flatten as though trodden upon by some colossal foot; the stagnant, slate-colored pools that dotted the marshes would churn and bubble and turn black as the night sky over Cornwall, and the bog islands buoyed up by the murky water would tremble.

These last were dangerous places, where, amid the now pale gold grass, tufts tipped with brown and sprouting tangled yellow strands grew to deceive the unwary, the unsuspecting. Here a man might step forward and find instead of earth beneath his feet only a thin layer of weeds and slime, and he would fall through it into the black, peat-tinged water and drown. I, who had been born and reared in northern Cornwall, knew every inch of this bleak, rugged terrain; but even I did not care to be upon the moors when the sky darkened and the fog rolled in from the sea to cover the grim, uncompromising land with a thick blanket of white.

From the tops of the tors, one could see the grey-green ocean shimmering in the distance and the long, gnarled fingers of black rock that dipped into the sea, where the ruins of Tintagel Castle rose at the end of the narrow causeway linking it to the jagged headland. Sometimes Draco and I explored the ancient fortress, too; and though, much taken with the legend of King Arthur, I would wish my Gypsy cousin to play Gorlois of Cornwall to my Igraine, always he would insist on being Uther Pendragon, come to take by trickery and force that which was not his.

Then at last the days turned shorter still and a hard white frost followed by icy sleet and then a layer of snow settled upon the moors; and we rode no more. Still, warm and snug in the manor, where logs sparked and crackled brightly upon the many hearths, I thought of Draco, huddled over a small peat fire in the cottage he shared with Hugh; and as the holiday season drew near, I labored over a wool muffler I was knitting and planned to give to my cousin on Christmas Day. Though I was sure he would receive Sir Nigel's gift on Boxing Day, when the servants were all given small presents as tokens of my father's esteem, I wanted Draco to know that I, at least, thought of him as family.

The Hall was already adorned with scarlet and gold ribbons, greenery, and beautiful decorations; ornate wreaths hung upon the front doors. The fresh, fragrant, wintry scents of mistletoe, holly, and bayberry, as well as the enticing aromas of mince pies, plum pudding, gingerbread, and other tasty foods baking in the oven under Mrs. Merrick's sharp eye, filled the air.

From the red velvet material Lady Chandler had purchased for me from Mrs. Faversham that summer, I had a hooded pelisse trimmed and lined with ermine, along with a pair of mittens to match. What was left was used to make a sash and ribbons for a new gown of white satin, which I would wear to Mass on Christmas Eve.

Welles came home from school for the holidays, and packed into my father's sleigh, all of us children, including Draco, went caroling. For once, there was no discord between us; and I felt a happiness I had never before known, standing between Esmond and Draco as, after alight-ing from the sleigh, we walked from cottage to cottage in the village, singing and delivering baskets to the poor families who should otherwise have naught with which to make merry. Still, no matter how humble each house was, we were always invited inside to warm ourselves by the fire and to drink a mug of steaming punch from the wassail bowl; and after our numb hands and feet had thawed, we trooped back outside to throw snowballs and make angels in the snow before trudging on through the frozen slush.

Then before I knew it, spring was upon us. Along with Sir Nigel and Aunt Tibby, Esmond journeyed to Eton to sit for the examinations for which Mr. Trahern, his tutor, had worked so hard to prepare him. I waited eagerly for my beloved cousin's return and was so distracted during his absence that Draco became quite provoked with me. Disgusted that I should be so attached to someone he termed a "baker-legged noodle," he avoided me for several days thereafter, much to my chagrin.

I saw him upon the moors, mounted upon the Dale he always rode, galloping alongside the herd of wild horses and ponies Black Magic had made his own; and I sensed my Gypsy cousin was becoming as obsessed as my father with the colt. Even now, when he thought of it, Sir Nigel sent men out to try to capture the animal, to no avail. But Draco, I knew, was different. He would bide his time, not wishing to tame the beast so much as to become one with it, as was the Gypsy way; and perhaps, in the end, Black Magic would be his.

I paid little heed to his pursuit of the colt. Esmond had come back from Eton, where, having passed his examinations, he was to attend school in the fall. I thought he would be happy at the prospect, knowing he had lived up to my father's expectations of him. But instead he was oddly downcast and told me he did not think he would fit in at the college. I did my best to cheer him, but it did not seem to help; and at last I gave up the attempt, hurt that Julianne, who smiled at him saucily and pooh-poohed his fears, appeared better able than I to rouse him from his doldrums.

Sir Nigel, on the other hand, was in much better

spirits, some of his vigor returning as he complained to Lady Chandler at the supper table about the political changes sweeping the country. So-called Luddites, named after one Ned Ludd, who, it was claimed, had started all the trouble by demolishing a piece of machinery, were rioting against the textile manufacturers who had replaced skilled craftsmen with machines at Nottingham. The dissidents had burned one of Richard Arkwright's factories and had broken into James Hargreaves's house to destroy his spinning jenny. My father predicted it was only a matter of time before the miners, who were always grumbling about something, turned violent as well.

"And then, I ask you," he thundered, glaring at us all, "who will protect us? That madman on the throne? That profligate standing in line to take his place?"

None of us answered, for it was well known that King George III suffered periodic fits of insanity, during which, on one occasion, it was rumored, he had leaped from his carriage to shake the limb of an oak and had spoken to the tree at some length, believing it to be the King of Prussia. However, as the malicious story had been put about by a page dismissed from the royal service, no one knew if it was true. None could deny, however, that at a dinner at Windsor Castle, the king, gibbering and foaming like a mad dog, had attacked the Prince of Wales and tried violently to beat his head against a wall.

Dr. Willis and Dr. Warren, the king's physicians, had treated his madness by threatening him, tying him to his bed, and putting him in a straitjacket when he did not behave properly. Later they had restrained him in a special iron chair and slathered him with poultices of Spanish fly and mustard that had been meant to draw out evil humors by producing painful blisters all over his body. Personally I thought it was a wonder the king had ever recovered, for surely the abominable attempts to cure him had been enough to drive even a sane person out of his mind.

As for the Prince of Wales, he was indeed a wastrel. All the king's sons were deeply in debt. In fact, when a statue of the Duke of York had been erected upon a tall column, people had joked that he had climbed up the pillar to evade his many creditors. The prince himself was notorious for his unpaid bills, his string of mistresses, his heavy drinking, and his gluttony. He had been hopelessly drunk at his wedding, and he was even fatter than his wife, Caroline, who did not have the slenderest of figures, although she was kind and the people loved her.

I did not think the prince would make a very good ruler, and I was sorry when King George III, who had lost his favorite daughter, Amelia, only last year and so had suffered a decline, was finally declared permanently insane and, under the terms of the Regency Bill passed by Parliament, was placed into the custody of his wife, Queen Charlotte of Mecklenburg-Strelitz.

But as my father had foreseen, the political situation did not improve, and the rioting of the defiant Luddites continued as the year wore on. Still the news meant little to me, for Sir Nigel did not own any textile factories; and besides, it seemed as though the whole world were in revolt.

England warred against France in Java, and on the Iberian Peninsula as well. In Africa, an Ottoman viceroy, Mohammed Ali, invited the Mameluke leaders of Egypt to a banquet in the citadel at Cairo, and there he massacred nearly all of them for plotting against him. In South America, Venezuela and Paraguay declared their independence from Spain; and in the United States, the Shawnee Indians were defeated during the absence of their chief, Tecumseh, by General Harrison and his troops at what soon came to be called the Battle of Tippecanoe.

In the evenings, at the supper table, my father continued to expound on the repercussions of these global events; but I must confess I paid him little heed. The boundaries of Cornwall were the limits of my world; and now that autumn was upon us and Esmond had gone up to Eton, far from the sphere of my existence, I had sunk into such a depression that Lady Chandler grew quite impatient with me and threatened to box my ears.

"For surely the world is dreary enough, Margaret,"

she rebuked me sharply, "without my having to look at your constantly long face!"

I dismissed her annoyance with me for what it was: an extension of her anger at Sir Nigel because he had once again refused to journey to London for the Season. The miners, he had asserted, were restless; and Mick Dyson, for all that he was an able head foreman and knew which side his bread was buttered on, was a vicious young brute clever enough to play both ends against the middle if it proved to his advantage.

"I'll not leave it to Heapes to deal with him, Gwyneth," my father had said, "and that's final."

Mr. Heapes was the manager of the mines, a thin, hunched man with a sly face and a whining disposition. I never knew why Sir Nigel employed him, except that the man had little care for the welfare of the miners but was interested only in getting a hard day's work out of them— and for half a day's wages if he could.

When I had heard enough of my father's tirades and my stepmother's remonstrations, I retired to my room to curl up on my chaise longue with my cat, Grimalkin, and read, for I was quite fond of novels. Esmond, along with his many lengthy missives to me about the difficulties he faced at college, sometimes sent a book he thought I would enjoy. The latest was called *Sense and Sensibility, A Novel by a Lady*, which had been published anonymously at London that year, although later it came to be known that the author was a Miss Jane Austen, a clergyman's spinster daughter.

Strangely enough, though now I seldom saw him, I felt I had grown even closer to Esmond somehow, for his letters were filled with accounts of his daily life and, more important to me, his thoughts and feelings. He was greatly enjoying his scholarly studies, he wrote; but as he had feared, he was not accepted by the more popular boys who held such sway with his peers, for Eton was a unique college in that its students governed themselves through elected representatives. Esmond had, he told me, earned the contempt of one such youth in particular when he had informed the boy he had no desire to try out for the cricket team.

I did not understand why my beloved cousin should be ridiculed because he was not interested in athletics; but Julianne, when I mentioned the matter to her, curled her lip scornfully and said Esmond would never get anywhere at Eton with that attitude. Though Welles did not have the best possible grades at the prep school he attended, he was the captain of the rowing team, which was undefeated, so he was well liked, she explained proudly.

To my dismay, Draco, who was listening to our conversation, for once sided with Julianne; and they spent the remainder of the afternoon poking fun at Esmond, which I thought was quite spiteful since he wasn't there to defend himself. I was thoroughly annoyed by them both; and later, when Draco confided to me that he was making a good deal of progress on the moors with Black Magic, I said crossly that I was glad, for he was fit company only for that uncivilized horse. My cousin did not speak to me for days afterward. But eventually we made up our quarrel and so were friends again.

Thus did the years of my life pass, quietly, uneventfully, until one ominous day in 1815, when Sir Nigel, who had never got over his obsession with Black Magic, was coming home from business in Plymouth and spied Draco, riding like the wind across Twelve Men's Moor—mounted upon the fiery black stallion.

Chapter Eleven

The Accident

Shot? so quick, so clean an ending?
Oh that was right, lad, that was brave.

—*The Welsh Marches*
A. E. Houseman

Dear reader, there was no peace in our house after that. My father, now knowing that a Gypsy bastard had succeeded where he had failed and so had bested him, would not rest until the horse had been captured and brought back to the Hall. As he had done on so many previous occasions, Sir Nigel sent out a group of men, under the direction of Hugh, to catch the animal; but this time, his hard, cold face set with grim determination, my father delivered to them an implacable ultimatum not to return unless the beast were in their possession. As the men were now aware that their jobs were otherwise forfeit, they pursued Black Magic for days, relentlessly, until the stallion was so exhausted that he was ready to drop in his tracks.

Tears stung my eyes on that terrible afternoon when, despite his weariness, savagely fighting them every step of the way, Black Magic was ignominiously dragged home after five long years of freedom and tied to the post in the center of the paddock. I could not bear to see the proud horse, grown more magnificent than ever, humbled so; and

Draco's face, when I looked at him, was both heartbreaking and terrifying, filled with anguish for the animal he loved so passionately and murderous rage against Sir Nigel, who was even now issuing orders to have Black Magic forcibly subdued.

At twenty years of age, my cousin was a tall, powerful man with massive muscles and a quick temper and fists; and there were many at the Hall who feared him and took great pains to keep out of his way. But my father, who, over the years, had rarely demonstrated anything but contempt for Draco, was not one of these. He paid no heed to my cousin's snarled epithets and fury, but merely laughed and jeered at him and told him scornfully to get out of the way. Thus Sir Nigel was taken by surprise when suddenly, to the utter shock and mortification of all those who saw it happen, having got nowhere reasoning with and then threatening my father, Draco attacked him violently, knocking him to the ground.

I was as stunned as everyone else as I watched the two men grappling with each other; and as vicious blows were exchanged, it seemed to me that all the pent-up hatred they had felt for each other since that stormy night when Sir Nigel had brought my Gypsy cousin to the manor was released and given full rein. Draco, growling and cursing, pounded my father's head brutally against the earth, while Sir Nigel, shouting and straining to free himself, grabbed my cousin's throat and choked him unmercifully.

At last Hugh and two of the other grooms, regaining their senses, ran forward to haul Draco, twisting and struggling wildly against them, off my father; and Sir Nigel, his face red with wrath, staggered to his feet and, grabbing his fallen riding crop, beat my cousin severely with it about the head and shoulders until, gasping for breath, Draco slid heavily to his knees, groaning and bleeding profusely. Still, to my horror, Sir Nigel went on hitting him like a crazy man until finally I leaped down from the fence upon which I was perched and raced across the enclosure to stay my father's arm.

"Stop it! Stop it!" I screamed and sobbed hysterically.

"You're killing him! For God's sake, Father! You're killing him!"

At that, Sir Nigel rounded on me, breathing hard, spittle flying from his lips; and such was the look upon his mottled face that for a moment, I thought he would strike me, too. But at last he slowly lowered his arm and tossed away his whip; and some semblance of sanity returned to his fierce, fervid eyes.

"Take him away"—he motioned with anger and disgust toward Draco—"and see that he's packed off the estate as soon as possible!"

Then he directed his attention back to Black Magic, demanding the beast be bridled and saddled immediately.

I rushed forward to help Draco up; and though I think in that moment he despised me because of my father and wanted no assistance whatsoever from me or my ilk, still he leaned against me heavily as we stumbled across the paddock to the gate that one of the stableboys, his eyes stricken, held open for us. I begged my cousin to come up to the house and let me tend his wounds, but he shook his head stubbornly and refused to go any farther, shaking off my arm and resting against the fence for support, his eyes closed, his breath coming in tortured rasps.

I remember very little after that, only bits and pieces of what occurred, for the remainder of the afternoon was like a horrid nightmare I had lived through once before, seeming to move too slowly, with shapes and shadows dark and blurred, as they are now in my memory, except for Draco's face, sharp and clear in those last terrible moments. . . .

But I get ahead of myself. I must tell you now how, with the greatest of difficulty, a bridle and saddle were eventually placed on Black Magic and how Sir Nigel mounted the horse, only to be savagely thrown off as he had been years before. I do not know how many times this process was repeated, grimly, brutally, with neither side giving any quarter, though both man and beast were dripping with blood from their many wounds; but it seemed like a thousand. Whip and spurs, teeth and hooves . . . all blended together like so many weapons in a melee, until it was impossible to distinguish one from another as the battle raged on relentlessly.

Then finally my father was tossed from the saddle one last time, looking strangely like a scarecrow as he was pitched through the air. He hit the earth with a thud and lay still; and as I watched, petrified, unable in that moment to grasp the reality of what was happening, the stallion came down viciously upon his sprawled figure, trampling him. This time, bruised and battered and bleeding profusely, Sir Nigel was unable to escape as before from those deadly hooves; and he gasped and cried out with pain, rolling and writhing as the animal ravaged him time and again.

To this day, I can still hear the dreadful sound of my own screams and the ghastly echo in my ears of Black Magic's high, shrill cries of agony mingling with mine as somehow my father, desperate to save his life and suddenly possessed of a brute, unnatural strength, reached up like a madman with bloody, trembling hands to clutch to his breast one of the beast's flailing forelegs. Crazed with his terrible power, Sir Nigel rolled over, heaving his weight against the limb, causing Black Magic, who was greatly hampered by his short lead, to lose his balance, stumble, and then fall heavily to the ground. The horse thrashed sickeningly upon the earth, squealing with anguish, before somehow he managed to struggle to his feet, his leg curled at an odd angle beneath him.

I did not understand at first what was wrong, that the stallion's leg was broken; everything still seemed so unreal. Through my tears, I could see Hugh running to my father's side; and then, above my terrified wails, I heard our head groom swearing and yelling that Sir Nigel was unable to rise and like to die and that someone should ride posthaste for the doctor.

The next thing I knew, Draco was staggering from the stables, his face contorted with rage and an agony so piercing as to be utterly unbearable. He held a shotgun purposefully in his hands, and I thought of nothing then but that he meant to murder my father. Screaming and crying, I raced into the paddock to stop him. But I was too late. Tears raining down his cheeks, he fired the weapon at point-blank range; and I, not knowing he had put the bullet through Black Magic's proud, beautiful head, heard naught but the horrible sound of the shot dinning in my ears as the world seemed slowly to spin away into nothingness and a merciful blackness swirled up to engulf me.

BOOK TWO

Upon a Moon-Dark Moor
1815–1819

Chapter Twelve

The Aftermath

I loved him not; and yet now he is gone
I feel I am alone.

—*The Maid's Lament*
Letitia Elizabeth Landon

Highclyffe Hall, England, 1815

That night, after killing Black Magic, Draco ran away; and though I grieved for him and wondered frantically for many long months afterward what had become of him, I neither saw nor heard from my wild Gypsy cousin. It was as though the earth had swallowed him up; and after a time, I realized that like his father before him, he had probably disappeared for good, never to return—except in a coffin perhaps. Mayhap even now, he lay dying or was already dead, I thought, and I wept at the notion of his bold, brave spirit being snuffed out like a candle, as Black Magic's had been.

After Draco's shooting of the horse, a pall seemed to fall over the manor, as it had the fairy-tale castle of Aurora, the sleeping beauty; and the following three years of my life were relatively quiet, if unhappy, ones.

Miraculously Sir Nigel somehow survived the stallion's lethal assault upon him, but he was left paralyzed from the waist down and so was confined for the remainder of his life to a wheelchair. An ugly, hulking attendant, Bascombe, who was, I often fancied, an escaped criminal (though I had no proof of this), was hired to wait upon him and carry him up and down the stairs when necessary. Yet although there were days when he appeared quite like his old self, my father was never to regain his former health. Almost overnight, it seemed, his thick black hair turned thin and grey and his hard body, which had always been a trifle on the heavy side, grew soft and slack and corpulent from lack of exercise and overindulgence in food and drink and the laudanum prescribed for his pain. His temper, never the most even at the best of times, worsened steadily; and when heavily drugged and deep in his cups, he took once more late at night to summoning me to his study, as he had used to do years ago. There he would rail at me violently, often confusing me with Draco—for there was, in truth, a resemblance between us—and frequently he muttered to me as though Black Magic were still alive, so I feared for his sanity.

I was not the only one to suffer from Sir Nigel's erratic outbursts, however. Julianne was often the target of his abuse as well. He told her meanly that for all her outward beauty and charm, inwardly she was sly as the proverbial fox and needn't cosset him with her fluttering eyelashes and dimpled smiles, for she did not fool him one whit.

"I may be crippled and bloated as a dead fish," my father would snarl at her, "but I've still got eyes in my head, and my wits aren't addled yet, despite what you may think! You don't find it so amusing now to sit beside me and regale me with clever little anecdotes, do you? No, now you find me pathetic and loathsome—too reminiscent of the sights and smells of Southwark and Bermondsey, eh, miss? Or perhaps I married your mother in time to spare you London's worst. Well, no matter. Whatever I may be, by God, I still hold the purse strings, and so you swallow your repugnance like a weasel does a chicken egg and play the ministering angel in the hope of winning my favor. Well, you needn't bother, miss, for I'm not planning to die any time soon, and 'tis not likely I'll change my will to suit *your* fancy anyway—whatever you may think!

"You've got no backbone, miss; you never have!

You're a cozener and a complainer—and I daresay you always will be! You want life handed to you on a silver platter, and when it doesn't suit you, you pucker up like a prune and indulge in histrionics. Well, I had little patience for your crocodile tears before, and I've got none at all for them now, so be off with you, you blood-sucking leech! Just because I'm stuck in this hideous contraption''—Sir Nigel would pound his wheelchair vehemently—''doesn't mean I'm a fool who'll let you drain me dry!''

At such times, Julianne, mortified at being spoken to in such a manner—and no doubt by having her secret thoughts so ruthlessly exposed as well—would flee, weeping hysterically, from my father, his mocking laughter ringing in her ears and echoing bitterly through the entire house.

I almost felt sorry for my stepsister on those occasions, for she had thought Sir Nigel loved her as a daughter. Now it was obvious he had never really cared one way or another about her; she had been little more than an amusement to him, and he had always seen straight through her.

Even Lady Chandler, looking drawn and harried these days, was not spared the cruel lash of his tongue. But to her credit, she never flinched when my father berated her, but gave back as good as she got. In the end, he would always harrumph and growl some uncharitable remark that turned into a gruff endearment, so I knew he admired and respected her and, in his own fashion, perhaps loved her, too.

Thus it was left to her to soothe and cheer him, especially on his worst days, when the constant pain he must live with was very bad indeed. Yet my stepmother dealt with him so efficiently and unfailingly that for the first time in my life, I could no longer despise her, but was grateful for her presence. I now realized that for all the luxuries she had received in recompense, her life with Sir Nigel had not been an easy one; and now, tied to an irascible cripple, her future must seem bleak indeed.

Before his accident, she had, for the last three years in a row, prevailed upon my father to journey to London for the Season; and while she had not taken the *haut ton* by storm, she had not earned their utter contempt either. In a small way, she had made her mark in society, and now to give it all up must be a bitter blow indeed. I did not expect her to do it. I thought she would leave Sir Nigel and take up residence at his town house in London, perhaps putting in an appearance at the Hall from time to time. Certainly I believed she would discreetly take one or more lovers.

To my surprise, however, Lady Chandler did neither. Like all those who aspired but did not by birth belong to polite circles, she followed slavishly the strict rules of propriety that governed society and that the gentry, secure in their rank and riches, frequently flouted. Thus, while casting off one's infirm husband might be considered acceptable, if scandalous, behavior for a duchess, it was to be arrogantly condemned in the unsuitable wife of a baronet.

In addition to this, I recognized that, though she may have married him for money, Lady Chandler had come, in her own way, to care sincerely for my father, who had spared her the indignity of being cast into Ludgate Prison, a pauper. Sir Nigel, it appeared, had understood his own attraction to women and my stepmother's nature far better than either Aunt Tibby or I.

If, during those years, the Hall seemed frozen in time, isolated from the rest of the world and locked in a perpetual circle that revolved solely around my father's unpredictable moods, the world did not know or care, but forged ahead ceaselessly, with little light to guide it through the darkness of the times.

The entire planet was affected when a volcano called Mount Tambora on a small island in the Far East exploded, producing whirlwinds and tidal waves that killed thousands. Clouds of dust and ash plunged the island into blackness for three days and altered the earth's climate worldwide, so that for nearly a year afterward, frost layered the ground long after spring had ended and snow fell in some places in the dead of summer.

On a smaller scale, the French emperor, Napoleon Bonaparte, was defeated at Waterloo by the Duke of Wellington, who became a national hero; and a banker, Nathan Meyer Rothschild, made a fortune on the London

Exchange after he received reports by carrier pigeon from Belgium of Napoleon's downfall. Rothschild depressed the worth of British consols by selling short. He subsequently bought all he could at distressed prices, only to sell again when news of Wellington's victory reached England's shores, sending the value of the consols soaring.

England, having won the battle against the French, lost another to the Americans at New Orleans in the war that had begun in 1812; and the warden of Dartmoor Prison, enraged over a minor incident at the penitentiary, ordered the Somerset militiamen to massacre hundreds of prisoners, most of whom were American sailors who had been convicted for privateering.

The Corn Law was enacted by Parliament; the income tax was abolished; and the Luddite movement that had been suppressed in 1813, when its leaders had either been hanged or transported after a mass trial at York, was revived, and rioting once more swept across England.

A man called Humphry Davy invented a safety lamp for miners, which had a metal shield around the flame to keep gas from being ignited and so helped to prevent accidents. Robert Stirling, a Scottish engineer, patented an engine that needed no boiler; and at Guy's Hospital, in London, a surgeon, Dr. James Blundell, performed the first successful blood transfusion on a human being.

The architect John Nash completed his work on Brighton Pavilion for the Prince Regent, and the oriental palace was both applauded and condemned in polite circles. Novels by an anonymous writer, said to be one Mr. Walter Scott, the son of a Scottish solicitor, and Jane Austen, who was by now much admired by the Prince Regent, were published and eagerly devoured by romantic young ladies especially. We in England danced the quadrille for the first time; and society was set atwitter with rumors and scandal when its adored fashion king, Beau Brummell, was forced to flee to Calais to escape from his creditors, who were dunning him for numerous gaming debts.

It was shortly after Julianne turned sixteen and was discharged from the schoolroom that Lady Chandler persuaded my father to allow my stepsister—and me also, though I was already betrothed to Esmond—to have a short Season in London. Though Sir Nigel grumbled heatedly about the expense, at last he relented and even permitted Sarah to accompany us, dutifully ensuring that she, too, was outfitted with the appropriate garments for a London debut. Although I did not care for either the city or society, the coming-out ball my stepmother arranged for us at Sir Nigel's town house was an event I should not have liked to miss. To my utter surprise and delight, for I had never before thought of myself as a pretty girl, I attracted nearly as many young bucks and dashing blades as Sarah and Julianne, the latter of whom was undeniably the toast of the Season.

Alas, it did not answer after all, for no one could take Esmond's place in my heart; Sarah had eyes only for Welles; and Julianne, for all her loveliness, had but a modest dowry and was the daughter of a mere merchant besides. Those suitors who could well afford to overlook my stepsister's lack of wealth could not manage to overcome their prejudice against her background; and those who cared not one whit for her lack of blue blood unfortunately had little more than their devotion to offer. She received three honest proposals of marriage: one from a handsome but tragically dispossessed young French *émigré*, and two from men who had nothing but their character to recommend them. She was also the recipient of several less-than-honorable propositions, which ranged from a lecherous old duke to a rather rapscallious actor she met in Drury Lane.

Thus when we returned home at the beginning of the summer of 1818, Julianne was greatly downcast and desperate beyond measure to secure her future. She could not bear to be dependent upon my charity; yet once my father was dead, the estate would belong to Esmond, my betrothed, and after our marriage, I—not my stepmother—would be mistress of Highclyffe Hall. The notion festered like an open wound in Julianne's mind, distressing her far more deeply and often than I realized, for I, knowing I was to wed

Esmond and so having little worry about my future, gave scant thought to my stepsister's plight.

Esmond and I corresponded as frequently as possible; I wrote rather more often than he, for having completed his studies at Eton, he was at King's College at Cambridge now and did not have as many free hours as I. Still he somehow found time to exchange letters with me, and with Sarah and Julianne, too, just as Welles wrote, albeit sporadically, to all three of us. My stepbrother had another year or two left at Harrow, where he was currently enrolled. Then, much to Lady Chandler's displeasure, instead of going on to Oxford, as she had hoped, he planned to take a job aboard a merchant ship, intending to follow in his father's footsteps.

Of Draco, I knew nothing. Sadly I believed he must be dead, for I thought that otherwise I should surely have had some word from him by now; and to my surprise, I felt a strange, hollow ache in my heart at the idea that I would never see him again.

Chapter Thirteen

The Return of My Gypsy Cousin

So on the ocean of life we pass and
speak one another,
Only a look and a voice; then darkness
again and a silence.

—*The Theologian's Tale (Elizabeth)*
Henry Wadsworth Longfellow

Sometimes I think that the ancient Greeks were right and
that there are indeed three Fates, robed in white, who
fashion the threads of life. It is said that of the three,
Atropos, the smallest, is the most terrible, for it is she who
cuts the threads with her shears and so brings death to each
of us in time. Yet now that I am old and, with the telling of
this story, looking back over the years, I have come to
believe it is the other two Fates who are most to be feared;
for it is Clotho, with her spindle, who draws out and twists
the fibers of all men into the threads of life, and Lachesis,
with her rod, who measures them; and between the two, we
who are the threads are turned and twined until our lives are
a tangled skein from which only Atropos can finally free us.
So did the gnarled fingers of Clotho and Lachesis cause my
life's thread to cross Draco's again at last and to become
once more interlaced with his.

It was a few weeks after I had returned from London

that I discovered that during my absence, my Gypsy cousin had come back without warning to northern Cornwall and had taken up residence at Stormswept Heights, the old, ruined manor some few miles to the southwest of Highclyffe Hall. Upon hearing the unexpected news, my emotions were mixed. I was surprised and happy, of course, to find out he was not dead after all, but lived and apparently had prospered. But more than this, I was deeply hurt that he had never once written or sent word to me, not even to tell me of his return. Draco was both my cousin and my friend, and I had thought we shared a special bond between us. But, then, I reflected, I had been just fifteen the last time I had seen him, older than my years but a child yet in so many ways that perhaps I had read more into our relationship than, in truth, there had been.

Draco was, I soon learned, the object of much speculation at both the Hall and the Grange, and in the village as well. No one knew where he had been, why he had come back, or how he had acquired the means to buy Stormswept Heights.

Even I never knew for certain the answers to these questions, for some days later, when I rode over to see him, I asked him about the three years he had been gone from us, and casually he replied only that he had "traveled here and there," that he had returned "for reasons of his own," and that he had had "a bit of luck at the hazard tables," which had enabled him to purchase the manor.

He offered no further explanation, and I did not press him for one, for he was so changed that I felt I scarcely knew him. He had withdrawn deeper than ever into his dark, brooding shell, and his demeanor was so stern and forbidding that even I, once his closest companion at the Hall, was more than a little afraid of him.

He kept a huge, savage mongrel that followed in his wake like a shadow wherever he went and that soon became well known in the vicinity for its ability to discourage visitors. Thus, so far as I could learn, with the sole exception of myself, no one save Mrs. Pickering, an aged widow who served as both his housekeeper and cook, and Renshaw, his caretaker, who was generally believed to be mad, went near the place, nor did my cousin invite anyone to do so.

He was laboring in the fields, naked to the waist beneath the warm summer sun, when I, mounted upon my horse, a handsome dapple-grey gelding I called Avalon after the mystical isle of King Arthur's legend, first trotted up the weed-ridden drive into the yard at the Heights. Draco saw me from the distant fields, I knew; but for a curiously painful moment, I thought he would pretend he had not and would go on with his work. At last, however, he slipped the harness from his massive shoulders, and bidding the sturdy, dark brown Dale hauling the plow to stay, he walked forward to greet me, the large grey, wolfish dog at his heels.

Strangely, as my cousin drew near, my heart gave a little lurch, then began to flutter in a most peculiar, inexplicable way; and suddenly I felt as nervous as I had before my London debut, uncertain of finding favor. I fussed with my hair and fidgeted with my riding habit, wondering what Draco would think of me. Would he find me much changed with the years, a woman fully grown now? Or would he still see me as a child? I did not know; I did not even understand why it seemed so important to me to know. Yet it did. But I had no time to analyze the reasons why, for now he stood before me. All the cool, clever things I had planned to say, so he would not realize how much I had cared that he had gone away with never a word to me, went right out of my head as I gazed down at him.

I had prepared myself to be disappointed in him, for over the years, I had discovered that one's childhood memories are deceptive things, drawn on a sweeping canvas and painted with colors more intense than they ever really had. Yet Draco was exactly as I remembered him, as though his bold, dark face had been forever engraved upon my mind in clear detail: his swooping black brows, like a raven's wings poised above his glittering jet-black eyes; his full, sensual lips twisted with mockery beneath his broken nose; his strong, square jaw shadowed by the faint, dark stubble of a beard. I thought how strange it was that I should recall him so sharply when my childhood images of Welles and Julianne, of Sarah and even Esmond were blurred at the edges, like vignettes. All I could remember of them were fleeting impressions: a look, a smile, a gesture. It was almost as though Draco's face had shimmered so brightly in my mind that he had somehow blotted out all the others, leaving them no more than silhouettes in my memories.

I did not know then what he thought when first he saw me. I knew only that when he reached me, he stared at me so avidly and fiercely—like a hawk, I thought—that I grew flustered and confused and suddenly wished I had not come. His eyes gleamed like hot coals when they raked me, and for an instant, I believed he meant to snatch me from the saddle and devour me, his expression was so nakedly savage. My breath caught in my throat, for no man had ever looked at me like that—as though he knew me intimately. At the thought, a slow, swooning sensation I had never before felt started at the very core of my being and spread through my body like a feverish chill, making me shiver with mingled fear and excitement. My pulse raced jerkily, and my mouth went dry. Without warning, it seemed as though the afternoon had grown abruptly still and the land and the sea beyond had faded into the background, leaving my senses focused acutely on Draco.

I became aware of the sweat that beaded his upper lip and glistened on his swarthy, bare upper torso, droplets dampening the dark mat of hair upon his chest and trickling down his powerful arms, where his muscles bulged and rippled beneath his skin. A slight breeze stirred, kissing my lips with the salty taste of the ocean, so it was almost as though I had pressed them to Draco's flesh; and for a moment, as the unbidden, tantalizing image filled my mind, I was overcome by a violent wave of some strange emotion I had never before experienced. I leaned toward him, drawn to him by the nameless thing that had seized me in its grasp and now sucked me down into itself, so I felt as though I were drowning in the dark, fathomless depths of Draco's eyes.

I do not know what I expected; but at last he swept his eyelids down to veil his thoughts, as I had seen him do so many times in the past, and the spell that had been cast upon me was broken, leaving me keenly disappointed, as though there should have been something more.

"Hullo, Maggie," he said.

As it had used to do, my heart leaped queerly as his deep, lilting, accented voice washed over me; and to my dismay, I felt myself blushing like a silly schoolgirl. I fancied he found some measure of satisfaction in that, for a peculiar smile curved his mouth as the color rose in my cheeks, and my eyes could no longer meet his. I glanced away, biting my lip and feeling oddly exposed and vulnerable. But when next I looked at him, his countenance was as hard and impassive as ever; and I was puzzled and hurt by his sudden coolness.

"Hullo, Draco," I responded softly.

After a minute or two of silence that seemed to stretch tautly between us, he invited me into the house; and as he assisted me from the saddle, I felt the strength of his firm, callused hands, like iron around my slender waist. I trembled a little at the power that was his, remembering how brutally he had pounded Sir Nigel's head against the ground that day of the accident. But I did not want to think of that. It was a day best forgotten, and so I pushed the terrible memory of it away.

Now that I stood before my Gypsy cousin, I realized how tall he was, as tall as I remembered, for the top of my head barely reached the middle of his chest, though I was not a small woman. Over the years, I had grown and filled out, so I was no longer the gawky girl of my childhood; and if I were not the dainty, blond-haired, blue-eyed beauty, like Julianne, that I might have wished to be and that was currently all the rage in polite circles, still I knew from the months I had spent in London that there was about me a certain, undefinable quality that attracted a second look. The thought gave me confidence now, and gently I pulled Draco's hands from my waist and clasped them in mine.

"'Tis good to see you again," I told him quietly. "I have often thought of you and wondered if you were well."

"Have you?" He lifted one black eyebrow, and for a moment, his dark visage had a devilish cast. "How very... gratifying. I had supposed that in time, you would forget me.''

He said nothing more; but I could tell he was pleased, for as, after relinquishing Avalon into the care of the lunatic but capable Renshaw, Draco and I strolled toward the manor, a faint smile lingered upon his mouth and his black eyes were like twin flames.

I studied him covertly as we walked along, noting the fine lines of time and dissipation that had not been there before, but that now etched his face, so he seemed older than his twenty-three years. Wherever he had been, whatever money he had made, his life had not been easy, I suspected, in the years since he had left us; and knowing Draco's background, I thought it was as likely that he had spent them in Newgate Prison as it was that he had lived them high on the hog in London, as people claimed.

Still, for all that the Heights was a shambles, it could not have come cheaply, so perhaps he had won a fortune in some gaming hell after all. I would not have put it past him to have earned his living as a sharp or an ivory-turner, for despite their calluses, his hands were smooth—he kept them so with a pumice stone—and no doubt they were deft at palming cards or switching dice if the need arose.

We went inside the house, where Draco led me through the decaying hall and down a short flight of stairs into the kitchen, where he mockingly bade me be seated, for there were only a crude table and a few rough chairs shoved against one wall to serve as furniture.

The Widow Pickering, who was half deaf and so shouted as a result, thinking no one else could hear either, greeted us loudly and, upon Draco's command, prepared tea for us, occasionally talking to herself as she bustled about. If she were surprised to see me, she gave no sign of it, but set the chipped mugs and a plate of oatcakes down upon the table as though it were every day she entertained the baronet's daughter. After that, she left us—to get on with her household chores, I guessed, though what she found to do in her desolate domain, I did not know—and Draco and I had the kitchen to ourselves.

We talked of this and that, trivial things mostly, for my cousin did not choose to reveal his past to me, and after my curiosity had been politely but firmly discouraged, I did not ask again. Instead I told him about Highclyffe Hall and Pembroke Grange and that Sir Nigel lived but was paralyzed and confined to a wheelchair.

"Is he now?" Draco remarked and said nothing more, though I sensed he felt it served my father right for his cruelty to Black Magic.

Discomfitted by my cousin's reticence, I chattered on like a raven to fill the silence, unable to halt the flow of words that tumbled nervously from my lips. I spoke of my Season in London, of Sarah and Welles's love for each other, of Julianne's failure to catch a husband, and of my own plans to marry Esmond once he had completed his studies at King's College and returned home.

"So . . . you still fancy yourself in love with the estimable Mr. Sheffield then, eh, Maggie?" Draco drawled in such a way that I knew he still felt nothing but contempt for Esmond. "Such devotion is to be greatly prized, surely. One wonders, then, why the worthy young gentleman comes so late to the altar. *Tsk, tsk.* If you were my promised bride, Maggie"—he took my left hand in his to study my betrothal ring, which Esmond had given to me some months past—"I would not be so slow to tie the knot, I assure you."

Something in his voice sent a shiver of that strange, undefinable emotion down my spine, and flushing, I snatched my hand away rudely.

"You never did like Esmond, Draco," I accused in order to hide my sudden confusion and consternation, "though I cannot think why, any more than I can think why *he* despises *you* so intensely."

"Does he? How very . . . interesting," my cousin said, his eyes alight now with a peculiar flicker of emotion.

"Yes, but I don't understand—"

"No," Draco interrupted curtly, his voice sounding oddly harsh and bitter now, "you don't—more's the pity." Then, seeing the concern and bewilderment upon my face, he sighed. "Ah, well. 'Tis neither here nor there, I imagine—

and certainly naught for you to bother your delightfully inquisitive mind about, my girl. Suffice to say that Esmond and I have never been friends and never shall be. Let's leave it at that, shall we, Maggie?''

I cursed both my tongue and my stupidity then, for of course, if not for his bastardy, Draco, not Esmond, would have been heir to Sir Nigel's estate. I did not know how I could have forgotten such a thing, except that I never thought of my Gypsy cousin, as everyone else did, in terms of his illegitimacy.

I started to apologize, then realized I would only make matters worse. So instead, observing how late the afternoon had grown, I took my leave of him, feeling his intense black eyes on me all the while as I reined Avalon hard about and galloped down the drive past the deserted lodge and through the rusty wrought-iron gates of the ruined manor.

Chapter Fourteen

Esmond

Betrothed, betrayer, and betray'd!

—*The Betrothed*
Sir Walter Scott

Although, after that day, I occasionally visited Draco again, he never rode over to the Hall, and I did not ask him to do so, fearing that Sir Nigel would have an apoplectic fit if he saw him. Though all of us at the manor, in tacit agreement, had kept from my father as long as possible the news of Draco's return, eventually he had learned of it—no doubt from Bascombe, who could not be thought of as being one of us anyway—and upon hearing that his bastard nephew had not only purchased, but had, bold as brass, moved into Stormswept Heights, Sir Nigel had worked himself into such a frenzy that even Lady Chandler had been unable to calm him. We had been forced to send for Dr. Ashford, who had told my father that if he did not learn to curb his temper, he should soon find himself in his grave. Sir Nigel, most provoked by this remark, had given the physician his heated opinion of it, whereupon Dr. Ashford, long accustomed to my father's rages, had merely shrugged, snapped shut his black bag, and said that as it was Sir Nigel's life after all, he must do with it as he pleased.

After that, my father had sent a note around to Draco,

demanding he present himself at the Hall forthwith to explain himself. I never knew what my cousin's reply was; but I had gathered from Sir Nigel's infuriated response to it that it had been rudely penned with the sole intention of refusing and insulting him, and so I thought it prudent never to mention my brief sojourns at the Heights.

It was shortly after this that the term at King's College ended and that Esmond returned to the Grange. I was overjoyed to see him, and it was with the greatest of happiness that we set our wedding date at last for the following summer of 1819, when it was thought that he would be finished with his studies.

Though our betrothal was a long-standing one, a formal announcement of our engagement and forthcoming marriage was necessary, so, accordingly, an appropriate engagement notice was written and mailed to London for insertion in the *London Gazette*; and Lady Chandler and I began shortly thereafter to make the initial preparations for the event.

Mrs. Faversham, the dressmaker, was summoned from Launceston to take my measurements and submit for my inspection the materials from which my trousseau was to be fashioned. Messages were dispatched to Mr. Earnhart, the vicar; Mr. Keefe, the caterer; and others to secure their services well in advance of the date Esmond and I had selected; and Sir Nigel addressed a letter to his London solicitor, Mr. Oldstead, requesting him to journey to Cornwall at his earliest convenience to draw up the marriage contracts.

During the weeks that followed, Esmond came as often as possible to the Hall, and we took long rides on the moors and walks in the park, where we spoke of our love for each other and dreamed of our future together. We decided to spend our honeymoon in Italy, in Venice and Florence, after which we would return to the Hall, where we would live and Esmond would be instructed in the management of the estate until such time as he came into his inheritance.

Often, as we strolled along, Esmond would take my hand in his, and a warm feeling of tenderness and security would envelop me at his touch. He had beautiful hands, fine and slender and gentle, in sharp contrast to Draco's, I thought, remembering the strength and hardness of my Gypsy cousin's hands about my waist. I was thankful there was none of Draco's coarseness and brutishness about my beloved, for even though Draco held a strange fascination for me, there was, as well, a streak of cruelty in him that frightened me.

He was not pleased when I rode over to the Heights to tell him Esmond and I were to be married next summer. At my news, his black eyes filled with some unreadable emotion and narrowed as his eyelids lowered to conceal his thoughts. For a moment, he paused in the act of lighting one of the cheroots he had taken to smoking. His mouth tightened, and a muscle twitched in his jaw before, realizing the match was about to burn his fingers, he drew on the thin cigar, exhaled, then quickly tossed away the flaming match, stamping upon it with his foot.

"Well," he drawled dryly, "I suppose I should wish you joy, Maggie; but as it is inconceivable to me that you will be happy with that dull stick you are determined to wed, I shall not do so, but will hope only that you are not made too miserable by him."

"I am sorry you feel that way, Draco," I answered coolly, "for I had hoped you would wish me well. But I see you are bent on trying to spoil my pleasure instead. Well, you shall not do so, no matter what you say, for I know 'tis only that you do not care for Esmond that makes you speak so." I paused, then continued.

"I fear you have grown even more bitter with the years, Draco—and are lonely, too, for the Heights is very isolated and desolate. Have you given no thought yourself to taking a bride? I'm sure there are many girls in the village who would be honored to have you as their husband."

"Perhaps," he agreed, his voice low. "But there is only one who takes my fancy, and she is pledged to another. If I cannot have her, I shall never marry."

I was surprised by his words, for I had not thought him to be suffering from unrequited love. I wondered who had won his heart and scorned it; but I did not ask, for I sensed he would not tell me.

"You are yet a young man," I said instead, laying my hand upon his arm. "No doubt you will change your mind in time."

He made no reply to that, so I knew he was neither comforted nor convinced by my words; and after a time, I took my leave of him, pity for him filling my heart.

I do not know when I first became aware there was something wrong between Esmond and me, though I suppose I must have sensed it long before I finally admitted it to myself. There were so many hints in his behavior to inform me that his feelings toward me had undergone a change that I could not have mistaken them for aught else. But still I kept ignoring them, making excuses to myself so I should not have to face the subtle discord in our relationship.

In the beginning, it seemed only that Esmond's fine hazel eyes, once so open and honest and shining with love for me, could no longer meet mine, but slid away from my adoring gaze in a manner most unlike him. At first I blamed myself for this, thinking I had grown bold and brazen with my love for him, allowing my affection and desire for him to show so nakedly upon my face that I had offended his shier, more refined sensibilities with my unseemly want of discretion. Yet when I mentioned my fears to him, Esmond hastened to reassure me otherwise, so presently I came to believe his ardor for me was such that he could not trust himself to control it, and I exulted in the way he trembled and grew pale at my nearness.

With the passing of summer, he became reluctant to take my hand in his, to kiss me, as he had sometimes done before, tenderly, sweetly, his lips soft as down upon mine. But this, too, I attributed to his yearning for me, for I knew from the gossip I had heard over the years and from what Linnet had told me, too, when curious, I had questioned her, that it was more difficult for a man to restrain his passions than for a woman. That was why young men were permitted without condemnation to sow their wild oats and why those unmentionable women who accommodated them were likewise repudiated for their lack of virtue. A lady remained chaste until her wedding night, lest her character be demonstrated as base and therefore undesirable by a gentleman, for a man must be assured his heirs were born of his own seed and no other's.

Esmond, of course, could not wish me to be compromised before our wedding or to have some undeserved scandal attached to my good name. How generous and unselfish, he was, I thought, to deny himself that which his longing for me urged him to take. I was touched by his care and concern for me. Such evidence of devotion was surely to be admired!

And yet sometimes I felt myself wishing he were not so protective of my maidenly modesty, my inbred sensibilities born of my status in life. Sometimes I secretly hoped that his desires would overcome his natural reticence, that he would take me in his arms and kiss me passionately, unrestrainedly, so I would know how much he wanted me. I longed for him, just once, to press me down upon the sweet summer grass and try to have his way with me, though, of course, in my daydreams, we would both come to our senses before our love was consummated.

I was shocked by my wanton thoughts; yet I would not be honest if I did not confess them, no matter how much it pains me to do so, and I have promised to be truthful in my telling of this story.

Therefore, much to my dismay, I must also admit that I was excited, as well, by these vignettes I imagined. I believed there must be something wrong with me to conjure such scenes in my mind, some lack of character or gentility in myself; and I began to understand why Miss Poole, long gone from us now, had discouraged the reading of those various romantic novels that were all the rage in polite circles. Yet time and again, the wayward images haunted me, and I could not put them from my head.

I said naught to Esmond of my fantasies, however,

knowing he would be deeply mortified by them and doubt the conviction of my morals. He would further, I suspected, consider it his duty as both my cousin and my fiancé to chide me gravely and point out the possible imperilment of my immortal soul; and I had no wish to be lectured by him. Yet I believe if he had pressed me, I would have given myself to him willingly during those halcyon days of our courtship.

Thus I did not know which of us was more relieved when at last autumn was upon us, cloaking us with her mantle of scarlet and gold, and Esmond must return to Cambridge. Our parting was more wrenching to me than it had ever been before. But he, I fancied, was glad of it since he should no longer be exposed to that which tempted us both; and my heart was filled with secret triumph and delight that I held such attraction for him. I smiled at him tremulously through my tears after I had kissed him good-bye, feeling much like any woman secure in the knowledge of her man's love; and I bade him write to me, as always, until the winter holidays, when we would again be reunited.

This, Esmond promised to do. But his missives, when they arrived, were not the impassioned love letters I had expected to receive; and once more an odd, niggling sense of perturbation assailed me, as though something were amiss between us. Again I searched my mind in an attempt to discover what it could be; but I could think of nothing, and finally, feeling that perhaps it was merely my imagination, I determinedly thrust the notion from my head.

It is no more than nerves, I told myself. *All brides are anxious as their wedding day approaches.*

And as nothing untoward occurred, I was, for the most part, able to content myself with my reassurances. Certainly the Hall did not share my slight sense of disquiet, but, as winter wrapped us in her white blanket of frost and the holiday season drew near, was merrier than I ever remembered it being.

For once, Sir Nigel was in a rare good humor, made so by the news of my impending marriage to his heir; and as a result, Lady Chandler's disposition was brighter, too, than it was usually wont to be. Even Julianne, who had initially been quite resentful, I thought, of Esmond's wedding me, seemed to have rallied her spirits from the depths of gloom into which they had sunk; and she went about the manor with that peculiar half-smile so like her mother's on her face, so occasionally I wondered at the cause of her good cheer. She looked, I mused, like someone possessed of a secret; but then, as the holidays were a time of secrets, I shrugged and thought no more of the matter, guessing she was planning some special surprise.

How could I know it was to bring me the worst unhappiness of my life? How can I tell you what rage and agony welled in my breast when I learned what she had done? Fool that I was, I never once suspected her treachery— or Esmond's betrayal of our love—until, having declined to read for honors and so having forfeited a chance at a fellowship, he took a pass degree from King's College and, several months earlier than I had expected, returned home to Cornwall, not just for the holidays, but for good.

He said naught to me at first to explain his leaving Cambridge so soon; but then a few days before Christmas, he rode over to the Hall and asked me to walk in the park with him, his manner so distracted that a sudden chill of foreboding clutched my heart.

I shall never forget his face as it was that dreary morning, pale and sickly damp as the leaden sky above us, as contorted with anguish as the twisted yews of the wood when he turned to me and took my hands in his.

"Esmond, what is it?" I cried, stricken, thinking he was ill. "What is it?"

"Ah, Maggie, dearest Maggie, I am not worthy even of your contempt!" he burst out abruptly, causing my heart to shrivel inside me with a different kind of dread now. "I despise myself, as you shall despise me when you learn what I have done—and I shall not blame you for it; no, I shall not, for no one knows better than I what a cad I am become! I am lower than the lowest blackguard!" He dropped my hands and, swallowing hard, looked away so I could no longer see his face. "I can do naught now but plead for your understanding—though I know I am undeserving of your forgiveness—and ask you to release me from our pledge.''

"You—you want me to cry off from our engagement?" I said stupidly, stunned. "But... why, Esmond? Why? I don't understand...."

"I love you, Maggie; you know I do!" he insisted, turning toward me once more. "But I have come to realize 'tis the love of a brother for his sister, a cousin for his cherished friend, as you have ever been to me—not as a man should love the woman he takes for his bride. I cannot offer you that—I see that now—not when my heart pines so fervently for Julie that I can hardly bear it!''

"Julianne. Julianne," I repeated dumbly. "Are you telling me you are in love with Julianne, Esmond?"

"Yes. *Yes!*" he wailed wretchedly. "I can put it no plainer than that! Now you know the great wrong I have done you! Oh, Maggie! Don't look at me like that, I beg of you! I never meant for this to happen; I never intended to hurt you, though I know I have done so—and more deeply than I care to imagine! But how can I marry you now, knowing I can no longer be that which you most deserve—a loving husband? I should make you miserable, Maggie, as miserable as I am at this moment!''

"How—how did it happen?" I asked, still unable to believe his words, for they did not seem real, but something from a nightmare.

"I have loved Julie for a long time, since we were children, I think," Esmond said, more quietly now. "She is so beautiful and fragile, like a delicate porcelain doll, and so charming and helpless that I have ever yearned to protect her from the harshness and cruelty of the world, so different from her own sweet and noble nature. No one has ever understood her, you know... how she suffered in her past, how she has always felt out of place at the Hall, dependent upon Uncle Nigel's charity, as I have been," Esmond declared bitterly, so I realized for the first time how ashamed he was of his lack of means, his inability to provide for Aunt Tibby and Sarah. He paused, then continued.

"This past summer, when I saw Julie again, I could no longer deny my true feelings for her, nor she for me, though bravely she tried to deceive me, to pretend as though she did not care. But I knew how she felt—I could see her grief and longing for me in her eyes whenever I looked at her—and at last, one day after I had ridden away from the Hall, I chanced upon her here in the park. I dismounted to speak to her, and after a time, emboldened by my desire for her, I dared to take her in my arms and declare my love for her. She broke down and wept then, confessing her own love for me and how she had attempted to hide it, for she could not bear to wound *you*, Maggie, who have been as a sister to her, and so she had borne her despair in silence.

"Then she thrust me away and cried out passionately that we must never speak of our feelings for each other again, that we must think of you, Maggie, only of you. Such generosity! Such unselfishness! What could I do? I rode away, as Julie had bidden me to do; but I could not put her from my heart and mind. I sought her out and pleaded with her to let me ask you for your blessing and understanding of our love. But she demurred and said that I must not, that you had never liked her and would accuse her of being a false sister to her, though the thought of your happiness was ever her utmost concern. She was determined to go away, after our wedding, for she could not bring herself to live at the Hall with you and me, to see me every day and know you, not she, were my wife.

"I was frantic with worry for her, for where would she go? How would she live? Her inheritance from her father, Captain Brodie, is not large, you know, and Uncle Nigel, who is not an overly generous man, has found great fault with her recently, though she has done her best to try to please him. Still Julie said that I must not be anxious on her account, that she would manage somehow, even if she must return to the poverty she had known in London.

"Autumn was upon us then, and I was forced to go back to Cambridge; but I was so downcast that I had little inclination for my studies. Time and again, I wrote to her, begging her to change her mind; and finally, after I had pointed out to her that your joy in our marriage must, of necessity, be painfully marred when you discovered I could not love you as my wife, she relented and said I might speak to you upon my return to Cornwall.

"Now I have done so—and feel the better for it, though I have hurt and misused you cruelly, I know. But I could not go on living a lie, Maggie. Surely you can see that! How could I bring myself to wed you in such ill faith when you have been, and remain, so dear a cousin to me? Oh, I do not blame you if you hate me! I deserve whatever loathing and anger you no doubt feel toward me now. I do not ask for your forgiveness. I beseech you only to let me go so Julie and I will be free to marry."

He fell silent then, and I . . . I was silent also, hurt and enraged, both pitying and scorning him in that moment. I saw everything so clearly now, how Julianne, desperate after her failure in London to secure a husband, and thus her future, had cleverly wormed her way into Esmond's heart, slowly turning him against me while all the time pretending she thought only of my happiness. I could imagine all too well how she had watched for him to leave the Hall, how she had waited in the park to intercept him and enact her tearful little charade. But it did not matter. There was nothing I could say to make Esmond realize what she had done, how she had schemed to ensnare him, wanting only that which would be his upon Sir Nigel's death. Were Esmond suddenly to be disinherited, my stepsister would not spare him a second glance, I knew. But he would not believe me if I told him that. He would think only, as Julianne had already shrewdly pointed out to him in order to protect herself, that as I had always disliked her, I would say anything against her, no matter how awful or untrue.

I thought of how I had believed Esmond trembling with passion for me, how I had been willing to surrender myself to him, if only he had asked me to do so; and I was filled with shame and mortification that all the while I had been imagining such wanton things, he had been holding and kissing Julianne. Dear reader, will you think ill of me if I tell you how much I hated her in that instant and wished her dead—dead and moldering in her grave, her beauty decaying from her bones, her black heart withering in her breast? I did—passionately, vehemently, with every ounce of my being. I had been a fool, I thought, an unutterably stupid fool! Thank God, I had never told Esmond how I had yearned for him! It was my only consolation, and small though it was, I clung to it as though it were my salvation.

Somehow I managed to pull myself together—how, I shall never know. But my voice, when finally I spoke to him, did not quaver, and somehow, as I laid my hand upon his arm, I held my tears at bay so he should never know how deeply he had wounded me.

"I release you, Esmond," I said quietly, with as much dignity as I could muster, "and I wish you joy of her, though I think you shall not find it in the end."

Then I turned and walked swiftly away from him so he would not see the tears that streamed at last, unchecked, down my face.

Chapter Fifteen

The Cliffs at the Edge of the Sea

And if you gaze for long into an abyss,
the abyss gazes also into you.

—*Jenseits von Gut und Böse*
Friedrich Nietzsche

Aunt Tibby and Sarah were my only comfort in those days that followed after Esmond and I announced our broken engagement and he asked Julianne to marry him. Both the Hall and the Grange, as well as the village, were set atwitter by the scandalous news. Wherever I went, I could feel people's eyes upon me pityingly, for though, out of guilt and respect for me, Esmond and Julianne's betrothal had not yet been made public, it did not matter. Somehow the servants always knew everything that occurred at the manor, and now was no exception; thus the entire village was aware of my plight.

I bore that knowledge as best I could, directing a cool, level gaze at any who sought to pry into the affair and saying only that Esmond and I had found we should not suit after all. Nothing more could be got out of me, and of course Esmond and Julianne said naught of the wicked trick they had played me.

They could not keep the truth of the matter from Sir Nigel, however, who guessed instantly what had happened and who, drugged and in his cups, cursed me savagely for it, with no regard whatsoever for my heartache and sorrow.

"You are a fool, Margaret," he declared coldly, "a bigger fool than I ever realized to let that devious little chit get the best of you. By God! Why didn't you fight for yourself, miss? Why didn't you tell Esmond you would sue him for breach of promise if he persisted in withdrawing from your engagement? Don't you know that's why he wanted *you* to be the one to cry off? He has turned his study of law and politics to some account after all, it seems!

"Well, there's naught to be done about it now; you've made your bed, and now you must lie in it, miss, so don't look to me to replace what you've handed to your stepsister on a silver platter! You'll have your dowry—if you can find someone to wed you now, though who would want a woman stupid enough to throw away Highclyffe Hall, I can't imagine! But not a farthing more, do you hear me?

"Christ! To think there was a time when I thought there might be something of me in you after all. But, no, you're your mother through and through, as weak and spineless as she ever was," Sir Nigel sneered, disgusted. "By God, how I rue the day I married that woman! *She* had no backbone either, the dreary little idiot! How I yearned for her to die so I would be rid of her, so I should no longer see her creeping around here like a timid mouse, starting and cringing every time I spoke to her. I should have known any offspring she produced would be as spiritless and imbecilic as she! I ought never to have tried to get an heir on her, for only look what I got for my pains!—*you*, Margaret, a daughter who has proved every bit as miserable as I ever thought, a daughter as misbegotten as that contemptible Gypsy bastard of my brother's!"

Stricken to the very core of my being, I staggered back from my father as though he had struck me a vicious blow. I had never before known how he felt about my mother. I had thought he loved her and blamed me for her death. Now I saw that in reality, he had hated her and longed fervently for her demise. He had been glad she had died; he was sorry I had not died along with her, for I was a constant reminder of his guilt over wishing her dead and his secret gratification and relief when she had been so. This was his sole, perverted reason for despising me.

How can I tell you how devastated I was by that knowledge? I could not bear it! I turned and ran from him, blindly, weeping, more wounded than I had been even by Esmond's confession to me, for Sir Nigel's revelation was by far the uglier, ravaging my past, as surely as Esmond had shattered my future. All those nights of my childhood when I had trembled before my father's wrath, I had comforted myself with the thought that he must have loved my mother very deeply to wish I had never been born so she might have lived. Now even this small solace had been stripped from me, brutally, with no thought of its merciless effect upon me.

I had no one and nothing, it appeared. My life lay in ruins about me, and I did not know how I should go on. The Hall I loved and of which I had thought to be mistress someday suddenly seemed so oppressive that I could no longer stand it. Heedless of the cold and the thin layer of snow that lay upon the ground, I grabbed my pelisse and ran from the house to the stables, where I did not even wait for Hugh to saddle Avalon, but threw myself upon the gelding's bare back and, gathering up the reins, galloped down the icy drive like a wild thing.

I do not know what demon drove me, what thoughts were in my mind as I struck out across the moors to the cliffs and the sea. Perhaps even then, such was my heart-break and despair that the notion of taking my own life had already occurred to me. I do not know. I know only that sometime later, I stood at the very edge of the headland, staring down into the wintry grey-green depths of the ocean and contemplating throwing myself from the sheer black rocks into the cold, dark water.

To this day, I still do not know whether I would truly have done it. I had no chance to find out. Above the cry of the gulls and the roar of the pounding surf breaking against the coast below, I heard behind me the sound of hooves thudding hard over the moors; and as I turned, my breath caught in my throat, for briefly, eerily, I thought it was the devil himself who rode toward me.

In the next moment, I realized it was Draco, mounted upon Black Magic come to life again; and I believed I must be dreaming or deluded by the thin mist drifting across the snowy heaths, for the magnificent stallion had been dead these many years past, as well I knew.

"Maggie!" my Gypsy cousin shouted, the many capes of his black greatcoat flapping so wildly in the wind as he drew near that he looked like a rook swooping toward me. "Maggie!"

The horse that was Black Magic's ghost reared and pranced as Draco yanked it abruptly to a halt, then flung himself from the saddle and strode toward me. Fury and fear such as I had never before seen upon his face were there now, and I shivered, frightened and thinking that my first impression had been right after all, that it *was* the devil himself who approached.

"You fool! What were you thinking of?" Draco cried as he reached me, grabbing my shoulders to drag me back from the cliffs, then shaking me roughly. "Did you not see how close you were to the edge? Did you not realize how easily you could have slipped on the ice and fallen into the sea? You might have been swept away and drowned!" His eyes narrowed suddenly as they took in my pale face and trembling figure. "Or is that what you intended?" he asked, his fingers tightening on my shoulders, digging into my skin cruelly through my cloak, hurting me. "Is it? By God, Maggie Chandler! Do not stand there and tell me you would kill yourself over that wretched Esmond Sheffield!"

He looked so wroth that for a moment, I was afraid he would hit me, and I swayed a little on my feet and closed my eyes so I should not have to see the terrible expression in his.

" 'Twas not just that," I murmured. " 'Twas not just that."

"My God! Something more, then? What?" he demanded angrily.

" 'Twas Sir Nigel . . . the things he said to me . . . dreadful things—Oh, Draco! He never loved my mother! All these years . . . his torment of me, his wishing I had never been born . . . it wasn't because he loved her and because my birth killed her. It was because he hated her and longed to be rid of her. All these years, I have been nothing to him but a reminder of his unspeakable wish to see her dead. I never knew, and I bore it all because I thought he loved her—'' I broke off, sobbing.

"Hush, Maggie, hush," Draco said more kindly, drawing me into his arms and smoothing my wind-tangled hair, while I wept against his broad chest. "He has never cared for anyone but himself—and perhaps Lady Chandler in his strange fashion, though I daresay he would sacrifice even her if he thought it were to his benefit. Don't you know that by now? Come. You are shaking from the cold. Let me take you to Stormswept Heights, where you can warm yourself by the fire and have some tea and regain your composure. This is not like you, Maggie. Where is your spirit, my bold, wild girl?"

"My father said I had none."

"Then he is an even bigger fool than I thought. Why do you care what he thinks? Come. It is starting to snow again."

Without protest, I allowed him to lead me toward the horses; but when I would have mounted Avalon, Draco lifted me instead into his own saddle. Then, catching my gelding's reins, he swung himself up behind me and put his arm about my waist to hold me steady. Gratefully I leaned against him, drawing strength and warmth from his body.

"Where did you get this horse?" I queried curiously, sniffing and trying to dry my tears as we started toward the desolate manor that was his home.

"I caught him—on Bodmin Moor. He's one of Black Magic's get, I'm certain. I call him Black Legacy."

Black Legacy. How fitting, I thought.

Black Magic was dead and gone, but he had left behind his son, both a beautiful mirror image of his dark, majestic self and a painful reminder of that dark, grim day of his death. Draco could not have chosen a more appropriate name. I was glad for his sake that something of Black Magic remained.

In silence, we arrived at the Heights, where Renshaw must have been watching for his master, for at the sight of us, the mad caretaker came running forward to take the horses and lead them into that portion of the stables that was still standing. Draco and I went into the manor, and as we walked through the hall and down the short flight of steps to the kitchen, I saw that here and there were places in the roof where the snow was coming in. My cousin sighed as he observed the trailing white flakes slowly melting upon the floor. Then he said he must finish his work of repairing the house before he was either washed away by the rain and sleet or buried alive by the snow.

"Why did you not think of that last summer?" I inquired, smiling at him tremulously.

"Because I wish to eat, come next year," he replied, "and I had to get the fields ready for planting in the spring, as I hope to raise whatever grains, fruits, and vegetables I can."

"Then why did you not hire men to help you till the soil and fix the house? That way, you might have accomplished both and been that much further ahead."

"Ah, Maggie"—Draco shook his head ruefully and laughed—"do not tell me even *you* believe all those indignant but envious rumors about my having a despicably acquired king's ransom stashed under my mattress!"

"Well, don't you?"

"Alas, no. Whatever disgraceful treasure I may have once possessed was spent on buying the Heights. I've little enough to my name now."

I did not know whether to believe him, for it was always difficult to determine Draco's thoughts, and he lied quite easily, often for no other reason than because he resented people poking into his affairs. That was the Gypsy in him, I supposed, though when I remembered how I had felt when the gossip had flown thick and fast about my broken engagement, I could not fault him for his wicked desire to confound the scandalmongers.

Mrs. Pickering was happy to see me—I think she often fretted over Draco's taciturn ways—and she bustled about the kitchen, chatting loudly as she prepared the tea, while I warmed myself by the fire that now blazed brightly in the hearth, my cousin having tossed more peat upon the flames to fuel them.

As she usually did, once Mrs. Pickering had set the mugs and a light repast upon the table (she had made barley cakes today), she left us to ourselves. We sipped our tea and spoke of inconsequential things until the last of the cakes had been eaten and Draco had shoved back his chair from the table to light a cheroot. Silently I watched as he drew on the thin cigar, then exhaled, the cloud of smoke wafting up to the rafters, while I twisted my hands in my lap, feeling a trifle shy and nervous now that I had regained my senses.

"Feeling better now, Maggie?" my cousin asked.

"Yes, much." I paused, then uttered softly, "I owe you my thanks, Draco. I won't forget what you did for me today."

"No?" He raised one thick black brow. "Well, we shall see." Then before I could ponder this odd remark, he changed the subject abruptly. "So, tell me," he said, "what are your plans now that the conniving Miss Prescott has done you such an unintentional kindness by relieving you of the tiresome burden of Mr. Sheffield?"

"That was not the way of it, Draco," I insisted, frowning at his sudden churlishness and wondering at its cause.

"Wasn't it?"

"No. 'Twas merely that Esmond and I decided we should not suit after all."

At that, my cousin laughed shortly, his teeth flashing white against his dark Gypsy skin.

"Don't give me that twaddle, my girl!" he jeered, his former consideration for me obviously having dissipated along with his cigar smoke. "It may suffice for the rest of the village, but I know better. Julianne has always been greedy as a vulture; and when she found out, much to her dismay, that society had nothing to offer her but a monthly allowance in exchange for her virtue—sans wedding ring, naturally, since she's got the vulgar taint of a Cit background clinging to her skirts—she shrewdly set her cap for the dreary but dependable Esmond, who, being heir to a mere baronetcy and having little taste for London society, could be persuaded to overlook the fact that her father was in trade. Before either you or Esmond realized what she was about, she neatly snatched the dull, besotted fool from your loving arms and wrapped her own about him as surely as a spider does a fly. Of course Julianne doesn't care a fig about Esmond one way or the other; but no doubt life as the wife of a Cornish baronet must have seemed eminently preferable to that of being passed around among the members of London's elite clubs!''

''How crude you are, Draco,'' I noted coolly, sorry, now, that I had come to the Heights, for even if my cousin *had* prevented me from taking my life, it did not give him the right to pry into it!

''I may be crude, my girl, but at least I'm honest, which is a damned sight more than you can say! Come now, Maggie. Admit it! Don't sit there and tell me that you don't find Esmond even the tiniest bit stupid for not being able to perceive Julianne's true character and the real reason behind her sudden penchant for him, that you don't believe he's a dolt for not realizing he has cast away a diamond for a paste bauble—and for, incredibly, thinking himself the richer for it!''

Draco's words hammered at me relentlessly and, what was even worse, dinned in my ears with a ring of truth I did not want to face, for I *had* thought such things about Esmond, no matter how much I longed to deny it. But I did not tell Draco that, for though I believed Esmond a poor dupe, I was not blind to the fact that Julianne's bedazzling beauty and calculated charm were enough to have cozened any man, especially one of Esmond's honest nature. It was she, I felt, who was to blame for what had happened. She was a common fortune hunter, like her mother, and she had used her wiles to that end. I only hoped Esmond would recognize that and come to his senses before it was too late, for I loved him still.

"I'm sure I don't know what you're talking about, Draco," I lied, forcing myself to speak calmly so my cousin should not guess how well he had discerned my thoughts. "There is nothing more to the matter than what I have told you: Esmond and I were not suited."

Draco laughed harshly again.

"No, by God, you weren't!" he declared, suddenly slamming his hand down hard upon the table, making me flinch. "And that is the only true thing you have said to me! Esmond was never man enough for you, Maggie. He would have bored you to tears within a fortnight, and you would have made his life a living hell. Regardless of what you may think to the contrary, you are well rid of him!"

His words hurt me, for the wound of Esmond's betrayal was still too fresh and grievous for my anger to conquer my anguish when I thought of what he and Julianne had done. I did not consider myself better off without my beloved cousin, for I had lost not only him, but my home as well. How could I live at the manor with him and Julianne? I could not; I should have to go away—but to where, I did not know.

"It seems you are determined to quarrel with me, Draco," I said stiffly, "and over something you must know is painful to me. 'Twas not just Esmond's wife I had hoped to be, but mistress of Highclyffe Hall, too, someday. Now I have nothing to look forward to but life as a governess perhaps, for I cannot remain at the manor."

"A governess! Why, Maggie, what a bleak future you have mapped out for yourself! Esmond Sheffield is not the only fish in the sea, nor is Highclyffe Hall the only estate in England. Surely you do not intend never to marry, then?" Draco's dark visage was now oddly still, and his eyes were shuttered so I could not read his thoughts.

"Yes, I mean just that," I rejoined, "for whom would I wed?"

For a moment, my cousin did not answer, and a peculiar tenseness in his face was revealed to me by the twitch of a muscle in his jaw. He started to say something—I do not know what—then decided against it and fell silent. At last he smiled at me mockingly.

"You are yet a young woman." He paraphrased the words I had once spoken to him and flung them back at me now. "No doubt you will change your mind in time."

I had no chance to respond, for just then, Mrs. Pickering returned to the kitchen to announce a visitor.

"Mr. Prescott, sir," she said to Draco.

Before she had even finished speaking, Welles, who had followed hard on her heels, appeared, his hat and greatcoat both sprinkled with snow.

"Welles!" I cried, jumping up to greet him. "Welles!"

Though my stepbrother seemed startled at first to see me, he soon got over his astonishment, and sweeping off his hat and smiling, he kissed my brow and hugged me close as I cast myself into his arms.

"Maggie, dear girl! What a pleasant surprise—and a vast relief as well, I might add. Frankly I've been quite worried about you," he confessed, ruffling my hair fondly. "Hugh said you'd galloped away from the Hall in something of a dither—to put it mildly—and bade me ride after you. We thought . . . well . . . I don't know what we thought. Still we ought to have known you wouldn't do anything foolish, for here you are, safe and sound after all, thank heavens."

"Yes, of course I'm all right. Why shouldn't I be?" I replied steadily, not daring to look at Draco, who alone knew what I had thought to do when I had stood upon the cliffs at the edge of the sea.

"No reason, Maggie. We were just concerned about you, that's all," my stepbrother answered lightly. Then he turned to shake hands with my cousin. "Hullo, Draco. Good to see you again. It's been a long time."

"When did you get back?" I asked Welles as, after the amenities had been got out of the way, we sat down at the table, while Mrs. Pickering hurried to fetch more tea and barley cakes.

Having completed his studies at Harrow, my stepbrother had been away at sea for the past year, with only sporadic visits to Cornwall in between. He had secured a job as a deckhand upon a merchant ship and had proved so skilled at seamanship and such a quick learner that when the second mate had fallen ill and had had to be left at a foreign port, Welles had been promoted to fill the vacant position.

"Only this morning," he responded to my question, giving Cerberus, Draco's mongrel shadow, a friendly pat as the dog, wagging its tail, approached my stepbrother and laid its head in his lap. "We docked at Plymouth three days ago, but we didn't finish all the business connected with the unloading and so forth until yesterday, what with the inspection, duties, reports, and what not—damned, infernal nuisance, that! Ought to be done away with, you know. After all, I doubt that any smugglers are so foolish as to be running their goods into an official port, else they would hardly be smugglers in the first place, would they? And why should a man be taxed for a decent glass of brandy anyway, I ask you? Parliament ought to abolish the excise, that's what! Save everyone a great deal of trouble, if you ask me. But of course no one does.

"At any rate, I went straight to the Grange first, naturally, to see Sarah, and she told me about you and Esmond, Maggie. I'm so sorry, dear girl. 'Twas an underhanded affair, that—as I shall certainly tell Julie when I see her! In fact, I was on my way to the Hall to do so; but then Hugh sent me to look for you, so I didn't have a chance to give her a piece of my mind. I searched for you for some time but couldn't find you; and as I was near the Heights, and cold, I decided to stop and avail myself of Draco's hospitality. 'Tis a good thing I did, too, else I might not have found you."

Such was the affection and anxiety for me I saw in Welles's eyes that I was heartened, despite myself, knowing there was someone who cared for me after all. I had the love of Aunt Tibby, Sarah, and Welles at least, I realized; I was not totally alone in the world.

Why, I could move into the Grange, I thought and

wondered why the idea had not occurred to me previously. No doubt I had been too distraught to think of it.

"Well, Draco, old boy, this is some place you have here," my stepbrother observed, abruptly changing the subject. His face, as he glanced about the kitchen, was thoughtful; his eyes were narrowed and veiled in a manner most unlike him. "'Tis quite a ruin, isn't it? And so isolated and out of the way that I shouldn't wonder if it was inhabited by ghosts."

"Yes, how odd that you should mention that, for only the other evening, Renshaw claimed actually to have seen one," Draco remarked, eyeing Welles intently, so it seemed suddenly and extraordinarily to me as though the two men were saying one thing to each other but meaning quite another.

Then my cousin laughed and shrugged, and I thought my brief, peculiar perception of their discourse must have been the product of my imagination after all. Moments later, however, I felt the strange sensation again, and this time, I was not so certain it was merely a whim on my part.

"Of course, since Renshaw is mad, I doubt that anyone believed his tale," Draco went on. "Still the Heights has a bizarre and violent history, so perhaps 'tis possible it is haunted. They claim murder has been done here in the past," he said, his voice low now, almost a whisper, and eerie somehow, so that without warning, a tiny, cold tingle of fear crawled up my spine, "and one young mistress of the house committed suicide, you know. She couldn't be buried in consecrated ground, of course; and so she does not rest easy in her grave, they say, but, when the night is dark and the mist hangs low over the moors, walks along the cliffs at the edge of the sea, crying for her lover. That's one of the reasons why the house stood empty for so long before I bought it."

"Yes, well, *I* certainly shouldn't care to come here at night at any rate!" Welles asserted, shuddering. "'Tis no wonder the village believes you a cold, wicked creature, Draco. Really! The least you could do is hang some mistletoe to brighten up the place a bit—or don't you celebrate Christmas at the Heights?''

At that, my cousin relaxed, flushing a little with embarrassment. Then he smiled wryly, and the queer, bewitching spell cast by his tale was broken.

"It hardly seemed worth the trouble," he explained sheepishly. "With the manor in such a state, 'twould only have been ludicrous to decorate it, I thought, and besides, there would have been none but myself to see it."

"And what are Maggie and I? Pilasters?" Welles queried indignantly.

"No, of course not. But, then, I so seldom have guests, you see—"

"Nor, from what I hear, do you encourage them," my stepbrother drawled dryly, grinning. "Not very friendly, are you, old boy, eh? 'Tis said you set that mutt of yours on anyone who thinks to pay you a visit—"

"Yes, and why shouldn't I?" Draco defended himself hotly. "'Tis no less than those nosy old busybodies from the village deserve—poking and prying into my affairs!"

"Yes, I should certainly discourage that if I were you," Welles asserted, no longer smiling and a curious note, surely, in his voice, I fancied. However, before I could ponder the matter further, he turned to me and said, "Well, we had best be on our way, Maggie. Hugh was really most anxious about you, and I'm afraid if we delay here much longer, he will send out a search party after you, which would cause a great deal of trouble since there is no need, especially in this weather."

I agreed this would be unjust, and presently we took our leave of Draco to return to the Hall.

It was not until later that night, when I lay in bed, unable to sleep because my mind was beset by turmoil, that I remembered Welles and Draco's singular conversation and wondered about it. After further reflection, I determined there had been, despite his quite reasonable explanation for his presence there, something peculiar about the whole matter of my stepbrother's coming to the Heights. Although he and my Gypsy cousin had always been friendly, they had never been particularly close; yet now, going over the afternoon again, I was puzzled and, for some reason, faintly disturbed by it. Now that I dwelled upon it, I felt more strongly than ever that a strange undercurrent of tension and emotion had lain between the two men during their discussion, as though they had actually been talking on two levels in order to conceal something from me. But I could not imagine what that might be, though I racked my brain ceaselessly. At last I decided I was so upset by Esmond and Julianne's betrayal of me that I must, as a result, be growing suspicious of everyone, envisioning secrets where none existed. What could Welles and Draco possibly have to hide from me? Nothing, surely. It was as my stepbrother had said: He had been cold and had thought merely to warm himself by the fire at my cousin's manor.

Still, despite my reaching this conclusion, a nagging doubt continued to plague me about the entire incident. I might have dismissed it, except for one thing: Cerberus, Draco's monstrous cur, had neither barked nor growled at Welles's entrance, but had greeted him like an old friend, and my stepbrother had petted the vicious beast fearlessly, as though quite accustomed to doing so. Because of this, knowing how long it had taken the dog to stop raising its hackles at the sight of me, I knew that Welles must have visited the Heights on several previous occasions and that he had done so without anyone else's knowledge, for Sarah would have told me about it otherwise. Now, despite there appearing to be nothing particularly sinister about it, I could not help but wonder how my stepbrother had come to be on such intimate terms with my Gypsy cousin—and why the two men had taken such pains to prevent the extent of their relationship from becoming known to me and everyone else.

Chapter Sixteen

Madness, Wild and Savage

O Love, O fire! once he drew
With one long kiss my whole soul thro'
My lips, as sunlight drinketh dew.

—*Fatima*
Alfred, Lord Tennyson

Spring came early to Cornwall that year, like an eager young housemaid, dusting the light powdering of snow from the branches of the trees and sweeping the dead leaves from the ground. Here and there, patches of black peat and ripening green grass showed upon the surface of the land, muddy and sodden from the melting frost and the rain that drizzled from the pale, leaden sky turning slowly to a wan, washed blue with each passing day. Early flowers bloomed upon the moors, their fragile petals fluttering as though they shivered with each gust of the cool spring air; for though the wind that had blown so coldly and cruelly all winter had lessened to a balmy breeze, it was still chilly, tinged with the tangy scent of the sea and the sad, sweet cry of the gulls that nested in the rocks along the coast.

Their mournful calls seemed to echo in my heart, for Esmond had not come to his senses, as I had hoped, and I knew, now, that he was truly lost to me as surely as though he had never been mine once at all. He was to marry

Julianne a few weeks hence, just as soon as the banns had been posted. She had been too cunning to agree to a long engagement from which he might at any time withdraw; she was too clever to let him escape, as I had done. I had been a fool; my stepsister was not disposed to follow in my footsteps.

How that knowledge wounded me! There was a great, empty space in my breast where my heart had used to be. It throbbed dully, constantly, so I thought I should never be free of the pain. Still somehow I got through the days; I was too proud to do otherwise. But at night . . . ah, at night, I wept quietly so none should hear me, and I felt my loneliness as though it were a tangible thing, suffocating me. My hand felt naked without my betrothal ring, which I had returned to Esmond, and its absence seemed to me a visible mark of my rejection, condemning me in the eyes of the world as unwanted, unloved, lacking in some significant manner. I felt as conspicuous and ashamed as though I bore the brand of a criminal upon my forehead.

Yet I think I gave no outward sign of my unhappiness. Indeed, several times, when they thought I was not listening, I heard the staff comment that I was bearing up quite well beneath the heavy burden that had been laid upon me. Yet how could I do otherwise, for what would wailing, tearing my hair, and gnashing my teeth have availed me? Certainly naught of which I was aware, other than to have made me an object of both embarrassment and further pity. No, what was done, was done. If I could not undo it, I must make the best of it, no matter how hard it might be to force my common sense to prevail over my emotions. Still I persevered and endeavored to behave as I normally did.

Only Lady Chandler was not deceived by my composed demeanor.

"You despise Julianne and no doubt wish she were dead," she commented matter-of-factly one morning after having asked my opinion of some fabric for my stepsister's trousseau and received a noncommittal answer from me. "No, do not try to deny it, Margaret, for if I were in your place, I should feel the same."

I made no reply; indeed my stepmother did not seem to expect one, but smiled that odd half-smile of hers and, rising from her chair, moved to close the doors of the morning room, where we were seated, so I knew she did not wish to be interrupted during the conversation she appeared determined to have with me. We were alone; I might have left her, rudely, with no one the wiser about my conduct toward her. But some strange curiosity to hear what she had to say stilled my flight, so I remained upon the sofa, my hands folded in my lap, and waited for her to speak again. Presently she sat down beside me, her crystal-blue eyes gazing at me steadily as she collected her thoughts.

"You think me hard and cold, Margaret," she said at last, "and perhaps you are right, for if I were not so, I think Welles, Julianne, and I should have starved after Captain Brodie's death. Oh, yes"—her laughter rang out wryly at the expression upon my face—"I know my many little extravagances were a good deal to blame for the unfortunate turn of our affairs. But you cannot know what it is like to be forced to pinch one's pennies, to have nothing with which to brighten the dreariness of one's days. Captain Brodie was a gregarious man, much like Welles in that respect; but he was also a merchant—and a successful one. He did not believe in spending money for the sheer joy of indulging caprices, but for garnering a profit instead. Further, he had no desire, as I did, to get on in the world, but was content with his life much as it was. So, much as I loved him—and I *did* love him, you know—still I was like a bird released from a cage when he died.

"As you may have guessed, I went a little wild without my first husband's restraint," Lady Chandler confessed, "and before I knew it, we were deep in debt. If your father had not come along when he did, I shudder to think what would have happened to us!" She paused for a moment, reflecting on the grim future she had narrowly escaped. Then she continued.

"Frankly I was surprised when Nigel took such an interest in me, the widow of a merchant," she disclosed, "but I did not then know how little he cared for society's opinion of him; and of course there was nothing the least bit disrespectable about my background otherwise, my father having been a squire and my mother a knight's daughter. Ah, you did not know that, did you? Well, 'tis true; so you see, though my family may have been countrified, we were not quite as common as you thought, Margaret. But unhappily, though we did not lack for bloodlines, we were like so many others whose fortunes have been depleted by generations of mismanagement, gambling, and drink; and as you have seen, men with both rank and riches do not usually choose as wives women who have neither.

"Were circumstances otherwise, I should not have married Captain Brodie, a chance business acquaintance of my father. However, as my family lived quietly in Kent and any hope of a Season in London was beyond me, there being no funds for such, I accepted my first husband's proposal and thought myself lucky to be wedding a kind man who would be able to provide comfortably for me. I did not then know that Captain Brodie, while shrewd, was not very ambitious; and he . . . well, he could not understand why I was not content with my lot in life. I'm afraid he thought me possessed of a greedy, grasping nature. He did not realize how hard it was for me to move to London, where he lived, to see the *haut ton* as they passed, and to know, but for the twists of fate, I might have been one of them.

"You see, Margaret, as Thomas Gray said, ignorance *is* bliss. Had I never known what I was missing, I should not have missed it; and that brings me to the point of my story, to which you no doubt grow impatient for me to arrive.

"You have little sympathy for me, Margaret," my stepmother observed. "To you, I am no more than an interloper who disrupted your quiet life here at Highclyffe Hall; and so I did. Yet I think you benefitted also by my marriage to your father, as did my own children. But just as you feel I did you an injustice by forcing my presence upon you, so I did Julianne a like iniquity in some ways by bringing her here to Highclyffe Hall.

"Wellesley will always land on his feet, no matter his status or situation in life, for that is the kind of reckless, devil-may-care rogue he is. But my daughter is another matter entirely. She remembers all too well the poverty into which we were cast upon Captain Brodie's death, and she has grown all too accustomed to the life Nigel has provided for her here at the Hall, a life that had I not wed your father, she would know little of and thus would not have missed.

"To ask Julianne to give it all up, then—and for something that was no fault of her own—was a cruelty you cannot imagine, Margaret!" Lady Chandler insisted. Then, at the stony expression upon my face, she sighed and went on. "I had hoped, for her sake, that during her Season in London, she would find an appropriate suitor. But, alas, it was not to be, for as you know, my daughter could not overcome the stigma of her father's having been in trade, though had she been possessed of a considerable dowry, I daresay some eligible bachelor might have been persuaded to turn a blind eye to her background," my stepmother declared dryly. "But that is neither here nor there. Despite her being the toast of London, her Season did not answer; no man of title and means offered her his name and his heart. What, then, was left to her but to set her cap for Esmond, who grew up with her and so cared naught for the fact that her father was a merchant?"

"But Esmond was mine!" I burst out, no longer able to remain silent now.

"Yes, so he was," Lady Chandler agreed calmly. "But despite what you may think, Margaret, he was never the man for you. You were always a strange, wild, fierce child, Margaret, like the moors themselves, I used to think; and you have become, I suspect, for all your quietness, a woman of deep and lasting passions. But Esmond has none of that fervent emotion that beats eternal in your breast. For all his study of law and politics, he will never stand for Parliament, but will be content here in the country, correctly playing his role as a dutiful, loving husband to Julianne and escaping to the library with his dull, dusty books whenever reality intrudes too closely upon him. Sooner or later, you would have found him lacking in some manner you would not have been able to understand, Margaret, while Julianne will be satisfied as the grand lady of the manor, too self-centered really to notice Esmond at all—much less to analyze his character—as long as he idolizes her and indulges her whims. If the two of them are adaptable, they will be happy enough together after a fashion.''

"As you and my father are happy?" I sneered, but my stepmother was not offended by my sarcasm.

"Yes and no, for Nigel and I are much alike, and we understand each other besides, Margaret, both of which are things no relationship between two strong, independent individuals can do without, as I believe you will learn in time.''

"How can you say that?" I asked bitterly. "Surely there is now little hope that I shall catch a husband!"

"On the contrary, Margaret," Lady Chandler declared firmly. "I think there is every reason to believe that you will eventually marry, that you will wed . . . a man who is quite suited to your passionate nature; and though I cannot feel your life will be an easy one, I suspect that in the end, you shall find it a great deal richer nonetheless. I promise you, now, that if and when a time ever comes that you should need my help, you shall have it, for though you may dislike me, I, on the other hand, have grown rather fond of you actually.

"Though as a child, you were a sore trial to me, I have always admired your spirit, Margaret. You are very like me, and Nigel, too, in that respect; I wonder that he cannot see it. But, then, one is so often blind to one's traits when they exist in others, especially when one is as stubborn as your father! Still that gritty determination will stand you in good stead in the future, I think."

Then before I could ponder her enigmatic words, my stepmother rose, indicating she had said all she was going to say. She picked up the bolt of fabric we had been discussing earlier and eyed it critically.

"Now, tell me truly, what do you think of this blue, Margaret?" she inquired as smoothly as though she had never revealed to me her innermost thoughts. " 'Tis a shade too dark, isn't it, for Julianne? Perhaps the lavender for her, after all, since she cannot abide pink, and the red velvet for you, of course. . . ."

The banns had been posted; Esmond and Julianne's marriage had taken place. Welles and Sarah stood up with them, for which I was profoundly grateful, for I do not think I could have borne it had Julianne been so unfeeling as to ask me instead of Sarah to serve as her bridesmaid.

Somehow I had managed to smile as inscrutably as Lady Chandler at the wedding that ought to have been mine, though I was glad—so very glad—that the guests who had come from far and wide for the ceremony at the village church could not see into my heart. Somehow I had talked and laughed brightly with those seated on either side of me at the lavish supper laid out at the Hall following the rite that had shattered my dreams forever. Somehow I had boldly flirted and danced with one partner after another in our grand ballroom, where the musicians in the minstrel gallery had played until the last of the revelers had retired; and I had taken a fierce delight in seeing the brief, wounded look in Esmond's eyes when I had allowed one handsome young man to lead me out onto the terrace in the darkness, though the impassioned words he had whispered in my ear had meant nothing to me.

Only now, alone in my chamber, could I cast aside the hard, brittle mask of gaiety I had worn all day and let my tears flow freely.

I had sent Linnet away, for I had not been able to bear the sly, avid look in her eyes when she had come to help me undress. She had been like a vulture, I had thought, watching me closely for any sign of weakness so she might gossip about me to the staff later and thus momentarily raise herself to a position of importance in the household. The cunning expression on her sharp, thin but vaguely pretty face had reminded me so much of Julianne that for an instant, I had been sorely tempted to dismiss her permanently from her post and, in the morning, request that I be given another abigail. But then I had realized Linnet was hardly to blame for my misfortune; it was not her fault if she seemed to me to resemble my stepsister in some indefinable way.

Now at last I rose from my bed, where I had cried long and hard; and after rinsing my tearstained face with some water from the pitcher atop my washstand, I sat down before my dresser and began slowly to take the pins from my long black hair.

I looked like a witch, I thought dully, for my reflection in the mirror showed me all too clearly the dark mauve rings around my sloe eyes, red-rimmed and swollen from weeping; the hollowness of my cheeks, for I had lost weight since Esmond's betrayal of me; and all the other ravages my misery over the past few months had wrought. My red velvet gown with its gold trim, which I had worn to supper and for the dancing afterward, seemed now so vivid as to have drained all the color from my face. My head ached horribly; I had drunk far too much champagne this evening, and my brain felt tired and muddled as a result.

Raggedly I ran my hands through my hair, smoothing it back from my face. Then I laid down my silver-backed brush and glanced at my door, fancying I could hear from across the hall Julianne's low moans of pleasure as she lay in Esmond's arms, for they were not to leave on their honeymoon until tomorrow. He was taking her to Italy, to ride in the gondolas on the canals of Venice, to walk hand in hand through the crowded streets of Florence, as I had once dreamed of doing with him. Worst of all, he would make love to my stepsister beneath an Italian moon and sky, as I had once dreamed of him making love to me. I buried my head in my hands at the images that rose before me, my shoulders shaking from the wrenching sobs I tried to smother. But still, unbidden, the unwelcome scenes of Esmond and Julianne together, now and forever, taunted me, tormented me, and I could not put them from my mind.

Were those two who had so deceived me lying, even now, naked and pressed close to each other in the darkness of their room? Was he even now kissing her, caressing her, filling her with desire for him, as once I had so wanted him? Ah, God. I could not bear it. *I could not!*

All at once, the walls of my chamber seemed to be closing in on me, crushing me, suffocating me. My face and hands were damp with sweat, as though I had suddenly been stricken with a fever. My red velvet dress clung to my body, the soft material feeling heavy and sodden, as though it were soaked with rain. I could not breathe; I gasped too quickly for air. My head reeled so, that my room appeared to spin about me, and I clutched the edge of my dresser for support.

Without warning, I longed desperately for the wide, open moors that were so much a part of me, that were in my very blood and bones. I yearned fervently for the feel of the cool night air, tinged with the salty tang of the sea, against my hair and skin.

I think I scarcely knew what I was doing as abruptly I leaped to my feet and rushed from my chamber to stumble blindly down the back stairs, out into the blackness of the night. I knew only that I must escape from the house, where Esmond and Julianne lay together, callously indifferent to my suffering. I was like a wild thing, driven by some dark demon as I raced down the drive, paying no heed to the gravel that bit into my bare feet; for earlier I had taken off my slippers and my stockings, too, and now, in my haste to get away, I had left them behind. I did not care. I cared for nothing but the strange, mad thing that had seized me in its fist and now compelled me recklessly forward.

Once, I tripped and fell, for there was no moon and I had only the faint gleam of the brightest silver stars to light my way, the others being occluded by the thin, drifting grey clouds of fog that rolled in from the sea. But I got up and kept on running anyway, panting for breath, sucking the cool spring air into my lungs in great gulps, as though I could not get enough of it. The ancient trees of the wood towered over me, amorphous black shapes and shadows in the darkness. Pale, diaphanous wisps of mist floated like ghosts among their gnarled branches; their leaves rustled with each soughing gust of the breeze, seeming to speak to me as I passed, mocking me, laughing at me. The sound echoed in my chaotic mind like a fragment from Tourneur's *The Revenger's Tragedy:* . . . *hurry—hurry—hurry/Ay, to the devil* . . . , urging me on, so I ran faster and faster, my skirts held high before me and my swift feet sending gravel flying.

The gates of the Hall stood open wide, as they always did when we had guests; and without pausing, I passed through the portals, crossed the road beyond, and struck out over the moors toward the cliffs and the sea.

I do not know why I headed in that direction, for certainly I had no thought of taking my own life, as I had contemplated doing once before. Yet something seemed to draw me toward the rugged headland all the same, some peculiar, irresistible force I could neither name nor deny.

The wind felt cold now against my skin; the grass was chilly beneath my feet. Behind me, my skirts trailed across the heather and bracken damp with the mist, so my hem was soon wet and dragging, snagging here and there on the thick clusters of gorse. I snatched it free and went on, breathless yet somehow feeling as though I could run forever; for in some dim corner of my mind, I thought irrationally that if I ran fast enough, the world would come to a standstill and Esmond and Julianne would become inanimate things, frozen in time and thus unable to hurt me anymore. But it was not so. Deep in my heart, I knew it was not so. Their images were with me still. I could not escape from them.

My head throbbed, my heart ached. Tears borne of the night air and my own unhappiness stung my eyes so I could not see my way across the treacherous expanse of dark moor I now traversed. My breath caught in my throat with fear as, without warning, a hazy shape cast in shadow suddenly detached itself from the shimmering mist like a specter to loom before me; and before I could halt my wild flight, I stumbled into it, not knowing whether to be frightened or relieved as my body made contact with solid flesh, bone, and muscle, and I realized the figure had form and substance and so was real.

Startled, I gasped and tried to draw back, a scream

rising in my throat as bulging arms grabbed me and I fell against a broad chest, unable to discern the face of my assailant.

"Maggie," a voice breathed in my ear. "Maggie, my girl."

"Draco! Oh, Draco!" I cried, whimpering a little with nervous laughter and overwhelming relief as I realized it was my Gypsy cousin who held me and not some phantom or scoundrel.

I did not know how he had come to be there. I did not care. He was warm and alive, while I felt cold and dead inside; and he, more than anyone, knew what it meant to be suffering and alone, with no one to turn to. I remembered how he had stood apart from the others at his father's funeral, as now I felt myself isolated from those at the Hall; and I knew he would understand the loneliness and grief that so bitterly engulfed me this night. If anyone could, Draco could take away the pain I felt. So, as I had once comforted him when his father had lain lifeless in our parlor, now I instinctively sought solace from him, clinging to him fervently, reveling in the feel of his hard, male body pressed close against my own soft, female one.

He did not question me, for which I was deeply grateful, but stroked my hair and crooned to me in Romany, so I was reminded of the night we had freed Black Magic, and I knew why the horse had been drawn to Draco alone, who sensed so much and offered what was most needed. Now I trembled in his arms and buried my face against his chest, thinking how strong and muscular it was, how wide and solid his shoulders were beneath my palms, powerful enough not to bow beneath the heavy burden of my anguish; and gradually, as I was consoled by his lilting voice, his soothing hands, I began to grow aware of him not just as my cousin, but as a man.

I could feel his warm breath, smelling faintly of wine and tobacco, against my skin, feel his chest move as he breathed. I could hear the steady, lulling beat of his heart beneath the ruffles of his crisp white shirt, and the sound reassured me as it does a child in its mother's womb, making me feel safe and secure. But I was no child. I was a woman fully grown—and aching with need—and Draco was a man, a man whose emotions and desires ran as strong and deep as mine. Something flickered in my mind at the thought; but before it could take flame, his corded thighs brushed mine, and without warning, a strange, feverish sensation quickened inside me and spread through my body so even my fingertips tingled, making me gasp and quiver and cry out softly.

I do not know what Draco thought, but abruptly he thrust me from him, and his fingers tangled themselves hurtfully in my windswept hair, forcing my face up to his, though I tried to turn away so he would not see the tears that lingered on my cheeks. His intense black eyes searched mine; and as the mist shifted, the pale starlight danced across his face, illuminating it as the lightning and lamplight had once done so many years ago that night he had first come to the manor. As I had then, I thought now how ugly and brutish his dark visage was, almost satanic in appearance, so different from Esmond's handsome, refined features.

Ah, Esmond! my heart keened silently. *Cruel, faithless Esmond, my beloved, lying now with Julianne instead of me.*

At the thought, emptiness washed over me like a tide, so I felt as though I were drowning in a sea of agony; and suddenly I did not care that Draco was coarse and common. I wanted to feel his mouth upon mine, his arms wrapped about me tightly. I wanted to lie with him, to snatch back some small measure of the happiness Julianne had stolen from me, and to hurt Esmond as deeply as he had hurt me. I wanted to know what they had denied me, those two who had betrayed me—the love, the sharing, the belonging. I wanted, too, in some darker, twisted way I did not care to understand, to strike back at my father, who had rejected me also. What better way than with Draco, whom Esmond and Sir Nigel despised?

I had no thought of tomorrow, only of here and now as my hands, fingers tensed and spread wide, slid up to my Gypsy cousin's face and wantonly, impetuously, I drew him to me, heedless of the consequences of my brazen actions. I had just brushed his lips with mine when he dragged his mouth away and caught my wrists so roughly that I felt certain I would have bruises upon them in the morning. His breath came raggedly, and his eyes were dark and opaque as he gazed at me with sudden, naked hunger, so I knew my own desire for him was plain upon my face.

"I'll not be teased, Maggie—not by you," he warned me, his voice low and harsh. "So be sure—be very sure—that this is what you want."

"It is. Oh, yes, it is! Hold me, Draco! Love me! Please," I begged. "Please. I need you so. . . ."

I do not know what I expected, but it was not the wild savagery I unwittingly unleashed with those words, for he kissed me then, and it was as though, without warning, some hitherto unsuspected thing that had lain sleeping within him, and within me, too, came fully awake to spring upon us both and devour us.

Draco groaned low in his throat as his lips swooped down to capture mine again and again, as though he could not get enough of me. His mouth was hard and demanding against mine, his tongue soft and insistent. His teeth grazed the tender flesh of my lower lip so I tasted blood upon it, and a thrill of pleasure and pain I had never before felt shot through me, arousing and exciting me, filling me with violent longing.

"Ah, Maggie," he muttered against my mouth. "Maggie, my girl, it was always you and me—both of us miserable, misbegotten misfits. What a fool you have been. You were never meant for Esmond, but for me. *Me*, Maggie! Oh, God! How I have loved you, wanted you, and thought never to make you mine, thought to lose you to Esmond when it is *we* who belong together! I have waited so long for you to see it—*too* long, damn you!"

I scarcely heard his words, only dimly comprehended them, for I was too caught up in the madness of the moment, the feelings he was evoking inside me, to force my dazed, wounded mind to deal with his declaration and what it portended. I realized only, wonderingly, that he loved me, passionately, as Esmond had not, and that I wanted desperately to be loved—tonight of all nights.

How strange that it should be Draco who cares for me, I mused, Draco, of whose existence I knew nothing until that night I pressed my ear, like any common eavesdropper, against my stepmother's door. Draco, my bastard Gypsy cousin whom Esmond so holds in contempt, and me, the household prier, the woman Esmond scorned and cast off. There is irony in that somewhere, surely. . . .

But then, as swiftly as it had entered my mind, the thought was driven from it by the man who held me in his arms as though he had every right to do so. And perhaps he did; perhaps it was as he had said: that we were two of a kind, that we belonged together. I did not know or care. I knew only that I wanted him and that I was painfully ignorant of the ways between a man and a woman. I had never before known what it was to be kissed, for certainly Esmond had never kissed me as Draco did now, fiercely, possessively, seeming to drain the very life and soul from my body and then to pour it back in.

Boldly his tongue ravaged my mouth, a new, half-frightening, half-exhilarating experience that dizzied me and set my knees trembling, so I thought I should have fallen had he not held me so tightly. I felt weak as a child and so pliant that it was as though all my bones had dissolved inside me as, of its own eager volition, my body molded itself to his. Draco was massively built, his body like iron against me, so I shivered at the strength that was his and felt myself small and helpless before his onslaught upon my senses; and in some dark corner of my mind, I wondered if, when the time came, he would hurt me very much, for I did not deceive myself that there would be only this and nothing more.

I shuddered faintly with apprehension at the thought, and he, sensing my sudden maidenly fear, tightened his hold upon me, as though to prevent me from changing my mind and drawing back. But I made no protest against him, although now, sometimes I think how different my life would have been had I left him then. But I did not. Instead, to my everlasting shame, I allowed him to spread his black greatcoat beneath us and to press me down upon the purple folds of its silk lining, where I gave myself up to him, my nemesis.

Time passed. I hardly knew how much as I lay in his arms and let him do as he wished with me. I knew nothing but the sensations that enveloped me as he touched and tasted me, expertly, so I knew instinctively that there had been other women—many others—before me, and a vicious stab of jealousy pierced my being because I was not the first to know his kisses and caresses. In sharp contrast to his skill were my own ignorance and uncertainty, the gnawing feeling that I should not please him. But when I would have spoken of these things, he bade me be silent and growled, "Do you think I would have you any other way, love?" So I knew he was glad no other man had left his mark upon me, and I forgot my fears and let him be my guide as he initiated me in the rite of lovemaking.

The sweet green grass felt cold and damp beneath the softness of his cloak; the wind brushed my naked skin with chilly fingers. But I no longer felt the coolness of the spring night. There was naught for me but the heat of Draco's body, warming me, filling me with desire for him. I relished the feel of him, his skin smooth as ivory in places, hard as horn in others where old scars I had not known he bore puckered his flesh. I wondered how he had got them, but he would not tell me, saying merely, "Some fight or other," before he stilled my questions with his lips.

I felt his hot breath upon my mouth and skin, wakening within me exquisite emotions I had not known existed, had never dreamed of in my wildest imaginings. He whispered in my ear, and the things he said made my blood sing, my heart soar, for I had never thought them or been told them before.

"You are so beautiful, Maggie," he murmured. "Even when you were a child, I could see the promise of the woman you would become, and I knew then that there would be no other for me, that I would wait for you to grow up. That day at Stormswept Heights, when I first saw you again, I wanted you so badly that it was all I could do not to seize you then and there and claim you as mine. Damn you—you, with your witch's hair and eyes, haunting me, tormenting me. Damn you.... Ah, Maggie, love ... yes, yes...."

He intoxicated me. The dark hair that matted his chest was like silk beneath my palms and against the sensitive tips of my breasts. He tasted of salt borne of earthy sweat and the wind and sea. It was as though he were the very elements themselves, ruthless, relentless, crumbling my maidenly defenses as surely and savagely as the breakers crash against the wild Cornish shore to change and shape it as they will. I was breathless in his wake, discovering him, touching him everywhere I could reach, yielding to him as the flowers upon the moors open to the sun and the rain. The fragrance of the budding heather and bracken that filled the sweeping heath, the tanginess of the sea beyond, permeated my nostrils, mingling headily with the masculine scent of him and the spicy aroma of sandalwood that clung to his skin, spurring me on.

I was like fire and ice, burning and melting beneath him, a mass of quivering sensation raised to a feverish pitch. My swollen breasts ached with delight and yearning wrought by his lips and tongue and hands; my body throbbed at its secret heart with an unbearable hollowness, so I longed instinctively to be filled by him. I writhed against him, driven by blind, primitive need; and at last he took me.

I gasped, then cried out at the shock of it, for despite all the stories I had heard, I had not truly known what to expect, had never understood until now this absolute invasion and surrender, this stretching and molding of oneself to accept the other. It was as though my body no longer belonged to me at all, but had become a part of Draco. His hands were beneath my hips, lifting them to meet his own; and in that moment, the world spun away into nothingness as I moaned and strained desperately for some nameless thing I did not understand, but felt I must find or die. Then suddenly a feeling of such painful intensity that I could not bear it quickened at the very core of my being, bursting inside me in waves of pulsing heat and pleasure that coursed through my body so violently that they took my breath away.

From someplace far beyond the moors, it seemed, I felt Draco's fingers tighten on me painfully, heightening the intensity of what we shared between us. His nails dug into my skin as he groaned, then inhaled sharply. Then a frenzied shudder racked the length of his body before finally he lay still, his heart pounding furiously against mine.

After a moment, he kissed me and pulled me into the cradle of his arms to share his warmth with me; and so it was some time before the chill of the night air seeped into my bones and I shivered, realizing that I was cold and wet, that it was raining gently and had been for quite a while. At the recognition, sober reality returned to me with cruel, crystal clarity, and abruptly the full import of what I had done swept over me, shaming and sickening me. I had lain with my Gypsy cousin, had given myself willingly to him—a coarse, common bastard. I recoiled in fright and revulsion from the thought as the consequences of my action struck me pitilessly. What had I done? No decent man would have me now; Esmond . . . Esmond would be appalled if he knew. I became aware of my nakedness, how I lay sprawled upon the ground, Draco's limbs entangled with mine, my clothes torn and crushed and soiled, strewn hastily to one side. Now that I could think clearly, what had, only moments before, felt so wildly passionate and glorious seemed vilely vulgar and degrading now. I was no better than the cheapest whore, I thought, stricken. Esmond had been right to reject me; I was not worthy of him.

"Oh, God," I moaned, not realizing I had spoken the words aloud. "What have I done? What have I done? Esmond. Esmond . . ."

I tried to wrench myself free of Draco, to sit up; but he yanked me back roughly and pressed me down, his face so contorted with pain and anger that he seemed even uglier and more brutish in the half-light, repelling me, making me ill as I thought of how I had let him kiss and caress me, how I had flung myself at him and begged him to take me. Yet perversely I could not deny that he possessed an animal magnetism that, to my utter mortification, attracted me even now, though I sought determinedly to crush it.

"Esmond," Draco snarled bitterly. "Always Esmond. By God, I'll drive him from your heart and mind, Maggie, if I have to kill you to do it!"

Without warning, he caught my sodden hair and twisted my face up to his, grinding his mouth down on mine, bruising my lips, for there was nothing loving in his kiss now, as there had been before, only rage and the desire to hurt me as deeply as I had hurt him. I fought him with all my strength, but I was no match for him, and so I learned what it meant to be taken against my will, without caring or tenderness; and when it was done, I hated him with all my heart.

Tears trickled from the corners of my eyes. I trembled with shock and fear and loathing; and suddenly the murderous look in Draco's eyes faded as he came to his senses at last and realized what he had done. He knew a moment's remorse, and despite how I shook and shrank from his touch, he tried to take me in his arms once more.

"Maggie," he uttered brokenly. "Maggie . . ."

But I wanted no part of him now.

"Don't touch me!" I spat and rolled away from him, groping for my clothes.

It was raining hard now, and I was grateful for that, for I thought that otherwise he would surely have attempted to restrain me. But now a brilliant flash of lightning illuminated the moors, and thunder cracked, and he knew, as I did, that we were not safe here, exposed as we were upon the open terrain. So he turned away to begin pulling on his shirt and breeches.

My teeth chattered. I shivered uncontrollably as I struggled into my own wet garments, knowing they were ruined and wondering frantically how I would explain myself if someone should see me returning in such a state to the Hall. I was desperate to get home, to blot this terrible night from my mind and pretend it had never happened. I no longer cared that Julianne lay in Esmond's arms at the manor; what I had done in my hurt and anger at my stepsister and cousin was far worse than their betrayal of me. They were guilty of nothing more than wounding me emotionally, while I . . . *I* had allowed myself to be disgraced and dishonored, for though Draco had said he loved me, he had not spoken of marriage.

Truly the fact that I would even for a moment have considered wedding him showed me the depths of despair and madness into which I had sunk; for then I would be as much of an outcast as he, scorned and despised for marrying beneath me, a discredit to the Chandler name. Certainly Sir Nigel would not permit such a thing, even had I wished it, which I did not.

The wind, which had risen ominously, lashed me unmercifully as I staggered to my feet and tried to fasten the hooks of my gown. I could not do them up alone, but still I twisted away from Draco when he would have helped me; and soundly he cursed me and caught hold of me, his fingers digging into my arms.

"Maggie, listen to me!" he shouted harshly over the roar of the wind and the rain, the maddened surf beyond the cliffs, his dark visage fierce as a demon's in the blackness shot through with streaks of lightning. "For God's sake, listen to me!"

But I did not want to hear what he had to say; and fueled by a strength born of my fear and shame, I struggled wildly against him, so we stumbled and fell. We grappled upon the rain-soaked earth like animals until at last I managed to loose one hand and slap him hard across the face, momentarily stunning him. Then, clawing blindly at the grass and heather, I dragged myself forward, intent on escaping from him. Draco, recovering, grabbed the hem of my dress to pull me back, but I snatched it free. Then I lurched to my feet and began to run, beyond caring that I was half naked. Somehow during our altercation, the top of my gown had fallen down about my waist. Without thinking, I clutched my bodice to my breast, knowing only that I must get away from him. If only I could reach the gates of the Hall, I could close and lock them so he would not be able to catch me. I was terrified that otherwise he would force me to accompany him to the Heights and would compel me to remain there overnight, thus completing my ruin.

My imagination ran wild, thinking of what else he might do. He hated my father—vehemently. Perhaps he intended to have his revenge on Sir Nigel through me. Perhaps after he was done with me, he would cast me aside, as Esmond had done, and laugh and boast to my father of how he had taken my virginity. The knowledge would kill Sir Nigel, and it would be my fault if it did. For the rest of my life, I would have the guilty burden of his death on my conscience as surely as he had that of my mother's on his.

Behind me, I could hear Draco yelling and swearing as he gave chase, the wind catching the words and carrying them to me; and gasping for breath, I raced on as though the devil himself pursued me. Somehow I outstripped him—I do not know how, though the darkness and the rain must have aided my cause—and at last I was through the gates of the Hall. But sensing my cousin was hard on my heels, I did not pause, as I had planned to do, but rushed on, leaving the gates open and unlocked, trusting I could reach the house in time; and finally I was inside the manor, my heart beating so strenuously that I thought it would burst in my breast.

I leaned against the side door for a moment to catch my breath. Then, knowing I dare not linger, lest someone spy me, I hurried upstairs to my room. Only when I was safely within its protective walls did I collapse with relief and exhaustion.

For a long time, I lay upon the bed, my mind a blank. But at last, jerking wide-awake, I realized that I had been drifting into sleep and that I must get undressed and cleaned up so Linnet's sharp, eager eyes would find naught to arouse their curiosity in the morning.

Embers smoldered upon the hearth, where the maid had laid a fire earlier to take the chill from the spring night. Now I rose, stoked up the flames, and added more wood to fuel them, grateful for their warmth and cheerfulness. Then I stripped off my clothes and spread them before the fire to dry. After that, I poured some water from my pitcher into the basin on my washstand and, with a cloth, sponged myself off, feeling, as I did so, that I would never be clean again, no matter how hard I scrubbed. I·winced at the slight soreness between my thighs and was pierced anew by the thought of what I had done. Numbly I stared at my reflection in the mirror before me, thinking it was a stranger who looked back at me. My dripping hair was a mass of tangles where Draco had ensnared it to hold me prisoner; my lower lip was cut and swollen where he had kissed me so brutally; purplish blue bruises shadowed my skin where his ironlike hands had crushed me to him. I blushed scarlet with shame at the memory; I could not understand what had possessed me. Surely I was a hopeless wanton to have behaved as I had.

Esmond was right to spurn me, I thought again.

Great sobs racked my body at the bitter realization. It was no wonder he had chosen Julianne over me—Julianne, who, desperate as she had been to secure her future, had not stooped as low as I had this night.

With shaking hands, I pulled on my night rail. Then I knelt before the fire to examine my ruined apparel. With a stiff brush and a cloth, I worked vigorously on the red velvet gown and the rest to remove the mud and grass stains from them. Then, with a needle and thread, I mended the rents as best I could so the garments' condition would not be so obvious. After that, I put everything away, hanging the dress behind all the others in my wardrobe and burying my underclothes at the bottom my chest of drawers. Linnet, who was a trifle lazy, would not look for what I had worn today, I thought, but be glad I had spared her the chore of picking up after me.

Then, both physically and emotionally drained, I climbed into bed, knowing dawn was but a few hours hence. Still my inner turmoil kept slumber at bay; anxiety ate at me fiercely. Now that I had regained some measure of sanity, I was like someone who had committed a crime: My biggest fear was not of the enormity of what I had done, but of being caught and made to pay for it. If what had happened

this night ever became known, I would become an object of
scandal and decent ladies would shun me. No gentleman
would marry me—though no doubt there would be many
who would make me offers of another kind. Why had I not
thought of these things before? Only now, when it was too
late, did I wonder like any other woman who had foolishly
given herself to a lover if the man would tell. Would he?
Would he? I did not know.

I shall call him a liar if he does, I thought boldly for
one in such a tenuous position. *He has no proof of what he
did. It will be his word against mine. Father will have no
choice but to believe me—if only because he won't be able
to bring himself to believe Draco. Surely Draco will realize
that, too. Surely he will say nothing....*

I comforted myself with the thought, but it was small
solace all the same; and at last, knowing I was achieving
naught with my speculations, I forced myself to push them
from my mind, to close my eyes and breathe deeply so sleep
would come. In time, I drifted into an uneasy slumber—and
dreamed of Draco, his satanic face blotting out the heavens
above me as he pressed me down upon a moon-dark moor
and took me again and again.

Chapter Seventeen

Ties that Bind

So for the mother's sake the child was dear,
And dearer was the mother for the child.

—*Sonnet to a Friend Who Asked How I
Felt When the Nurse First Presented
My Infant to Me*
Samuel Taylor Coleridge

To my great relief, for reasons I could only guess, Draco told no one what had passed between us that shameful night, so all my fears of being disgraced and ruined came to naught. But despite his silence, I now knew I was undone just the same, for of all the repercussions I had recognized that I might suffer for my folly, there was one that had never occurred to me: the cessation of my monthly courses. I was going to have a child.

At first I could not believe it. My menses had never been very regular, and initially I had thought my flux was merely late again. It was only when it had not come at all that deep down inside, I had suspected the reason why. Still I had refused to face the facts. It was not uncommon to miss a month, I had reassured myself, especially when one had been as distraught as I. Besides, I had no other symptoms— no morning sickness, no tiredness, no faintness.

But soon I could deceive myself no longer, and now I

was cast into panic and despair at the realization that my body was indeed changing to accommodate the child who grew within me.

As usual when I was troubled, I had sought the moors to think. But today even they had no power to soothe me, for I could no longer find any comfort in the sweeping expanse of heather and bracken that had witnessed my downfall. Now, reining Avalon about, I turned away from that lonely stretch of heath where I had given myself to my Gypsy cousin and rode on until I reached the edge of the cliffs along the shore. There I dismounted and walked forward to stare down at the vast, shifting sea far below. For aeons upon aeons, the mighty breakers had eaten away at the headland, eroding the earth so it had crumbled and retreated before their onslaught, leaving behind only the gnarled black rocks that protruded from the water like tentacles, the final remnants, perhaps, of the fabled lands of Lyonnesse and Ys. Mayhap someday Cornwall, too, would lie fathoms deep beneath the waves, I mused, no more than a legend, its inhabitants long dead and forgotten. I was saddened by the thought, for it made me realize how truly insignificant I was. I had been born, and I would die; and still the sea would go on battering the headland until even the place where I now stood was no more than a memory.

Today the ocean was so clear and blue, so calm and smooth that it was hard to believe it was such a constant, pitiless force. Yet I knew I had but to step forward and I would plunge to my death beneath the deceptive water. Once there had been a time when if Draco had not prevented me from doing so, perhaps I would have taken that fatal step. But not now—not when I no longer had just my own life to consider. I had not yet felt my child stir within me; it was too early for that. But I knew with every fiber of my being that it lived and breathed inside me just the same; and while I was dismayed by the knowledge, aware of the scandal that would ensue at the discovery, to my surprise, I was filled also with an utterly overwhelming joy and a deep, fierce protectiveness toward this tiny, fragile new being that depended upon me for survival.

I shuddered as I thought of the stories I had heard of women who found themselves in my situation, women so desperate to rid themselves of the indisputable evidence of their shame that they would risk anything—even death—in an attempt to expell the unwanted fetus from the womb. Every other day, it seemed, the newspapers reported that some poor, unfortunate woman, cast off by her lover and destitute, had been found dead in the meaner streets of London, the victim of some filthy butcher masquerading as a doctor or midwife.

When I thought of the agony these women must have endured before dying, I could not help but wonder how much more their unborn children had suffered before relinquishing their tenuous hold on life. Now, sickened by the thought, I turned from the sea, knowing with certainty that that way was not for me or mine. I could not destroy myself, and thus my baby, too, in the process, no matter what hardships I must face because of my plight. To do so would be to commit murder—I had no doubt of that—and I would not have that sin, too, upon my soul. Even now, when I had only just become sure of its existence, I loved my child too much for that. Even the thought of bearing it and giving it up afterward tore at my heart like the sharp talons of a hawk, and I knew I could not do it. My baby's face would haunt me forever then; I would always wonder if it was well and safe and happy. I would long to see it, to hold it, to let it know how much I loved it—A sob of torment caught in my throat. Regardless of what happened, I would never part with my child. *Never!*

Gathering up Avalon's trailing reins, I remounted the horse, pausing a moment uncertainly as I gazed at Stormswept Heights in the distance. I had not seen Draco since that fateful night upon the commons. Now, though I knew I must, still I hesitated to seek him out. He had loved me, and I had scorned him. Perhaps I had hurt him as deeply as Esmond had me. I did not know. I knew only that he had been right when he had said we were much alike. He was as

proud as I, and that pride had kept him from coming to me,
I felt sure, just as it had kept me from Esmond after he had
betrayed and rejected me. Now I knew that if I were to have
any relationship at all with my Gypsy cousin, it must be I
who humbled myself.

Under different circumstances, I should not have done
so. But I had my child to think of now, my innocent child,
as blameless for its conception as Draco and I had been for
ours. The thought bolstered my resolve. There was nothing
I would not do to prevent my baby from suffering as we had
suffered for sins not our own, nor did I think Draco would
feel otherwise. Even if he now hated me, I did not believe
he would cast me aside as Esmond had done. Draco knew
all too well what it meant to be illegitimate. Surely he
would not want his child to bear that stigma also; surely he
would wed me to prevent it.

I shivered at the thought of marrying Draco, wishing
there were some other way to secure my baby's future. But
there was not. I knew no other man who would have me,
especially now. Nor did I have any money with which to go
away to someplace where I was unknown and could pass
myself off as a widow. Esmond and Julianne were still in
Italy, and I would not have asked them for aid in any event.
Aunt Tibby and Sarah had nothing more than what my
father gave them; and Welles would not come into his
modest inheritance until next year. I did not even consider
applying to Sir Nigel and Lady Chandler for assistance,
knowing they would be enraged by what I had done. They
would, I thought, send me away to give birth to my child
secretly. Then afterward they would see that it was taken
from me and placed in a convent or an orphanage. They
would not care about my feelings for my baby; they would
never allow me to keep it. If Draco refused to help me, I
must run away. Though I would be alone and penniless,
somehow I must make my own way in the world—for my
child's sake.

But surely it will not come to that, I thought now.
Surely Draco will marry me.

That there was another, more shameful choice he might

compel me to make, I did not want to contemplate. Yet in my heart, I knew I was so desperate that I would become Draco's mistress if only he would support me so I would not have to give up my baby. Squaring my shoulders determinedly, I urged Avalon forward toward Stormswept Heights.

I found Draco in the fields, planting the rows he had tilled last summer, though I did not know what he hoped to grow in the harsh, inhospitable climate of northern Cornwall, which was much better suited to the raising of cattle and sheep than grains, fruits, and vegetables. He glanced up silently at my approach, and such was the bitterness upon his face that I realized I had wounded him far more than I had suspected. My heart sank at the knowledge; my resolution faltered. It was useless to have come here; I had availed myself nothing by it. Then I remembered the child I carried, and I forced myself to continue toward my Gypsy cousin, though he had returned to his work and was now studiously ignoring me, his jaw set in a hard, arrogant manner that told me more plainly than words how grievously he felt I had wronged him.

He looked tired, as though he had not slept well for many nights, I thought as I drew near to him. A faint hope stirred within me at the notion. Perhaps he still cared for me after all, then, if only a little. But if this were so, he gave no sign of it, and my spirits once more failed me as I recognized that he did not mean to make things easy for me.

Slowly I dismounted and moved to stand beside him. Still he paid me no heed, and finally I dared to lay my hand upon his arm, knowing he would not let that pass unchallenged. He stiffened at my touch and ceased his sowing and raking. His black eyes burned with pain and anger when he turned them upon me scathingly. But still he did not speak; and though I swallowed hard, neither did I quail in the face of his wrath nor deliver the apology he so obviously expected me to make, for I saw it would do me little good.

Instead I said quietly, without preamble, "I'm going to have a child, Draco."

He inhaled sharply at the words. Something unfathomable flickered in his eyes, so I knew he was not as indifferent to

me as he would have me believe. He stared at me intently
for an instant. Then abruptly he tossed aside his seed sack
and rake, and he grasped my shoulders so tightly that I
winced.

"God help you if that's a lie, Maggie!" he hissed,
giving me a savage little shake.

"I would not be here if it were—and you know it!"

He was silent for a moment. Then he nodded.

"Yes, I suppose that's true," he agreed.

He looked away. A muscle worked tensely in his jaw,
so I knew he was thinking, as I had thought, of what this
unexpected baby would mean to us, how it would change
our lives forever; for he knew as well as I why I had come
here. He must marry me. *He must!*

I wondered now if Draco could relive that night we had
shared upon the stretch of moor, if he would still press me
down among the heather and bracken and make love to me,
knowing the price we would have to pay for that brief, mad
moment of passion. We had never thought of that then.
Only now, when it was too late, were we forced to consider
the cost of what we had done.

His hands still gripped my shoulders painfully; I could
feel his fingers digging into my skin, reminding me of how
he had clutched me to him when we had lain together
beneath the black, raining sky, naked and feverish with
longing. Despite myself, a wave of unbearable emotion
swept through me at the memory. The afternoon seemed
suddenly to have grown very quiet, the hush broken only by
the sighing of the sea in the distance and the cries of the
gulls along the shore. Acutely I became aware of Draco's
sweat-dampened shirt, unbuttoned to reveal the dark mat of
hair upon his chest. Even now, I could recall the silky feel
of the crisp curls brushing against my breasts, the weight of
his body atop mine. My breath caught in my throat.

Hearing the small sound, he turned back to me; and in
that instant, it seemed as though the world faded into the
background around me and there were naught for me but
Draco. Try as I might, I could not look away from him. It
was as though I were held spellbound by his eyes, entranced

by the desire I now saw smoldering in their depths. I
shivered at the sight, but relief rushed through me, too, for I
understood that despite whatever else he might feel toward
me now, Draco still wanted me. He would not leave me to
face my fate alone. It was enough, I told myself; nothing
else mattered. I must do whatever was necessary to protect
my child.

Slowly my cousin's hands slid up to cup my face; his
thumbs traced tiny patterns on my cheeks. I stood very still,
my heart pounding so violently that I thought surely he must
hear it. His eyes and mouth mocked me, dared me to escape
from him while I still could. But I made no move to do so,
silently offering myself to him instead, knowing that if I
were honest with myself, I must confess it was not just
because of the baby that I made no protest against him. I did
not love him; it was Esmond who held my heart. But some
dark, atavistic thing inside me was drawn to Draco just the
same. I could no longer deny that, no matter how much it
shamed me to admit it.

Time slipped away as he kissed me, roughly, possessively,
so there could be no mistaking what he wanted from me—or
what I could expect from him if I gave myself into his
keeping. I was painfully aware of his intent to make me
aware of that. But still I made no attempt to free myself,
and at last, his breath coming quickly, he released me.

"So, Maggie. You are now willing to be mine, then—
for the sake of the child, of course," he muttered, his eyes
regarding me in a way that made me blush and glance away.

"Yes," I whispered, trembling at the thought of what I
must endure for my answer. But what else could I say? It
was why I had come after all. "Yes."

"And what makes you think I would have you now?"
he asked cruelly, callously, so I blanched and stared at him,
stricken, my stomach feeling as though the earth had suddenly dropped from beneath my feet.

Had I misjudged him after all, then? Did he truly mean
to spurn me, as I had him, even though he knew I was
carrying his baby? I felt cold and sick with dread and panic
at the thought. Deep down inside, I had never believed it

would come to this. What would I do? Where would I go? I had no money; yet I could not stay here, at Highclyffe Hall, where my child would be wrested from me.

Draco laughed harshly at the fear upon my face, so if I had not truly hated him before, knowing I, as much as he, was to blame for that night upon the moors, I hated him now with a passion. I cried out and flung myself at him blindly, my hands curled like claws to scratch the jeering grin from his face. But he grabbed my upraised arms easily and pinioned them behind my back, pulling them tight until, breathing hard, my eyes flashing, I ceased struggling against him. Then, though I tried to jerk away, he caught my jaw with one hand and forced my face up to his.

"You really must learn to control your emotions, Maggie," he drawled, "lest one day, they prove your undoing." Casually he flicked his forefinger against my cheek, angering and humiliating me as I realized how powerless I was against him. "Be at ease, my girl," he said. "Much as you may deserve it, I'll not throw you to the wolves. But understand this, Maggie," he continued, his eyes growing hard, his hands hurting me. "Neither will I settle for however little of yourself you may think to give me. I will have all of you, or so help me, I *shall* cast you off to fend for yourself rather than wed you, for I'll not have even the shadow of Esmond Sheffield stand between me and mine! Is that clear?"

With difficulty, I bit back the heated words that tumbled to my lips, knowing that to utter them would be the height of foolishness. No matter how fervently I might long to fling his crude proposal back into his face, Draco was not a man to be twice scorned. He had agreed to marry me, and I was in no position to dictate his terms. Swallowing hard, I nodded.

"Yes, quite clear," I replied stiffly, for I despised him more than ever for frightening me so maliciously when he had meant from the outset to wed me. How I wished that I were not with child, that I could spit in his face and give tongue to my fury. But I could not. I could do nothing but submit to his demands. It did not matter, I thought again;

Esmond was irrevocably lost to me anyway. What good would it do me to go on pining for him? "I shall—I shall do my best to put him from my heart and mind, Draco," I said.

"See that you do, Maggie," he insisted tersely, "for mark me: If ever I find out differently, you shall regret it, I promise you. By God, I'll have your loyalty at least, if nothing else!" He paused, and then his eyes appraised me meaningfully. "But of course," he went on more softly, "I will have more than that, won't I, Maggie?"

My cheeks grew hot with shame and embarrassment at his words. I could no longer meet his eyes; and when he drew me to him, I shook with apprehension and tried to pull away, uncertain what he intended. Did he mean to take me here and now, in the fields, knowing how deeply debased by the act I would feel? I could not bear it if he did. Yet if I refused him, perhaps he would withdraw his offer to marry me—or, worse, would merely laugh and force me down upon the ground anyway, as he had that night upon the moors. Well, and what if he did? Hadn't I now, as I had then, given him every right to do so? I shrank from the answer, not wanting to face it. Yet I could not deny it, any more than I could truly blame him for wanting to strike back at me for my previous rejection of him. I knew that if given the opportunity, I, too, would retaliate however I could at those who had wounded me. Had that not been my intention when I had lain with Draco to begin with—to hurt Esmond and, if I were honest with myself, my father also in some deeper, distorted way I did not care to examine? Had I not chosen to seek comfort from a man I knew they both despised? Had I not surrendered to him my honor, which society charged them, my nearest male relatives, to defend? Yes, I had. But still, understanding Draco's motive for misusing me did not lessen my instinctive rebellion against it.

"Don't, please, don't," I whimpered as his lips brushed mine and I felt his breath, warm and provocative, against my skin.

Deliberately he pressed his body close to mine; his

thighs grazed my own suggestively. With one hand, he caught my hair so I could not turn away as his mouth burned across my cheek to my ear.

"Don't what?" he asked, his voice low and husky, making me quiver like a high-strung filly in his arms. His palm slid down to cup my breast through the thin material of my riding habit. "Are you denying me, Maggie?"

"Yes. No." I bit my lip, blinking back the tears that had started in my eyes at my helplessness against him. Once more I yearned desperately to lash out at him, and once more I thought of my child and restrained myself. "I—I will do whatever you want," I consented reluctantly at last, feeling more demeaned than ever. "But please, Draco, not here. Someone might see. Let us go inside at least."

"You were not so particular that night upon the commons," he remarked, making me flush scarlet again. But to my surprise and relief, having wrung such a confession from me, he shrugged and let me go. "It matters not. I can wait. After all, under the circumstances, you will doubtless want to be wed as quickly as possible, will you not? When can you be ready to leave?"

"L—l—leave?" I stammered, confused. "I—I don't understand."

"Oh, come now, Maggie. Think! You are but what . . . just turned nineteen? You cannot marry in England without Sir Nigel's consent, and surely you do not suppose he shall give it. The baronet's daughter wed a Gypsy bastard?" Draco laughed unpleasantly at the thought. Then he said, "No, I'm very much afraid it shall have to be Gretna Green for us, my girl."

I stared at him, stricken, for this had never occurred to me. Still I knew he was right: I was underage, and no English priest would perform the wedding without my father's permission. We must travel to Scotland if we were to be married.

"Father will come after us," I murmured, blanching at the notion.

"Let him," Draco snarled, as though he relished the prospect. "By then, it will be too late. You will be mine."

The realization filled me with trepidation, but still I nodded.

"Yes," I breathed. "I will be yours, Draco." *To do with as you please*, I thought, shivering again; but I did not speak the words aloud. Instead, after a time, I said, "I must think. I must think how I can best get away without arousing suspicion. . . ."

My cousin shrugged.

"You need say naught but that you are riding over to the Grange," he suggested. "By the time anyone discovers you are missing, we will be long gone from Cornwall."

"There will be a dreadful scandal."

"Not if Sir Nigel is clever enough to hush it up; and if he is presented with a fait accompli, he would be a fool to do otherwise. My God!" Draco burst out suddenly. "How I shall enjoy seeing his face when he learns we are married! I daresay he shall find it a bitter pill indeed to swallow!"

At the thought, his mouth curved in a sardonic smile that did not quite reach his eyes, making me shudder as I recognized that I was indeed to prove his instrument of revenge against my father. Inwardly I cringed as I thought of Sir Nigel's wrath upon realizing this also, as he surely would when he learned Draco and I were wed; and though, just minutes before, it had been my cousin I feared, now I moved closer to him, instinctively seeking his protection from my father, of whom I was even more afraid. Upon seeing this, Draco's manner toward me softened for the first time.

"You don't have to be frightened of him ever again, Maggie," he declared, his voice kinder now than it had been previously. "Unlike those more careless than I, I defend what is mine. Do you truly believe I would let anyone hurt you or our coming baby?"

"I—I don't know. Even now, I feel I dare not displease you, lest you cast me aside after all, as you threatened to do—"

"I spoke in anger then. I always intended to have you, Maggie, one way or another. Do you really think I would let you go now, especially when you are carrying my child? My

God! I may be a lot of things, my girl—and not all of them pleasant—but I'm not such a brute as that!'' His mouth tightened with ire, but I knew it was not directed at me, so I did not cower from him as I had before. ''Sir Nigel may have beaten me to my knees in the past,'' he went on grimly,''but he shall not do so now, I assure you. Nor will I allow him to ill-treat you, Maggie. He will answer to me for it if he does, I promise you!''

Strangely, considering his behavior toward me earlier, a warm feeling crept through me at Draco's words. For the first time, I thought perhaps our marriage would not prove as disastrous as I had feared. Though I recoiled from the idea of his confronting my father, still I was grateful he had offered to do so. It informed me that regardless of his own conflicting emotions toward me, in the eyes of the world at least, he would show me every respect to which I was entitled as his bride. I need never be afraid that as my husband, Draco would publically subject me to ridicule, as so many men did their wives.

''Thank you for that at least,'' I uttered quietly. I paused for a moment. Then I said, ''I—I know so little of how a thing such as this is done. What must I do to prepare? Will I need papers . . . money—''

''No. I shall make all the necessary arrangements. Do not concern yourself about that. You need do naught but pack one small bag with whatever few essentials you will require for the trip—but no more than that, Maggie. We must travel fast and light if we are to reach Gretna Green before we are overtaken by any who may prove so unwise as to pursue us.''

''I—I understand.''

''Then in three days' time, I will come for you. Be ready and waiting for me early that morning on the road at the edge of the wood.''

''So—so soon?'' I queried tremulously. ''I—I do not know—''

''Waiting will only postpone the inevitable, Maggie— not prevent it,'' Draco reminded me, growing hard and cold toward me once more. ''If you wish to draw back now, then say so. You know what I am; I've never pretended to be aught else. If you can't accept that, then why did you come here?''

"Because I had no one else to turn to." I spoke honestly.

His face whitened as though I had slapped him, and for a moment, I feared he would strike me. His eyes blazed; a muscle twitched in his cheek. Then his eyelids swept down to conceal his thoughts, and he laughed bitterly.

"But of course," he sneered. "Why should there have been any other reason? So you came to me out of fear and desperation, did you? And no doubt after you return home, you will have second thoughts. Well, pay them no heed, Maggie, for though I kept silent before about what passed between us—to spare you disgrace—I shall not do so again. The child is mine after all, and I would, of course, be forced to claim it as such if you were to do aught foolish. Do not think, therefore, to deceive me in some manner. Be very sure that I shall not permit you to wed another, nor by running away can you escape from me. A woman alone and penniless is easy enough to trace, and you must know I would find you and bring you back. I do not think that under the circumstances, even Sir Nigel would stand in my way then. No matter how much he hates me, I don't believe he would care to see his only daughter ruined."

"No, I don't suppose he would," I responded. "For the baby's sake, then, if nothing more, I will make no attempt to cross you, Draco. I am not such a fool as that."

"Be sure of it, my girl, for once we're married, there won't be any going back, you know."

"Yes, I know." Then, as it seemed there was nothing else to say and the afternoon had grown very late besides, I turned to take my leave of him, calling to Avalon, who was grazing idly nearby. The gelding came to me, and I gathered up the reins, preparing to mount. "I will be ready and waiting for you in three days' time," I told Draco after he had assisted me into the saddle.

"You do that," he said, catching hold of the reins firmly so I could not ride on. Then, grinning mockingly, he drawled, "Chin up, Maggie, my girl. You might have done worse, you know. I may be a coarse, common bastard, but I'm smart and ambitious and not afraid of soiling my hands with a bit of hard work, so I fancy I shall get on in the world in the end. And with you at my side to provide a touch of grace and gentility, who knows what we may accomplish? It may be that we shall do very well together after all, for we are immensely well suited, I have always thought."

"Indeed?" I rejoined coolly. "I cannot imagine why. Certainly *I* have never thought so!"

With that, I yanked Avalon back hard, so the reins were wrenched from my cousin's hands and I was free to go. Then, wheeling my horse about, I galloped from the fields. I did not look back; but even so, I knew instinctively that Draco watched me steadily until I was out of sight.

Chapter Eighteen

Gretna Green

Thus grief still treads upon the heels of pleasure:
Marry'd in haste, we may repent at leisure.

—*The Old Bachelor*
William Congreve

I remember little of our terrible journey to that small, notorious town across Scotland's border, for from the start, the entire trip was like a nightmare from which I could not awaken.

Draco had got a coach and four strong horses—I knew not whence or how—and mad Renshaw and two other dubitable men I did not recognize were with him when, from a pale grey veil of mist, he appeared on the appointed morning to claim me as his. Despite myself, a wave of relief swept through me at the sight of my Gypsy cousin, for in my heart, I had half feared he would not come. Still I shivered as the carriage drew to a halt before me and he stepped down from the vehicle, the folds of his black greatcoat swirling about him like a shroud beneath the slowly lightening sky. My teeth chattered, and my skin was cold as ice when he touched me. He swore softly at that. Then he made some risqué remark to me, and when I blushed furiously and hissed at him to hush, a low laugh emanated from his throat.

"I thought that would revive your spirits, my girl," he noted with cool amusement. "For a moment, I was afraid I was about to run off with a corpse! For God's sake, Maggie! Why didn't you wear a heavier cloak? Into the coach with you. You'll be warmer inside, and there's a flask of hot tea besides. Here, Ned." Draco tossed my bag up to the hulking escort. "Strap that on top." Then he turned to Renshaw, who now stood beside him. "Take Miss Chandler's gelding back to the Heights," he directed slowly, stressing each word, "and keep it hidden there until I tell you otherwise. Do you understand?"

The stooped ruffian nodded, his eyes like those of a sly, dumb beast, so it was only now and then that he seemed to be crazy, I thought as, gratefully sipping the hot, sweet, savory tea from the flask Draco had provided, I watched the two men from the carriage. I suspected Renshaw had moments of lucidity; perhaps, in his own way, he was even capable of a strange, twisted sort of reasoning and comprehension. Certainly Draco appeared to think so.

"Repeat my instructions then." He spoke as though the old lunatic were a child who must be told things several times before he grasped them.

"If that be yer wish, sir. I'm ta take t' missus's horse ta t' Heights, an' no one is ta see him till 'ee tells me dif'rent."

"That's right. Now, do you recall what else I told you do?"

"Aye, sir. I've got yer note right here in me pocket, I do." Renshaw patted his filthy, tattered coat proudly.

"Good. And what are you to do with it?"

"I'm ta take it ta Sir Nigel at t' Hall . . . er . . . long about suppertime this eve."

"Well done, Renshaw." Draco smiled at him kindly, and the fellow beamed so like a faithful dog that I almost expected him to lick my cousin's hand, but he did not. "Be off with you now." Draco waved him away brusquely. "And keep your lip buttoned about this morning's doings, else you shall regret it, I promise you."

Leading Avalon and babbling incoherently to himself

under his breath, Renshaw began obediently to shuffle down the winding road, apparently having taken no offense at his master's rudely delivered threat. Draco watched him briefly, then climbed into the waiting vehicle, pulling the door shut behind him. After he had settled himself beside me on the comfortable, upholstered seat, he leaned forward and pounded with his cane on the box above us.

"Spring them, Will," he called to the thin, wiry driver.

At that, a whip cracked, the horses leaped forward, and with a lurch, the coach started to move, its body swaying, its wheels clattering upon the rocky dirt road. The cold, sick feeling of fear at the pit of my belly hardened and shriveled into a tight little knot then, for I knew my last chance to escape that which lay ahead of me was gone. There would be no turning back now. For better or worse, I was committed to my fate.

"Cheer up, Maggie," Draco urged jovially upon observing my pale face as he took the now half-empty flask of tea from me, recapped it, and set it aside. "You look as though you are on your way to a funeral—not a wedding."

"I can't help how I feel, Draco."

His good humor vanished abruptly at my words. His black eyes narrowed, and his mouth tightened perceptibly with anger.

"Then I shall order the carriage about and return you to the Hall at once!" he snapped, half rising from the cushioned seat. "I told you before: I will not marry a woman who thinks to withhold a part of herself from me!"

"No! No, wait! Please." I bit my lip, putting one hand upon his arm to restrain him as I thought of the child I carried. "I'm—I'm sorry. I didn't mean that the way it sounded. I—I *do* want us to be wed. 'Tis just that I'm so . . . scared."

To my relief, Draco resumed his place beside me, casually sliding one arm about my shoulders and tipping my face up to his with his free hand.

"Of what, Maggie?" he inquired more gently. "Me? Surely not. After all, you already know all my flaws, do you not? And if 'tis Sir Nigel you are worried about, well, then, put your mind at rest. I have taken care of him."

"How?" I asked. Then I remembered. "The note you mentioned?"

"Yes."

"What did it say, Draco? Will you tell me, please?"

He was silent for a time, his face so closed and unreadable that I thought he did not mean to answer. Then at last he shrugged.

"It said merely that I have you and that if he wishes to avoid a scandal, he will do nothing until he hears from me."

At first I did not understand. But after I had dwelled upon the message for a few moments, I grasped the full import of what Draco had intended, and I gasped.

"Do you mean you insinuated to Father that you have—have *kidnapped* me?" I cried. "That you are holding me at your mercy until you should choose to release me? Oh, Draco! How could you have been so cruel? Do you know what he will think?"

"I know precisely what he will think, my girl, and I bloody well hope his miserable soul squirms every time he thinks it! Oh, I daresay at first he shall not believe it. He shall not *want* to believe it. But when night falls and you have not returned home, he will go to bed knowing deep down inside that you are lying in my arms and that he is powerless to prevent it. He will know what I am capable of doing to you, because he is a man such as I, and he will wonder if I mean to make an honest woman of you afterward or if I will cast you out instead and boast of your shame. By tomorrow, he will be racked with both anger and fear, and by the day after that, he will be absolutely frantic. He will think of the scandal attached to his fine, old name—a scandal not of his own making, one he shall not be able to snap his fingers at and haughtily dismiss—and he will do whatever is necessary to avoid that besmirchment, even if it means swallowing his pride and permitting me to beat him to his knees, as he did me. Oh, yes, I know what he will think. I counted on it, my girl!"

"The shock will kill him," I whispered, stricken,

closing my eyes as the interior of the vehicle seemed suddenly, strangely, to spin about me. "And to think I gave myself to you . . . willingly, that first time. . . ."

"Don't waste time blaming yourself for that, Maggie. Make no mistake about it: If you had not come to me of your own volition, sooner or later, I would have taken you anyway, just as Sir Nigel will believe I have taken you now. I would have abducted you and forced you, if for no other reason than to prevent you from marrying Esmond Sheffield."

There was a deadly ring of truth to Draco's words, and I shuddered as it pealed over me, for I knew now, far more than I had ever known before, the terrible things he was capable of doing. Once more my head reeled, and I shook it in a fruitless attempt to clear it, bewildered by the odd sensation.

"You are a monster," I said, trying without success to free myself from his embrace.

"A monster who adores you, Maggie," he murmured in my ear, nibbling at my lobe. "Come. Can you not love me just a little?"

"How can I—when you shall be the death of Father?"

"Why should you care? He does not love you. You shall see when we return to Cornwall that it is only his pride and his name that matter to him. Besides, he is too mean and stubborn to die. He will be enraged that I have bested him. He will want to live so he can get even with me."

"He will kill you."

"He may try," Draco corrected me arrogantly. "He shall not succeed."

"I should not care if he did."

"Wouldn't you?" he asked huskily, his eyes hooded, his mouth very close to mine.

"No."

My cousin laughed softly at that.

"Shall I prove to you that you *would* care, Maggie? That you would, in fact, care very much?"

"No! Leave me alone!"

"Ah, Maggie. If only I could. But you are in my blood

like a drug, I fear, and the more I have of you, the more I crave.''

Then before I could protest again, his lips captured mine, imprisoning them. I was taken by surprise, for I had not expected this—not yet. Indeed I had clung to the desperate hope that Draco would not touch me again until after we were married. I should have realized the futility of that wish, I thought with a sinking heart. I knew what sort of man he was; he had never made any attempt to deny it. To the contrary, he had deliberately gone out of his way to show me his demoniac nature—and now was no exception.

Surely he will do no more than kiss me, I thought.

But I did not know, and I trembled at my lack of knowledge, feeling his mouth, hot and insistent, against my own, yet unhurried, for indeed, why should he not take his time? I could not escape from him, and even if I could, I would not be so foolish as to jump from the coach when it was traveling at such a furious pace, and he knew it. Still I tried to elude his encroaching lips, his ravaging tongue, but to no avail. He did not mean to let me slip away so easily.

Slowly he untied the ribbons that held my hat in place, removed it, and tossed it aside. His hands caught my hair; one by one, he pulled the pins from the tresses, loosing them. His fingers wove themselves into the dark cloud that tumbled free, entangling the silken strands, tightening upon them so I could not turn away. My head felt light and dizzy in his grasp; it was as though I were drunk or dreaming. I seemed to have no will of my own. I could not understand what was happening to me, why I should feel so dazed.

Draco's tongue traced the outline of my mouth before he compelled my lips to part again, invading me, swallowing my breath with his. Licking tongues of fire smoldered in my mouth, burning me with their molten flames. A low moan escaped from my throat. At the sound, my eyes flew open wide and I struggled against the waves of lethargy that assailed me. I fought my cousin, too, in vain, for my mind was clouded by confusion; my limbs appeared to have gone numb and leaden.

And then I knew.

"The tea," I breathed. "The tea was drugged."

"A small amount of brandy and laudanum . . . to calm you," Draco admitted without a trace of conscience or regret.

"You are no gentleman to treat me thus." To my mortification, the words were languid and slurred.

His laughter sounded mockingly in my ear.

"Did you really think I was? What a pity, then, to disabuse you of the notion."

"But . . . we are not yet married."

"Within the next few days, we shall be. Besides, it did not matter to you before that we were not."

There was nothing I could say to that. Shame swept through me at the thought that I had no one but myself to blame for my predicament.

Relentlessly Draco pressed me down upon the carriage seat. I tried to rise, but I could not. He was too strong for me; I could not help but be aware of my own weakness in comparison. There was naught I could do to resist him; I was powerless against him. He undid the ties at the throat of my cape and folded its edges back. Then his hands moved to the buttons on my spencer. Deftly he unfastened them.

"It seems you have had a lot of practice at that," I heard myself say and could have bitten off my tongue with horror.

Draco lifted one eyebrow with amusement.

"Jealous, love?"

"I'm not your love!"

"Oh, but you are. Be glad of it, for otherwise I should not wed you."

Somehow my blouse was open. I was dimly conscious of that fact as I stared up at the ceiling of the vehicle that was carrying me farther and farther from home. Now that the early morning mist had faded, the spring sun shone in shades of pink and yellow against the pale blue of the sky. Mellow rays reached in through the coach windows to caress my full breasts as Draco pulled down the top of my chemise to bare them to his appraising gaze. Embarrassed, I tried to cover myself with my arms, but he caught them easily and pinioned them beneath me, making my back arch and my breasts strain and swell above the ruffled edge of my corset. He knelt over me, his face a dark shadow wreathed in a halo of sunlight, his powerful inner thighs pressing against the sides of my legs so I could not move.

"Maggie," he muttered. "Ah, Maggie."

I felt his hands close over my breasts, and I cried out in protest, as though expecting someone to come to my aid. But there was no one save the coachmen, my cousin's hirelings, and if they heard me above the pounding of the horses' hooves and the churning of the carriage wheels, they ignored me. The vehicle rattled on.

"They will not help you," Draco said, reading my mind. "They have been well paid to turn a blind eye and a deaf ear to your pleas. You are helpless against me. Why do you fight me?"

"I—I must!"

"You are behaving foolishly. I have already taken your virginity. There is no part of you that I do not know, my girl, that I have not claimed as mine."

"But there is. You do not hold my heart, Draco."

"I shall, Maggie," he vowed. "I shall."

"No. I will never love you."

"You love me now; you would not have given yourself to me otherwise. Come. You know it is true; you just do not want to admit it. You have always loved me."

"No . . . nor will I ever!"

"We shall see, my girl. We shall see!"

His palms cupped my breasts, glided sensuously over their dark, twin peaks so they puckered and stiffened as though touched by the cool spring air. I shivered—with revulsion, I told myself. But deep down inside, I knew better. Even now, against my will, my treacherous young body was awakening beneath his expert kisses and caresses. Draco lowered his mouth to one breast; his tongue stabbed me with its heat. Shooting sparks of atavistic longing and intense delight radiated through my body; I was like a catherine wheel set aflame, spinning and burning. The gradually warming sunlight streamed in upon us in streaks of deep rose and vivid gold, so it seemed as though the coach itself were on fire.

This is not happening, I thought. *This is not real.*

But it was.

I floated in a timeless place where light and dark and color came together in a kaleidoscopic swirl of emotion and sensation, ancient, primeval, the patterns ever changing, ever deepening as Draco molded me to his will. Earlier he had cast aside his greatcoat and jacket; now, impatiently he yanked loose his cravat and unbuttoned his shirt down to his waistcoat to expose his matted chest. Then slowly he unfastened his breeches to reveal the evidence of his desire for me. Blushing, I quickly averted my gaze, and he laughed softly as he bent over me again.

"Soon, Maggie, love," he promised throatily. "Very soon now..."

My skirts felt like raw silk as he shoved them up roughly over my thighs. In sharp contrast to this were his hands, hard as horn, touching me where no other man had ever dared to trespass. I trembled as his skillful fingers stroked me, invaded me, heightened my readiness to receive him. I did not know he was capable of arousing me still further, in a way I had never dreamed.

"No, Draco," I sobbed brokenly at the realization. "Please, no...."

He ignored me. His lips and tongue were like cognac trickling over ice as brazenly he tasted me. Warmth and moisture met and mingled as I quivered and melted beneath his indecent onslaught upon my body and senses. I whimpered with shock and mortification that such a thing should be done to me. But still I reveled in it, writhing beneath him as he tormented me until I was like a mad thing, moaning with want, frantic with need. Blindly I strove against him, aching to be filled by him. He rose to his knees then and lifted my hips. His bold black eyes raked me hungrily, possessively. His mouth parted.

"Maggie..." he groaned.

Without warning, he impaled me so suddenly, so savagely that I felt as though I would be torn asunder by his assault. But I did not care. I was consumed by passion, driven by desire as I took him deep into me, my breath catching sharply in my throat at the glorious pleasure and pain of it. I cried out my surrender; but still, deliberately, tantalizingly, he withdrew, then swiftly entered me again, watching me all the while.

Slowly, joined to me, he lowered us both back down to the carriage seat; his weight pressed me into the soft velvet cushion. I could feel his hot breath against my throat and upon my breasts as he dragged his mouth across my flesh to suck my nipples greedily and lave them with his tongue. Wildly I bucked and arched against him, my head thrashing from side to side as inexorably he began to move within me, rocking me as the jolting vehicle rocked me, each thrust harder and deeper than the last, until I was panting for air and clutching him wantonly, my nails digging into his broad back as I reached for rapture and seized it with a vengeance.

A roaring tide of exhilaration washed over me, engulfing me; exquisite surges of sensual delight swelled within me, merging into a massive wave of unbearable sensation that swept me up ruthlessly and bore me aloft. I rushed mindlessly toward its crest, clung to it desperately before suddenly it peaked and shattered within me, leaving me gasping, drowning in the dark, whirling depths of its deluge. Draco's hands tightened upon my hips as I stiffened and shuddered beneath him. Faster and faster, he plunged into me before at last he spilled himself inside me, then collapsed against me, his heart pounding like a violent surf against my own.

After a time, he withdrew, his eyes coolly triumphant as he gazed down at me. Dimly reality penetrated my befuddled mind as I tried to collect myself, to struggle against the stupor that enveloped me still. I wanted nothing more than to close my eyes and go on lying there. I did not even care how I must appear, sprawled half naked upon the carriage seat, with my skirts rucked up vulgarly about my thighs. But still the knowledge that I had been conquered so easily and thoroughly intruded upon my senses, and I began to cry, ashamed.

"Hush, Maggie," Draco said, helping me to rearrange

my clothing. "Hush, love. It was nothing that had not happened between us before or that will not happen again."

But neither that truth nor the prospect that accompanied it comforted me, and I wept until finally sleep overtook me.

When I awoke, it was dark, and for a moment, still languourous, I thought that I was back in my own bed at the Hall, that I had suffered a nightmare. Then slowly I became aware of the swaying of the coach, and of Draco's presence beside me, and I recognized that it was no dream, that I was indeed on my way to Gretna Green to marry my Gypsy cousin. Now, too, I recalled this morning's events and was stricken anew by them. A sob rose in my throat; with difficulty, I held it back so Draco would not know I was conscious. But I must have made some small sound or movement nevertheless, for presently he turned to me and spoke.

"So, Maggie, you are awake at last," he observed. "Good. I was beginning to think you intended to sleep all the way to Gretna Green. Are you hungry? There is an inn just ahead—the St. George and the Dragon—where we can dine if you like."

To my surprise, I realized I was famished, for I had eaten nothing all day. Sitting up, I voiced my agreement to his suggestion. In response, Draco lowered the window and leaned out to give Will, the driver, the necessary instructions. I shivered a little as the night air struck me, for now that the sun had set, the spring breeze had once more turned cool. Finding my cloak in the darkness, I drew it on for warmth and set about making myself presentable. I smoothed my crushed traveling ensemble beneath the folds of my cape and made sure all my buttons, hooks, and tapes were fastened. Then I searched the carriage seat for my scattered hairpins and wound my loose tresses up as best I could in a chignon at my nape. After that, I placed my hat upon my head and tied its ribbons beneath my chin. Lastly I retrieved my gloves and reticule from one corner of the vehicle.

There was nothing more to do after that, so I sat quietly, watching the shadows that danced across Draco's face as the flickering light cast by the bouncing coach lanterns shone through the dark, gleaming windows. I wondered how far we had come, but the countryside was shrouded in blackness, so I had no way of knowing and was forced to ask my cousin.

"We are just outside of Highbridge," he told me.

I could scarcely credit the fact that we had covered nearly a hundred miles of road. But as I could think of no cause for him to lie to me, I saw no reason to disbelieve him.

We must have stopped to change horses several times, I thought.

Yet the effects of the brandy and laudanum had been such that I had not awakened. I wondered if that had been part of Draco's motive for drugging me, so that in case I changed my mind about wedding him, I should be asleep and unable to beg for aid until I had been gone from home so long that it would not matter if I did attempt to escape from him? I decided it probably had been, for I would not have put such a thing past him. I was all too familiar with his devilish nature for that.

At last the coach turned off the main road and came to a halt before the St. George and the Dragon. Upon hearing our arrival, an hostler hurried from the stables to unharness the lathered horses and lead them away, while Draco assisted me from the carriage. By the cheerful glow of the inn's lamps, I saw that while small, it was clean and well kept and not a place I would hesitate to enter, as, suspecting the type of establishment my cousin was prone to frequent, I had half feared. We opened the door and went inside, and the portly innkeeper came forward from behind his desk to greet us. Draco, displaying a weighty purse—I wondered how he had come by so much money—bespoke the private dining room for us, as well as a single bedchamber. My heart sank at the implication of this last, but even I realized how strange it would seem if he were to request adjoining rooms when I had no abigail accompanying me.

"I want the best you have, my good man," my cousin insisted. "My wife is with child, and I should like her to rest comfortably. We have had a harrowing day. My wife's maid fell and sprained her ankle and so had to be left behind; and my wife herself felt faint earlier and so has not eaten." The lies rolled so smoothly from his tongue that I half believed them myself. "Thus, although I know it is late, I should like some sort of supper served to us also."

"Never you fear, sir," the innkeeper declared, having judged the cut of Draco's jib and the extent of his purse and thus being eager to please. "The bedchamber is the largest in the inn, and the bed itself has a fine feather mattress. As for supper, why, you shall find no better cook than my wife. She can prepare something in a trice. If you'll step this way, sir. . . ."

He led us past the brightly lit common room, where a few male travelers were hunched over tankards of ale, to the more intimate private dining room. We had not waited very long when the innkeeper's wife appeared, bearing a tray laden with steaming bowls of thick mutton stew and early sweet peas, and plates of fruit, cheese, and bread. The innkeeper had not exaggerated about his wife's cooking ability, and Draco and I fell upon the savory fare with relish, though I scarcely sipped my wine.

Afterward we retired to our bedchamber, where, despite my objections, Draco tossed me down upon the soft feather bed and made love to me until I moaned with ecstasy—and hated him more than ever for making me feel as though perhaps I did not truly hate him at all. Silently he smoked a cheroot afterward, while I wept quietly into my pillow, thoroughly bewildered by my conflicting emotions toward him.

Thus was established the pattern of the days that followed. They continued to have an unreal, dreamlike quality to me; I seemed to live them in a perpetual state of torpor. Though I felt certain Draco did not drug me again— nor did he ply me with liquor—still I could not rid myself of the sluggishness that permeated my being. My mind felt as though it were full of cobwebs, my body dragged down by heavy weights. I did not know what was wrong with me; I was afraid I had been beset by some strange wasting sickness.

"It is the child growing inside you, Maggie," Draco said when finally I grew so scared that I told him of my fear. "Did no one ever tell you how mentally and physically draining pregnancy is?"

Of course I had expected tiredness—but nothing like this. Everything I had ever heard had centered on the unpleasantness of morning sickness, of which I had none. Nothing had ever prepared me for this haziness of mind, this leadenness of limbs. I felt like a sloth; I did naught but sleep and eat—this last so ravenously that I was mortified by the amount of food I consumed. But Draco only laughed and said teasingly that he hoped he would be strong enough to carry me over the threshold upon our return home. Certainly my enormous appetite did nothing to diminish his desire for me. He took me when he pleased, undeterred by my protests.

Yet, curiously, for I had not expected it, he was kind to me. He saw to my every need and comfort, arrogantly demanding—and paying for—the best whenever we stopped at a posthouse to change horses, dine, or spend the night. I did not ask where my cousin had got the money he showered so freely upon hostlers and innkeepers alike, sensing he would not tell me the truth, but would fob me off with some careless remark. Still I wondered at the source of his funds and thought perhaps there was some veracity, after all, to the stories of his having a king's ransom stashed under his mattress.

Now that some of my initial fright had receded, I observed, too, that during his three-year absence from northern Cornwall, he had acquired some taste and polish as well. His clothes were very fine and, surprisingly, impeccable, though he had no valet to assist him; and his manners would have found favor in any fashionable drawing room. It was small wonder that merchants and lackeys alike scurried to do his bidding, never dreaming they bowed and scraped before a Gypsy bastard. From the supercilious twist of his mouth, I suspected that their attitude amused Draco no end, that he took perverse delight in deceiving them, as, with his insolent note, he had deceived my father.

I felt a sense of impending doom whenever I thought of Sir Nigel, for even though we had seen no signs of pursuit, I could not help but think he was hard on our heels, despite the fact that Draco's missive had specifically warned him against this. I realized my cousin also did not expect my father to do as instructed, for we continued to travel at a furious pace, so that by the time the coach rolled across Scotland's border into Gretna Green, we had journeyed roughly four hundred miles in four days.

By then, I was so exhausted that I remember little of our wedding, except that it was not at all what I had dreamed of as a child or planned with Esmond when I had thought he loved me. Scottish law required neither the posting of the banns nor a special license in order for two people to marry. No vicar officiated at the ceremony. Instead, just after midnight, Draco and I repeated our vows in the shabby parlor of the village blacksmith, who, though he grumbled about being roused from his bed at such an hour, was obviously used to being wakened by runaway couples desirous of being married as quickly as possible. Will and Ned, the coachmen, served as our witnesses.

I was appalled by the entire hole-in-the-corner affair. I felt degraded, as though I had been the victim of a crime. I could not believe we had traveled so far for so little.

Even after the wedding was over, I found it difficult to grasp the fact that Draco and I were truly married. There had been no Mass; the yawning blacksmith had made a hasty jumble of the ceremony itself. Only my husband's heavy gold ring upon my finger and his bold black signature scrawled upon our wedding certificate were real to me. *Draco Chandler*, he had written, as though he had every right to use the family name. How Sir Nigel should rant and rave upon seeing that, I reflected wryly. Still it would avail him nothing. The deed was done. I was legally married to my Gypsy cousin, and even my father would not be able to untie the knot that bound us.

I did not know whether to laugh or cry over that.

Chapter Nineteen

I Leave Highclyffe Hall

Revenge is a kind of wild justice,...

—*Of Revenge*
Francis Bacon

I had been gone for nearly a fortnight when at last I returned to Highclyffe Hall. The hour was late, but lights still shone through the windows of the manor, evidence that Sir Nigel and Lady Chandler had not yet retired; and weary to the bone, I realized with a sinking heart that I would not be spared the ordeal of facing them this night. In sharp contrast to my anxiety, Draco's demeanor, as he assisted me from the carriage, was one of grim satisfaction, and I knew he, at least, relished the prospect of the imminent confrontation.

I trembled with apprehension as I stood upon the doorstep of the house from which I had dared to run away; but my husband's stance was bold, and he pounded the brass knocker so peremptorily that I thought it would fall off the massive oak portal. In response, Iverleigh, deeply affronted, jerked open the door, intending, I had no doubt, to deliver a sharp rebuke to the culprit responsible for the disturbance. But his heated words died on his lips when he caught sight of us.

"Miss Chandler!" His eyebrows flew up with astonishment. "M–M–Mr. Draco—" Flustered at hearing himself address a former stableboy in such a manner, the butler broke off abruptly, and my husband's upper lip curled jeeringly.

"Is Sir Nigel at home?" he inquired of Iverleigh curtly.

"In the library, but—"

"Excellent," Draco drawled, smiling unpleasantly. Then, taking hold of my arm, he imperiously shouldered our way past the discomposed butler. "You need not bother to announce us; we shall show ourselves in. Oh, and, Iverleigh, see that we're not disturbed, won't you? There's a good fellow."

Although he had not set foot in the manor since his father's death, my husband had not forgotten the arrangement of its rooms; and now, half dragging me along, he strode swiftly through the hall, down the corridor past the small drawing room and the billiard room, to the library. Without bothering to knock, he flung open the door.

My father was seated in his wheelchair before the hearth, where a fire burned to take the chill from the cool spring night. Close at hand on an occasional table sat a silver tray with a decanter of whiskey and a half-empty glass upon it. A book lay open on his lap, but I did not think he was reading, for he was not turning the pages, but, rather, staring into the flames. I drew up short at the sight of him, shocked by his appearance. In the short time I had been gone, he seemed to have aged twenty years. Surely his hair was whiter and thinner than it had been before I had run away. Surely his eyes were more bloodshot, puffier, and ringed with darker circles, his jowls heavier, slacker. Had he always been so corpulent and slovenly? Surely not. I did not remember him being so. His collar was open, his cravat was askew, and he had spilled whiskey down the front of his white cambric shirt. His waistcoat seemed too tightly stretched across his girth, and the shawl draped over his knees was disarranged. I could not credit the change in him; I would have felt sorry for him had I not known how he would scorn my pity.

Now, angered at being so rudely intruded upon, Sir

Nigel's head jerked up fiercely. Then slowly, at our entrance, he swung his wheelchair around to face us and propelled himself forward until he came to a halt in the middle of the room, his wintry eyes and set jaw the only outward signs of his deep rage. He spared not even a glance for me, his only child; instead, coldly, his gaze met and held Draco's, so it seemed the two men were locked in a contest of wills that would be ended only when one of them looked away. For an extremely long, tense moment, no one moved and the room was deathly still. My mouth was dry with fear that violence should be done, for though I knew he was physically incapable of such a thing, I half expected my father to leap from his wheelchair and lunge savagely at Draco's throat. And though I could not imagine even Draco attacking a man unable to defend himself bodily, still I could not be certain of my husband's actions if provoked. Finally, to my relief, a log sparked and cracked in the hearth, and Draco's mouth curved wolfishly.

"*Samson Agonistes*, sir?" he asked mockingly, breaking the silence that lay heavily upon us as he observed the open book upon my father's lap. "An interesting choice. I prefer *Les Liaisons dangereuses* myself. Let me see . . . how does that line go? Ah, yes. 'Revenge is a dish best served cold.' "

"I shall see you hanged," Sir Nigel ground out suddenly through clenched teeth, his hands tightening on the metal tires of his wheelchair.

"I think not," my husband rejoined dryly, a taunting smile on his face. "You see, sir, I found that Maggie pleased me very well, and so I married her."

My father inhaled sharply at the news; his face drained of color, as though he had been struck a stunning blow. Then, and only then, did he glance at me, his eyes hard and unrelenting as they appraised me. I knew only too well what he saw, for I, more than anyone, was painfully aware of the spectacle I presented.

In the coach, before our arrival at the Hall, Draco had once more chosen to demand his husbandly rights of me; and afterward, when I would have straightened my appear-

ance, he had bidden me refrain from doing so, threatening
me with dire consequences if I disobeyed. Now I clutched
my crumpled gloves and reticule in one hand; my cloak, as
Draco had insisted, was draped over my arm so my
dishevelment was fully exposed. With my loose, tangled
hair, my spencer open, my blouse unbuttoned at the collar,
and my skirts wrinkled, I looked exactly as my husband had
wished me to look before Sir Nigel, as what I was: a woman
who had recently been made love to—thoroughly and well.
Two bright spots of color rose high in my cheeks as my
father's eyes calculated the extent of the damage that had
been done to me. Then, his mouth tightening with marked
distaste, he disdainfully dismissed me.

"Leave us, Margaret," he ordered icily, no longer
staring at me, but at Draco.

"But—but . . . Father—" I beseeched, unable to believe he intended to say nothing more to me than that.

"Leave us, I said! This matter no longer concerns you!
Indeed it never did. You have been but a pawn this blackguard used to his advantage!"

"No—"

"Do as he says, Maggie," Draco commanded softly.
"Sir Nigel is right: This is between him and me. Go on.
Fetch whatever you may need from your room, and direct
your abigail to pack the rest. You shall not be staying here
or ever returning to this house again."

His eyes were filled with understanding and pity for
me; and in that moment, I could no longer deny what we
had both known all along: that my father had no love for
me, his daughter, but cared only for his pride and his name.
Yet deep down inside, I had still hoped somehow for more
than that, and now that it was not forthcoming, Sir Nigel's
rejection hurt far more deeply than I would have thought
possible. I could not believe he had no concern for me when
he had every reason to suppose that I, gently bred and, to
the best of his knowledge, a virgin, had been brutally
kidnapped and ill-used by his bastard nephew. Tears stung
my eyes at his lack of regard for me, but I was too proud to
let them fall. I would not give my father the satisfaction of

seeing how he had wounded me. Biting my lip to keep from sobbing aloud, I turned away, and the reassuring squeeze Draco gave my hand as I did so was small comfort indeed. With an aching heart, I left the two men alone together in the library, no longer caring if they killed each other; for it was in that moment that I was made fully and bitterly aware of what it meant to be a woman in a man's world and that I came as close to understanding my stepmother and Julianne as I ever would.

Though dimly I had realized these things before, now I saw with cruel clarity that because I had had the great misfortune to be born a female, I was a prisoner as surely as though I were shackled by chains, legally bound first to my father and now to my husband. I had no rights of my own. I could not vote, and so I had no voice in the laws that governed me. I could not own property, and so I must be dependent upon whatever some man chose to bestow upon me. I could be bartered by Sir Nigel to salvage his pride and his name, and no one would care, for it was the lot of a woman to be bought and sold to the man who would best endow her family with power and wealth or spare them the agony of scandal and disgrace. I could be beaten, locked away in a madhouse, or raped by Draco, and no one would lift a finger in my defense, for it was the lot of a woman to be nothing but her husband's chattel, to belong to him as surely as his house, his carriage, and his velvet smoking jacket did. Within the next few minutes, how I spent the remainder of my life would be determined in my father's library, and I was not even to be permitted the privilege of being present while the decision was made.

It was not to be borne. Yet somehow I must bear it, as all women must. It must be enough that I had secured my future by my marriage, that my husband was reasonably able to provide for me so I should not want, and that while he might be hard and cold, he was unlikely to black my eye, have me declared insane, or install a mistress under my roof, as many men had been known to do to their wives. It must be enough that I was content with my house and my child, no matter how bored I might grow with nothing more than domestic matters—more often than not adequately attended to by a staff of servants in any event—to occupy my time and challenge my bright mind. It must be enough that I appeared at all times serenely composed and well groomed, that I sit at the foot of my husband's table and make polite conversation with his guests, and that I be ready and waiting in his bed when he chose to retire. And if by some chance I should ever long for more than that, well . . . I must suppress my longings, because there was nothing I could do about them anyway in a world where women existed solely to make men's lives more comfortable.

I was Mrs. Draco Chandler, a woman of scandal perhaps, but a woman wedded to a smart, strong, ambitious man, even if some did think him nothing more than a Gypsy bastard. I would not be separated from my child, forced to labor in a sweatshop, to sell myself upon a street corner, or be cast into a workhouse. And if ever being Mrs. Draco Chandler, mistress of Stormswept Heights, mother of my child, and the proud possessor of some new trinket was not enough, well . . . it *must* be enough, because it was all I—or any other gentlewoman—had.

Slowly, ignoring the curious, speculative glances of Iverleigh and Mrs. Seyton, the housekeeper, who had busied themselves in the hall, pretending duties they did not have, I trudged up the stairs to the second story and made my way to my bedchamber in the south wing. There I was greeted by a fat bundle of fur bounding into my arms.

"Grimalkin!" I exclaimed, burying my face against the cat's soft, silky black coat. "Grimalkin! How could I have forgotten about you?"

The cat was nine years old now, but it still retained much of the vigor and playfulness of its youth. Now, happy to see me, it licked my face exuberantly with its rough tongue, its loud, intermittent purring sounding like the rattling of bones in its throat. My own throat tightened with emotion at the familiar noise, and now the tears I had held at bay in the library slipped down my cheeks to drip freely upon Grimalkin's fur. But finally, not knowing how much time I had before Draco sent for me, I forced myself to place the cat in its basket, latching the lid shut. Then, taking a portmanteau from the bottom of my wardrobe, I began to pack my most treasured possessions, too upset even to wonder why Linnet had not come to help me.

Shortly thereafter, a knock upon my door interrupted me, and before I could ask who stood without, Lady Chandler swept into my chamber. I had never before witnessed her in such a state, and for a moment, I could only stare at her, speechless with shock. Her long hair was unbound, the first time I had ever seen it so, and a startling streak of white that had not been there previously now sprang from her forehead to cut a visible swath through her blond locks. Her eyes were swollen and red-rimmed from weeping, and she looked gaunt as a chimney sweep. So distracted was her manner that I feared at first that she had lost her reason. Still she seemed sane enough as, twisting a damp lace handkerchief nervously in her hands, she stepped forward to greet me.

"My God, Margaret!" she burst out, grasping my hands tightly in hers. "Are you all right? No. what a stupid question! How could you be? Oh, that dreadful, despicable man! That diabolical Gypsy bastard! How dared he? *How dared he?*" Her voice caught on a sob. Trembling, she turned away, pressing her handkerchief to her mouth as she tried to compose herself. After a moment, she continued raggedly.

"Nigel blames me for everything, you know," she confessed, revealing the cause of her extreme agitation. "He has been so cruel to me—*me*, his own wife!—that I've hardly been able to bear it!" She sniffed pathetically at the injustice she felt had been done her. "It just isn't fair. It just isn't fair at all—" She broke off abruptly. Then, pacing the floor, she went on.

"My God! I shall never forget Nigel's face when he received Draco's vile note. He grew so enraged, so mottled with red that I thought—I thought that he was having an apoplectic fit, that he would drop dead on the spot! Oh, it was horrible, Margaret! *Horrible!* You—you have no idea. . . . He read the note to me. His eyes—his eyes were so terrible. They felt like hot coals burning me when he glared at me. He said that it was all my fault, that I ought to have been a better chaperon to you; and indeed I—I suppose I should have paid more attention to your comings and goings and not allowed you to dispense with the groom on these jaunts of yours! But I was so busy with Esmond and Julianne's wedding—Besides, who would have thought? I mean . . . you didn't have any suitors," she pointed out uncharitably. "It wasn't as though you were sneaking off to conduct an *affaire de coeur* or anything. So to what harm, really, could you have come upon the moors—you, the baronet's daughter? Why, Nigel would have killed any man who dared to lay a hand on you! Who would have dreamed, then, that Draco would prove so barbaric as to spirit you away and—and—"

"Please, Stepmama," I murmured soothingly, sensing she was on the verge of hysterics. "Please. Sit down, and let me fetch you a glass of water. You are overwrought, and that is not like you. There is nothing for you to worry about. Draco and I are married—"

"Married? *Married!* You fool!" she wailed, turning on me without warning. "You utter fool! Do you think that makes everything all right? Why, even if Draco found favor in Nigel's eyes, marriage to a Gypsy bastard cannot be thought other than an appalling misalliance for a baronet's daughter; and no doubt under the circumstances, Nigel would rather see you dead than wed to his illegitimate nephew!"

"Yes, no doubt," I agreed dryly, remembering how my father had dismissed me as though I no longer existed for him. "Still it is done, and there is no undoing it now."

"But there is. *There is!*" Lady Chandler cried suddenly, her eyes lighting with hope. "You are underage. We can have the marriage annulled, hush up the scandal somehow. No one who matters knows the truth of the affair. When you didn't return home, we told everyone you had been taken ill at the Grange and were convalescing there. Tiberia and Sarah won't say anything to the contrary—Nigel would throw them out to fend for themselves if they did—and we can get rid of those few servants who know differently. Oh, how fortunate it was that Nigel was forced to take to his bed after receiving Draco's note and so could not pursue you. How very wise he was not to send anyone else in his stead, knowing none but he was a match for Draco or could be trusted to keep quiet about the deed. Yes, you'll see, Margaret," Lady Chandler babbled on eagerly. "Things can be put aright, and then perhaps Nigel will forgive me—"

"No, Stepmama, the marriage will stand, I assure you," I said. "I was not underage in Gretna Green; I did not require Father's consent there to wed. And as the marriage has already been . . . consummated, there are no other grounds for an annulment."

At that, Lady Chandler finally sank down in a chair, stunned.

"Oh, Margaret, you wretched girl!" she moaned at last, blanching. "Why did you ever agree to such a thing? Oh, not—not . . . the consummation part. I'm sure that evil Gypsy gave you no choice about that. He is no gentleman; that much is patently clear. But . . . marriage . . . and—and Gretna Green? Such a long journey . . . all the way to Scotland's border. . . . Did you have no chance to escape, then? Surely someone would have helped you had you informed them of your plight. And—and how could a man of the cloth perform a wedding ceremony you were unwilling to undergo?" She massaged her temples tiredly. "I'm—I'm afraid I don't understand. . . ."

"No, I know you don't, and perhaps 'tis best that way. Just believe me, Stepmama, when I tell you I had good cause to act as I did. I made no attempt to escape—I had no wish to do so—and besides, Draco made sure it was impossible. Further, as I was quite willing to marry my husband, there was no reason for the village blacksmith— we had no priest; none is needed in Scotland—to refuse to perform the ceremony."

"I . . . see," she stated slowly. My words had angered and puzzled her, I knew, for now she ceased to cry and stiffened her spine, regaining a good deal of her composure. "Well, perhaps I am not as much to blame, then, as I thought, for this underhanded affair," she declared, calculating, I could see, how best to turn this realization to her advantage. "Indeed, quite frankly, I have always suspected you and Draco cared for each other with far more than just cousinly affection, Margaret, even though you were betrothed to Esmond and professed to love him. Now it seems clear to me that I was right. Certainly you wasted little time after Esmond and Julianne's wedding in flinging yourself into Draco's arms. No doubt, if the truth were known, he neither abducted you nor forced himself on you at all!" Her eyes narrowed suddenly, shrewdly. "Yes, that is it, isn't it?" she breathed triumphantly. "You and Draco planned this together—in the hope that the shock and the scandal would destroy Nigel. Yes, yes! I can see it all now. You have always despised him—the both of you! And all because of that unnatural horse—may it rot in hell! You have hated Nigel ever since it had to be destroyed. You never cared that it left him paralyzed, that he suffers every day of his life from excruciating pain, which he must take more and more opium to subdue. You would stop at nothing to see him brought down!"

"That's not true, Stepmama!"

"Isn't it?" She laughed scornfully, in full control of herself now that she had spied a way to redeem herself in my father's eyes. "Oh, don't bother to deny it, Margaret. You've always had an easy face to read." She paused. "Well, you shall learn that Nigel is made of sterner stuff than that, you wicked girl! And to think he was finalizing arrangements for you to marry Lord Broughton, whom you met in London and whom I had at last succeeded in persuading to wed you! Oh, yes. You didn't know that, did you? It was to be a surprise—to console you for losing Esmond to Julianne. Only consider, Margaret, what you have thrown away because of your stupidity and spite! You might have been Lady Broughton, a rich and powerful countess! And I . . . I would have helped you make your mark in society; I would have taught you how to use your position to become one of the leaders of polite circles! You had the necessary background and the spirit; all you lacked was the knowledge, the means. Nigel shan't live forever, you know. Together we could have accomplished a great deal, secured our future. We could have had it all. . . .'' Her voice trailed away as she realized how much she had revealed to me.

The depths of her ambition and scheming astounded me, for I saw only too well now why she had developed a fondness for me, had offered to help me if ever I should stand in need. When my father died, she had planned to use my rank and wealth as Lady Broughton to catch herself a third husband. No doubt she had hoped for an earl or even a duke. The woman was incorrigible!

Still, understanding now, so painfully, what it meant to be trapped in a female body, I could not find it in my heart to condemn my stepmother. She was as much a victim of circumstance as I. What, indeed, would be left to her upon Sir Nigel's death but to find another husband? If she did not, she would be nothing more than the Dowager Lady Chandler, subject to Julianne's whims and Esmond's purse. How could I blame her for wanting more than that and for using whatever means she had at her disposal to achieve it? Perhaps in her place, I should have done the same.

Now, seeing that I had guessed her ulterior motive in befriending me, she shrugged in the French fashion.

"Ah, well." She sighed, dismissing the matter as though it were of little importance. " 'Tis too late now for all that, Margaret. You have chosen to make yourself an object of notoriety and derision instead, and no decent person will have anything to do with you in the future." Abruptly she rose. "I wish you joy of your Gypsy bastard, Margaret," she said coolly. "Indeed I begin to believe the two of you are eminently well suited!"

With that parting shot, she lifted her chin haughtily and sailed from the room, headed, I felt certain, to inform my father of her speculations about Draco and me. I should have been upset by the notion. But oddly enough, I felt nothing but an overwhelming relief that because of my husband, I should be spared marriage to Lord Broughton, a man I remembered as being much older than I, with hot, greedy eyes; thin, cruel lips; and groping, clawlike hands. The thought that Sir Nigel had actually intended me to wed such a horrible old man destroyed my last shred of feeling for him. I no longer cared that he did not love me. For the first time, I was *glad* I had given myself to Draco and run away to marry him. Fervently I hoped my father choked on that knowledge!

I quickly finished cramming my things into my bag. Then, gathering it up, along with Grimalkin's basket, I gave one final look around the chamber that had been mine since childhood. Draco was right; I should not be coming back here. Stiffening my spine, I walked from the room, not bothering to close the door behind me. But after turning the corner of the hall, I discovered I was not yet to make good my escape. Sir Nigel, his interview with Draco obviously having concluded, was poised at the head of the stairs, blocking my path. Bascombe, his hulking attendant, had carried him up the steps just in time for my stepmother to intercept them; and now, silently, the servant hovered behind my father's wheelchair, waiting for him to indicate whether he wished to be pushed to his bedchamber. Nearby stood Lady Chandler herself, her head flung up victoriously, that inscrutable half-smile upon her lips. So, she had indeed told Sir Nigel her suspicions, then; and now that she believed she had won his forgiveness with the news she had hastened to impart to him, she felt secure in her authority and position once more.

Taking a deep breath, I continued on down the corridor, my heart pounding as though I were still a child and had been summoned to my father's study for some transgression. I would have passed him by without stopping or speaking, but he motioned to Bascombe to detain me, effectively preventing me from eluding him. That he would have his attendant lay hands upon me showed me the extent of his contempt for me. But still I faced him unflinchingly, coldly jerking my arm from Bascombe's grasp. The brute started to grab me again, but Sir Nigel stayed him with an upraised hand.

"I have spoken with your stepmother, Margaret," he

said, a subtle note of menace in his tone, "and she has told me an entirely different version of this sorry affair than I had previously been led to believe. I should like to hear from your own lips now the truth of the matter, miss. Did that—that *despicable scum*"—he pointed to Draco, who now stood at the foot of the stairs, leaning against the newel post—"forcibly remove you from this estate or not?"

For a moment, from long habit, I was tempted to lie to protect myself. Then I thought: *I have nothing to fear from this man, and I no longer care what he thinks of me. Why should I defend myself? I am done trying to win his favor. He has hurt me for the very last time.*

"No," I replied tersely, surprised to hear how calm my voice sounded. "And what's more, I'm glad, Father. I'm *glad*, do you hear?" I repeated the words fiercely, savoring the sound of them.

Sir Nigel's face whitened with incredulity at my temerity; he had not expected it, I could tell. Then he turned scarlet with wrath, an ugly blue vein popping out on his forehead and pulsing so hard that I thought he should have a stroke. His eyes blazed.

"By God!" he thundered. "You brazen hussy! I'll blot your name out of the family Bible for this if it's the last thing I ever do!"

"Then do it—and see if I care, you hateful old tyrant!" I shot back, shaking with the sudden intensity of my emotions. "That's what you tried to do to my mother, wasn't it? Pretend that she didn't exist? But she did, and I do. And nothing you say or do is ever going to change that! But you can't accept that, can you? No, you can't. You're pompous and mean. You have to dominate everyone and everything around you—just as you tried to dominate my mother, and Black Magic, too. But you couldn't crush *them*, could you? No, you couldn't break them to your will, because they died rather than submit to you, you—you *despot*! And now they're free, just as I am!"

"Free!" my father snorted, enraged that I had dared to speak to him in such a manner. "They're not free—and neither are you, you execrable chit! They're dead, and you're shackled to a no-good Gypsy bastard who doesn't give a damn about you one way or another—except as a means of revenging himself on me. My God! What a fool you are! Your mother, pathetic as she was, was worth ten of you! Why, you're no better than a common whore!"

"How dare you?" I shouted, my head now throbbing so furiously with anger that I thought I would faint. "Shut up! Shut up, or you'll be sorry, I promise you."

"Don't threaten me, miss," Sir Nigel sneered, "especially when you haven't got the guts to back it up with."

At that, something inside me snapped so violently that it was as though I had received a crushing blow to my skull. A red mist formed before my eyes, my head reeled, my heart pounded so hard that I thought it would explode. A great roaring sounded in my ears, and I seemed to lose all control of myself. It felt as though the tiny part of me that was still sane wrenched itself from my body, and I had the strangest sensation that I was floating in midair, looking down at myself and watching with horror as I suddenly went as berserk as a rabid dog.

I shall never forget the surprise and disbelief on my father's face in that moment as I dropped my portmanteau and Grimalkin's basket where I stood and sprang at him wildly, meaning to seize him and shake him until he took back the ugly things he had said about me and my mother. But Sir Nigel did not scare easily. With one powerful fist, he hit me so hard that I staggered and fell, dizzy and breathless from the stunning blow to my head. Then, his face murderous at the thought that I had dared to raise a hand against him, he propelled his wheelchair toward me, determined, I realized dazedly, to roll over me and crush me if he could. I was only dimly aware of Lady Chandler's terrified screams as she stood rooted to the floor; of the stricken expressions of Draco, Iverleigh, and Mrs. Seyton below; of Bascombe's lunging forward to try to haul me from beneath the wheels of the contraption as I struggled blindly to escape. As though in a dream, I saw myself grab one metal tire in a futile attempt to stop its ominous turning motion, even as Bascombe yanked me away, causing me to lose my grip on the tire, making the vehicle spin about crazily from the impetus. His mouth hanging open ludicrously, my father clutched the sides of the seat to keep from being pitched off as the sudden, erratic shifting of his weight made the wheelchair tilt alarmingly. It teetered on one tire before crashing down upon the floor and smashing into the balustrade that enclosed the landing. Desperately Sir Nigel clung to the railing in an attempt to halt the careening contraption, but it lurched around the corner of the bannister, the left tire bouncing from the landing to the top stair, throwing him brutally against the railing as the wheelchair rocked dangerously on the edge of the step. Then suddenly Draco was there, lifting man and vehicle as one and shoving them back onto the landing, while I wept with shock and fright that my husband would not be strong enough to save my father; for despite all he had done to me, I did not wish for his death.

"Hush, Maggie, hush," Draco crooned quietly, enfolding me in his arms now as Bascombe released me. "It's all over, my brave-hearted girl. It's all over. Come, love. Let me take you home."

Retrieving my bag and Grimalkin's basket, Draco guided me down the stairs, one arm wrapped about my waist to hold me steady, for now that the terrible incident had ended, I trembled, weak with fear, at what had nearly happened, how close Sir Nigel had come to toppling down the stairs. No sound but my father's labored breathing broke the silence as we crossed the hall and Draco opened the front door, pausing for a moment on the threshold to gaze back at Sir Nigel.

"You are a fool, old man." He spoke with a strange note of pity in his voice to my father. "A very great fool indeed, for out of all you ever had, we were the best."

After that, we walked out into the night, leaving Highclyffe Hall behind.

BOOK THREE

A Woman's Naked Truth
1819–1820

Chapter Twenty

By Our Beginnings

Youth, what man's age is like to be doth show;
We may our ends by our beginnings know.

—*Of Prudence*
Sir John Denham

Stormswept Heights, England, 1819

I have heard it said that when a door in one's life closes,
another opens, and so it was for me. I had left Highclyffe
Hall behind, but Stormswept Heights lay ahead, and to my
surprise, I now looked forward to its refuge. I needed a
haven where I could assess my life and come to grips with it.

The drive to the manor was quiet, Draco understanding
that I was still in a state of shock born of my father's savage
attack upon me and his resulting near accident. Even now, I
could not believe he had truly wanted to hurt—perhaps even
to kill—me. Yet he had. And still if he had fallen down the
stairs in the attempt, I should have felt somehow to blame; I
should have carried the guilt of his death upon my conscience for the rest of my life, as surely as he bore the guilt
of my mother's death upon his. I did not want to be like
him, but now, because of my own stormy outburst toward
him, I feared there was more of my father in me than either

he or I had hitherto suspected. I had not known I was capable of such anger, such violence.

It was not a pleasant revelation, and though I yearned to put it from my mind, I knew I must face it and deal with it instead. The Chandlers had always been a ruthless, hot-tempered lot, and I, it seemed, was no exception. Perhaps Lady Chandler's assessment of Draco and me had not been so wrong after all. Perhaps we were indeed well suited.

From beneath my lashes, I stole a glance at my husband. He had once saved my life, and now he had taken me away from my father, who hated me. Surely I owed Draco more than I could ever repay for that. Yet he had asked for nothing in return but my loyalty, had taken nothing from me that I had not already given to him freely that night upon the moors. I had thought I knew him, but now I realized I scarcely understood him at all. What manner of man was he, this strange, brooding cousin I had married? Perhaps I would never know; he kept so much locked inside himself. Yet now, to my surprise, I found myself wanting to learn more of him. But I did not know how to tell him that, how to breach the walls of pain and emotion that stood between us; and so in silence, we rode on toward the Heights.

Previously I had paid little heed to the ruined estate, for it had held no significance for me. But now, as the coach clattered through the open gates and past the lodge to wend its way up the drive flanked by tall, twisted trees, I leaned forward with an unfamiliar eagerness as my new home came into sight.

The Heights was very old, having been built during the thirteenth century, and although various improvements had been made over the years, especially during the reign of the Tudors, its origins as a fortified manor were still evident in its archaic structure: in the finely carved and timbered gatehouse, in the crenellated curtain wall, and in the two large, round towers at its north and south ends. More than this, I could not see until we had passed beneath the gatehouse itself into the stone courtyard formed by the curtain wall. Then the rest of the manor was revealed to me.

With the exception of its half-timbered additions, it was constructed entirely of granite that gleamed eerily where struck by the silver moonlight, making the stone cast in shadow seem even darker and greyer in comparison. The house, which was three and a half stories high, counting the attic, loomed over the carriage and was dwarfed in turn by the massive twin Cornish elms that stood like sentries in the courtyard, where the paving blocks had been carefully laid to preserve the ancient trees. The tall, narrow lancet windows that lined the front of the Heights on the two main floors appeared to stare out at us curiously as Draco and I alighted from the coach; light reflecting off the glazed, lozenge panes made them glitter like a thousand eyes in the blackness. An equilateral arch at the center of the manor framed the single ponderous oak door upon which hung a brass knocker carved in the shape of a seagull. The small, square windows of the half story, the remainder of which was below ground, ran along the bottom of the wings.

On the second floor, on either side of the stained-glass cathedral window mounted in the stone facade above the door, were the half-timbered additions. These were fashioned of heavy black beams and stucco that, over the ages, had weathered to a pale silver grey. Set into the steep front peaks of the black slate hip-and-valley roof were the round dormer windows of the attic. Square chimneys protruded from the roof itself; at either end, the towers rose like spires to surmount the manor. Centuries ago, they had served as open watchtowers; now they were capped by turrets, and the crenels bordered twin parapet walks from which one could look out over the land or sea, as I would discover in the coming days. The north turret, encircled with windows, had functioned as a lighthouse in years past, Draco informed me as he pointed it out, saying he hoped to continue this practice once he had completed his restoration of the estate.

He must have sent word of our impending arrival, for the Heights was ablaze with lights and Mrs. Pickering and Renshaw were on hand to welcome us. Now, as my husband swept me up in his arms and carried me over the threshold into the hall, where the two servants waited, Renshaw, tugging his forelock and making an awkward little bow, presented me with a small bouquet of flowers, mumbling how pleased he was to have me as the mistress of the manor. Mrs. Pickering dropped me a curtsy, adding her effusive greeting to his. Then, clucking at Draco and fussing over me like a mother hen, the housekeeper led me away, grumbling under her breath about my husband's lack of sense in bringing me home at such a late hour.

Though I *was* tired, still I could not help but gaze around me with interest, for previously I had seen nothing of the manor except the hall and kitchen. The great hall, as it had properly been called in centuries past, was the oldest and largest room in the house. Its vaulted ceiling soared to the roof, exposing the supporting rafters and curved beams, blackened over the years by the smoke of open fires, though the hearth that had once stood in the center of the room had long since been torn out and a fireplace constructed in the west wall. Because the room was in poor repair and virtually empty, its age and immensity were even more apparent. Here and there, layers of plaster had cracked and fallen away to reveal the original stone walls; and Mrs. Pickering's voice, as she continued to chatter over her shoulder to me, echoed in the cavernous chamber. Stone staircases, with more recent balustrades of oak, angled steeply up the north and south walls to the wings. As I followed the housekeeper up the initial short flight of steps to the north, I could not resist pausing on the bottom landing to peek through an open doorway into what must be the dining room, since it was directly above the kitchen. However, as it was dark inside, I could see little except that it, too, was devoid of trappings, so I turned to continue the long climb to the second story, feeling slightly dizzy as I glanced over the railing at the hall far below, where Draco was relaying orders to Renshaw and the coachmen.

Mrs. Pickering led me down a corridor past several closed doors to an oak portal set into a circular wall, which I guessed formed part of the north tower.

"Here we be, missus," she announced, flinging open the door. "This be Mr. Chandler's bedchamber—and yours, too, now, I expect, since none of the others has any furniture," she confided airily, "though no doubt the master will remedy that, now that he is wed. Will you be wanting a bath before retirin', missus?''

In truth, I was exhausted and longed for bed, but the thought of soaking the journey's dust and strain from my body was appealing, and I was hungry besides.

"Yes, if it's not too much trouble, Mrs. Pickering," I replied, "and a pot of hot tea and something to eat would be nice."

"I'll bring a light repast at once, missus, and instruct Renshaw to fill the bathtub. He's quite good at understandin' things, you know, provided you tell him two or three times. Poor fellow. 'Twas a blow to the head what addled him. Many a year ago now, 'tis been since it happened. Ah, well." She sighed and shook her head. "Ned will bring up your bags shortly, I imagine. If you need anything else, missus, the bell rope's right over there." She indicated a narrow, tasseled length of tapestry hanging from the ceiling. "It *does* work, though a body wouldn't think so around here. Pull once for me. Renshaw seldom comes to the kitchen—spends most of his time in the gatehouse—so he won't hear you, no matter how loud you ring."

Remembering that Mrs. Pickering was deaf, I wondered if she would hear me either, but I merely nodded and thanked her, relieved that circumstances were such that I must share my husband's room. I should not have liked to sleep alone in this desolate old house, with only a deaf woman and a madman to summon in case of need.

After Mrs. Pickering had gone, I took stock of my surroundings. Draco's chamber was quite spacious, and though time and neglect had taken their toll here, as elsewhere, still I could understand why my husband had chosen this room as his. Through the windows, I could see the moon reflecting off the sea just beyond the cliffs that fell away sharply at the edge of the sweeping lawn far below, unkempt now, and overgrown, so it seemed a part of the moors themselves. The tall grass stirred in the breeze, rippling like the quicksilver waves in the distance, and I knew that tomorrow, when the sun had risen, the view would be breathtaking.

Although the chamber was sparsely furnished, its contents had obviously been selected with care, and I saw much to admire in the old and valuable appurtenances. A massive, dark walnut bed, with a huge canopy, a solid headboard carved with a labyrinthine design, and the distinctive melon-bulb footposts of the Tudor period, dominated the room. At its foot was a closed-sided wooden wainscot chair. A single heavy night table stood to one side; an ornate press cupboard sat nearby. Flanking the stone fireplace, where, upon the mantel, a beautifully framed painting of a savage sea reposed, were a washstand and a hammered-brass bathtub. A curved stone stairway led to the lighthouse above and to another empty chamber below, neither of which I wished to explore this night.

After I had finished perusing the room, Mrs. Pickering appeared with a laden tray. Hard on her heels were Ned with my bags and Renshaw with my bathwater. Wondering what had become of Draco, I inquired after him and was told he had retired to his study, where some business matters required his attention. I tried to wait up for him, but the meal and bath proved soporific, and at last, my weariness taking its toll, I could no longer keep my eyes open. Yawning, I climbed into the big bed alone and scarcely stirred when, toward dawn, Draco finally slipped in beside me.

I was startled to awaken in the morning and see Linnet laying out my garments as usual. For one wild moment, hope leaped in my breast, and I thought perhaps my flight to Gretna Green with Draco and what had followed had been a nightmare after all. Then I saw the circular walls that surrounded me, the bright sunlight that streamed in unchecked through the curtainless windows, and I knew it had been no dream. I was indeed married to my Gypsy cousin and lying in his bed in the north tower of Stormswept Heights. Bewildered, I sat up and rubbed my eyes, half wondering if my abigail was a delusion.

"Good mornin', missus," she greeted me cheerfully, "and a fine mornin' it be, too. Feels like spring is here to stay at last."

"Linnet, what are you doing here?"

"Why, I've brought the rest of your things, that's what, and come to wait upon you, just as I always have."

"Do you mean—do you mean you are planning on *staying*?" I asked, incredulous.

"But of course. Sir Nigel will hardly take me back, now that he's discharged me, will he? Turned me off without a reference, he did, the mean old sod! Not that it mattered, mind you, for I'd already told him that I was leavin', that I had no wish to be demoted to a housemaid just because you'd upped and wed Mr. Draco . . . er . . . Chandler, and there wasn't any place for me as an abigail at the Hall anymore. Of course I heard all the commotion last night; who at the Hall didn't? No offense intended, missus, but 'tis too bad the bloomin' nob didn't fall down the stairs and break his bloody neck! 'Twould have served him right! Well, anyway, realizin' what your being married to Mr. Chandler would mean to me, I crept downstairs and slipped outside to ask his coachmen to deliver a message to him for me—that's why I wasn't there to help you last night when you arrived—and this mornin', Mr. Chandler sent a note over offerin' to hire me if I'd pack up the rest of your clothes and such and have them ready and waitin' when Ned and Will came for me. That I did, missus, though 'twas no easy feat, I tell you, tryin' to persuade Tim, the footman, to help me lug your trunks down to the gate. So here I be—and a good thing, too, because from what I've seen, you can use the help, missus."

That, I thought, was true. But still I did not know whether I was glad of Linnet's presence. I had never got over my feeling that she was a sly, devious girl, much like Julianne in that respect, and I had never been able to trust and confide in her as most women did their abigails. Still it seemed unlikely that I would manage to get a respectable girl from the village to take her place. Indeed Draco's servants were an incongruous lot, and now that I had married him—and under such scandalous circumstances, too—I had little doubt that I should be as shunned as he. In truth, I wondered why Linnet wished to become part of such a dubious household. I had not thought her so devoted to me.

"Aye, well, Mr. Chandler's payin' me a pretty penny, missus," she said when I questioned her. "I'd not be makin' so much someplace else—and what's a bit of gossip to the likes of me? I've no care for what the village folk think."

It was then that I remembered Linnet had come from the miners' rows. Sir Nigel had taken her on when her father had been killed in a mining accident; and now, having been turned off without a reference, she was unlikely to find another position.

"Very well." I nodded. "We shall go on as before, then. But, mind, Linnet, you're to do as you're told—and without complaining. I'll have none of your airs here, miss. As you can see, there's a great deal of work to be done—and precious few hands to do it—so we all must pitch in wherever we're needed. Further, I'll not have you blabbing to Sir Nigel's staff about the Heights. 'Tis none of their business what goes on here." I eyed her sharply, for I did not mean to give my father or stepmother the satisfaction of learning any hardships I must now endure as Draco's wife. "If I hear one word spoken in this household repeated elsewhere, out you go."

"Aye, missus. I understand."

"Good. Then we will begin by touring the house and making a list of what needs to be accomplished. But first, I must dress, then speak with . . . er . . . Mr. Chandler." The name Draco had appropriated felt strange upon my lips. "Have you any idea where he is?"

"I believe he be in the study, missus."

The study, I discovered, was on the bottom floor of the south wing, in what I supposed must have originally been the armory. Sunlight shone through the small, high windows of the portion above ground, but still the study was shadowed and gloomy, swathed in dust and debris. Draco sat at a massive desk, a stack of ledgers and papers spread before him.

"Ah, Maggie, I'm glad 'tis you," he said as I knocked

and entered. "There are some matters we must discuss. Sit down." He indicated a chair. "I trust you rested well?"

"Yes. I feel much better today."

"Good. I'm glad to hear it. I've been worried about you, you know. These past few weeks cannot have been easy for you. Fortunately they are behind us now, and we can get on with our lives." He paused, collecting his thoughts, then continued. "Maggie, were you aware that in her will, your mother left you a respectable sum of money to be given to you upon your marriage?"

"Why, no," I answered, startled.

"Well, she did. It was one of the things Sir Nigel and I discussed last evening. He is making arrangements now to have it transferred to you from the trust in which it has been held since her death. I have instructed that it be placed in your name in an account at the bank in Launceston. I want you to understand that it is *your* money, Maggie, to do with as you please. I have no need of it, and I'll have no one saying I married you to get my hands on your inheritance. Under the circumstances, there will be gossip enough as it is without adding fuel to the fire," he remarked dryly. "However, as I have some knowledge about business, while you, I suspect, have none at all, I will, if you like, be happy to advise you with regard to various matters you may want to consider, as I'm sure you will want to continue some of the investments Sir Nigel has made over the years. While I have little liking for him, honesty prevails upon me to admit he has done very well by you with his management of the trust, increasing the original amount your mother left you to five thousand pounds."

"Five—five thousand pounds!" I gasped, stunned.

"Yes, as I said, a respectable sum of money—not a fortune by any means, but enough that you could live comfortably for some time if ever it became necessary. However, as I am in perfect health and well able to provide for you and our coming child, I see no cause for you to worry about your future."

"But you led me to believe you were a pauper, Draco!" I accused.

He smiled with amusement at that.

"Dear Maggie—and to think you married me anyway. Will you hate me very much if I confess I deceived you just a little?"

"But . . . why?"

"Because, my sweet," he rejoined lightly, "I wished to ensure that you wanted me for myself, as I did you."

He was still smiling, but his hooded eyes were watching me in a way that made me think he had spoken truly, and I did not know what to say. I could hardly deny that I wanted him, when after a fortnight in his bed, we both knew differently. Still that was something I did not yet want to face. Swallowing hard, I glanced away, a blush staining my cheeks and my heart suddenly beating too quickly in my breast. For a moment, a strange, curiously expectant silence lay between us. Then Draco leaned back lazily in his creaking chair, and the spell was broken.

"I'm not rich, but I *do* have money, Maggie," he admitted, "enough to keep you and the baby, I promise you."

"Enough for me to begin setting this house to rights as well?"

He laughed.

"Yes, even that, my girl," he consented. "Just don't try to bankrupt me in the process."

"Perhaps I shall at that," I teased, getting to my feet, "for only think what fun I should have if you should suddenly find yourself dependent on *me* for a change. I vow I should show you no mercy, but deal with you as . . . uncharitably as you have me."

"Come now, Maggie," he chided, rising and walking around his desk to take my hands in his. "Confess. Have I truly treated you so terribly?" When I made no reply, he caught my jaw with one hand and tilted my face up to his, stroking my cheek with his thumb. "Have I?" he asked, his voice low.

"No," I whispered.

He bent his head then; his lips brushed mine in a lingering kiss that left me breathless and trembling in his arms.

"I—I must go, Draco. The house is all sixes and

sevens, and I—I have work to do," I stammered, flustered, and tried to pull away from him; but I could not escape so easily.

"Close the door, love," he said softly, his eyes dark and gleaming in a way I had come to know well. "The morning is young yet, and the house will keep."

And so my life at Stormswept Heights began, quite unlike the life I had been reared to expect and certainly would have lived had my husband been anyone other than Draco. I suppose those who knew of it thought our marriage odd; indeed I often thought so myself. But Draco, when I mentioned the matter to him, merely laughed and said as he was quite confident in himself and his abilities, he had no cause to feel threatened by any man—or any woman either, even if she were his own wife and as intelligent and capable as he.

"I am proud that you are, Maggie," he told me. "I should not have wanted you otherwise. I've little use for scatterbrained chits and simpering misses."

His words filled me with pleasure, for I had been praised so seldom that I was like parched earth soaking up the rain of his admiration. I could hardly believe he found the very traits that had often earned me the condemnation of others not only desirable, but actually worthy of his approval. He never talked down to me as Sir Nigel, and even Esmond, had been wont to do, but encouraged me to express my thoughts and emotions, no matter how shocking or ill-considered. Then, if he did not agree with me, Draco would argue with me fiercely; but he never dismissed my opinions as foolish and undeserving of attention.

He gave me a generous amount of pin money, and unlike my father, he did not make me account for a single farthing of it. It was mine to do with as I pleased, just as my inheritance from my mother was; and when the banker in Launceston treated me rudely, he, in turn, was treated to a visit by my coldly enraged husband, who soon set him straight about just who was in charge of my five thousand pounds. Thereafter it was all I could do not to laugh when the banker bowed and scraped before me, hastening to attend to my every financial need.

I could well understand how Lady Chandler had felt after Captain Brodie's death, for now I, too, was like a bird released from a cage. As my stepmother had once told me, ignorance *was* bliss, for now that I knew what I had been missing, I realized just how oppressed I had been before my marriage, and I wanted to weep for having previously been denied what I had now. I had thought Draco would prove my jailer; instead he had set me free. Like a determined fledgling, eagerly I tried my wings, flying high as I dared, secure in the knowledge that although he refused to catch me, my husband would be there to help me up if I fell. With each new experience, I learned my strengths and weaknesses, as well as Draco's.

More than anything, I was, as Lady Chandler had once said, a woman of deep and lasting passions, wild and impetuous, more often than not ruled by my heart instead of my head. I was not made to live life tamely, but to seize it with a vengeance and bend it to my will. My emotional heights were rapturous, my depths all too filled with despair. Yet now that I saw all that life had to offer, I was glad I was not other than what I was; and if sometimes I thought, with faint, disturbing perception, of Esmond, I pushed the dim, unpleasant realization hovering at the edges of my mind away. Esmond was a gentleman and, as such, was not to be compared to Draco, who though he might be a charming rogue was a rogue just the same. Yet I must confess that as time went on, I was not displeased with my husband. I saw a great deal of my father in this iron-willed man I had wed, for he was every bit as shrewd, as clever, as proud, and as arrogant as Sir Nigel. But Draco's character was tempered by an understanding, a compassion, and a sense of humor my father lacked. Draco knew what it was to suffer and want, to be forced to prove himself time and again; and so he did not scorn my own need to reach out, to expand my horizons, to grab life by the throat with both hands and hang on until it was mine to command. Instead he cheered me on with a cool, amused enthusiasm, applauding my victories, commiserating with me over my defeats.

I was both fascinated and frightened by my discoveries, for I soon found that even freedom had a price—the acceptance of responsibility for one's choices—and this burden, my husband did not permit me to thrust upon his shoulders, but forced me to take upon my own, often to my chagrin. Ruthlessly he stripped away my childishness so I became not only a woman, but the woman I truly was, the woman that under different circumstances, I must have subjugated to conform to society's expectations of me. But society had cast me off, and this, too, I soon learned was a blessing in disguise; for I saw that social acceptance was simply another means of compelling women to submit to the authority of men, and in this, men were aided and abetted by women themselves, who would rather be tyrannized or dead than ostracized, so great was their fear of becoming an outcast. But I, who *was* an outcast, discovered there was nothing very much, after all, to fear unless one were bent on being a painted porcelain doll with no words or actions but those given to it by its owner. And so if there were women who swept their skirts aside and crossed the street to avoid me when I passed by, I did not care, but pitied them and their blissful ignorance instead.

In truth, even had I not been tarred by the brush of scandal, I had little time for socializing. I do not think any bride ever worked as hard as I did those first few months at the Heights. Certainly I had never before known what it meant to do manual labor, and for the first time in my life, I understood fully the perpetual exhaustion of the working class and the poor. There were days when I thought I should never again know what it was not to ache with weariness in every bone in my body. But still I drove myself, and the servants, too, relentlessly. It was as though I were compelled by some inner force to set my house in order before the birth of my child. Even Draco, laughing at what he called my "nesting instincts," was pressed into helping.

Beginning with the north tower, we repaired loose and crumbling stones; we ripped out rotten beams, cracked molding, and broken boards and replaced them; we patched, plastered, and painted the walls; we scrubbed, swept, and dusted the tower until it shone as though new. Draco and I turned the room below our bedchamber into a comfortable sitting room for ourselves. I bought furniture, rugs, and material for curtains and linens, and I kept Mrs. Pickering and Linnet busy sewing in the evenings, while I embroidered. For our coming child, Draco carved a beautiful cradle and made no demur when I insisted on its being put in our bedchamber, for the walls at the Heights were a foot thick, and I feared I should not hear the baby crying if it were in a nursery in some other part of the manor.

Indeed I did not want a nursery or a nanny—at least, not as a substitute for myself. I remembered all too clearly my childhood at the Hall, with only my old nurse to love and care for me, and I did not want that for my baby. More than anything, I wanted it instead to feel secure in the knowledge that I loved it deeply, that there had never been a moment when I had not wanted it and joyed in its coming. For I did. In truth, despite all the hardships I must now endure, I was in some ways strangely happier than I had ever been in my life. I was no longer alone; my child grew inside me, and I talked to it often, marveling at its existence in my womb. To think that Draco and I had created a new person seemed a miracle to me. I wondered what it would be like, this tiny being so dependent upon me for survival. Would it be a boy or a girl? Would it look like Draco or me? Would it be exuberant or introspective? I feared for it, for there were so many things that could go wrong, and I prayed every day that it would be a healthy baby. I could hardly wait for it to be born. Much to Draco's amusement, in my anticipation and excitement, I began preparing for our child's arrival long before it ever became necessary.

Because, despite my father's wealth, I had had relatively few possessions growing up, I could scarcely restrain myself when it came to things for the baby. It must have the best of everything: the softest mattress, the finest linens, a sterling silver cup and spoon. When I was not busy working on the house, I made one small garment after another and knitted so many caps and bootees that Draco joked I must be expecting a litter. I did not care. I knew there would be precious few christening gifts forthcoming for my baby, and I was determined it should not lack for aught simply because Draco and I were shunned.

With the exception of Sarah and, more rarely, Welles, no one visited us at the Heights, nor were we invited anywhere. Aunt Tibby, fearing Sir Nigel's wrath, was too scared to associate openly with us and took to her bed, prostrate with nerves, whenever Sarah dared to ride over to see us. Welles, though unafraid of my father, came and went like a shadow, at odd hours, during which time, for the most part, he stayed closeted in the study with Draco or disappeared with him for hours on end, I knew not where. In this only, when I questioned him about it, did my husband refuse to humor me, saying bluntly that I would be wise not to pry into affairs that did not concern me. Thereafter I became so curious with regard to the two men's activities together that my imagination ran wild whenever Welles appeared, and had I not been so certain of Draco's sexual inclinations, I think I should even have suspected him and my stepbrother of unnatural behavior. The notion that doubtless they went whoring together crossed my mind more than once, and for some peculiar reason, the thought of my husband's being unfaithful to me hurt me terribly. I had no proof that he was, but I could not help noticing he desired me less frequently as time passed and I grew heavier with our coming child; and because I was wounded by his withdrawal from me, I knew I was not as indifferent to him as I sought to make us both believe.

I had come to recognize that despite his brutishness, Draco was possessed of a strange magnetism that drew me to him. I no longer thought him ugly, for now I saw that though he lacked the refined features that would have won the hearts of many a fashionable matchmaking mama and her daughter, he was handsome in a coarse, carnal way that appealed to something primitive and earthy in me. There was nothing now in his looks to offend me, nothing about his hard, muscular body to shock me when he strode naked

across our chamber in the mornings, the golden sun streaming in through the windows, turning his dark skin to bronze
and making his black hair shine like jet, damp and slick
from his ablutions. True, his flesh was marred by scars in
places, puckered and white now with age, but I saw in the
slashes and crescents a beauty I would not have seen before,
for they were a testimony to his will to survive.

Draco had begun life in the mean streets of London,
cheated of his inheritance by an accident of birth, and
somehow he had managed to claw his way up out of the
muck in which society would have seen him buried. I could
not help but respect and admire him for that, for the grit and
determination that even now kept him fighting long after
another would have conceded defeat. He worked harder than
anybody I had ever known, rising at six o'clock each
morning and sometimes not retiring until two or three.
When he was not helping me with the house, he was busy
elsewhere: in the fields, where he had planted wheat, oats,
and barley; on the commons, where small herds of black
cattle and white sheep that bore his mark roamed; or in his
study, where he made constant entries in his ledgers. Of
those who served him, he asked naught that he would not or
could not have done himself; of the rest of the world, he
asked nothing. He was what society most hated and feared:
a self-made man—and proud of it. I began to think he had
been right when he had said there was nothing we could not
accomplish together—and the rest of the world be damned.
Society had spit in our eye, and if Draco had anything to say
about it, there would come a day when those who spurned
us regretted it. In the meantime, we must survive as best we
could the circumstances that had set us apart from others of
our ilk. Irrevocably bound together, we must struggle to get
ahead, with only each other for companionship and support.
Once, I had found the thought of wedding my husband
frightening. Now I was as determined as he to join forces
against the world, no matter how fragile our alliance might be.

There were mornings when Draco woke me up and
teased me, tickling me until I begged for mercy and warned
him he would rue his behavior once I had grown fat as a

cow with my pregnancy and could sit on him and weigh him down. There were afternoons when he told me I worked far too hard and he tossed aside my apron to whisk me away in his carriage for an alfresco luncheon upon the moors or to Launceston for some other amusement. There were nights when we sat and talked and he revealed to me more of his thoughts and emotions than I suspected he had ever let anyone else know. But still he held a part of himself aloof from me, a part that was not mine; and oddly I was hurt and troubled by the thought. I felt there was something missing from our relationship, though I would not have cared to give it a name; and in defense, I, too, held a part of myself back, unwilling to risk committing myself totally into Draco's keeping. Though, now and then, he spoke of his love for me, still I could not bring myself to believe him. I knew what manner of man he was, how callously he had used me to gain his revenge on my father, and I would not allow myself to fall prey to his lies. Words meant nothing to him. In truth, I suspected he had said—and still did say—them just as easily to other women, for the less he sought my bed, the more certain I grew that he took his pleasure in arms other than mine.

How quickly he tired of me once I was his! I thought. *He treats me well only because I am his wife. He has no real care for me.*

I told myself I did not love my husband, and so it did not matter whether he loved me; but somehow, strangely, Draco's lack of feeling for me was more painful than either my father's or Esmond's had been. Sometimes, despite the fact that I was, for the most part, happy, I felt horribly ugly and unwanted, and then I would find myself crying over the slightest upsets and worrying that my tears would in some way affect the baby I carried.

It did not help that I knew the entire village gossiped about Draco and me. Sir Nigel, Sarah had informed me, had scotched the scandal of our marriage as best he could. But still where there were servants, there were always whispers of their betters' doings as well, and by now, most everyone was aware that Draco and I had eloped to Gretna Green.

Because there were those who had pitied me when Esmond and I had broken off our engagement, some were disposed to be generous toward me now. Sighing romantically, they insisted I had loved Draco for years and had finally run away with him because my father would not consent to our wedding. But others were not so kind, and they circulated vicious rumors about us and speculated about whether I should have a seven-month child. Worse, the stories about what had happened upon our return to the Hall were so wild and distorted that even those who sympathized with us did not befriend us, fearing reprisals from Sir Nigel if they did so. It was common knowledge that he had stricken my name from the family Bible and, except for my inheritance from my mother, which he could not legally keep from me, had cut me off without a penny for making such a dreadful misalliance. As my father wielded a great deal of power in northern Cornwall, no one wished to offend him, so Draco and I were avoided as much as possible.

Still I refused to be intimidated by the scandalmongers and held my head high whenever I accompanied Mrs. Pickering to the marketplace. Draco, afraid I might lose the baby, had forbidden me to ride and had bought me a pony and trap so I could drive myself wherever I wished. But even so, I confess I did not go as often to the village as I might have. To get there from the Heights, I must pass the miners' rows, and this I did not like to do. Now that my own baby grew inside me, I could countenance even less the pathetic condition of the poor children who worked at Sir Nigel's china-clay mines and the squalor in which they lived.

Once, I thought I spied Linnet coming out of one of the run-down cottages that formed the miners' rows. As it was her day off, I assumed she must be visiting her family. Though she seldom talked about them, her mother and siblings still lived there, I knew. Her brothers were all miners, and her older sisters were married to miners. She must, I guessed, be glad to have escaped their lot. She did not see me, and I, thinking the matter unimportant, did not mention it to her later. Now, looking back, I wonder what tragedy might have been avoided if only I had spoken to her that day. I might have prized a good deal of the truth from her then, if only I had realized . . . But such thoughts are futile. All that happened is long since over and done with now, though you shall hear of it by and by, and then you may judge for yourself how much I might have prevented if only I had known then what I know now. But hindsight is useless, as I have come to recognize and accept.

Now I know how ignorant I was of what went on about me during those bittersweet, halcyon days when I was a young bride wrapped up in my coming child and my preparations for its birth. But that year of 1819, I knew little beyond the gossamer dreams I spun endlessly in my head as I sang softly to myself in the evenings and rocked my baby's empty cradle, smiling as I thought of the child who would soon lie within it. The Heights was even more isolated than the Hall. I lived like a caterpillar in a cocoon, and the world forged ahead without me. I should not have cared if it fell to pieces about me as long as my baby were safe. It was all I had, the only person who had ever truly belonged to me.

Now that work on the north tower, including the lighthouse, was finished, the servants, Draco, and I moved on to repair the hall, and as we labored, I envisioned how my husband and I would sit here by the fire in the wintry evenings, our child perhaps sleeping peacefully on the rug I intended to lay before the hearth. It was a pleasant daydream, and I resented its interruption by a knock upon the door and then Mrs. Pickering's subsequent announcement of visitors.

"Mr. and Mrs. Sheffield," she said, her voice ringing loudly through the now still, expectant room.

For a moment, I stood there stupidly, thinking I must have heard her amiss. Esmond and Julianne had returned over a fortnight ago from their honeymoon, I knew, but I could not believe they would be so brash and insolent as to call upon Draco and me, despising him as they did and after betraying me as they had. Yet there they stood, Julianne smiling smugly as she glanced avidly, with ill-concealed disdain, about the hall, and Esmond shamefaced, looking awkward and ill at ease, so I knew he had not wanted to come.

"Cerberus!" Draco snapped his fingers and sharply called the dog to heel as it growled and raised its hackles at the unwelcome intruders.

My face flushed with embarrassment as I sought to compose myself. My hands flew self-consciously to my untidy hair as I hurriedly tried to arrange it. Then, sensing with dismay the futility of this, I abandoned the attempt, wiping my hands nervously upon my apron, mortified as I saw the grimy streaks I left behind. No doubt my face was filthy, too; certainly I knew I reeked of sweat from my labors. I wanted to sink through the floor that I should be caught in such a state—and by Esmond and Julianne of all people!

"Hullo, Maggie, Draco," Julianne greeted us with condescending sweetness as she picked her way carefully across the floor littered with debris. "Goodness gracious. What a mess you are in!" Her laughter trilled gaily. "I see we have chosen a poor time indeed to call, but Esmond and I had no idea you were in the midst of remodeling, though, of course, with the Heights being such a ruin, perhaps we ought to have guessed...." Her voice trailed away as she gazed as me with pretended wide-eyed innocence. "Dear Maggie. I hope you are well. I should give you a sisterly kiss, you know, to congratulate you on your most... surprising marriage; but of course you will understand why I do not. My new dress... it's from Paris, you see, and I should so hate to have it mussed."

"Yes, of course," I replied coolly, her remarks proving precisely the impetus I needed to regain control of my flustered emotions.

She had lied, I knew, about being unaware of our restoring the estate. Draco and I had certainly ordered enough supplies from various merchants that our endeavor was no secret. No, Julianne had known exactly what she was about. Unlike everyone else, she had no reason to fear Sir Nigel; his estate was entailed, and he could not legally disinherit Esmond. Secure in that knowledge, she had been unable to contain her curiosity about Draco and me when she had learned of our marriage. She had come here solely to pry, and to gloat over the lowly state to which I had sunk;

and somehow she had managed to drag Esmond along with her in the hope of further disconcerting me. Despite my bedraggled appearance and the shambles of my home, I drew myself up proudly, for I had no intention of humbling myself before my stepsister, who had taken what should have been mine and now sought to twist the knife in the wound.

Still, despite myself, a sharp pang of envy pierced me to the core as the cloying fragrance of her lavish French perfume assailed my nostrils and my eyes took in her rakish, plumed hat and modish gown of sarcenet—both a deep wine red in color, I was wryly amused to see, wondering what Lady Chandler's reaction to the stylish ensemble had been. Sir Nigel must have increased Esmond's allowance handsomely, I reflected, for Julianne to have so indulged herself. Indeed she looked as though she had sated not only her craving for fashion, but for food, as well, on the Continent, for she had grown plump as a partridge during her absence. Then suddenly, stricken as though I had received an arrow through my heart, I realized she was not fat, but heavy with child.

Esmond's child, I thought, feeling sick and faint.

Of course he had lain with her, made love to her. He was her husband, was he not? Yet somehow, despite all my imaginings otherwise, a part of me had hoped he had not touched her. If only he had not, he would still in some small way have been mine.

Now my eyes turned to him accusingly, as though he had betrayed me anew, and with bitter triumph, I saw he could not meet my gaze, but stared at the floor, all too conscious of the awful faux pas he had committed in bringing my pregnant stepsister here. It was not like him to act so insensibly, and I wondered how Julianne had persuaded him to accompany her. No doubt she had subjected him to one of her petulant tantrums, I decided, curious as to whether, if such were indeed the case, he had finally perceived her true nature and recognized how cleverly she had duped him into wedding her. Certainly, for all that they had extended their honeymoon by several weeks, traveling on to France from Italy, Esmond did not look like a happy bridegroom, I thought. I felt a fierce, swift stab of gladness at the notion, for now, more than ever, I devoutly hoped Julianne made him miserable.

"Hullo, Esmond," I uttered quietly, relieved that my voice sounded as calm and unemotional as though I had never been betrothed to him, had never loved him as other than a friend. "I trust you are well, Cousin."

I spoke the last word with cruel deliberation, so he would know he meant nothing more to me now than that. Yet I could take no pleasure in wounding him, for such was the dejection in his silently pleading eyes when he looked at me then that I knew suddenly, painfully, how bitterly he regretted choosing Julianne over me. With certainty, I understood he had not only recognized his terrible mistake, but the fact that it was I he really loved. My heart should have leaped with joy at the realization. But it did not. Instead, without warning, fury at him, pity for us both, and an overwhelming grief for what we had once shared and lost swept through me.

Damn you, Esmond Sheffield! my heart cried out to him in despair. *Damn you for loving me—and for letting me see it now, when 'tis too late for us!*

Yet how shortly I had mourned his defection, how quickly I had allowed myself to be consoled by another, I realized as his anguished, recriminatory eyes lingered on my belly swollen to rival Julianne's. I had not played the part of a jilted lover and worn my heart upon my sleeve for all to see. I had not been faithful to his memory. Instead I had given myself to Draco, and by now, Esmond would have heard the rumors about my wild flight to Gretna Green and what had followed upon my return to the Hall. Now it was my eyes that fell before his as a lump rose in my throat, choking me. Swallowing hard, I glanced away, struggling to mask my emotions.

But I could not conceal my thoughts from Draco; and I was all too aware of his strolling lazily as a cat to my side, of the somehow sexually proprietary arm he slid around my waist, of the sardonic smile he directed at Esmond, a smile that did not quite reach his hard eyes as the two men exchanged reserved amenities, a wealth of underlying meaning in their tone. The air seemed abruptly to crackle with tension, as before a battle, and my breath caught in my throat with apprehension as the two men went on assessing each other. Julianne felt the tautness of the atmosphere but did not understand it, I knew, for her eyes were puzzled and she had withdrawn a little from us, as though to escape from the intangible thing that now enveloped us with its mockery and menace. She, who was so selfish and shallow, thrilled to the coquetry of the hunt, I thought, not the reality at its end. She had never truly comprehended Draco's nature, would have been appalled by it if she had. But Esmond had guessed at it years ago, though boy that he had been, he had not fully grasped its essence, sensing only that something in Draco posed a threat to him. Now I saw he understood completely the sort of man my husband was and chafed at his own character in comparison, his helplessness to prevent Draco's possession of me.

Trembling, I bit my lip, blushing with shame that Esmond should suspect the passionate nature of my relationship with my husband. I wanted to make some protest, some explanation, but there was nothing I could say to him. I was as powerless as he against Draco. I could do naught but hope Esmond would look into my eyes and see it was he I still loved.

At the thought, guessing how I betrayed him with my heart and mind, if not my body, Draco's arm tightened around my waist; a muscle twitched in his cheek, revealing his sudden anger toward me.

"Won't you stay for tea?" he asked Esmond and Julianne politely, so only I was cognizant of the deep rage he suppressed. "Though we are all sixes and sevens here, I'm sure Mrs. Pickering can manage something. She has proved herself an admirable housekeeper."

The Sheffields murmured their excuses, but Draco, perversely, would not hear of their declining; and so at his insistence, we sat in the kitchen and had tea and scones together, he the only comfortable one among us. Even Julianne, all the plumes on her hat seeming abruptly to droop and the hem of her smart frock smudged with dirt from all the debris, sensed she had somehow failed in the object of her visit and was now anxious to take her leave of us. But still she remained in her chair, reminding me so of a butterfly pinned to a board that I almost felt sorry for her.

"Well, this is quite like old times, isn't it?" Draco commented to no one in particular after Mrs. Pickering had left us. "We lack only Welles and Sarah to be complete. What a pity they aren't here to join us. We see them so infrequently these days, it seems; but, then, Welles is so rarely home that he and Sarah must make the most of what little time they have together, I imagine. No doubt that will change when they are married and settled."

"I do not expect that to happen any time soon," Esmond rejoined coldly, "since upon my reaching my majority, Sarah's guardianship passed from Sir Nigel to me, and she must have my permission to wed. Even if he is my brother by marriage, I do not consider Welles a suitable husband for her. He is a madcap and a wastrel, second mate on a second-rate merchant ship. I doubt he has two shillings to rub together. I shall never consent to his wedding Sarah."

Draco arched one eyebrow devilishly.

"How unfortunate for your sister, then," he declared. "But perhaps Welles's pockets are not so sadly to let that he cannot hire a carriage and a fast team of horses. Gretna Green is, after all, not so very far."

I inhaled sharply at my husband's temerity. Julianne tittered nervously, and Esmond's mouth tightened with severe disapproval.

"I can understand your stooping to that remark, Draco," he asserted grimly, "for you are no gentleman and never have been. But I cannot believe you have so little regard for Maggie's feelings that you would mention such a thing. Under the circumstances, she can scarcely wish to be reminded of it."

"To what circumstances are you referring, Sheffield?" Draco asked, his voice suddenly low and silky and subtly threatening. "Surely you have more sense than to listen to spiteful gossip. 'Tis true enough that Maggie and I eloped.

But after all, what else could we do when we were in love and could not obtain permission to wed, eh, my sweet?" He turned to me and took my hand in his, kissing my palm.

I would have drawn my hand away, but he held it too tightly. Across my palm, his fierce black eyes bored into mine, daring me to contradict his words. I would not, of course. He had known I would not, no matter how much Esmond might be hurt by them, as Draco had intended. I could do naught but hope Esmond would understand. Draco was my husband, the father of my child; I must live with him and make the best of it, for he would never let me go. He was not a man careless with his possessions. Had he not told me that? Even if Esmond were somehow to free himself of Julianne, there was no hope for us. Draco would still stand between us.

"Nothing, Draco," I replied softly. "There was nothing else we could have done."

It was the truth. But somehow that did not make the pain and reproachment that clouded Esmond's eyes any easier to bear. His silent condemnation of me wounded me to the core. Instinctively I rebelled against it; sudden rage rose within me. He was as much to blame as I for what had come to pass! Had he not been so blind to Julianne's true character, so gullibly ensnared by her false charms, so eager to scorn me for her, I should never have flung myself at Draco that night upon the moors. I lifted my chin. I would not permit Esmond to salve his guilty conscience at my expense, as my father had so often tried to do. I would shoulder the burden of my own mistakes, but never again would I do more than that.

Angrily, accusingly, I looked at Esmond, longing suddenly to be gone from the kitchen, where the sunlight streamed in through the small, high windows to illuminate the dust motes that swirled like golden mist in the air; where my beloved cousin's hazel eyes lingered on my face like those of a dying deer; where Draco lounged in his chair and drew casually on his cheroot, only his eyes, alert as a hunter's upon his prey, belying his languid demeanor; where Julianne sat still as a mute china doll forgotten on a shelf, her eyes watchful but uncomprehending, her painted mouth twisted in a sullen pout because she could not understand us, knew only that she was not the center of attention, as she wished to be.

I drank my tea—and my fill of Esmond's countenance, too, paler, thinner than when he had gone away, I thought. Mauve circles ringed his eyes, like bruises upon his fair skin. A stray lock curled over his forehead, as it had used to do when he had bent over his studies in the library at the Grange. As abruptly as it had arisen, my ire dissipated at the sight; my heart ached with sorrow and yearning. Oh, to have back those misspent days of youth! So wasted on the young, who know nothing of life; so regretted by the old, who know too much.

Youth, what man's age is like to be doth show/We may our ends by our beginnings know.

The fragment from Denham's poem echoed in my mind, making me shiver a little; for it was an ill-made pattern we had woven together, we four who sat now in the kitchen, a pattern of fragile fabric rent with flaws and sewn with ragged stitches, a pattern begun in our youth and fashioned of our sins. Dull needles and weak thread indeed, they had been: Julianne's vanity and greed, Esmond's fool- ishness and faithlessness, my pride and wrath, Draco's lust and revenge. Still we had employed them. How much more wretchedly would they serve us? I wondered.

Without warning, I felt an insane desire to laugh—to laugh until I cried at the bitter irony of our lives. Stranger still was the knowledge that if I were indeed to give way to my wild, inexplicable mirth, Esmond would be mortified and Julianne offended. Only Draco would understand, as somehow he always understood me. How odd that it should be so, I thought, when it was Esmond I loved.

At last the Sheffields left us. I was relieved to see them go, for the day had turned as dark and grey as my thoughts and I wanted nothing more than to lie down and rest; I suddenly felt so tired and old, far older than my years.

Murmuring my excuses to Draco and the servants, I hurried upstairs to the north tower. The new curtains in my bedchamber were open, and through the western windows, I could see black thunderclouds massing on the far horizon of the leaden sky. Below, the moors rippled and bowed with each gust of the rising wind, and foam crested the churning waves that rushed in upon the shore.

I knew if I were to turn to the eastern windows, I would see Esmond's horse and chaise, its calash top no doubt pulled up against the coming rain. But I made no move to watch the vehicle that must even now be wending its way down the drive, taking Esmond away from me, back to the Hall, where I was as dead now as though I lay in the cemetery at the church.

"Perhaps 'tis better so," I whispered to my unborn child. "For when all is said and done, in truth, I am glad you are not to grow up beneath my father's roof."

For the first time, the baby stirred in response to my voice, and I felt a small fluttering within me, quick and light as the beating of a butterfly's wings. Holding my breath, I stood very still, pressing my hands to my womb and waiting for the sensation to happen again. When it did, I smiled slowly with wonder and joy at the tiny being who grew inside me, safe and warm in its own world, as yet untouched by the harshness of mine.

A new life. A new beginning.

Determinedly I vowed that both would be better than mine.

Chapter Twenty-one

Interlude Before the Storm

And they are gone: aye, ages long ago
These lovers fled away into the storm.

—*The Eve of Saint Agnes*
John Keats

Silent as the fog that had begun to roll inland from the sea, Draco slipped into our bedchamber and strode across the floor to where I still stood gazing out the western windows, sleep having eluded me, despite my weariness. Though I had known he would waste no time in seeking me out, still, lost in my reverie, I did not hear him come in, and I was startled when he laid his hands upon my shoulders and spoke, his voice low in my ear.

"'Twas quite an entertaining little charade enacted here today, was it not?" he asked mockingly. "Poor Esmond. He has had a rude awakening, I fear. Like a pirate, Julianne has run up her true colors at last, and 'tis too late now for Esmond to raise his boarding nets. She has got her grappling hooks securely in him. The fool! He shall be sunk without firing a single shot in his defense!" Draco paused for a moment. Then, angry that I made no reply, he continued harshly, giving me a small, rough shake. "We had a bargain, you and I," he grated.

"Yes, so we did."

"I shall expect you to keep it, my girl."

"I did not think otherwise, Draco."

"Didn't you?"

"No."

"Yet I could have sworn there was a softness upon your face when you looked at Esmond Sheffield that you have never shown to me."

"If that is so," I began, turning at last to face him, "then it was born of my memories—nothing more. I do not deceive myself that there can be anything between Esmond and me now. I know you too well for that, Draco."

"Then you must know that I would kill him, Maggie, if I thought you were unfaithful to me with him." He spoke quietly enough now, but still there was a serrated edge to his voice that sent a sudden chill through me as, without warning, an image of Esmond lying dead at my feet, his life's blood flowing from him, rose to haunt me.

"Yes, I know."

"Then you would be wise to do nothing foolish, my girl, no matter how much you may be tempted."

"Yet you do not think what is sauce for the goose is also sauce for the gander, Draco," I ventured boldly.

His eyes narrowed.

"And just what do you mean by that, Maggie?"

"Do not seek to play the innocent with me, Draco," I uttered, my voice abruptly fierce with emotion, my body trembling at my daring. "I know you have other women—perhaps even a mistress! Yet you expect me to turn a blind eye and a deaf ear to that fact. Well, I won't, do you hear? Just as soon as another bedchamber can be made ready, I shall have my things moved into it and lock my door against you!"

To my surprise, for I had thought he would be enraged by my words, a strange smile curved his lips instead.

"Do you really believe that would keep me from you, love?" he inquired softly, looking at me in a way that brought a blush to my cheeks. "And what makes you think I have other women . . . a mistress?"

"I am not a fool," I said stiffly. "I know you have

tired of me—and quickly enough at that! Don't you think I can guess where you and Welles disappear to for hours on end when you come back reeking of smoke and sweat and brandy? And once, you stank of French perfume, too, Draco!'' I accused hotly. ''I've heard the rumors about that place in Launceston, that—that house of . . . ill-repute. Do not think I have not! No doubt you are quite familiar with it! Indeed I expected nothing better of you, for that is the sort of indecent man you are. But to drag Welles along with you—'' I broke off, scowling with disapproval. ''Well, I only hope Sarah doesn't learn of it, for her heart should be broken; she loves him so. I think you might consider her feelings, at least, if not mine, though, of course, I don't care one way or another what you do.''

Draco's eyes glinted oddly at that—with satisfaction, I thought, confused, for it was not what I had expected.

''But if that is the case, my sweet,'' he remarked lightly, ''then I confess I fail to understand this indignant tirade to which you have subjected me. Can it be that despite your claims to the contrary, you harbor some tender feelings for me after all? Can it be that you are, in fact . . . dare I suggest it? . . . jealous?''

''Don't be ridiculous!'' I retorted more sharply than I had intended. Biting my lip, I flushed and glanced away. '' 'Tis only that I have no desire for our marriage to provide any more grist than it already has for the gossip mill.''

''Indeed?'' Draco quirked one satanic eyebrow. ''Then let me set your mind at ease, love. There are no other women. I have no mistress, nor do I have any desire for one. I thought I had made it clear to you that it is you—and you alone—I want. If I have been reluctant of late to seek your bed, it is not because I have tired of you, but because I have no wish to do some injury to our unborn child. As for Welles . . . well, we are involved in a small business venture together, and we would prefer to keep it secret for the time being, as we have no desire for Sir Nigel to learn of it and thrust a spoke in our wheel. You know your father has no cause to wish me well, Maggie,'' he drawled dryly.

How strange that I should be filled with such joy at my

husband's words; yet inexplicably, maddeningly, I was. I could not understand it, for only an hour before, I had gazed upon Esmond's fair countenance and known I loved him still. Why, then, did I make no demur when Draco swept me up in his arms and carried me to our bed? Why did I feel such a sudden thrill of anticipation and excitement when his lips claimed mine? I did not know.

The storm that had threatened earlier broke at last as we made love, the rain pelting against the windows with such fury that it seemed as though the glass panes must shatter beneath its onslaught. Yet inside the north tower, I lay sheltered in Draco's embrace, safe and warm as the child in my womb and, curiously, just as content.

Chapter Twenty-two

Mick Dyson and the Miners' Rows

I am one, my liege,
Whom the vile blows and buffets of the world
Have so incens'd, that I am reckless what
I do to spite the world.

—*Macbeth*
William Shakespeare

It was an uneasy summer that followed hard on the heels of the spring showers. In sharp contrast to the previous mist and drizzle, now the sun shone hotly, relentlessly, as it was wont to do in Cornwall, beating down upon the scarred headland to suck the moisture from the moors, leaving them parched and withered and pale gold as hay. Only occasionally now would a wild wind blow, bringing a blanket of fog and rain that lashed the land in quick but brutal summer storms. Then the day would darken, and the sea, turned angry, would roar along the coast, the whitecapped breakers crashing against the rugged cliffs. Afterward the mournful cries of the gulls and curlews would echo in the sudden stillness as though they wept for the brutality done to the land.

We did not work as hard on restoring the Heights now, for the heat and the weight of my growing child pressing against me made it hard for me to breathe, and Draco would not allow me to push myself as I had before. Mrs. Pickering was surprised by his concern for me, for I suspect she had not thought him capable of any gentler feelings, nor do I think most husbands behaved toward their pregnant wives as mine did toward me. It was quite amusing, really, to see how Draco looked after me and waited on me hand and foot, as though I were an invalid. He was forever plumping up the cushions on the chairs and bed to make certain I was comfortable, and once, despite my protests, he threw into the dustbin a pillow he deemed too hard for me to rest upon. He bought books for me to read to pass the time away and played games with me to entertain me in the evenings. He indulged my cravings for various foods, though after he had eaten chicken for supper four times in one week, he did remark dryly that he hoped he would not turn into one. He rubbed my back, which had begun to ache dully now, and my feet, because it soothed me; and sometimes, when nothing else seemed to bring me ease, he brushed my hair and sang softly to me in Romany until I fell asleep. Even I found it difficult to equate this kind, caring man with the one who had drugged me and forced himself upon me before I had been his wife and who, through me, had ruthlessly revenged himself on my father.

As time passed, I began to recognize that there were depths to Draco's character that although I had glimpsed as a girl, I had deliberately blinded myself to as a woman because it had been easier to despise him that way. But now, to my surprise, I realized that somewhere along the way, I had ceased to hate him, for though I knew him for a devil, he was not wholly wicked. He could be tender and compassionate when he chose, and these days, I seldom saw the hard, cold Draco who filled me with apprehension and loathing.

Still I soon had reason to be glad of his demoniac temperament. Times were hard, and all England was rife with unrest. The Duke of Wellington, who had earned himself a hero's name after defeating the French emperor, Napoleon, at the Battle of Waterloo, had returned home to enter Parliament; and there he had demonstrated his opposition to free trade, winning the widespread approval of his aristocratic peers, who had good cause to support him. The Corn Laws were upheld; the importation of cheap foreign grain was not allowed. Thus the landed gentry remained assured of a profit from their own fields, and the price of bread continued to rise at an exorbitant rate. This, in turn, enraged the manufacturers, who were hounded by their laborers into promises of higher wages. Then if the manufacturers did not or simply could not afford to make good their word, they became the target of violence and bloodshed.

I shuddered at the news that reached my ears even at the isolated Heights, for I had heard of the food riots of 1795; and during much of my childhood, a series of bad harvests had exacerbated the already tense situation. Quite simply, the working class and the poor were hungry, and when people were hungry, they tended to commit rash acts against those they blamed for their misfortune. The matter was not helped by the fact that with progress came machines that could be run by women and children, who worked for lower wages, displacing men who could find no other jobs to support their families. Increasingly, Irish refugees flocked to England's shores, as well, and proved an additional source of cheap labor, for some would work for as little as four shillings a week rather than starve.

Jobless, and soon homeless as well, destitute men flooded the workhouses in the cities and roamed the roads of the countryside. Some took to the high toby, robbing the rich at gunpoint, or became smugglers who led the dragoons a dangerous chase. Others, their ears filled with the talk of liberty and equality brought home by England's redcoats who had fought the French, fomented rebellion, inciting downtrodden men to rise up against those who oppressed them.

Sir Nigel, I knew, must find himself in a difficult position, for he belonged to the landed gentry, and to no one but the king would he bend his proud, stiff neck. But because my astute grandfather, Sir Simon, had been farseeing enough to grasp the fact that progress would come, regardless of the aristocracy, my father had inherited not only his estate, but the china-clay mines Sir Simon had bought as insurance against the day when the rights of the common man should prevail over those of the privileged class.

Though he felt nothing but distaste for the mines and the fact that my grandfather had stooped to their purchase, Sir Nigel was nevertheless too much the businessman to sell them when they enriched the Chandler coffers. He had placed the weaselly Mr. Heapes in charge of them and given him a strong, brutish right arm in the form of Mick Dyson, the head foreman, to help run them. Then, so he would not be soiled by the vulgar taint of trade, my father had washed his hands of the entire matter, permitting Heapes and Dyson to do as they pleased, so long as the mines turned a profit.

I doubt that Sir Nigel, if ever he thought of it, suffered any pangs of conscience over the miserable lot the miners endured beneath the harsh yoke of Heapes and Dyson. Certainly it must have been inconceivable to him that the miners would revolt against their grim, uncompromising treatment. After all, he paid them a day's wages for a day's work, didn't he? And if his idea of a day's wages was not theirs, why, they were free to go elsewhere, weren't they? I thought it was no wonder, then, that my father's carriage should be stoned as he and Lady Chandler were returning home late one evening. Neither of them was injured, but the warning note wrapped about the rock that had smashed through the coach window was clear: The miners' conditions must improve, or there would be further trouble.

I shivered when I learned of the threats directed against Sir Nigel, for I knew he would pay them little heed, and I feared further violence would be forthcoming. Perhaps it would not be only he who suffered, I thought, but all who were related to him, too. Still, although my father did nothing, to Mick Dyson's credit and my surprise, the head foreman took swift charge of the situation, cooling hot tempers as best he could with his level-headed reasoning.

"Oh, you should have heard him, missus," Linnet
gushed to me after returning home from visiting her mother.
"He had them in the very palm of his hand, Mick did,
tellin' them that it wouldn't do no good for them to walk off
the job, that they'd not be likely to find another, what with
even the most highly skilled laborers out of work and all.
They should think of their families, he said. Would they
want to leave their wives and children without a roof and
starvin' to death in a ditch somewhere, while they themselves were strung up on the gallows or, at the very least,
transported to Australia for crimes against Sir Nigel? Mick
told them he and Heapes would talk to the baronet, would
try to reason with him. In the meanwhile, the workers must
sit tight, Mick said, for times are tough all over, and they'll
not find it any easier elsewhere, nor will they be doin' the
rest in the miners' rows a favor by makin' Sir Nigel so
angry that he shuts down the mines completely."

"Well, frankly, Linnet, I am surprised to learn Mick
Dyson advised caution in the matter, for I have always
perceived him to be a hotheaded scoundrel who would slit
his own mother's throat if he thought it were to his advantage to do so."

"Well, you're a fine one to talk, missus!" she shot
back impertinently, her green eyes flashing with sudden
anger. "Somebody who nearly caused her own father to fall
down the—"

"That's enough, Linnet!" I spoke sharply, shaking
with emotion at her outburst, for she would never have
dared to speak so to me at the Hall. "What happened that
night was not my fault, as well you know. You forget
yourself, miss. I ought to dismiss you at once!" Then,
realizing I was unlikely to find another abigail, especially
one who, besides caring for my wardrobe, would also assist
with repairs to the house, I forced myself to breathe deeply,
continuing on a calmer note. "However, I shall overlook the
matter just this once. Obviously I offended you with my
comments about Mick Dyson, and for that, I apologize. I
didn't realize the two of you were so close."

Oddly my abigail's face blanched at that. Then, biting

her lip, she flushed scarlet, and her eyes fell before mine.

"We're not . . . not really," she insisted. " 'Tis just that he—he was so kind to me and my family after—after Pa was killed at the mine. I thought—I thought you would be glad to hear how he spoke up for Sir Nigel, for if there's trouble," she went on, her eyes glancing at me slyly now, "some of it's bound to be aimed at Mr. Sheffield as well, him bein' the baronet's heir and all—and him havin' taken on some of Sir Nigel's duties as the local magistrate now, too."

I had not thought of this, that Esmond, especially since he had assumed some of my father's responsibilities as magistrate, would be singled out for persecution; and now a cold hand of fear wrapped its fingers around my heart. I had no way to warn my beloved cousin, to urge him to take care, for there was no one in my household whom I could trust to take a note to him and not tell Draco. Even Linnet had shown me she could be disloyal. I had always suspected it of her, but now that I was sure of it, I disliked her more intensely than ever, thinking her resemblance to Julianne was more than just a vague similarity in appearance. Annoyed, I sent the abigail away, wishing I did not need her services.

She had lied about her relationship with Mick Dyson, I thought, and wondered why. Were they perhaps lovers, then? I did not know. I did not care, though later I wished very much that I had.

It was a few days after my conversation with Linnet when I learned it was not only Esmond for whom I must be afraid, but myself as well. It was market day, and as Mrs. Pickering was busy, I had offered to go to the village myself. Now I sat beside Will on the seat of the trap, my parasol spread wide against the rays of the morning sun, my mind drifting aimlessly as we rode along. Though I liked Mrs. Pickering immensely, I was glad she had not been able to accompany me this day, for she was a garrulous woman,

and because of her deafness, I was often forced to shout my
replies. I much preferred a quiet drive, during which I could
delight in the scenery about me and daydream to my heart's
content. Since Will, who had stayed on with us after my
marriage to Draco, was not given much to talking, he suited
me well enough, though I thought him a rapscallion and
often wondered what sort of life he had led before coming
to the Heights. But I did not ask, sensing that even if he
should decide to tell me, which no doubt he would not, I
should not like the answer.

Alongside the road, the moors stretched out about us
like an endless sea, the greenness of spring faded now to a
pale gold by the summer sun. To the southeast, the tors rose
in the distance like massive obelisks against the blue horizon. I could see Brown Willy, which Draco and I had
sometimes climbed in our childhood, and I thought how
long ago those days seemed now. It was almost as though
someone else, not I, had lived them. Now and then, I
yearned to have those days back, for I thought I should
never know their like again. I was no longer the young girl I
had been then, blissful in my innocence and ignorance, but
a woman grown, with my eyes opened to the reality of the
world, no matter how callous or cruel it might be.

The trap rattled on. The miners' rows were in sight
now, and as always, I was struck by the deterioration and
neglect of the cottages: crude, two-room boxes so poorly
constructed that even from a distance, I could see the cracks
and chips in the exterior walls, which had once been
whitewashed but were now a dingy grey and streaked with
grime from smoky peat fires lit in hearths for heat and
cooking. The hovels were packed so close together that each
scarcely had room for a tiny, weed-ridden garden that
yielded little enough sustenance in northern Cornwall's
harsh climate but that kept starvation, if not hunger, at bay.

Strung between the plots were lines on which laundry
was drying, garments far more dreary and ragged than any I
had ever owned. In the scraggly patches of yard, women
were bent over hot tubs of water acrid with strong lye soap,
scrubbing the clothes against washboards, then lugging full,

heavy baskets over to the lines. The faces of even the youngest females looked old and worn, and I thought pityingly that no matter my lot in life, it was far better than theirs.

In the narrow lanes between the rows, scrawny children played, none of them more than five or six years of age at the most, for those older than that were put to work at the pits. Their families needed the wages, and though children who toiled in the shafts more often than not were soon twisted and crippled by work far too strenuous for young bones and bodies that had not yet reached their full growth, the pain they must endure counted for little when there were hungry mouths to feed.

I was not unaccustomed to the silence that always descended when I passed the miners' rows; but now I became uncomfortably aware that the stares directed at me this morning were strangely hostile, some even openly belligerent, and a small chill of foreboding tingled up my spine. These people were poor and hungry—and angry at my father, the source of their meager livelihood, the target of their complaints. My heart began to pound with fear. No doubt one Chandler was the same as another to these people. Suddenly the crunch of the vehicle's wheels sounded overly loud in my ears as I forced myself to look straight ahead, to ignore the sullen glares of the women and children standing before the squalid cottages. Now, though it was not Sunday, from the corners of my eyes, I noticed several men, too, huddled in a little group, and I wondered what they were doing home at this hour. Work at the mines began each morning at five o'clock, and anyone who was not present by then was fined accordingly. Had the men walked off their jobs, then? I did not know. I did not want to find out. Perspiration beaded my upper lip; I could feel my palms sweating through my gloves in the summer heat. Beside me on the seat, Will sat hunched over the reins, whistling through his teeth as though he hadn't a care in the world. But I noticed that his alert eyes missed nothing and that his shotgun lay on the floor wihin easy reach. Glancing down at it, I wondered, if it became necessary, whether he would use the weapon, and my mouth went dry with terror that he would not. For all that Will had served as my coachman now for months, I did not know him well. Certainly I did not trust him. He looked like the sort of rascal who would abandon me to my fate if he thought it would save his own neck. I did not relish the prospect of having to depend upon him to defend me if there were trouble. Besides, even if he were not so dishonorable as to leave me to my fate, what could he, a lone man, accomplish against an enraged mob?

I did not realize I was holding my breath until, without incident, we left the miners' rows behind and I exhaled with relief. Will threw me a sharp, inscrutable glance but said nothing, and I wondered what he was thinking. But he was as guarded as his master, and I knew he would not tell me.

Though by the time we reached the village, I had regained some measure of my composure, still I was so shaken by the enmity I had felt at the miners' rows that I botched the marketing, coming off the worse in my bargaining with the vendors and thus being cheated of several shillings I might otherwise have saved. I had no doubt that Mrs. Pickering, who considered it her business to look after me in my dead mother's place, would chide me severely for allowing myself to be taken advantage of in such a manner.

When it came time to return home, I searched the marketplace for Will, half afraid he had left me. But at last I spied him waiting at the edge of the square, and after he had tossed my purchases into the trap and climbed up beside me, we started off, I tense and nervous, and Will, I fancied, fortified with a good deal of ale for the journey back; though perhaps I was unfair to him in this, for his clear blue eyes were keen as ever, and his hands upon the reins were steady.

Still he spoke scarcely two words to me, and as the vehicle rolled down the road toward the miners' rows, I became increasingly uneasy, wondering if we should be permitted to pass again unmolested. The morning had grown very late; much might have happened while we were in the village. Perhaps, like Will, the delinquent men at the miners' rows had been drinking to allay the effects of the summer heat. My heart sank at the notion. Perhaps they would be emboldened by the liquor they had quaffed and so would not be constrained by the fact that I was a gentlewoman, and with child, but would set upon me and haul me from the trap and, in their inebriated state, viciously misuse me, never thinking of the price they would have to pay for their crime. My imagination ran wild, fueling my fear, and at last I could contain myself no longer.

"Take the long way home, Will," I directed as calmly as I could so he should not guess the extent of my trepidation.

He was silent for a moment as thoughtfully he considered my words. Then, reluctantly shaking his head, he spoke.

"Nay, with all due respect, missus, that I will not do," he declared firmly. "T' master be expectin' us, an' he shan't be happy if we tarry. Besides, 'twill do 'ee no good not ta go back t' way we come. If them miners think they've frightened 'ee, they'll be like a pack of wild dogs scentin' blood. Thee'll not be safe then, fer they'll hound 'ee just fer t' fun of it, thinkin' ta get a bit of their own back against t' gentry. 'Tis better 'ee face 'em now, missus, afer they've screwed up their courage ta do somethin' rash. I'll not be runnin' away an' leavin' 'ee ta their mercy, if that's what thee art a-thinkin'. T' master would have me hide if I was ta do such a thing, so 'ee can rest easy on that account. Besides, 'ee an' t' master have been good ta me, missus. It ain't just anyone who would have give me a second chance after I got out of prison, an' I reckon I got some loyalty."

I confess I was horrified by the fact that Will was a former convict, for even I had never suspected Draco of hiring such a man; but still I felt deeply shamed by my driver's little speech, for I realized he must have guessed my uncharitable thoughts toward him and had his feelings hurt. At any rate, I reflected, if Will had survived incarceration in one of England's horrible jails, a gang of ruffians was unlikely to hold many terrors for him.

"Very well, Will," I said, lifting my chin defiantly, "we shall do it your way—the miners be damned!"

If the small, wiry man were shocked by my coarse language, he gave no sign of it, but nodded his head with approval, clucking to the pony and slapping the reins down upon its back to urge it on; and I sensed I had gained a friend and an ally in this rough servant of mine.

A few minutes later, the miners' rows came into view, and now, as the trap drew near, I saw among the men faces that were unknown to me. Despite my brave words earlier, my heart beat fast at the realization, for I suspected the strangers were insurgents who traveled about the countryside, giving speeches about unions and strikes and reforms; men who urged rebellion and incited riots; men who had already lost all they had and had nothing more to lose if they should be put into prison, transported, or hanged for their unlawful acts; men who did not care who fell victim alongside them so long as a blow against tyranny and oppression was struck. Dangerous men, they were, men who would blow up a mine, smash the windows and machinery of a factory, or put a torch to a textile mill. I had not seen such men hereabouts before; I had no wish to see them now. But it was too late now to turn back.

"They'll not harm 'ee, missus. I shall see ta that," Will vowed, and at his reassuring glance, I squared my shoulders and fought down my rising panic.

Silence descended upon the miners' rows as we approached, but this time, when we were halfway past the cottages, a catcall rang out, causing me to stiffen with anger and mortification at the rude words. I saw that it did indeed mean nothing to these people that Sir Nigel had disowned me. In the end, I was still my father's daughter, and if they could not vent their wrath and frustration upon him, I would serve just as well. Soon other shouts and ribald laughter followed, and before I realized what was happening, someone threw a stone at us. It struck the pony, who started and shied, and only Will's strong hands forcibly restraining the animal prevented it from bolting, perhaps from overturning the vehicle and killing us both. I thought of the baby I carried, dead before it had even had a chance to live; and suddenly I was no longer afraid of this rabble. Before Will could stop me, gripping the top edge of the seat to maintain my balance, I stood up in the trap to face my tormentors.

"For shame!" I cried heatedly. "What sort of men are you to set upon a woman heavy with child?"

There were those who flushed guiltily at my words and turned away, their eyes downcast, unable to meet mine. But there was one man bolder than the rest, and he was not chastened as they were. Brazenly he sauntered toward me, a big hulk of an Irishman with bulging muscles born of years of hard, grueling labor in the mine pits. His long, unkempt hair was red as flame; his eyes were like bits of green glass in his face. His nose had been broken so many times in fights that it was impossible to tell how it had originally been shaped. His lips were twisted in a mocking leer as he looked me up and down in a way he should not have done, appraisingly, disrespectfully, as though he would like to bed me and teach me my place. Revulsion crawled up my spine at the notion. Even had I never seen him before, I should have known at once who he was: Mick Dyson, my father's head foreman.

Now that I saw him at close range, I understood fully why the miners feared and obeyed him, for he looked like a man who was quick to take offense and to use his fists when provoked, a man who had fought and clawed his way up to a position of authority at the mines. But still he was not, I knew, one of those men who remembered whence he had sprung and sought to ease the lot of others beneath him. Instead he felt nothing for them but contempt. He hated them for reminding him that he was no better than they; he despised them for not having the willpower to haul themselves up out of the muck, as, in a limited fashion, he had managed do.

I recalled what Sir Nigel had once said about Dyson, that he would play both sides of the fence if he thought it were to his advantage, and now I did not doubt the truth of that. He seemed to me a man who would seize any opportunity to get ahead, no matter how vile or whom he injured in the process. I suspected that deep down inside, the Irishman loathed my father and all he represented; but still he was clever enough to recognize that Sir Nigel had little liking for the mines and would simply shut them down if the workers caused him any trouble. As Dyson was unlikely to find another job as a head foreman, it was not, therefore, in his best interests to antagonize my father by disputing the long hours worked or the meager wages paid at the mines. Still, despite the speech Linnet had heard him give to the laborers, now I wondered if perhaps Dyson fancied he could push Sir Nigel just enough to force him to accede to a few of their demands. Certainly I could not understand why the Irishman would allow the miners to harass me otherwise. If this were the case, however, he had made a grave error in judgment, I knew, for my father was unlikely to be swayed in his decision by any violence that might be directed at me, who had ceased to exist for him. But I did not know if Dyson would believe me if I told him that, and I trembled at his approach, unsure of his intent.

When he had reached the road, he moved to stand before the vehicle. Then deliberately he caught hold of the pony's harness, preventing the trap from continuing on.

"Good day ta ye, missus," he greeted me impudently, as though he were my equal, and my knees suddenly weak, I sank down upon the seat, clutching my parasol tightly, my knuckles white.

I thought that of all the men I had ever known, this one was the most frightening, for I did not think he cared for aught but himself. He was not bound by the rules of society, to which even Sir Nigel must bow in the end if he wished to remain a part of his class. Nor did Dyson have Draco's compassion, his Gypsy affinity with the earth and its wild creatures.

Though born and bred an Irishman, Dyson, I had heard, had left his homeland years ago and had made his way to England, along with so many others of his ilk, immigrants hoping to find a better life than the one they had left behind, for Ireland was a harsh country in which to survive, wild and rough and perpetually torn by strife. To my knowledge, no one had ever heard him speak of his life there, so I could only imagine what he had endured as a youth to make him as he was now. Nor did he ever mention his family, so I assumed they must be dead. He had had a wife once, however, whom I had seen years ago in my childhood, a woman not much older then than I was now, a pale wraith of a woman, her face pinched with hunger and drawn with weariness, her breathing labored and racked by a nagging cough. She had died in childbirth, and the thin scrap of a baby with her. Dyson had grown even more bitter after that, it was said, and he had flung himself furiously into his work doing the job of three men. I did not know what he did with his wages, for though he could raise a mug of ale with the best of them, he did not frequent the taverns as often as the other miners did. I suspected he hoarded every penny he could in the hope of rising still further in the world. But I did not even begin to guess the depths of his ambition and determination; indeed I should have been horrified if I had.

I knew only that he was a dangerous man to cross and that I had crossed him. Now I shook at my temerity, wishing I had never dared to reproach those who had taunted me, but had ignored them and driven on. But as always, my heart had ruled my head, and now I must face the consequences of my impulsive action.

"You're blocking the road, Mr. Dyson," I said, startled but relieved to hear how calm and cool my voice sounded.

"Indeed I am," he agreed, unruffled, "fer sure an' I've a mind ta give ye a piece o' advice, missus. Yer a pretty colleen, ye are, an' I've no grudge against ye, so I'd not like ta see some . . . mishap befall ye. So ye give yer man a message fer me, then, will ye? Tell him he would do well ta stay home nights an' look after his wife. Sure an' these be hard times, missus, an' there be dangerous men abroad in this countryside."

Yes, I thought, *and you one of them.*

But I did not say the words aloud. Instead I nodded, swallowing hard at the veiled threat against me that I had perceived in Dyson's warning.

"Very well, I shall give my husband your . . . message.

Now, step aside, if you please. You've delayed me overlong as it is. My husband will wonder at my lateness, and I should not like him to be put to the trouble of coming to search for me, as he surely shall if I don't return home presently.'' I let it be known that despite what Dyson might think to the contrary, I was secure in the knowledge that Draco would indeed defend me if necessary.

To my relief, the Irishman released the pony's harness and stepped back from the trap. At that, Will slapped the reins down smartly upon the animal's back, and it broke into a brisk trot. With an abrupt jolt, the vehicle moved forward. I did not look back; but even so, as we left the miners' rows behind, I sensed that Mick Dyson still stood in the road, his green eyes hard and narrow as they bored into my back.

Chapter Twenty-three

The Ghosts at Stormswept Heights

About the dead hour of the night
She heard the bridles ring; . . .

—*The Ballad of Tam Lin*
Traditional

Draco was anxious about my lateness, I knew, for upon my return to the Heights, he came striding out into the courtyard, his face dark with anger to conceal his concern. Despite his forbidding expression, I was glad to see him, for there was something very comforting now in the determined set of his jaw, the sight of his broad shoulders and muscular arms.

"Where have you been, Maggie?" he asked tersely as he assisted me from the trap.

"I was unavoidably detained," I said, laying my hand upon his arm. "Come into the house, Draco. There is much I have to tell you."

He must have guessed from the sound of my voice that something was wrong, for he made no demur, but merely nodded silently, his eyes searching mine intently for a moment before he led me into the manor. Once inside, I explained to him about the upsetting incident at the miners' rows, and after I had repeated Mick Dyson's message word for word a second time, his eyes narrowed and his mouth tightened into a thin, grim line.

"It is a dangerous game Dyson plays," he observed once I had finished my tale. "He had best tread carefully, lest someone beat him at it." He paused, drumming his fingers thoughtfully upon the kitchen table as he considered the matter. At last he spoke again. "I don't want to alarm you, Maggie, but neither will I pretend to you that Dyson is harmless, for I do not think he is; and while I do not believe he would be so foolhardy as to attempt to do you any real injury, there is no point in taking any chances. From now on, you must be very careful," he told me. "Do not drive out in the trap again. Use the coach if you must go somewhere, and be certain both Will and Ned are with you—and armed. In the meantime, I shall pay Dyson a visit—just to make certain he understands whom he's dealing with. Let us see how bold he is when it is *I* he must face!"

I never learned what Draco said to Mick Dyson, but after that day, the Irishman did not bother me again. Still I took care to keep out of his way, avoiding the miners' rows as much as possible. When I must, of necessity, pass the cottages, Ned displayed his shotgun prominently and Will whipped the horses to a gallop, so the coach swept by at such a furious pace that it was evident it would run down anyone who got in its way. Now, when they spied my carriage coming, none of the inhabitants of the miners' rows ventured too near to the road, and I no longer had to fear I would be set upon by them. Even so, I retained a strong sense of disquiet, and I should not have gone anywhere at all but for the fact that I was accustomed to roaming the moors and would not easily relinquish this freedom.

Since learning of my mother's bequest to me, I had paid a portion of my inheritance to the village church to be certain her crypt was given special attention by the caretaker of the cemetery. The chiseled granite block that sealed her resting place in the Chandler vault was to be cleaned each week, and every Sunday, I visited the cemetery to make sure that this was done and to hang a wreath of flowers upon her tomb. On other days, I went just to talk to her, as I had done since I was a child.

Now I knew how unhappy she had been, how unloved by my father; and so she had died. Yet she had loved me dearly, as Sir Nigel had not. In my heart, I had always felt it to be so, but I was certain of it now. My mother, too, had known what it meant to be a woman in a man's world, trapped in a marriage from which there had been no escape but death; and I knew without a doubt that she had left me her legacy upon my own marriage to ensure that if I were made miserable, I had another way out than the one she had taken.

But though I was glad of my inheritance, I never thought of using it to leave Draco. I was, as I have said, strangely happy at the Heights, and if I had not loved Esmond, I would have been content with my lot in life.

I had not seen him since the day he and Julianne had come to the manor, but sometimes I thought of him and wondered if he was well. Still, oddly, I did not daydream about him as often as I had used to do, nor did I grieve for him as deeply as I had in the past. But I did not examine the reasons for this too closely, sensing deep down inside that if I did, I would discover too many things I was not yet prepared to face.

But there were other things—strange things—in my life, which I could not so firmly force myself to dismiss. Over the years, I, like everyone else, had heard the peculiar stories told of the Heights and its violent history; Draco himself had related many such tales to me. But previously I had paid them little heed. In recent months, however, I had begun to wonder if it were not true, after all, that the manor was haunted by ghosts from its past; for sometimes in the dead of night, when the moon was dark and the mist blew in from the sea to hang like a shroud over the moors, I would awaken from a deep sleep, roused by some unfamiliar noise sounding faintly at the fringes of my subconscious.

For a moment, I would lie still in my bed, my eyelids

heavy with sleep, and when my ears discerned nothing more, I would think I was dreaming. So I would drift back into slumber, telling myself it was only the creaking of the house or the soughing of the wind or the sea that I had heard. But eventually there came a night when I knew it was none of these things that had disturbed me, and as my mind swirled up from its somnolent state to come fully awake, I was beset by puzzlement, curiosity, and, because of the unrest in all England, a twinge of fear, too. I could have sworn it was the soft jingle-jangle of a bridle, quickly muffled, that I had heard below in the yard. I turned and stretched out one hand to waken Draco, only to find he was not there. Had he not yet come to bed, then, or was he already downstairs, investigating? Surely he had not gone out at such a late hour, for I had left him in his study earlier, and he had said nothing to me to indicate he would be absent later.

Silently I rose and, fumbling in the darkness, lit a candle. The flame flickered eerily, casting elongated shadows upon the walls of the north tower. I moved to the windows that overlooked the lawn and, pulling aside one edge of the curtains, peeked out through the bezeled glass panes. The moonless night was black as a witch's cat; the stars were obscured by fog. Yet Draco had not lighted the peat we kept laid in the round, open stone hearth of the lighthouse, so I could see little. I was just about to turn away when I spied the dim glow of a lamp filtering through one of the windows on the first floor of the south tower.

But that is impossible, I thought, startled, for Draco had shut up the south tower and forbidden anyone to enter it. It was in such poor condition, he'd said, that he feared it would collapse.

The light vanished so suddenly that I wondered if my eyes had deceived me. I stared at the south tower intently for several minutes, but the light did not reappear, and at last I let the curtain fall back into place. Then, drawing on my wrapper, I hurried downstairs to the hall. Lamps still burned here, so I knew my husband was up and about.

"Draco," I called softly. "Draco."

Moments later, to my relief, he appeared in the doorway that led to his study.

"Maggie! What are you doing here?" he asked.

"I—I heard a noise. Is . . . everything all right?"

"But of course. Why shouldn't it be?"

I explained to him about hearing the sound of the bridle and then seeing the light in the south tower. He listened quietly, then smiled a little with amusement and shook his head.

"Go back to bed, my sweet," he said calmly. "There's naught for you to concern yourself about. 'Twas nothing more than the ghosts of poor Aislinn Deverell and her lover, Joss, who haunt the south tower."

"G–ghosts?" I stammered, confused.

"Yes. Do you remember I told you there had been murder done here once?" At my nod, he continued. "During the time of the Plantagenets, Aislinn Deverell came as a young bride to the Heights. But she was very unhappy here, and with her husband, who, it is said, sorely misused her. One evening, as she was returning home from some soirée, her coach was set upon by a highwayman, Joss, who treated her so gallantly that she fell in love with him; and since she was very fair and graceful, Joss loved her, too. They began an affair that lasted until finally Aislinn's husband discovered them one night in Aislinn's chamber in the south tower. He was so enraged by her betrayal of him that he flung the two lovers into the dungeon, and there he kept them until a gallows was built. Then he forced Aislinn to watch as his men hanged Joss, and while Joss still dangled from the rope, slowly choking to death, Aislinn's husband took his sword from his scabbard and struck her head from her shoulders before Joss's dying eyes.

"Now, or so 'tis claimed, in the still of a summer's night, when the moon is new and the fog rolls in from the sea, Aislinn's ghost lights a candle in the window of her room and waits for her lover, Joss the highwayman, to come riding up to the south tower."

I shivered at Draco's story, saddened by it, though, since I doubted the existence of ghosts, I found it hard to

believe. Still, not knowing why he should wish to deceive
me, I made no further protest when, saying he would
follow shortly, he again suggested I return to bed.

The next morning, I went down to the kitchen to
discover Renshaw hunched upon a stool in one corner,
rambling to Mrs. Pickering about the ghosts in the south
tower. The housekeeper merely snorted and shook a wooden
spoon at him in disgust.

"Aye, an' what would 'ee be knowin' about it, missus?" Renshaw asked slyly. "Deaf as a stone, 'ee be.
'Twould take more than a pony ta wake t' likes of 'ee.
People think just 'cause me wits is addled, I don't know
nothin'. But I do—an' I know t' ring of a bridle when I
hears it. Besides, if 'tweren't no ghost rider, what was it?
Eh? Answer me that, then. Thee'd like ta know, wouldn't 'ee,
an' I could tell 'ee, too, if I was of a mind t'—"

"That's quite enough, Renshaw," Draco, entering the
kitchen, cut him off smoothly, staring so hard at him that the
caretaker's face filled with fright and he mumbled some
vague apology I could not catch. "Mrs. Pickering has better
things to do than listen to your babbling about ghoulies and
ghosties and long-leggety beasties."

"Aye, master." Renshaw nodded, his eyes downcast as
he abruptly slid from his stool and scuttled off like a
cockroach, banging the kitchen door behind him in his haste
to escape.

I gazed after him thoughtfully for a moment, wondering curiously why he had grown so fearful at Draco's
admonishment and what he might have revealed had not my
husband interrupted him. Then, as I observed Draco watching
me intently from beneath his half-closed eyelids, it suddenly
occurred to me that perhaps he had indeed had some reason
to lie to me last night, that there had indeed been someone
besides a ghost in the south tower. But, who? And what had
it to do with Draco? I did not know, nor could I even hazard
a guess. Still I could not shake off the nagging suspicion
that my husband had been untruthful with me, and it once
more crossed my mind that perhaps Renshaw was not really
quite as mad as he appeared.

Chapter Twenty-four

Death and
the China-Clay Mines

Then, with no throbs of fiery pain,
No cold gradations of decay,
Death broke at once the vital chain,
And freed his soul the nearest way.

—*Written by Samuel Johnson, on the
death of Mr. Levett.*

As soon as I could, I tried to question the caretaker, but the
poor lunatic grew so frightened at my interrogation that I
could get nothing from him but gibberish; and after that,
more than ever convinced Draco was indeed hiding something
from me, I resolved to get into the south tower if I could. I
had a set of keys to the house, so this did not seem initially
to pose any problem. But after I had retrieved the chatelaine
from the new desk in my chamber, I discovered that none of the
keys upon the ring fit any of the doors to the south tower.
That in itself was quite odd and served to strengthen my
suspicions, for if my husband *were* using the tower for some
purpose he wished to conceal, he would, of course, have
taken my keys to it—and no doubt Mrs. Pickering's as well.

Still, like a hound pursuing a trail, I did not give up
easily. I went out to the stables and returned with a crowbar,
with which I attempted to pry open the door on the second
floor of the tower. But the stout portal refused to budge, and

this made me aware that the tower was in much better condition than Draco had led me to believe, for surely I could have forced the door from its frame otherwise. Undaunted, I went outside, where I tried to peer through the tower windows. But they were so coated with dust on the inside that I could see nothing. I considered smashing one of the glass panes, but then I realized that if Draco spied the damage I had done, he would know I had been prying into his private affairs, and he would be furious with me. So at last I was reluctantly forced to abandon my plan to penetrate the tower.

Still all was not lost, for nearby the stone stairs that wound around the outside of the tower, permitting entry to its two exterior doors, I discovered stamped into the ground a single fresh, deep hoofprint, that of a pony whose shoe matched none of those with which our own horses were shod. There *had* been someone here last night, then, I thought triumphantly, and it had not been Joss the highwayman's ghost, a notion, as I have said, that I had found difficult to credit anyway. And Draco—not the ghost of Aislinn Deverell—must have been in the south tower, waiting for whoever had come. Who had it been? I wondered. Welles? But surely he was away at sea.

I had many more questions than I had answers, but I decided I would not confront my husband—at least not until I had gained enough evidence to compel him to admit the truth. Nevertheless I was consumed by curiosity, and I spent many long nights in my chamber, pretending to be asleep but, in reality, lying awake and listening intently for the soft jingle-jangle of a bridle in the yard below. I accomplished nothing but tired myself so greatly that I must spend a good part of my days napping in order to recover. Fortunately Mrs. Pickering attributed my fatigue to my advanced pregnancy. But once or twice, I caught Draco eyeing me speculatively, and I wondered a trifle uneasily if he suspected I was spying on him. I felt a twinge of guilt at the thought, because he was my husband, and although I did not love him, he gave me no cause to despise him either. I could not help feeling slightly ashamed of myself when after several weeks of my watching and listening, nothing untoward occurred; and at last I began to believe that perhaps my imagination had once more run away with me, after all, that despite my doubts, it truly *had* been ghosts I had seen and heard in the south tower. Exhausted, and feeling a trifle foolish as well, I gladly abandoned my role as the household detective in favor of a good night's sleep.

Unfortunately the rest of the country was not, like the Heights, devoid of incident that summer. The cost of food had continued to rise steadily, and as a consequence, industry was depressed. All year long, there had been a series of rallies calling for political changes, leading many to believe England was on the verge of a Jacobin revolt such as had occurred in France some years past. It was obvious to everyone that sooner or later, there would be trouble.

Finally, on August 16th, at St. Peter's Fields, in Manchester, a group of approximately sixty thousand people gathered to protest against the Tories, demanding reform of Parliament and repeal of the Corn Laws. None of the insurgents was armed, and the demonstration was a peaceful one; but still the magistrates present, alarmed by the size of the throng and its rebellious mood, insisted that the Manchester yeomenry arrest the seditious speakers just moments after the meeting had begun. In their zeal to carry out their orders, the untrained yeomenry not only seized the speakers (thought to be the leaders of the radicals), but, wielding sabers, set upon the crowd itself. Naturally what had initially been little more than an orderly assembly immediately degenerated into a panicked mob. Stricken, the chairman of the bench of magistrates called out the 15th Hussars and the Cheshire Volunteers and commanded them to join the yeomenry's attack. Five hundred persons were injured and eleven killed in what soon came to be known as the Peterloo Massacre. Even so, the government took no action against either the magistrates or the soldiers. In fact, the entire affair so incensed the Tories that there was a great deal of talk of taking stringent parliamentary measures to prevent any further revolt of the common man, who had plainly forgot his place in the scheme of things.

Like a pebble thrown into a pond, shock waves from the incident rippled through the country, and in many parishes, such as mine, the result was tragedy.

As I had feared, Sir Nigel would not be dictated to by the miners, and he refused to accede to their demands. I learned from Linnet that although he condescended to meet with Heapes and Dyson, he informed them in no uncertain terms that he saw nothing wrong with either the miners' wages or the conditions under which they must labor, and that if they persisted in causing trouble, he would indeed simply shut down the mines entirely. Heapes and Dyson related Sir Nigel's position to the workers, Linnet said, and for a while, it seemed as though they realized they had little choice but to accept their defeat.

Still an undercurrent of tension remained in the air at the miners' rows and, some weeks later, an unexplained explosion occurred in one of the pits of Wheal Penforth. Fortunately no one was injured or killed, and of course accidents could, and often did, happen in the mines. But naturally, under the circumstances, everyone suspected the explosion had been deliberately caused by the miners themselves. My father was infuriated. Because the pit must be cleared of debris and structurally reinforced before it could be reopened, a shipment of china clay he had expected to deliver to a porcelain manufacturer was delayed, and he was compelled, through Heapes, to make excuses to the factory's owner. Again he warned Heapes and Dyson that he would tolerate no further insurrection on the laborers' part, and to demonstrate that he did indeed mean business, he closed Wheal Penforth, thereby causing several men and children to lose their jobs.

Heapes was most upset and Dyson highly angered by Sir Nigel's decision, Linnet reported, but there was nothing either man could do about it. As he read aloud to the miners the names of those for whom there was no longer any work, Dyson told the hapless men and children they had no one to blame for their bad luck but whoever among them had sewn the seeds of rebellion and set off the explosion.

But there were those who did not see the matter that

way, and on October 13th, a dark and dreary autumn eve, as my father was returning home from business in Launceston, an unknown assailant, in an infamous act, set upon his carriage. After ordering both coachmen—old Phillip, the driver; and Bascombe, Sir Nigel's attendant—down from the vehicle and ruthlessly dispatching them each with a bullet in the back of the head, the attacker then ripped open the door of the coach and, in cold blood, shot my father straight through the heart, killing him instantly.

Though he had not loved me, still I was deeply shaken by Sir Nigel's brutal murder. I could not believe he was truly gone. He had survived so much that would have killed another man that somehow I had expected him to live forever. Even Draco was stunned by the news. He was strangely regretful, too, for though he had hated my father, he had respected him as a worthy adversary; and now that Sir Nigel was dead, Draco was like a man deprived of his principal chess opponent.

Grim-faced, he accompanied me in the carriage to Highclyffe Hall, where, half crazed with shock, grief, and anxiety about her future, my stepmother, now the Dowager Lady Chandler, instructed Iverleigh to refuse us permission to enter. Upon hearing her violent outburst to the butler, Esmond himself, thinking to spare my feelings, I suspected, came to the door. His face was pale and drawn, and filled with pity for me, too, for he knew that despite my father's cruel behavior to me, I had never wished him ill and had come to forgive him and make what peace I could with him now, even if it were only in my own mind. Esmond's eyes lingered on my countenance, drinking their fill of me as though he were a man dying of thirst. His love for me, his anguish at being forced to deny my request to keep vigil over my father's corpse, showed plainly upon his face as he suggested as kindly as he could that since Lady Chandler was not herself, perhaps it would be best if we did not disturb her just now.

It was in that moment, I think, that I truly looked at Esmond for the first time in my life without the aura of my love to soften and sweeten his image in my mind's eye. I saw a fair, slender, boyish man, with brown locks that curled gently over his forehead and a pair of fine hazel eyes clouded with pain and emotion; a quiet, graceful man wearing an elegant black silk suit with a froth of snow-white lace at his throat; a bookish man with soft white hands that had never done a hard day's work in his life. It occurred to me suddenly, startlingly, so I wondered why I had never realized it before, that there was no strength in this man. His was the path of least resistance, one that wended its way among the placid streams and still ponds of life; and with that, he was content. He would never boldly strike out upon a hard, rocky road, climb the highest tor, or sail the wildest seas, as only the bravest dared to do. These things did not cry out to him, challenge him, as they did me, but instead disturbed him in a way he did not understand. He had never been a fighter, but a dreamer; I saw that now. His love for me was like something in a fairy tale, unburdened by reality. In truth, he was content to worship me from afar. But I was not a goddess. I was a woman of flesh and blood, of desires and needs aching to be fulfilled. Without warning, I wanted to grab him and shake him and demand that he look at me, *really* look at me! And sadly I knew now, somehow, that he would be appalled if he did. He would find me—as subconsciously he had always found me—too passionate, too headstrong, too impetuous, ruled by my heart instead of my head. I was everything he was not and secretly wished to be, even while he despised himself for wishing it, knowing he lacked the courage to defy the world into which he had been born. He was weak, and his weakness was greater even than his love for me. It had always been so.

It was upon realizing this that my heart began slowly but surely to harden itself against him, that my respect for him began to diminish. My need to try one last time to understand and accept Sir Nigel's implacable hatred of me was as great as my stepmother's desire to carry it on for her dead husband's sake. But upon my father's death, Esmond had become master of Highclyffe Hall. He might admit whom he wished within its walls. Yet I saw clearly now that despite his love for me, he had chosen to bow to the wishes of Lady Chandler—and thus to avoid having to explain to Julianne, his wife, why he had not.

Julianne. Always Julianne.

I lifted my chin proudly, and when Draco, his jaw set with anger, would have forced our way inside the manor, I laid my hand upon his arm, staying him.

"No, Draco," I said, gazing coolly at Esmond. "We shall not intrude where we are not wanted."

With that, I turned away, and though I heard Esmond call my name softly, brokenly, I did not look back.

As it was sometimes wont to do in Cornwall, autumn seemed to have been chased away almost overnight by early winter nipping at its heels. The morning of Sir Nigel's funeral was cold and grey, made bleak and bitter by a biting wind that had brought with it a lowering sky and a chill drizzle. A veil of mist drifted in from the rough sea to enshroud the moors, where the heather and bracken had turned black and soggy as the marshes with the dismal weather. I suspected my father would have been pleased by the grimness of the day and by the mourners' suffering beneath the lash of the sharp wind and pelting rain as they paid their last respects to him. No doubt he would have thought it served them right, since in all likelihood, one of their ilk was his murderer. In truth, I could almost hear his mocking laughter at their discomfort ringing up from hell as he was laid to rest.

Although he had been my father, how little I had known him, I reflected numbly as I stood there shivering in the cemetery. Always he had kept me at arm's length, and I could remember but one act of caring and kindness he had ever shown me in my life, when he had given me my cat, Grimalkin. Still I mourned Sir Nigel, blinking back my tears as I thought sadly of all we might have shared had he not so despised me; and my heart ached for that which had ever been beyond my reach.

I shall not describe his funeral, for it was much as my uncle Quentin's had been, except that because it was so late in the year, there were chrysanthemums instead of roses and lilies on his casket, and this time, Draco did not stand alone, but with me at his side.

I clung heavily to my husband's arm, for the birth of my child was drawing near, and I was so bloated that it was difficult for me to be upon my feet for any length of time. My legs and feet swelled so badly that if I did not put my stockings and shoes on first thing every morning, I could not get them on at all later in the day. I could barely bend over, nor, once I sat down, could I rise without assistance. I was, in fact, helpless as a beached whale. Had it not been for Draco's taking such pains with me, I should have wept with frustration at my inability to perform even the simplest of tasks. But somehow he always succeeded in making me laugh, if ruefully, at my futile efforts to behave as though I were not incapacitated by my pregnancy; and when I felt fat and ugly, he reassured me that I was more beautiful than ever. Indeed my black hair shone as it never had before, and my dark skin bloomed, so that when I gazed into my mirror, I knew I looked well, despite my heaviness.

After Sir Nigel's funeral, to my surprise, his solicitor, Mr. Oldstead, who had come down from London to handle my father's legal affairs, paused on his way from the cemetery to request that Draco and I be present that afternoon at the reading of Sir Nigel's last will and testament.

"I'm afraid I . . . don't understand, Mr. Oldstead," I said, puzzled. "To the best of knowledge, my father disinherited me upon my marriage, and certainly he and Draco were never on the best of terms."

"Yes, well, that may be, Mrs. Chandler," the solicitor agreed. "But in fact, Sir Nigel, for reasons quite unknown to me, later had me draw up a codicil to his last will and testament, and as it concerns you and your husband, I shall expect you at the Hall at three o'clock."

"That's all very well and good, Mr. Oldstead, but I believe you will find that Mrs. Chandler and I are not welcome there," Draco stated coolly.

"Have no fear, sir. I have spoken to Lady Chandler, and since she is, of course, quite . . . er . . . eager to learn what provisions Sir Nigel made for her," the solicitor declared dryly, "she has assured me she will voice no objections to your being present."

After that, though both Draco and I were consumed by curiosity over the matter, Mr. Oldstead would not enlighten us further, but hurried on, his hat pulled down low over his eyes and his coat collar turned up defensively against the wind and rain. Draco handed me up into our carriage, and as Will cracked his whip over the horses' heads and the vehicle moved forward, I wondered aloud what was contained in the codicil to which the solicitor had referred. Draco shrugged and, as he secured a wool blanket about me so I would be warm enough on the drive home, made some noncommittal reply. Nevertheless I could tell he was as interested as I in learning why we were named in my father's will.

When we arrived at the Hall at the appointed hour, we were indeed admitted without hindrance, and after all the beneficiaries were gathered in the library, Mr. Oldstead proceeded to read aloud Sir Nigel's will. Esmond, of course, had, under a separate, lengthy document been deeded the bulk of the estate, which was entailed and so could not be otherwise dispersed. But trust funds were to be established for Lady Chandler and Aunt Tibby, from which they would each be paid an adequate, if not extravagant, allowance; and there were small bequests to Sarah and various servants as well. Welles and Julianne, much to her anger, received nothing, for they had been suitably provided for by their father, Captain Prescott, and, in addition, had been so handsomely supported by Sir Nigel during his lifetime that he believed he had dutifully discharged any and all obligations to them; this, the solicitor explained as he turned the pages of my father's will.

Finally Mr. Oldstead paused and, removing his silver-rimmed spectacles, slowly wiped them clean with his handkerchief. Then he carefully positioned them on the bridge of his nose once more and cleared his throat.

"Originally," he announced, "that was the end of Sir Nigel's will. However, recently he instructed me to draw up a codicil to said will, which I did and which was duly signed by him and two witnesses. It reads as follows: 'To my illegitimate nephew, Draco, son of my brother Quentin Chandler, and to my lawful daughter, Margaret Amélie Chandler, I do hereby bequeath the Chandler china-clay mines, known as Wheal Anant and Wheal Penforth, which are not part of the entail binding my estate and so are not therefore subject to any of its restrictions. This bequest shall be unconditional, with one exception: Said mines are not to be sold, but are to remain in the possession of Draco and Margaret Chandler for their lifetime and, in the event of their deaths, are to pass to their legal heir or heirs. Should Draco and Margaret Chandler find themselves unable to agree to this clause, said mines are to revert immediately and irrevocably to my estate. In such an event, I do hereby instruct my solicitor, Mr. Roger Oldstead, to draw up any and all legal documents necessary to make said mines a part of the aforementioned entail. *'À vaincre sans péril, on triomphe sans gloire.'*'"

After Mr. Oldstead had finished, I sat in stunned silence, unable to believe my ears. My father had left Draco and me the china-clay mines, counting, I felt sure, on Draco's stubborn will to hold on to what was his. Sir Nigel had been certain Draco would not allow the mines to revert to the estate, and thus to Esmond; and so, in essence, by refusing to permit us to sell them, he had cast down his gauntlet before us and challenged us to make them pay. He had known, I surmised, that Esmond would not be able to handle Heapes, Dyson, and the miners, and so would be forced to shut both mines down permanently. But Draco was a fighter. Not only would he brook no threat to his authority, but he would do whatever was necessary, no matter how difficult or dangerous, to wrest all he could from the mines, for he would see them as a means by which to accomplish a great deal more.

"*A vaincre sans péril, on triomphe sans gloire,*" my father had said: When there is no peril in the fight, there is no glory in the triumph. He had known Draco far better than I had ever realized.

My husband had been cheated of his due by an accident of birth, but one way or another, he meant to have it. Like Mick Dyson, he was hungry to get ahead in the world, and acquiring Stormswept Heights had but whetted his appetite for all that should have been his by right. Now I believed he was driven to prevail in making the desolate manor not only rival Highclyffe Hall, but surpass it; and for some strange reason, Sir Nigel had handed him the means by which, if he were willing to take the risks involved, he might succeed.

I did not know why my father had done such a thing. But still I could not put from my mind the image of Draco telling him that out of all he had ever had, we were the best, and I wondered if in the end, Sir Nigel had believed him after all.

Chapter Twenty-five

Jarrett

Gloomy night embrac'd the place
Where the noble Infant lay.
The Babe look't up and shew'd his face;
In spite of darkness, it was day.

—*Hymn of the Nativity*
Richard Crashaw

There was, of course, an investigation into Sir Nigel's murder; but little more was learned by the dragoons who arrived to look into the matter than Esmond, now the local magistrate, had already discovered: From the evidence gleaned at the site, it was clear that my father's carriage had been waylaid by a single culprit, who, it was presumed, had taken the coachmen—old Phillip and Bascombe—by surprise, forced them at gunpoint to climb down from the vehicle, and then had killed them both. After that, the unknown attacker had yanked open the coach door and mercilessly shot Sir Nigel, who, being paralyzed, had had no means of escape. But who had done the savage deed, or why, was not so easily determined, although it was the general concensus that my father had been set upon by one of the miners he had thrown out of work when he'd closed Wheal Penforth. No one envied Draco's and my inheritance; indeed many prophesied darkly that my husband would be the next victim if wages and conditions were not improved at the mines.

Certainly Draco took far more of an interest in them than Sir Nigel had ever done. Where previously my husband had risen at six o'clock, he was now up and gone from the Heights by four-thirty in order to be at the mines at five, when work started each morning. The first day, he began by meeting with Heapes in the mining office to examine the records and accounts, and what he learned of the manager's shoddy practices and shady bookkeeping so incensed him that he fired Heapes on the spot, thereby earning the miners' grudging approval. After that, much to the annoyance of Mick Dyson and the surprise of the laborers, he inspected the mines themselves. Although he knew relatively little about mining, what Draco saw appalled him, and he set about at once to educate himself about the process of digging china clay from the earth and to initiate the first of many changes he intended to make at the mines, letting it be known that although he was a hard man, he was also a just one and would deal fairly with those who accorded him the same treatment. Those who still opposed him were swiftly shown the door, and soon it became clear to all that Draco was a different breed of master from Sir Nigel. The inflammatory grumbling of the workers ceased as, for the time being, they decided to give the mines' new owner a chance to make good on his promises.

I breathed a sigh of relief at the respite, for in truth, I found the prospect of someone murdering my husband horrifying; and as I remembered the way Mick Dyson had looked at me that day at the miners' rows, I shuddered at the thought of having to fend for myself and my unborn child without Draco.

There is no life without death—and no death without life— for in the end, all things come full circle. Like the seasons, the new spring follows the old winter, and so it was in northern Cornwall that year, for a month after Sir Nigel was killed, on a grey November day sullen with the hint of a brewing storm, my labor began as my child struggled to push its way into the world.

At first I did not understand what was happening to me. The stories I had heard about giving birth had not truly prepared me for its reality. In the beginning, I thought it was simply that the baby was pressing down upon me so uncomfortably that neccessitated my frequent trips to the chamber pot. But presently, after I had changed my undergarments several times, only to have them soaked through again in moments, I realized my water must have broken. I was mildly surprised, for somehow I had expected this suddenly just to happen all at once, and even now, I felt none of the pain I had been told accompanied the onslaught of labor.

Certain my time was at hand nevertheless, I went in search of Mrs. Pickering to request that she send someone for Draco and Dr. Ashford. Minutes later, both Will and Ned were riding out from the stables, and Mrs. Pickering was hustling me back upstairs to my bedchamber, calling for Linnet. Together my housekeeper and abigail efficiently stripped me of my clothes and bundled me into my nightgown, then insisted I get into bed, although I did not feel the least desire to do so. Instead I was filled with a strange mixture of euphoria and apprehension, and I longed incomprehensibly to run and dance and laugh aloud with joy, while at the same time, I wanted to curl myself up into a tight little ball in a corner somewhere and remain absolutely still, for fear that otherwise something would go wrong and I or the baby should die. Quickly I pushed the frightening thought from my mind, reassuring myself that there was no reason to suppose I should not have an entirely normal delivery and a perfectly healthy child. Still I knew I would not rest easy until Draco and Dr. Ashford arrived.

While I, asserting my authority and stubbornly disdaining my bed, paced the floor like an anxious lioness, Mrs. Pickering scurried about, stoking up the fire and setting a kettle of water on to boil. As she busied herself with these preparations, she kept up a constant stream of garrulous chatter that under the circumstances, I found most distressing, especially when I must shout most of my replies, for I wished to concentrate instead on what was happening inside my body. I did not realize then that the housekeeper's intentions were kindly, that she sought but to relieve my mind of worry and to distract me from my first twinges of inevitable pain when they began, filling me with such anguish that I could scarcely believe the worst was yet to come.

Unlike Mrs. Pickering, Linnet proved worse than useless as, heedless of my discomfort and dismay, she perched avidly on a chair, her sly eyes dark with portent as she related to me with a good deal of relish the dreadful details of the births of her youngest brother and sister, at which she had been present. In truth, my abigail was really a rather heartless young woman, the serrated edge to her character born of her being reared in the miners' rows. She was not, I believed, truly wicked, but because she had suffered enormous hardship in her life and despised those who had not, she took a mean, petty satisfaction in the misfortune of others, her self-esteem somehow bolstered by the knowledge that their lot in life was little better than hers.

Thus I could not disguise my relief when, sometime later, Draco appeared in the doorway and, overhearing Linnet's horrid remarks, curtly ordered her from the room.

"Draco!" I cried, flinging myself into his arms. "Draco!"

"There, there, love," he murmured against my ear, stroking my hair soothingly as he hugged me close to hold me steady upon my feet when I swayed against him, gasping as another mild contraction coursed its way through my body. "Don't fret. There's nothing for you to worry about. Linnet's just a spiteful cat, that's all. I should have realized it sooner and sent her packing. I shall dismiss her at once if you wish. Shhhhh, Maggie. I'm here now, and I shan't let anything happen to you or the baby, I promise."

I could not help but believe him; there was something so strong and comforting about his broad shoulders, his warm embrace. He had always leaped to my defense. I had no cause to think he would not do so now. Without protest, I allowed him to tuck me into bed, since he insisted on doing so and I was only too happy now to lie down. But when he would have left me to see whether the doctor had come, I clung to him fiercely, tugging him back, and begged him to stay by my side.

"Don't let them send you away, Draco," I pleaded, clutching his hand tightly, Linnet's tales still preying on my mind. "I want you here to speak for me and the child if—if something should . . . happen."

"Nothing's going to happen, love. But I'll not leave you, then, never you fear."

And so, when presently my pains became so bad that they struck sharp as a knife ripping through my body, he was there to hold and encourage me, to rub my aching back and wipe the sweat from my forehead; and when at last Will returned to say that Dr. Ashford could not come, that he had driven over to an outlying farm to treat a seriously injured man and would not be back before nightfall, if at all, it was Draco who broke the news to me as gently as he could and informed me that he and Mrs. Pickering, who had some small experience as a midwife, were going to deliver my baby.

There was a wealth of concern for me in my husband's black eyes when he looked at me, and a flicker of fear, too, for I was his wife, and it could not be an easy thing for him to know my well-being, and that of our child, too, now lay solely with him and our housekeeper, who was muttering to herself and shaking her head with anxiety at the doctor's inability to be present at the birth. Still Draco had never been one to run away from a difficult situation, and now was no exception. Smiling at me crookedly, he shrugged off his jacket and waistcoat and laid them aside. Then he took my hands in his and gazed at me steadily.

"We shall see this thing through together, love, you and I. Have faith, Maggie. I'll not let you and the baby down, I swear it." Tremulously I nodded and smiled, biting my lip as I tried hard not to let my fear show upon my face. "That's my brave girl," he said. "I knew I could count on you."

And so, because I did not want to fail him, I fought down my rising panic as best I could and set about, like so many other women before me, to prepare myself to give birth to my child.

My labor was long and hard. I had never before known such excruciating pain, and though I tried not to cry out, in the end, the screams were torn from my throat by the agony that clawed at me so ferociously that I believed with all my heart that my baby and I were going to die.

As darkness had fallen, so had the brewing storm loosed its fury upon the land. The ominous wind shrieked and howled like a banshee, whining through the cracks and crannies of the manor so the flames of the lamps flickered wildly and cast eerie, dancing shadows upon the walls. The rain beat ruthlessly against the windows, tearing at the shutters and rattling the glass panes so violently that I thought they would shatter. In fact, though I, immersed in my pains, did not realize it, several of those in the light-house were indeed broken.

Draco had, as I have said, stripped down to his shirt and breeches. Yet even so, his brow and upper lip were now beaded with sweat from the stifling closeness of the hot, humid chamber, where the fire blazed against the dank chill of the storm. Perspiration trickled down his bulging fore-arms revealed by his rolled-up shirtsleeves, and once or twice, he wiped his face with the back of his hand.

"Push, Maggie, push!" he ordered grimly above the roar of the wind and the rain.

And so I bore down again and again, and finally, just when I knew I could bear no more, red, wrinkled, and squalling louder than the storm with anger at being so tortuously expelled from my womb into the world, my son, Jarrett, was born. Tears ran down my cheeks as Draco voiced his triumph and lifted him up so I could see him, so big, so bold, so beautiful, a patch of jet-black hair on his head, his small fists waving with indignant rage at his inability to return to his safe, snug nest.

"Is he all right? Is he all right?" I asked weakly, my

heart bursting with immeasurable joy at the sound of his lusty cries, my arms aching to hold him.

"Yes," Draco declared proudly as, cradling our son gingerly, he gently lowered him into the basin of warm water Mrs. Pickering had prepared to wash the blood and mucus from his chubby little body. "Yes."

"Are you sure? Count his fingers and toes!" I demanded, wanting to make sure and having a suspicious notion that men really were not very concerned when it came to such things.

"I already have," my husband replied softly. "He has ten of each. He's a beautiful baby, Maggie, the most beautiful baby in the world." Then, as Mrs. Pickering finished tying off the cord and swaddled the child, Draco kissed me tenderly. "The two of you have made me the happiest man alive," he said.

He handed our son into my outstretched arms, and as I hugged him to my breast, I marveled at his soft, downy hair, his tiny fingers and toes, the way his palm gripped my finger securely when I reached out to him. Instinctively he sought my nipple; awkwardly, for I was as inexperienced as he, I helped him find it, only to feel him lose it almost at once. His face turned scarlet with wrath, his eyes screwed shut, and he resumed bawling with frustration—and now hunger, too—until I once more guided his open mouth to its goal, and he latched on firmly and began eagerly to nurse.

"We will learn together, little one, you and I," I whispered and pressed my cheek against the top of his silky head, my heart overflowing with indescribable emotion at the sight of him suckling at my breast.

My child, I thought. *This is my child, a miracle. Thank you, God. Oh, thank you for this wonderful new being.*

I glanced at Draco, who, propped up on one elbow, was now lying next to us on the bed, watching us silently, his dark eyes shining unashamedly with tears, his face unmistakably aglow with his love for us. I had never before felt as close to him as I did now, and impulsively reaching out, I took his hand in mine and squeezed it tightly, swallowing hard at the sudden, overwhelming emotion that choked my throat. In that terrible moment when I had learned the doctor was not coming and I had been racked with agony, sure I was going to die, and my baby with me, this man had held our lives in the palm of his hands and had brought us safely through our ordeal. He had been there for me, and for our son, too, just as he had said he would be. For almost as long as I could remember, Draco had always been there for me, I realized suddenly—protecting me, loving me, giving me his all, and asking for so little in return. Why had I deliberately blinded myself to that fact? I wondered. Because of Esmond? Oh, God, I had been a fool, such a fool, I thought, for now, without warning, sweeping over me as strongly and sweetly as the touch of my husband's hand in mine, came the deep, certain knowledge that I loved him with all my heart—and always had.

Chapter Twenty-six

Days of Sweetness and Light

Between the dark and the daylight,
  When the night is beginning to lower,
Comes a pause in the day's occupations,
  That is known as the Children's Hour.

—*The Children's Hour*
Henry Wadsworth Longfellow

Dear reader, I cannot tell you how full were those glorious days following the birth of my son: abounding in joy, in eagerness, in difficulty, in frustration, and, above all, in love. If ever you have had a child, you will know of what I speak, for your life is irrevocably changed by the event. You are no longer the master or mistress of yourself and your fate, but responsible for and to another human being, a human being who, in the beginning, knows nothing but its own wants and needs and so makes constant demands upon you, ignorant of the fact that you have a life of your own. And so, at a time when I needed most to think, to dwell upon and to savor the discovery of my love for Draco, I had no chance to do so. Jarrett consumed me utterly, totally. I was fearful in my ignorance and inexperience of loving him too much or not enough, of spoiling him or neglecting him, of feeding him when his linen needed to be changed or vice versa—in short, of making some dreadful mistake that

334

would blight his life forever; and when I thought of Draco at all, it was with a guilty pang of conscience that I thought of him so little.

I knew there was much that needed to be put right between us. But wrapped up in Jarrett, I spoke no word to my husband of my love for him. I had withheld my heart from him for so long that now, at this wondrous, trying time, I did not know quite how to go about relinquishing it into his keeping. I could not bring myself simply to say "I love you," for the revelation that I did indeed love Draco was too new and fresh for the words to come easily to my lips, as they do to lovers of long standing. Nor did I dare to broach the subject of Esmond, for even though now I knew he had never truly won my heart, I had certainly behaved as though he had; and I could not imagine how to explain to my husband that in reality, Esmond had been nothing more than the fairy-tale prince of my childhood, as I now realized, someone I had made up and fallen in love with—and who had not really been Esmond at all.

So in the end, I said naught and cursed my wretched tongue, which had never failed me before, when it ought, and let me down now, when I needed it.

Still, although we had precious few moments to ourselves, curiously, Draco and I were closer than we had ever been before, drawn together by the tiny red scrap that was Jarrett. Never had there existed a sweeter, more beautiful child—or so we told each other repeatedly whenever we looked at him, certain in our hearts that it was true. Previously I had thought all babies were alike, and so, although I had dutifully smiled and cooed at those I had seen, I had paid them little heed. If they could not walk and talk, they were not very interesting, or so I had believed. Now I knew differently, for Jarrett was special right from the start; and until his second birthday, after which he seemed overnight to turn into a perverse little demon who did not understand the meaning of the word "no," I pitied other women, who must make do with rather less extraordinary children.

From the beginning, Draco and I petted and pampered

our son. The first few weeks after his birth, we hardly slept at all, lying awake instead in the darkness, our ears straining to hear the sound of his breathing so we could reassure ourselves that he had not suddenly, inexplicably, died in his cradle, as some babies had been known to do; and when we could not hear him, we leaped from our bed to shine upon him the lamp we left burning on the night table, and we poked and prodded him gently to be certain he yet lived. He must be fed, too, when he awoke, hungry and screaming, not knowing or caring if it was three o'clock in the morning; and at first, because I did not know any better, I woke him up myself several times during the night, as well, in order to change his linen, until kindly Mrs. Pickering, shaking her head over my ignorance, showed me how to pad the cloth so he did not need a fresh one until morning.

It was no wonder, then, that after scarcely a fortnight, Draco and I were exhausted, and at last, out of desperation one evening, we took Jarrett into bed with us so we would not have to check on him constantly. This arrangement suited us so splendidly that we continued it thereafter, for when Jarrett stirred and began rooting for my breast, I could feed him swiftly, forestalling his cries of hunger. Often the two of us would drift back to sleep while he suckled, never waking Draco at all. Jarrett, lying snug and warm between us, was so content that except for his single feeding, he slept through the night from then on.

Mrs. Pickering was scandalized by what she called our common behavior.

"No better than them what live in the miners' rows, missus, parents and children all in one bed—for lack of any other!" she declared stoutly when she learned of the matter, and silently I observed with some amusement that Draco was not the only one at the Heights who wished to get on in the world, but had surrounded himself, as well, with servants who considered themselves the equal of Iverleigh and Mrs. Seyton at the Hall. " 'Tis a disgrace, that's what!" the housekeeper continued. "For the Heights be no ramshackle cottage, and there be many an empty chamber here what might serve as a nursery! I suppose Master Jarrett shall grow up eatin' with his fingers and wipin' his nose on his sleeve, too—and you the late baronet's daughter, missus, and proper born and bred!''

She insisted Jarrett ought to have a decent nanny; and despite my love for my child, because I was young and in love and knew Draco and I did indeed need some time to ourselves, I at last allowed her to engage a girl from the miners' rows. My husband was pleased by my decision, for he felt it earned him another mark in the miners' favor to have provided a job for one of their own; and the girl, Annie, was clean and hardworking and proved to have a sensible head on her shoulders. So secure in the knowledge that Jarrett was in her kind, capable hands, I was able to get out and about a little, as I had not done for a while.

We were well into December now, a time when the wild, savage coast of northern Cornwall was at its most bitter, when snow lay upon the moors and ice encrusted the shingle along the beach, when the wind lashed like a whip across the land and, beyond the cliffs, the sea was dark and angry. I pitied the tall ships I sometimes spied in the distance from the lighthouse, their sails flogging violently in the wind, their hulls tossed hazardly upon the waves. Every night now, if Draco were not home to do so himself, I lit the peat fire laid in the round, open stone hearth of the lighthouse, and I hoped its flames would prevent the vessels I had seen from wrecking upon the rocky shore. Following the storm the night of Jarrett's birth, we had replaced the damaged windows in the lighthouse, only to find the glass panes lying shattered upon the floor a few weeks later, apparently broken once more by the force of the bitter wind. So we had repaired them yet again, for Draco had been strangely insistent that the lighthouse signal its ominous warning to distant ships, and the peat fire was difficult to keep burning without the windows to protect it when the gales of winter blew.

Otherwise the holiday season was a quiet time for us, one spent basking in the glow of the Yule log, Jarrett sleeping peacefully on the rug I had laid before the hearth in the hall, his thumb tucked lightly between his tiny, parted rosebud lips, his many presents, which Draco and I had opened and exclaimed over in his stead, lying scattered on the floor beside him.

Shortly after the New Year, mounted upon Avalon, I set out across the snowswept moors toward the Grange to call on Aunt Tibby and Sarah. I found them in good health but low spirits, for even though by the end of January, Welles would have reached his majority and come into his inheritance at last, Esmond remained firm in his refusal to permit Sarah to wed my stepbrother. Sarah was understandably most distressed by her brother's decision, and Aunt Tibby, not wishing to choose sides, was torn between the two. Still my aunt and cousin were delighted by my visit and plied me with endless questions about Jarrett, whom they had not seen since his christening. I gladly expounded upon the joys of motherhood until finally, fearing I sounded like one of those annoying women who go on and on about their marvelous children, I turned the conversation to topics upon which my tongue would be less apt to run away with me.

After learning from Aunt Tibby and Sarah that Highclyffe Hall was like a tomb now that Sir Nigel was dead and Julianne was miserable with her pregnancy, I rode over later that week to the Hall, too, knowing how my stepsister must feel and thinking that perhaps it was time now to let our past differences be bygones. After all, she had got what she wanted, and much to my surprise, strangely, so had I. There was no longer any need for hard feelings between us. There never had been, if only I had realized sooner that it was not Esmond, but Draco I desired; and since Julianne and I were related by marriage and must live out our lives together here on these wild moors of Cornwall, it seemed ridiculous not to be on speaking terms at least.

To my surprise, for I had half feared I would be turned away again at the door of my childhood home, Julianne was glad to see me and invited me to take tea with her in the small drawing room.

"Do sit down, Maggie," she urged, indicating a spot beside her on the sofa, "for I am like to die of boredom in this dreary old house, and it cannot be thought disrespectful of me to be entertaining you at least, since you are my stepsister and therefore family."

I gave a guilty little start at that, for it was customary to observe a period of six months' mourning for the loss of a parent, and though Linnet, whose services I had retained after all, had quite correctly laid out the proper clothes for me this morning, I had scarcely paid them any heed, nor, in the weeks following Jarrett's birth, had I truly thought of my father at all. I had made what peace I could with him at his grave, as, after a fashion, he had made his with Draco and me in his will, and no amount of crepe veils or black ribbon could alter the fact that I had long ceased to weep for him. My only regret now was that the person responsible for his terrible murder had never been apprehended.

But Julianne, I knew, must observe the necessary proprieties, for Lady Chandler would have insisted on it; and it was obvious from her apperance that currently my stepsister lacked both the will and the energy to oust her mother from a position of authority at the Hall. I estimated that Julianne weighed upward of ten stone if she weighed an ounce, and she was not one of those women who, like me, bloomed with pregnancy. Her face was puffy and swollen, her eyes were shadowed with dark mauve circles, and her fingers had got so plump that she had been forced to lock away her rings in her jewel box. She was tired and, I suspected, unwell.

"How are you, Julianne?" I asked, stripping off my riding gloves and laying them aside.

"How do I look? No, don't answer that, Maggie, for I know only too well that I am hideous as a leper. Oh, how I wish this miserable baby had never been conceived! I told Esmond I shouldn't like to have my figure ruined, but, then, men are such brutes, aren't they? They don't care a fig for anyone but themselves—the selfish swine!—and they marry women solely to get little replicas of themselves—as though we needed or wanted any more of them! Daughters don't count for anything, no matter how beautiful and intelligent they are. God, how I hope this one's a boy so I won't ever have to go through this again! I hate babies!'' my stepsister burst out, on the verge of tears, and though I pitied her, still I was stricken by her words.

I thought of the joy I found in Jarrett, in the sweet, milky scent of his breath and the fresh, powdery fragrance of his skin, in the curious wonder of his eyes and the delightful gurgle of his voice; and the idea of someone hating him appalled me.

"You don't mean that, Julianne," I said.

"Oh, but I do. I do!" she cried passionately. "Babies are horrible. They make you eat like a horse and put on weight, and they stretch your body all out of shape and cause you to swell up like a toad! Then, as though that weren't enough, they nearly tear you in two being born, perhaps even kill you, and half the time, they're born dead themselves or die shortly thereafter. And that's just the beginning of it! If they *do* survive, once they get here, they wail like howling cats until you'd just like to tear your hair out, and they drool and spit up all over you, mussing your clothes and making them reek of sour milk, and they soil their linen and expect you to clean them up afterward—Lud! I just don't know why any woman wants one!"

It was evident to me that she was overwrought, so I restrained from speaking any word of disagreement or rebuke, and I was quite relieved when Iverleigh appeared with the tea tray, my stepmother hard on his heels.

"Hullo, Margaret," she greeted me politely, as though there had never been any discord between us. "Motherhood must agree with you. I don't know when I've ever seen you in such good looks. And how is little . . . Jarrett, is it? I have been under such a strain that I'm afraid my memory plays tricks with me these days. With . . . Nigel's death, the funeral, Julianne's pregnancy . . . well, it's all been quite overwhelming, to say the least."

"Yes, I understand, Stepmama. Jarrett is well and thriving, a delightful child."

"I am glad to hear it. You must bring him to see me,

Margaret, for I am the only grandparent he has, you know, and so, of course, I must take an extra special interest in his welfare.''

"Of course," I said, as though this were the most natural thing in the world; but I confess I was much startled by her behavior.

She, Esmond, and Julianne had been at Jarrett's christening, of course, for it had taken place during the church service the Sunday following his birth; and somewhat to my surprise, they had sent an appropriate gift: a sterling silver rattle. But I had not expected anything more than that. Certainly I had not imagined Lady Chandler would express any interest in pursuing her relationship to my son, and I wondered at her apparent change of heart toward me, for since my marriage to Draco, she had made it clear to me that I was of no use to her. Still she was not one to burn bridges she might need later on, and now that Draco possessed the mines and it was plain he had every intention of making a success of them, perhaps she felt we might be turned to some account after all. There were, too, those who still believed he had a fortune stashed under his mattress.

Suddenly, for the first time, I wondered how Esmond was faring as master of Highclyffe Hall. If he should fail in his responsibilities, Lady Chandler stood to lose a great deal, I suspected, for I did not doubt that her trust fund would eventually prove inadequate for her needs and that she was depending upon Esmond and Julianne to provide her with an additional source of income. Without warning, the childhood memory of Draco boasting that he would manage the estate far better than Esmond rose in my mind, and inwardly I smiled ironically as Lady Chandler's thought processes were revealed to me. Really! Did she suppose that just because she was my stepmother, Draco would feel some obligation to discharge her debts if Esmond could not? In truth, I would not have put such a notion past her. Yet even so, I could not now find it in my heart to despise her. Rather, I felt sorry for her, as I did for Julianne, because they would never truly be a part of the society they craved, while I, who might have been, had spurned it and now thought myself the richer for it. Sighing, I wondered briefly why God didn't do a better job of ordering the world, for it was clear to me that it was sadly in need of attention.

After tea, I took my leave of the two women, glad to escape from the repressive, depressing atmosphere that surrounded them and to return to the sweetness and light of the Heights. I spent the remainder of the afternoon playing with Jarrett and thinking how my home, for all its ruin and lack of grace, was a much happier house than the Hall had ever been.

Chapter Twenty-seven

Dangerous Intrigue

The heights by great men reached and kept
Were not attained by sudden flight,
But they, while their companions slept,
Were toiling upward in the night.

—*The Ladder of Saint Augustine*
Henry Wadsworth Longfellow

With the birth of our son, Draco worked harder than ever, putting in long days at the mines, and at the manor, too. He had reopened Wheal Penforth, hiring back many of its former laborers, and he had found a new manager to replace Heapes as well, an honest, industrious, well-spoken man by the name of Franklin Vaughan, a man who was not easily intimidated or swayed by the opinions of others. Together they managed somehow to honor the delivery dates of china-clay shipments to the various porcelain manufacturers with whom Sir Nigel, through Heapes, had completed negotiations before his death; and so Draco turned a tidy profit and was well pleased with himself.

With the money earned, he engaged masons and carpenters to continue repairs on the manor, and since I insisted on the dining room being completed first, I could now look forward to serving a proper meal at the Heights at last. Mrs. Pickering had got two girls from the miners' rows to help her with the cleaning and cooking, too, and with the additional servants, we managed to get on fairly well, so I was now able to devote the majority of my time to my husband and son.

Whenever we could, Draco and I spent a quiet evening together, often with Jarrett, who was, however, still so new to us in so many ways that more than once, we glanced with surprise at him lying on the rug before the hearth in the hall and wondered whence he had come and why his parents hadn't arrived to take him home.

We played chess and piquet, and occasionally I read while Draco sang softly to Jarrett in Romany. Strangely, as I watched the two of them together, my emotions were mixed, for though I loved them both, I thought of Jarrett as my domain, and sometimes I felt a twinge of jealousy that he reached for Draco's hand as easily as mine. Yet I was glad it was so, for I did not want my husband and son to be strangers, as Sir Nigel and I had been; and I knew there were many women who would have envied me Draco's active interest in and deep attachment to Jarrett, things my husband felt because of the lack of such in his own troubled childhood.

How misbegotten indeed, we had been. How determined we were that Jarrett should not suffer that same feeling of being unwanted, of not belonging, which we had known during our youth. Yet even now, understanding that we were, in truth, two of a kind, I could not bring myself to speak to Draco of my love for him. Despite the growing closeness Jarrett had brought us, we were in some ways further apart than we had ever been before. My husband had not made love to me since before our son's birth, and now I felt as though we were in some peculiar fashion strangers to each other. I was once more shy of undressing before him, and when he touched me or kissed me, I trembled a little with fear, as I had of old, feeling as though I were a maiden and uncertain what to expect. Did he find me unattractive now, since I had borne a child? I wondered and studied my reflection in every mirror I passed, assessing my face and figure critically.

I looked a little tired, I thought; but other than that, I could find nothing wrong with my appearance. I had lost whatever weight I had gained during my pregnancy, and now my body was as slender as it had been before, its curves even softer somehow, more appealing, I thought.

But still Draco did not seek my bed, and so, thinking he no longer wanted me, I kept silent about what was in my heart—and ached desperately at the knowledge that I had recognized my love for him too late.

In late January of that year of 1820, Welles turned twenty-one, and with his inheritance from his dead father, Captain Brodie, and the investment of an unknown silent partner (whom I suspected but could not say for certain was Draco), he bought a fleet schooner, which he christened the *Sea Gypsy*. But to Esmond, my stepbrother's apparent progress in the world, from second mate to captain of his own ship, was still not sufficient to gain Sarah's hand in marriage. I daresay Julianne might have influenced her husband otherwise if she had chosen to do so, but as she liked Sarah as little as Esmond did Welles, she adamantly refused to aid her brother's cause. A fortnight ago, she had given birth to a daughter, christened Elizabeth, who was a tiny replica of her; and Julianne, who had hoped for a son and heir so she could be done with that side of her marriage, was therefore in no mood to listen to Welles's cajolery and threats. He had no one else to turn to for assistance except his mother, who, although she could find nothing objectionable in Sarah's background or breeding, since her father had been the Honorable Worthing Sheffield and her mother the daughter of Sir Simon Chandler, Bt., saw much to complain about in Sarah's modest dowry and so did not encourage Welles in that direction.

"Don't look so downcast, Welles. There's always Gretna Green," Draco pointed out to my stepbrother, who was still at home, winding up the legal matters concerning his inheritance and the purchase of his vessel, and who had ridden over from the Hall to visit.

"Yes, well, I daresay it was all very well and good for you and Maggie, old boy," Welles uttered glumly, "but the thing is . . . there would be a great deal of talk, you know, and while the gossip of old biddies doesn't matter one way or another to any of us three, Sarah wouldn't be able just to shrug it off. She's a sensitive soul and takes things like that too much to heart."

"Yes, I suppose that's true," I said, for even now, when Draco and I had begun to wedge a place for ourselves in the village, there were still those who shunned us and scorned our pretense that Jarrett had been premature, as we had claimed for his sake.

Though, by now, I had got used to that sort of thing, there were still times when the hateful rumors stung nevertheless, and I knew that Sarah, so wrenlike in her blithe, gentle nature, would be deeply hurt were she to be exposed to such viciousness.

It appeared there was no hope for the two young lovers, then; and Welles, when he finally took his leave of us, was in such a reckless, devilish mood that even Draco remarked upon it as he accompanied him outside into the courtyard and warned him somewhat sharply to have a care what he was about.

"Don't worry about me, old boy," my stepbrother rejoined as he flung himself onto his horse's back. "I can take care of myself."

It seemed as though he were about to say something more. But glancing at me standing in the doorway, my eyes filled with concern, he apparently thought better of it and, biting back his words, set his spurs to his gelding's sides, galloping off in a swirl of flurrying snow and mist.

It was later on that week that once more in the dead of night, I heard the ring of a bridle in the yard below my bedchamber. Though I had listened in vain for the sound these many months past and had finally doubtfully attributed it to the ghosts of Aislinn Deverell and her lover, Joss the highwayman, after all, I now recognized the noise at once for what it really was. This time, I awakened swiftly as the soft jingle-jangle roused me from my slumber. Instantly I rose and glanced about the room illuminated by the low flames that crackled in the hearth. As before, Draco was nowhere to be found, and after slipping on my wrapper and rearranging the pillows on the bed so Jarrett, who still slept peacefully, would not roll off, I hurried to the window and drew back the curtain.

I noticed immediately that the fire in the lighthouse was not burning, although Draco was usually so insistent upon keeping it lit after dark that Renshaw was required to rise and check it several times a night to add more fuel. As it was the dark of the moon and the mist and snow obscured the stars, I could see little. But still what I glimpsed was enough to set my heart pounding, for the glow of a lamp shone from a window of the south tower, and slowly, as I watched, the lower door to the stairs that wound about the tower's exterior began to open on well-oiled hinges. Moments later, Draco appeared upon the landing, holding the blazing light high to guide the shadowed figures who tramped across the snowswept yard in the blackness, Welles at their head, his blond hair gleaming like a beacon in the night.

In single file, the men moved quickly, furtively, toward the tower. Silently they came, and I saw that the bridles and hooves of the heavily laden ponies they led were wrapped with cloth to muffle the sounds of their passing. A few of the men carried lanterns, but the glimmer of these only heightened the eerie appearance of the group. Yet although they were coarse, common men, they were not, as one might have expected, a motley crew. Instead they seemed to be plain, rough farmers and shepherds, fishermen and miners, cobblers and tailors, the kind of hardworking men who must struggle to make ends meet and knew no other way than that to which the poor and the desperate, the daring and the ambitious had always turned in Cornwall; for I had no doubt of the men's occupation this night as wordlessly they began to unload the goods burdening the ponies. Hastily I drew back from the window, lest I should be seen.

My God, I thought, *Draco and Welles are smugglers!*

Yet, though somewhat frightened for their sake, since it was a hazardous, sometimes deadly, business in which my husband and stepbrother were engaged, I was neither shocked nor horrified by my discovery. In truth, I realized that deep down inside, I had half suspected that the two men must be involved in something like this, else they would not have been so secretive about their activities. But there had been smuggling in Cornwall for centuries, and it was a rare Cornishman who truly considered it a terrible crime. It was, if not an honorable profession, at least a widely accepted one, one that primarily injured the government, who deserved to have its coffers cheated for not repealing the Corn Laws and thus making it difficult for an honest man to earn an honest wage; and if it put food on the table and clothes on the back during these hard times, well, so much the better! Even Sir Nigel, the local magistrate before he had been murdered, had turned a blind eye and a deaf ear to the smugglers' comings and goings, for he had liked his brandy and cigars as well as the next man and had disliked just as fervently the hefty excise tax that must be paid on them.

Pulling my wrapper more closely about me, I sank to a chair, the wheels of my mind clicking furiously. I must say nothing about what I had inadvertently stumbled onto tonight, I decided, for if Draco had wished me to know of his stealthy enterprise, he would have told me about it himself; and I did not think he would be very happy to learn I had ferreted out the truth of his and Welles's joint venture. My husband was well acquainted with my inquisitive mind; no doubt he would believe I had been deliberately spying upon him. I must tread warily, I thought, if I were to keep his secret and thus avoid incurring his wrath.

But I had no time, just then, to reflect further upon my chosen course of action, for now at last Jarrett stirred and awakened, his cries no more than soft mewing noises initially. But if he was not fed, he would soon rouse the entire house with his screams, and I feared that then the smugglers would be observed by eyes other than mine. Rising rapidly, I cast aside my wrapper and untied the laces of my night rail. Then, crooning to Jarrett as I shifted the pillows on the bed and lay down beside him, I put him to my breast. Unlike Julianne had done her daughter, I had refused to relinquish my son to a wet nurse, for I enjoyed our closeness during this special time together, and I did not care if I was thought common for nursing my baby. Gently, as he suckled, I stroked his gossamer hair and sang to him softly a lullaby my nanny had used to sing to me:

> "Hush-a-bye, don't you cry,
> Go to sleep my darling baby.
> When you wake, you shall have
> All the pretty little ponies,
> Blacks, browns, and bays,
> Dapples and greys,
> All the pretty little ponies."

The words reminded me of the string of ponies in the yard below, and as my mind returned to what I had seen, I heard the tread of footsteps in the corridor to the north tower. Moments later, Draco opened the door of our bedchamber.

"Maggie!" he uttered abruptly, startled. "I did not think you would be up at this late hour."

His eyes narrowed thoughtfully as he gazed at me and the child, and I knew he was wondering whether I had heard Welles and the rest of the smugglers delivering their illegal goods to their temporary hiding place in the south tower.

"I should not have been if Jarrett had not been hungry," I replied quietly so as not to wake the baby, who, his appetite now sated, had drifted back to sleep, unaware of the dangerous intrigue that had taken place at the Heights this night.

My breath caught sharply in my throat at the thought, for if the excise agents or the dragoons should become suspicious of Draco and Welles and catch them in the act of smuggling, the two men would be imprisoned or transported or, at the very worst, hanged; and Jarrett would grow up branded the son of a common criminal. Swallowing hard, I hugged my baby close, pressing my cheek to the top of his downy head so my husband could not see the expression upon my face.

"You worked very late tonight," I commented as calmly as I could, knowing that there was a door in his study that led to the south tower and that he must have used it often enough when I had believed him to be bent over his desk piled high with his books and ledgers. "You must be tired. Come to bed, Draco."

"Is that an invitation, love?" he asked softly, quirking one eyebrow. Then, observing my surprise at his question, he said, "I have waited patiently, my sweet, for you to recover from Jarrett's birth, but I confess it has not been easy. Give me the child, Maggie. He is strong and healthy, like his father, and old enough now that he is not likely to die in the night. He shall do well enough in his cradle from now on, don't you think?"

Slowly, shyly, suddenly nervous as a bride, I nodded and handed him our son. After he had laid Jarrett gently in his cradle, Draco undressed, then blew out the lamp and slipped into bed beside me, the weight of his hard, muscular body settling into the soft feather mattress, causing it to dip so I slid into the indentation, feeling the touch of his skin against mine.

"Ah, Maggie," he breathed as he rolled over to take me in his arms, his chest crushing against my breasts, one thigh covering mine. "It has been so long since I held you like this. Too long. I have missed you, love...."

My heart leaped with joy at his words, for surely he would not have spoken them if he no longer cared! Trembling like a maiden, scarcely daring to believe he still wanted me, I parted my lips for his kiss and felt his warm breath brush my cheek in the darkness before inexorably his mouth closed over mine—hungrily devouring me with a rapacity whose wild exhilaration I had almost forgotten. Now, without warning, memories of his lovemaking came flooding back to me to mingle so intensely with the reality

of this night that for a moment, I did not know whether it
was truly his lips I felt upon mine or whether I only
dreamed he kissed me, his weight pressing me down upon
the bed, his fingers entangling my long black hair roughly
as he lifted my face to his. Again and again, his mouth
claimed mine, as though he were a man starving. His teeth
sank into my bottom lip, drawing blood, salty and bittersweet upon my tongue. Pleasure and pain erupted within
me, sharp and poignant as, more gently, he kissed away the
droplet beaded like scarlet dew upon my mouth. His tongue
traced the tremulous outline of my lips that opened eagerly,
vulnerably to his, swallowing his breath as a thousand
exquisite sensations swept through me, arousing my body
that had lain dormant these months past, sleeping, waiting
for him to waken it once more. Deep into my mouth, his
tongue plunged, searing me like hot honey, sweet . . . sweet,
melting my tongue until it flowed against his and I knew the
dulcet taste of nectar. It moistened my lips and trailed down
my throat to drip slowly between my breasts and spread in
rivulets to my nipples, laving them, engulfing them.

Heaven, or something very like it, I thought dimly in
some distant corner of my mind. *Eden, yes, Eden.*

For I was Eve, and Draco was . . . not Adam, but the
Serpent, dark and beguiling, tempting me, impatiently tearing away the virtuous modesty of my nightgown to expose
my nakedness and to feast upon that which was forbidden
fruit to all save him. I clung to him wantonly, reveling in the
sinfully delicious feeling of his mouth and tongue and hands
exploring the peaks and valleys of my body; and I roamed
his own flesh where I willed, making him gasp and quiver
and catch hold of me fiercely so I would know, despite my
power to excite him, which of us was the stronger.

"Enchantress," he muttered hoarsely against my throat,
"you would enslave me if you could, as I would you—and
shall. There is no part of you that is not mine. . . ."

Exultant, he showed me the truth of his words, pressing his mouth to the delicate arch of my foot as his eyes,
blacker than black with passion, lingered on my face,
mesmerizing me with their velvet depths. Deliberately his

lips burned their way up my leg, his licking tongue like flame, stabbing me with its heat. In its wake, light as a feather, his hands moved up my thighs, brushing like silk against the secret heart of me, then cupping my breasts, palms gliding over their dark, rigid buds swollen and bursting to unfold. Sweat trickled down the hollow between them, and slowly he lapped up the moisture with his tongue before teasing one taut nipple and then the other.

The sandalwood fragrance of him emanated from his bronze skin, permeating my nostrils as he buried his head between my breasts. My fingers burrowed through his hair, clutching him to me as I savored the closeness of him, writhed beneath him, yearning for more. My hands stole down his broad back, delighting in the feel of his powerful muscles that bunched and rippled beneath my palms as I dug my nails into his flesh, spurring him on. I kissed and touched him everywhere, intimately, as he did me, feverish in my aching need.

Time had no meaning for us, and the world spun away into nothingness, as though we had been cast out from its earthly realm into a place of blackness primeval, where all things began and ended with each other, where I was Draco's to command, his to bully and break and possess however he pleased, and he was mine to stroke and taunt and ensorcell until, with a low growl, he flung himself upon me, his desire for me and mine for him, honed to an unbearable edge as he thrust into me with a suddenness that took my breath away. I gloried in my helplessness against him, willingly cried out my surrender as he invaded me savagely, triumphant in his conquest.

Afterward we lay still, our hearts beating as one, damp skin gleaming in the dim light of the embers that smoldered in the hearth. Silently Draco drew me into the cradle of his embrace. My head nestled against his shoulder; one hand rested upon his matted chest, which gradually rose and fell more slowly and steadily beneath my palm.

"I love you," I whispered in a voice both tentative and longing, for I was half afraid he would mock me, and I knew I could not bear it if he did; yet I could no longer refrain from telling him of that which filled my heart to overflowing.

Holding my breath, I anxiously awaited his reply. But there was none, and at last, biting my lip to keep from laughing, and weeping, too, at the irony of my chosen moment, I realized I might as well have spoken to an empty room, for my husband was fast asleep, oblivious of my words.

Chapter Twenty-eight

Renshaw Speaks

It is not in the storm nor in the strife
  We feel benumb'd, and wish to be no more,
  But in the after-silence on the shore,
When all is lost, except a little life.

> —*On Hearing Lady Byron was Ill*
> George Gordon, Lord Byron

In the morning, when I awoke, Draco was gone, and had it not been for the slight soreness between my thighs and the deep feeling of contentment that pervaded my body, I should have thought I dreamed last night. Now I yawned and stretched like a cat, smiling to myself as though I were a child with a secret, so Linnet glanced at me sharply more than once as she busied herself preparing my bath and laying out my clothes. But I paid her no heed, determined that she should not ruin my day with her avid interest in poking and prying into other people's affairs. Instead I rose and fed Jarrett before turning him over eagerly for once to Annie. Then, after I had completed my morning toilet, I hurried downstairs, realizing that since today was Saturday, Draco would not have gone to the mines, for though the laborers worked six days a week and repaired machinery and so forth on the seventh, my husband was usually to be found in his study on Saturday and, like the Lord and masters, rested on Sunday.

After reaching the hall, I fairly skipped down the short flight of stairs to the corridor that led to Draco's study, my heart beating fast with joy and a nervous anticipation that caused my hands to shake so badly that I was forced to ball them into fists to still their trembling. When I stood before the closed door of my husband's private retreat, I paused and took a deep breath, anxiously smoothing my hair and gown, though I already knew from the dresser mirror in my bedchamber that there was nothing wrong with my appearance, that in fact, I glowed with the unrivaled radiance of a woman in love. I poised my hand to knock, then, frowning a little with puzzlement, slowly lowered it to my side as the sound of voices within reached my ears.

"We must take care, master. It be a foul, evil thing ta jibber t' kibber." I heard Renshaw speak, and for a moment, stunned like a person who has received a terrible shock, I thought my ears had played me some wicked trick. Indeed I prayed fervently that they had. But then the madman, muttering to himself, repeated the words. "Jibber t' kibber. Jibber t' kibber," he chanted as though it were some children's rhyme, "an' soon, thee'll preach at Tyburn's cross, with none in t' world ta mourn yer loss! Eh, master?" he asked, giggling slyly.

It was nonsense, I thought, meaningless babble, some foolish delusion of the lunatic's mind; and then suddenly I grew deathly still, cold and sick with horror and disbelief as Draco replied.

"Yes," he agreed grimly—chillingly. "But what does that matter to one who has committed so many murders that he can never wash his hands clean of the blood? You are right, Renshaw. We must take care. The excise agents and dragoons have grown suspicious and are on the alert. Inform the men to pay heed to what they're about, lest the jig be up before I can be rid of blame and we all find ourselves hanging from the gallows."

Fearing I was going to vomit, I did not wait to hear anymore. Stricken to the very core of my being, all of my happiness destroyed as utterly as though it had never been, I turned and ran blindly from the corridor, up the stairs to the hall, fighting down the bitter gorge that rose in my throat.

Jibber the kibber. Jibber the kibber. The words rang in my mind like a hideous death knell, hammered like nails into my heart, piercing it with such cruel agony that I could not breathe. *I could not breathe.* The walls of the Heights were closing in on me, and I was suffocating, I thought. As I had always done when attacked by the panicky sensation, I raced abruptly out of the house, banging the front door behind me in my haste to escape, uncaring that I had no cloak, that my thin slippers were unsuited to the layer of hard rime and powdery snow that encrusted the earth. After glancing wildly about the courtyard for a minute, I dashed through the open portals of the gatehouse, heading across the moors to the sea, sucking the cold winter air into my lungs painfully as, on and on, I ran, faster and faster.

At last when I could run no more, I slowed my pace to a walk, gasping for breath, a debilitating stitch in my side, an unbearable anguish in my heart. Dear God. It could not be true, I thought. My husband, Draco, was a murderer! I was in love with a cold-blooded killer!

There must be some mistake! There must be some mistake! my mind screamed over and over in protest at the notion.

But I had heard with my own ears the dreadful conversation in his study this morning; I had seen with my own eyes the evidence of his smuggling last night. I had been born in Cornwall. I had lived here all my life. I knew what it meant to "jibber the kibber." There was not a soul in Cornwall who did not, for it was the most heinous crime imaginable, so simple and yet so ghastly that I blanched at the thought of it: how, on a moon-dark night when the mist drifted like a ghost over the land and sea, vile men would row a boat out into the ocean and silence the warning bell buoys by wrapping thick flannel about their clappers. Upon returning to the coast, these same men would then lead a horse down to the shingle, where they would hang a lighted lantern about the beast's neck and tie up one of its forelegs so that when the animal moved, the lantern would appear like a ship's light, deceiving distant vessels with its false signal. By the time a prize so lured broke through the fog to realize its mistake, it was too late. It was already floundering helplessly in the brutal trough of the sea, caught by the pounding surf, a terrified prisoner being driven forward relentlessly to smash upon the perilous rocks protruding like sharks' teeth from the whitecaps, sails shredding, masts snapping, hull splintering as the slowly shattering ship rolled and plunged, was ripped and gouged until, groaning in agony, it shuddered and sank to its watery grave. And if all those aboard did not drown in the churning backwash of the sea that sluiced into the narrow channels between the rocks, the wreckers, as the sinister men who committed this monstrous offense were called, would take up their cudgels and wade out into the ocean to club the vessel's hapless victims to death as the poor, desperate wretches struggled to reach the shore. Then the depraved villains would retrieve the ship's cargo and rob the bodies floating on the waves. . . .

It was horrible! *Horrible!*

I buried my face in my hands, sobbing at the dark image in my mind of Draco among the wreckers, the maddened sea swirling high about his waist, his powerful arms, wielding a heavy stave, rising and falling again and again as he crushed the skulls of pleading, defenseless men, women, and children, or broke their arms and legs, so even the pitifully few among them who knew how to swim would drown, unable to move their limbs or even to stand so they could keep their heads above water.

No! *No!* My husband could not possibly be one of those inhuman men! Please, God. Surely he could not! I thought of his hands soothing Black Magic, caressing my body, cradling Jarrett. Those same hands had done murder, I realized now, shivering uncontrollably, and without warning, I doubled up and retched violently onto the ground. Afterward I wiped my mouth off with the back of my hand, then sank to my knees in the snow, hugging myself and rocking back and forth like a child. I was in a state of shock, I knew. My mind would not accept what it knew must be true. I could not believe it. It simply was not possible that Draco was a ruthless killer, though I knew full well the demoniac things he was capable of doing. "Gallow's bait," Sir Nigel had once called him, and in the village, there were those who said darkly that he had a "damned Tyburn face." No, it was not true! Draco would never do such base, abominable things, nor Welles. . . . No, not Welles, too; I shrank with horror at the idea that my stepbrother was a murderer as well, though I knew him for a rash, devil-may-care rogue. . . .

After a while, somehow, I forced myself to get up, to walk back to the manor, though it was the longest journey I ever made in my life, for the thought of returning there, to Draco, was frightening and abhorrent to me now. But where else could a woman with little family and few friends go? To Esmond, who was too weak to defend me? To Julianne, Lady Chandler, or Sarah, whose love for Welles would not permit them to believe me even if I were to bring them proof of what I had learned? To Aunt Tibby, who was afraid of her own shadow? To the vicar, who would merely listen to my confession and counsel me to have faith? No, there was no one to whom I could turn in this, my darkest hour. There was nowhere I could run that Draco would not find me. Like all women bound to vicious men, I must bear the knowledge of my husband's terrible crimes alone, in silence—and pray that it would not destroy me in the end.

Chapter Twenty-nine

A Heart Racked and Rended

Curst be the heart that thought the thought,
And curst the hand that fired the shot, . . .

—The Ballad of Helen of Kirkconnell
Traditional

I was not yet quite twenty years of age, but after that morning outside Draco's study, I felt as old and tired as though I were a hundred, and I longed for death just as fervently. There were dark crescent smudges beneath my eyes and hollows in my cheeks from too many nights of lying awake now and listening for the sharp ring of Black Legacy's hooves over the cobblestones in the courtyard to tell me Draco had gone out at some late hour; and when he returned, with the mist and rain of the slowly burgeoning spring clinging to his greatcoat, I would force myself to breathe evenly and pretend to be asleep so he would not touch me with his murderous hands. I cringed whenever he slipped into bed beside me, and I kept to its far edge as much as possible so I should not accidentally brush against him in the night. And when, inevitably, he demanded his husbandly rights of me, I lay cold and still as marble beneath him, seeing in my mind's eye the haunting images of the drowning men, women, and children fallen prey to his malevolence.

359

Draco did not understand my lack of response to him. How could he? For I dared not speak of what I had learned, but remained silent—and suffered as I had never suffered before. Sometimes when he saw he could not arouse me as of old, he grew angry and cursed me, accused me of lying with Esmond, and pressed me down upon the bed roughly to take his pleasure of me with a skill and deliberateness calculated to break through my defenses; and in the end, my treacherous body gave way to his demands, while I, in my shame, wept and longed for death as I lay beneath him. Then I thought of Jarrett, left to my husband's mercy, and I wanted desperately to live, so I swallowed my pride and fear, and I bore Draco's torment of me as best I could. At other times, sensing how appalled I was by him, he snarled at me viciously and flung me away from him in disgust. I was terrified of him, horrified by him, and whenever possible, I went to great lengths to keep out of his way. There was not a day that passed that I did not think of taking Jarrett, driving into Launceston, withdrawing my five thousand pounds from the bank, and running away. Only the frightening knowledge that my husband would surely pursue me and, upon finding me, as he doubtless would, would loose his merciless rage upon me prevented me from fleeing with my child.

And when, now and then, upon a moonless night, I heard the muffled jingle-jangle of a bridle in the yard below my bedchamber, I pulled the covers up over my head and forebore to look out the window.

But the heart knows no rhyme or reason, and sometimes, to my mortification and distress, I would find myself gazing at Draco and yearning achingly for the days and nights when, in my ignorance of his crimes, I had loved him; and then I must seek out some private place in which to shed my tears for all I had once known and lost.

And so time passed, the days one much like another, empty except for Jarrett. He was all my heart and joy now, and I clung to him as shingle clings to the shore. He at least was mine, if nothing else.

Spring was upon us now, the dormant land awakening

like a child from slumber, stirring gently, fretfully. The leaden sky of winter paled; the rains came to wash the scent of death from the earth, and in the air was the fresh, sweet smell of all new things. Slowly the sodden black moors grew green again, and the heather and bracken ripened until they were like a king's mantle of purple and gold spread upon the ground, folds rippling with each soughing breath of the wind. In the distance, the tors, stood like ancient gods surveying their domain, and the massive granite stones that were nature's megaliths and dolmens rose in splendor to cut a jagged swath against the far horizon. The ever-changing sea swept in to kiss the shore, and the slender black fingers of rock reached out to caress the lapping waves. In the cliffs that fell away to the beach, the gulls nested and sang their piercing song, and the melancholy melody echoed in my heart as I roamed the moors in solitude, and sorrow, and looked ahead to the long, lonely years that stretched before me.

Had I never known what it meant to love, I could have borne them if not gladly, at least stoically, I thought, believing that it was the lot of a woman simply to endure in a world that did not treat its women kindly. But now my heart battled my head, tearing me apart inside, for my eyes had been opened; I knew there could be more to life than mere existence, and I was restless as a bird who sees through the bars of its cage to the endless sky beyond.

How terrible would it be, I wondered, if I were to forget what I had learned that morning outside the door of Draco's study, if I were to blot from my mind the visions of broken ships and nameless faces that harried me? Would I then stand accused before my Maker, guilty as my husband, though my only sin lay in loving him, in being a woman weak as all women are when it comes to affairs of the heart? For it is a fragile, foolish thing—a woman's heart. Now I understood those reckless wenches of old who had offered themselves in a gallows wedding, those daring few who even in this day and age chose to stand at their man's side, though he be a pirate or rode the high toby, their love

stronger, in the end, than their fear of the brutal men they
had rather die for than live without.

I was torn by the realization that I should be a woman
such as they. But I could deny it no longer late one night in
March when Draco rode into the courtyard, his face white
as death, his life's blood pouring out of him from a bullet
hole in his chest. It was Renshaw who came to fetch me,
rousing me from my sleep and babbling so incoherently that
I could scarce make head or tail of what he said. I heard
only that "t' master be in a bad way, missus, fair ta turnin'
toes up, methinks," grasped only that Draco needed me and
begged me to come at once; and though my head counseled
me to remain in my room, to turn my back on my husband
and let him die as he deserved for his crimes, my heart,
beating queerly, refused to listen and instead compelled me
to respond to the lunatic's urgent tug upon my sleeve.

Somehow Draco had got to his study, where he lay
upon his horsehair sofa, his eyes closed, his dark skin
ashen, his chest rising and falling so shallowly that for a
moment, my heart leaped to my throat because I thought he
did not breathe at all. The folds of his greatcoat lay open to
reveal the blood that seeped from his wound, staining his
jacket and the snow-white lace of his fine cambric shirt with
crimson, and at the sight of all that blood, my head spun so
that I feared I would faint.

"Renshaw, wake Will," I said, hurrying to Draco's
side, "and tell him to ride for Dr. Ashford."

"Nooooo," Draco groaned, startling me, his voice
low, his eyes opening slowly, with effort. Deliberately he
gritted his teeth against the searing agony of his injury.
"No . . . doctor . . . Maggie."

"Don't be a fool! You're like to die!" I spoke more
sharply than I had intended. "Are you so eager, then, to
make me a widow?"

"Never you . . . fear, love." He smiled at me weakly.
" 'Twill take . . . more than a—than a bullet . . . to finish me.
Do whatever . . . needs to be—to be done, my sweet, but
no . . . doctor."

Then he gasped and winced with pain, and realizing I

would only waste time by arguing with him, I forced myself
to gather my wits and set about tending my husband. I had
little experience in such matters, certainly none at all with a
gunshot wound. Nevertheless I rolled up my sleeves and,
taking a pair of scissors from a drawer of Draco's desk,
began carefully to cut away his garments so I could judge
how much damage had been done. Sweat beaded his brow
and upper lip as I worked, and more than once, I had to
pause and wait for the trembling of my hands to cease
before I could continue. But though I knew I must be
hurting him terribly, he made no complaint; and at last,
slowly, I pulled away his shirt sodden with blood to reveal
his injury. My breath caught in my throat at the sight of it,
for I saw that had the bullet entered a few inches lower, it
would have pierced his heart.

"Draco, who did this to you?" I asked, for it was
obvious this had been no accident, but a deliberate attempt
on his life.

But he either would not or could not answer, and I
frowned at him with concern, certain his silence indicated
that this assault upon him was somehow the result of his
smuggling—or worse—and this last, I did not wish to reflect
upon. If he were to confess to me that he was, in truth, a
wrecker, I knew I should be sick unto death, for there was
still some part of me that refused to believe it, that hoped
and prayed it were not true. Taking a deep breath, I turned
to address Renshaw.

"Fetch a basin of warm water and some clean cloths
and bandages—quietly, so as not to waken the household,"
I instructed, as though to a child. "Do you understand me,
Renshaw?"

"Aye, missus." He nodded and shuffled off.

I had my doubts about whether he did, but finally he
returned, bearing the items I had requested; and I began to
wash away the blood upon Draco's flesh so I could examine
his wound more closely. Fortunately the bullet had gone
straight through his chest and out his back, for which I was
deeply thankful, for I should not have liked to attempt to
remove a piece of lead from him. Thus there was actually

very little for me to do besides cleanse the injury and staunch the bleeding. After I had got most of the blood wiped away, I took a bottle of brandy from a nearby cabinet and, uncertain how much was sufficient, poured almost half the amber liquid into the small hole in my husband's chest. Then, after folding the bandages into several thick pads, I pressed them to the wound, front and back, and bound up the whole.

By then, Draco was unconscious, I thought; but to my surprise, he once more opened his eyes and, fumbling like a blind man, reached for my hand, giving it a small, weak squeeze that I somehow found more painful than anything else, knowing the power that was normally present in the grip of his strong fingers.

"I knew you'd . . . not let me . . . down, my brave girl," he murmured, looking so proud of me that I was suddenly stricken by shame when I thought of how, earlier, I had considered leaving him alone to die.

"Draco, who did this to you?" I inquired again.

"I don't know," he replied, veiling his eyes, so I knew he lied. "It was . . . too dark . . . to see. Help me upstairs . . . to bed, Maggie."

"I'll do no such thing!" I spoke tartly, knowing that to press him further for answers to the many questions that plagued me was useless.

"Yes, you will, for . . . if you do not, I shall . . . attempt to get there on . . . my own, and I shall—shall no doubt fall down the—the stairs, rousing the servants. More grist for the . . . gossip mill. You wouldn't . . . like that, would you, love?" He grinned at me crookedly, causing my heart to turn over in my breast, and once more I thought to myself that surely I had made some dreadful mistake in believing him a wrecker, a murderer.

Sighing and making it plain I thought him a stubborn fool indeed, I helped him to his feet, and with Renshaw on one side and I on the other, we managed somehow to get him upstairs. He was nigh to swooning from shock and loss of blood, and so was only too glad to collapse upon the bed. His pale, perspiring face was gaunt and drawn, and quickly

I poured him a small glass of wine from the decanter upon the night table. He drank gratefully, then, moaning a little, finally drifted into slumber.

But I . . . well, I stayed away a very long time after that, examining my conscience and my heart, torn between the two and wondering if God would understand if I pressed my husband's hand to my cheek, just once, without thinking of sinking ships and bodies floating on the waves of the sea.

Despite his injury and my admonishments, Draco perversely insisted on getting up in the morning, dressing himself, and going to the mines. I railed at him heatedly over the matter, to no avail. He staggered to his feet, stumbled toward the wardrobe, and stubbornly began to struggle into his garments. At last, realizing that my protests were futile, that he was in great pain but determined to have his way whether I helped him or not, I finally relented and assisted him with his clothes, thankful he was neither a coxcomb nor a dandy who must have his jackets cut so tight and narrow that even a clever valet would have difficulty fitting them on him.

"You are behaving foolishly," I scolded nevertheless, scowling at him. "If you persist in this madness, your wound will break open and begin bleeding again. Then everyone shall know of your injury, which I'm sure you do not want, since you would not let me send for the doctor last night—no, nor Esmond either. He is the local magistrate, whether you like him or not, and should be informed of this scurrilous assault upon you so the culprit responsible can be ferreted out and punished as he so justly deserves. Oh, do get back into bed, Draco! Do! You can barely keep your feet. The mines will not fail if you are not there to oversee them. Mr. Vaughan is an excellent manager—or so you have certainly told me often enough—and Mick Dyson, for all that he is a vicious brute, must be a capable head foreman as well, else you would not have retained him after my father's death."

"Indeed," my husband uttered dryly. "Dyson has a cool,

clever head on his shoulders, I'll grant you that. 'Tis not just anyone could have survived as he has.''

"Yes, well, I suppose he is a fighter, like you, Draco."

"No, Maggie. Not like me. Never like me," he replied grimly, his black eyes glinting fiercely, a strange, frightening look coming over his face, so that without warning, the cold, sick hand of fear once more reached out with cruel fingers to close around my heart.

Chapter Thirty

Dark Before
the Rising Sun

> Straightway I was 'ware,
> So weeping, how a mystic Shape did move
> Behind me, and drew me backward by the hair:
> And a voice said in mastery, while I strove—
> 'Guess now who holds thee?'—'Death,' I said.
> But, there.
> The silver answer rang—'Not Death, but Love.'

> *—Sonnets from the Portuguese*
> Elizabeth Barrett Browning

It was on the eve night of my twentieth birthday that Esmond came to arrest Draco.

A dreary spring night, it was, of chill wind and mist and rain; a moonless night upon which I should not have been surprised to hear the muffled ring of a bridle in the yard, for Draco, scarcely recovered from the bullet wound in his chest, had ridden out earlier, saying not to wait up for him, that he would be late returning home. A fatal night, it was, one that was to change my life forever, though I did not know it then, when I first heard the knock upon the door.

"Sir Esmond, missus," Mrs. Pickering announced as she showed my visitor into the hall.

I glanced up, startled, from the book I was reading, for

it was nigh on ten o'clock and I could not think why Esmond should be calling at such an hour—or, indeed, at any hour. My heart gave a queer little lurch; my hands flew to my throat, for I knew there must be something very wrong.

An accident, I thought. *There has been an accident—or worse*—the terrible memory of that bullet hole in my husband's chest, of his life's blood flowing out of him haunted me—*and Draco is dead.*

And because at the idea that my husband lay cold and still forever, such a vast, terrible emptiness gripped me, I knew at last, with certainty, that my love was stronger than my fear of him, that if all in the world should perish tomorrow and only Draco remain, I should be glad beyond my wildest imaginings. Slowly I laid aside my book and rose.

"What is it, Esmond?" I asked, surprised to hear how quiet and composed my voice sounded as I crossed the room to greet him. "What has happened? Is something wrong, Cousin?"

Then I saw that Hugh and several other men from the Hall and the Grange accompanied him—armed men—and though I was still afraid, hope now leaped in my breast as some dim inkling of their purpose glimmered in my mind. Draco was alive! Esmond should not have needed armed men otherwise. There was upon his handsome countenance a look I had never before seen, a look of alertness, of eagerness, of triumph, as upon the face of a hunter when he closes in on the wily fox; and I thought: *He has ever hated Draco and longed for me, though when I was his, he scorned me. Now somehow he has learned Draco is a smuggler, a wrecker, a murderer, and he is here to seize him in the hope of claiming me. . . .* Yet I was not filled with joy, as I would have been once, at the realization. Instead I felt nothing but contempt for my cousin, who must come like a thief in the night to the Heights and bring armed men to do his dirty work. But I said naught of my thoughts, revealed no trace of them upon my face. If Esmond had come here to do some injury to me and mine, I would hear it from his lips.

"I am not here as your cousin, Maggie, but as the magistrate," he announced coolly, confirming my suspicions, jerking his head toward his men, who began grimly, efficiently, to search the house. "Where is Draco?"

And because I was certain now that if my husband were to be dragged away in chains and hanged, my heart would lie with him in his lonely grave, I did not at once answer, but played for time.

"What is the meaning of this, Esmond?" I queried sharply, indignantly. "I think you owe me some explanation— do you not?—for invading my home at this hour—and with armed men who have set about to poke and pry into every nook and cranny of the house. What is it that you think to find?"

"Dearest Maggie," he began, taking my hands in his and leading me to a chair. "Sit down, for I fear that what I have to tell you will come as a great shock to you, though in the end, you will be overjoyed to be rid of that monster who is your husband."

"I'm afraid I do not understand you," I remarked with pretended confusion as I sat, my heart thudding very hard and fast in my breast, my mouth dry, my palms damp with sweat. "Whatever can you mean, Esmond?"

"Sweet Cousin, I do not know how to soften the dreadful blow of what I must tell you, for naturally you can know nothing of what that vilest of creatures, Draco, your husband, has done." He ran one hand raggedly through his hair, a sure sign of agitation, so I knew he was not as calm and collected as he would have me believe, but was frightened, too, of Draco; and I felt some small but keen satisfaction that the taste of Esmond's victory should have an acid edge.

"Have you ever heard of the wreckers, Maggie?" he asked suddenly, his voice low and tinged with revulsion.

"But of course," I rejoined. "Who in Cornwall has not? What has that to do with Draco?" I paused as though considering, then opened my eyes wide. "Oh, Esmond!" I whispered and prided myself that my voice was appropriately faint and aghast. "Are you—are you saying that he—that he . . . is one of—one of those depraved men?"

He nodded, his face filled with disgust and loathing.

"Yes, unfortunately I'm afraid I am," he admitted. Then, rushing on, he cried, "Oh, dearest Maggie, to be forced to tell you such a thing! You cannot help but be shocked and horrified, as I was, by the knowledge! I have suspected it for some time now and have been watching him, hoping to catch him in the act. But he has been very cautious, very clever in carrying out his abominable crimes. I have learned little. But then, some days ago, your abigail, Linnet, came to me, in a state of the greatest distress, and reported that she had spied Draco and his reprehensible followers on the beach one night, had actually witnessed them in the very act of sinking a ship and murdering all those aboard! She was utterly terrified—and who could blame her? But somehow she summoned her courage and kept her wits about her. She followed the wreckers to the Heights, where she discovered that Draco was using its south tower as a temporary hiding place for his ill-gotten cargo."

Oh, sly, wretched girl! I thought with fury. *Evil snake whom my husband gave a place in his household when Father turned you off without a reference. To bite the hand that has fed you! For shame! For shame!*

Her betrayal stung me like a whip; but still I did not falter, was not swayed in my purpose of learning from Esmond all that I could in the hope of somehow saving the man I loved. Yes, *loved!* Dear reader, I confess it to you willingly, gladly, with all my heart. Though I might burn in hell for all eternity, I now knew I would cast my lot with Draco—be he murderer or no—uncaring if I were damned for my sin.

"And just what was Linnet about," I questioned, "that she had so little care for her virtue—her very life!—that she wandered along the coast after dark, unwittingly stumbling on to such deadly intrigue and exposing herself to further danger by sneaking after the wreckers, as you claim? A foolhardy act, that, surely, if it is true."

"Yes, indeed. But still one cannot help but admire the risk she took. As to why she was roaming the coast—" Esmond shrugged. "She did not say so in so many words, but I surmised that she must have been meeting a lover. Have you so little heed for your household, Maggie, that you are unaware of your servants' surreptitious comings and goings?"

I stiffened at his criticism.

"Decent maidens do not slip away after dark to rendezvous with lovers, Esmond. I had no reason to suppose Linnet was other than chaste. But I see now that she will have to be dismissed posthaste, for I will not have Annie and the housemaids, who are good girls, led astray by her brazen behavior," I declared, conveniently forgetting the fact that I had been guilty of such folly once, too.

He made no reply, for just then, we were interrupted by his men—Hugh chief among them. As he stepped forward to address Esmond respectfully, the groom's eyes lingered on mine compassionately, for he had ever loved Draco and me, and he had his doubts about my husband's guilt.

"We be finished with our search, sir," he said to Esmond, "exceptin' the south tower, fer which Mrs. Pickring claims she has no key. Mr. Draco is not ta be found. I've posted guards around t' house, as 'ee directed. He'll not be gettin' past 'em, sir, if he thinks ta return here tonight."

"Well done, Hugh. We shall be taking our leave, then. I want you and those men not watching the Heights to accompany me to the coast. It appears Miss Tyrrell was correct when she informed me that she overheard Mr. Draco and Mr. Prescott planning another attack to be carried out tonight! Yes, Maggie"—he noted my sudden start—"as difficult as you may find it to believe, Welles is in on the malignant plot, too. Did I not tell you he was a rash scapegrace, no fit husband for Sarah?" Esmond's voice was smug, and I had never despised him as I did then, for in that moment, I saw clearly that he was not only weak and a coward, but petty and spiteful to nurse all these years a grudge born of his childhood argument with my stepbrother at the Launceston fair. "Draco and Welles shall not get away with their diabolical scheme this time, however, for we shall be there, patrolling the coast, and we shall catch them in the very act of crime!'' He stood.

''I will bid you good night, sweet Cousin,'' he declared, ''and apologize for the ill tidings I have brought, for I know they are as repugnant to you as they are to me. But still you cannot help but be glad to be released from your vows to Draco, Maggie,'' he insisted, lowering his voice as he gazed at me with naked yearning, ''for I know you have never loved him. When you are free—But, no, now is not the time to speak of such things, I know. I must hold my tongue and bide a while yet. Nevertheless, rest assured, dearest Maggie, that you have ever held my heart,'' he confessed softly.

I was stunned by his words, for I had thought him resigned to his marriage to Julianne. Now I saw that instead he had built up in his mind a great, unrequited romance between us and had made Draco the villain responsible for keeping us apart. Somehow Esmond had reached the erroneous conclusion that I would be his if he but removed my husband from the sphere of my existence. Calling to his men, my cousin turned on his heel and departed, leaving me dazed and appalled, as he had known I would be, though it was not Draco's crimes that caused my chagrin, but the things Esmond had said, for I would not have him now—no, not even if I were free, and he also.

I do not know how long I sat there in the hall, mulling over all he had told me and pondering what I must do, consumed by despair at my helplessness to save my husband, to warn him that within hours, he and Welles would be walking into a trap Esmond had so mean-spiritedly laid and intended to spring shut upon them; for I knew that though it was his duty as the magistrate to apprehend criminals, my cousin had demonstrated to me that he relished his job tonight far more than the role required. He was, in fact, exultant at the idea that Draco should hang and that I should be released from the bonds of matrimony. What could Esmond be thinking of? I wondered. Did he plan, then, to divorce Julianne for me, no matter the scandal, or did he hope that I should suffer no qualms about becoming his mistress since, after all, I had lain with a murderer these many months past? This last must be the case, I decided slowly, for I could not imagine that Esmond's love for me would prove stronger than his desire to avoid having his reputation tarnished. I was infuriated by the idea that he believed I could be brought to his bed without benefit of clergy.

There must be some way to elude the guards he had posted, I thought. But none came to mind; and at last I rose, having some dim notion that there might be something in Draco's study to assist me, a gun perhaps, which I might use to get past the sentries, who would not know whether my husband had taught me how to load and shoot the weapon. In truth, I knew little about firearms. I was even less certain of my ability to point a pistol at any of the guards and to shoot one or more of them if it became necessary. I knew only that I was determined to escape from the manor however I could, to find and warn Draco of the danger that awaited him on the coast.

Now, as, taking a lamp from the hall to light my way, I moved quickly but surely down the short flight of steps to the corridor that led to my husband's study, I thanked God that Esmond believed that I still loved him, that I would be so horror-stricken as to be rendered insensible by his revelations, and so he had not bothered to set one of his men to watch over me. But I was neither weeping nor hysterical, as I should have been had I not already known much of what my cousin had told me. In fact, now that I had made my passionate decision to stand by Draco regardless of the cost, I discovered that my mind was calm and clear as it had not been for weeks; my thoughts were logical and deliberate as I set down the lamp and began methodically to search my husband's desk and cabinets.

At last, tucked away in the slender drawer of an occasional table, I found that for which I had hunted: a small, pearl-handled silver pistol that could fire two shots. The gun felt cold and heavy in my hands as I examined it carefully, not knowing whether it was loaded. How innocent in appearance, it was, and yet how deadly. To think that a bullet propelled from one of its chambers would actually kill someone! To my surprise, I was morbidly fascinated by the thought, and briefly I was tempted to pull the trigger simply to see what would happen. But of course I did not. Instead I gingerly dropped the pistol into my skirt pocket. Then I turned to go.

I froze, holding my breath as, without warning, the door to the south tower started to swing open on well-oiled hinges. Instinctively I doused the lamp, my heart pounding with fear as I stood there listening intently in the darkness, wondering whom—or what—would appear before me.

"I told t' master 'twere bad business ta jibber t' kibber," I heard Renshaw, to my relief, mutter to himself as he slipped into the study, lantern in hand. "Now t' jig be up, methinks. Hee, hee! There'll be them what dangle in a Tyburn string fer it, aye—But, wait! Did I not hear tell that t' Tyburn tree be torn down now? Curse me, I cannot remember. . . . Well, no matter, there'll be them what pay t' piper right enough, an' then we'll see if there's them what say I don't know what's what!"

"Renshaw!" I hissed, causing the poor madman nearly to start out of his skin.

"Eh? Who's there? Who's there?" he shrieked excitedly. "Oh, it be 'ee, missus, be it?" His crafty eyes narrowed suddenly with suspicion as he observed me. "What be 'ee doin' here? Can 'ee not see t' master ain't here? He'll not like 'ee pokin' yer nose inta what don't concern 'ee, missus. What did 'ee see? What did 'ee see? Nowt. Nowt, fer there's nowt in t' south tower ta see save ghosties. 'Tis ghosties, missus, that's all, what haunts t' tower on a moonless night." Furtively he reached out to grasp my arm. "Nivver tell t' master I said otherwise, missus, will 'ee not, eh? I meant no harm, none—I swear it! I would have waited fer 'em—them what brings t' cargo—just as t' master bade me. But there's men outside, missus, men what would hang a poor old sod, 'cause they don't know—they don't know what I could tell 'em if I had a mind ta. But I don't, 'cause they'd not listen ta me anyway, me, an innocent fellow who did nowt but follow t' master's orders. Aye, that's what I thought—an' said ta meself, 'Renshaw, if 'ee get back ta t' gatehouse, they'll not know nothing' of yer part in it, an' so thee'll be safe then. Thee'll be safe.' So I thought. Lud, missus! Thee'll not tell 'em 'ee seen me, will 'ee?'' he sniveled, wheezing, his eyes abruptly wide with alarm as he tugged pathetically at my sleeve. ''Thee'll not tell 'em aught of me, will 'ee, then, eh, missus?''

''No, Renshaw, no,'' I said, bewildered by much of his babble, but not mistaking his terror. ''I shall say nothing. But listen sharp now, for the master's very life depends upon it! Those men—the ones you saw outside—they mean to harm the master. Do you understand me, Renshaw? If the master returns here tonight, those men shall take him prisoner and kill him!''

''Aye, missus.'' He nodded sagely, mumbling to himself again. ''He did fear t' jig'd be up afer he'd got a chance ta put matters aright.''

''I must find him, Renshaw, and warn him—before it's too late! Somehow I've got to get out of this house and into the stables without being seen!'' I pondered the matter aloud, knowing, even so, that it was impossible.

But then, to my astonishment, Renshaw announced, ''Aye, well, if it be ta help t' master, I reckon 'tis all right, then, missus, if yer privy ta t' secret. But, mind: Yer ta say nowt of it ta t' rest, fer Miss Linnett . . . she's not ta be trusted, nay, fer t' master said she was not.'' Then, satisfied at last that I should mention nothing of what he showed me, he led me into the south tower, and there he pulled up a trapdoor in the floor to reveal a set of steep, narrow stone stairs that disappeared into a dark, yawning chasm. '' 'Twas used in t' olden days ta reach t' stables durin' t' rain an' snow,'' he explained. ''Follow t' tunnel, missus. It'll take 'ee ta where 'ee wish to go—me life on it!''

Then, without warning, his fear finally getting the better of him, the lunatic thrust his lantern into my hand and scuttled off before I could stop him. Biting my lip anxiously with sudden indecision, I glanced after him with some annoyance for his desertion. He had at least been someone to talk to. Now, knowing his wits were addled, I was not certain I could trust him. Perhaps he had lied to me. I did now know. Still, finally, aware that I was wasting time and seeing no other alternative but to follow Renshaw's directions, I turned back to the aperture that gaped before me. My heart thudding, I started slowly to descend the stairs.

The tunnel was dank and musty, thick with slime and dust, and rank with decay. As I moved forward apprehensively, small stones from the crumbling walls crunched and skittered beneath my feet, and rats chittered angrily and scurried away. Cobwebs brushed like sheer ghosts against my face and arms, making my skin crawl. Above me, I could hear the rain pitter-patter upon the earth, and eerily I thought: *That is how it would sound to one buried in a grave*. The idea unnerved me. Suddenly feeling as though I would suffocate in the close confines of the corridor, I abandoned all caution, hastening my pace until I was practically running through the dark passage, the lantern swinging wildly as I held it up high to light my way.

To my relief, I reached the tunnel's end within moments and, after racing up the steps at its terminal point, pushed open the trapdoor above me and clambered out, gasping for breath as a chill draft swept over me. Incredulous, I saw that I was indeed inside the stables, as Renshaw had vowed. He had known what he was about after all. Sending a silent prayer of thanks to God for that, I set down the lantern. Crooning to reassure the horses, I took a bridle from the tack room and approached my handsome Welsh pony, Patch. Normally he pulled the trap, but as he was sturdy, surefooted, and less likely than Avalon to be spied by Esmond and his men, I entered the pony's stall and coaxed a bit between his teeth. Then, after glancing out the stable door to be certain I was unobserved, I led him quietly outside. Once I was safely away from the yard, I mounted his bare back and set off at a rapid trot across the moors.

Unlike Highclyffe Hall, the Heights was not entirely surrounded by a stone wall, so it was possible for me to ride west toward the cliffs at the edge of the sea without having to pass through the front gates of the manor. Once I had gained the jagged headland, I kicked Patch into a gallop,

riding like the wind along the cliffs. The pony's hooves
thudded deeply into the wet, spongy ground, sending turf
flying, but I knew the sound would not be heard above the
roar of the ocean, and so I had no fear. Instead a thrill of
something wild and daring and utterly exhilarating shot
through me as I bent my head low over Patch's neck, feeling
the cool spring wind damp with the sea and the drizzle
tear ruthlessly at my hair, while the spindrift cast up
by the whitecapped surf sprayed against my face, soft as a
lover's kiss; and I thought of Draco, his lips upon mine, and
I lashed the pony on as though the hounds of hell pursued
me.

Hurry, hurry, hurry! my mind chanted over and over;
and then, unbidden, came Tourneur's answering line: *Ay, to
the devil.* . . . And I remembered how the words had goaded
me on toward my nemesis and my downfall that night upon
the moon-dark stretch of moor where I had first lain with
Draco, and I saw clearly that I had lost not only my
maidenhood to him then, but my very soul, else I would not
now have embarked upon this mad race against time and
Esmond.

For a moment, some spark of sanity flaring in my
mind, I almost turned back. But my heart was like a hawk
swooping across the sky, crying out and soaring recklessly
on, and I knew I had no choice but to follow. Driving Patch
harder still, I pressed on through the fog and rain.

I headed north, some instinct urging me in that direction, though I knew if I had chosen wrongly, I should be
forced to retrace my steps and so would no doubt be too late
to save my husband. Still the northern coast was wild, rocky,
and isolated; no villages lay along it, so there were no prying
eyes to spy the wreckers at their work. There would be none
but I—and Esmond and his men—peering through the misty
darkness, searching intently for the deadly, deceptive glimmer of a lantern moving like a ship's light; and so I rushed
on, my hair, pummeled by the wind and rain, tumbling loose
from its pins to whip savagely back from my face. The cool
night air stung my eyes, filling them with tears, blurring my
vision so that I could scarcely believe it when at last, my

heart leaping to my throat, I saw the dim, intermittent flicker of a flame just beyond in the distance. That was it! It must be!

And now, like a madwoman, hearing the hands of time ticking ominously in my mind, I struck Patch again and again with the trailing ends of the reins, so he stumbled and nearly fell, then recovered to lunge forward with all his might, his breathing labored, white foam flying up from his lathered coat. I was not cruel, but I think in that moment I did not care if I rode the brave little pony to death.

The lantern flashed its false signal, and now, through the fog, I could glimpse the white sails and slender masts of a tall ship that, lured by the vile light, slowly approached the coast, unaware of the danger that lay ahead.

No! Turn back! Turn back! my mind screamed, but still the fleet schooner came on, tossed upon the surging waves.

Far below, dark, amorphous figures began to emerge from their hiding places among the rocks, a tall, massively built man at their head. It must be Draco, I thought, and strained to discern his features in the darkness, a horrible sinking sensation suddenly knotting the pit of my stomach.

I felt chilled to the very marrow of my bones, for deep down inside, until this dreadful moment, I realized some part of me had clung desperately to a fragile thread of hope that he was not truly guilty of his terrible crimes. Yet even now, when I could see him standing there upon the beach, his face concealed by the shadows of the night, I could not bring myself to abandon him to his fate.

I had no care for myself, only for the man that—right or wrong—I would love with my last, dying breath. Galloping toward a place where the cliffs fell away to the shore, I found a steep, narrow path that led down the coast. For the first time, Patch balked; but I had come too far to be cheated now, and with all my strength, I forced him on to the treacherous, winding track. It was slick with rain; my numb hands were like ice upon the reins. The pony slipped and slid until I thought we should plummet over the edge in the blackness to be broken upon the rocks below. But then gallant Patch got his footing, and we leaped on to the solid shingle that encrusted the beach. His hooves clattering sharply upon the stones, we raced toward the wreckers.

The doomed vessel drawing nearer and nearer rose and fell upon the waves that carried it ever forward toward the perilous rocks that thrust up like thick, spiny bramble along the coast. Its sails flogged in the wind; its elegant bow sliced through the sea. Sick with dread, I knew that in moments, it would be caught by the pounding surf and dashed against the fatal boulders. The wreckers, howling with glee, gathered like sharks who have caught the scent of blood, waiting to fall upon their prey and rip it to shreds.

"No!" I sobbed, my voice rising to a scream. "No, Draco, no! It's a trap! It's a trap! For God's sake—"

And then suddenly I was rolling upon the hard shingle, knocked violently from the pony's back by a powerful black form that rose like a giant bat from nowhere to fling itself upon me. The impact of the brutal blow was horrendous. As Patch, whinnying shrilly with fright, ran on heedlessly, I lay stunned and helpless beneath my unknown attacker, flattened against the beach by his weight, the breath forced out of me painfully, a jagged edge of shingle gouging cruelly into my cheek.

"Lie still, damn you!" a man's voice snarled murderously in my ear, as a hand clapped over my mouth. "And if you value your life, don't make another sound!"

And petrified, certain it was death that tangled its fingers roughly in my hair, pressing my head against the sand and stone, I did as I was bidden. My heart beat with terror as, held captive, I could do naught but watch as the ship the wreckers had so wickedly tricked plunged forward upon the frothy, churning sea to break free of the fog at last.

So this is how it ends, I thought with despair, a sob catching in my throat as the schooner rushed toward the rocks that loomed before it menacingly. *In seconds, it will be finished.*

But to my utter amazement, at the last minute, like a miracle, the vessel heeled hard to starboard in an astonishing feat of daring and seamanship that prevented it from being imprisoned by the trough of the ocean; and then all hell broke loose as armed men in uniform—dragoons—came running from every crack and crevice of the scarred headland to surrounded the wreckers. Chaos reigned as shouts and shots rang out in the night and men scrambled over the wet boulders and grappled upon the beach. I did not understand what was happening, for now I could see Esmond, and the men from the Hall and the Grange, too, arriving at the scene, looking as startled and confused as I; and upon the deck of the ship, his feet planted wide apart, a rifle held purposefully in his hands as he fired at the wreckers on the shore, Welles stood recklessly, his blond hair unmistakable.

Without warning, the man who held me fast lunged to his feet, snatching me up and shoving me savagely behind a rock. Then incredibly he growled "Stay here, you little fool, for I intend to beat your pretty backside black and blue when this is over!" And I glanced up with shock and disbelief into the bold, gleaming eyes of my husband.

"Draco!" I breathed, then cried out, *"Draco!"*

But he was already racing down the coast into the melee, his greatcoat flapping about him wildly in the wind.

The Misbegotten
1820

Chapter Thirty-one

Better Days
and Happy Endings

> Grow old along with me!
> The best is yet to be. . . .
>
> —*Rabbi ben Ezra*
> Robert Browning

The Cornish Shore, 1820

And now, dear reader, I am come at last to the end of my story.

It was not Draco who led the wreckers, but Mick Dyson, as I learned when the dragoons finally managed to round up all the men on the beach. Draco and Welles were only smugglers, a crime that paled into insignificance when I thought of what I had once feared. I discovered that it was Dyson, as well, who had tried to kill my husband and had murdered Sir Nigel, for the vicious Irishman had been using various abandoned regions at the china-clay mines to store his foully obtained cargo. How my father found out about Dyson's hideous activities, I shall never know. Perhaps one of the miners, angry at the Irishman's lack of support for their cause, somehow stumbled onto the knowledge and reported it to Sir Nigel in the hope of a reward. But that is only conjecture. Dyson, suspecting that my father had learned of his activities and intended to arrest him, had

384 • REBECCA BRANDEWYNE

killed him. Draco, of course, had taken far more of an interest in the mines than Sir Nigel, and so he had become curious as to why there were certain areas into which the Irishman never permitted the laborers to venture. After that, it had been a simple matter for Draco to spy upon him and ferret out the truth.

It was through his mistress, my traitorous abigail, Linnet, who was hand in glove with him, that Dyson had first learned of my husband's own smuggling. Fearing that Draco was on to him and meant, when he had collected sufficient proof, to expose him for his wretched crimes, the Irishman had sought, by his threats to me that day at the miners' rows, to warn Draco off. Then, when that had failed, Dyson, like all such men who cannot resist boasting of their cleverness, had begun to drop various hints here and there, so Draco had realized the Irishman meant to turn the tables on him by making it appear as though my husband were the wreckers' leader. Draco had known then that he'd have to work fast if he were not to be hanged himself—not only for smuggling, but for murder. It was Renshaw's remarks to him in this regard, and his own reply, that I had overheard that morning outside his study and so horribly misinterpreted.

Seeing that Draco was not to be scared off, Dyson had then tried to kill him. When that had failed, the Irishman had made one last-ditch effort to incriminate Draco in his stead as the wreckers' leader. Knowing, along with the rest of the village, how Esmond despised Draco and Welles, Dyson had brazenly sent Linnet to Highclyffe Hall with her misleading tale of my husband and stepbrother's deeds.

Meanwhile the two men themselves had finally gained enough evidence to convince the dragoons in Launceston of Dyson's guilt. Together they had devised a plot to ensnare the Irishman. For a fortnight, while Draco and the dragoons had waited upon the shore, Welles had sailed the *Sea Gypsy* up and down the coast, watching for Dyson's false light. Upon observing it at last, Welles had signaled to Draco the wreckers' location, and my husband had alerted the dragoons, who made their way to the spot and hid until the Irishman and his followers should show themselves.

It was bitterly ironic that Linnet, eavesdropping on Draco and Welles discussing their scheme to entrap Dyson, had caught no more than the words "the dark of the moon" and "watch for my signal" and had presumed the two men were planning another smuggling run on the night of the new moon. She had dutifully informed Esmond of this, and naturally he had come with his men to the Heights to catch Draco in the illegal act. In the meantime, Dyson, thinking my husband and the magistrate both would be otherwise occupied for the evening, had seized what he had considered an excellent opportunity to deceive yet another ship and relieve it of its cargo, with very little risk to himself and his men.

Welles, of course, knowing the northern coast of Cornwall like the back of his hand and not being taken unaware by the wreckers, had been able to prevent the *Sea Gypsy* from smashing upon the deadly rocks.

Of his and Draco's own smuggling, the dragoons knew nothing; and though they would no doubt wonder about it, as Esmond had, when Dyson and Linnet finished telling their own story, there was no proof to condemn my husband and stepbrother. The south tower was empty; and if at one time it had not been, the dragoons, satisfied with this night's work, would probably not delve too deeply into the matter.

All this, I discovered from Draco as I sat, shivering and wrapped in his greatcoat, upon one of the boulders, watching numbly as the dragoons snapped manacles on the last of the prisoners and herded them away.

"I know that Dyson and his men will hang, but what will happen to Linnet, Draco?" I asked softly, feeling a strange pity for her, for none knew better than I why she had stood by her lover's side.

"I imagine even now that some of Captain Latham's men are on their way to the Heights to arrest her," my husband averred. "She'll plead her belly, of course, and if by chance she actually *is* with child, she'll save herself from the gallows for a time at least. Mayhap they'll transport her in the end."

I nodded, swallowing hard, thinking of the difficult life

she would have if she were spared the gibbet and sent to an Australian penal colony instead.

We fell silent then, for now Esmond approached, looking so sick and ashamed that I almost felt sorry for him. His eyes were filled with deep regret when he gazed at me; but I saw in them, too, a sad, bittersweet resignation at the realization at last that whatever love we had ever shared years ago in our youth was irretrievably lost to us now, as those halcyon days of our childhood were gone, never to come again.

I had thought Esmond weak and a coward; but now, as hesitantly he held out his hand to Draco, I knew that I had misjudged him, that he was but a man, and thus flawed, as we all were. He had made mistakes, as we all had; that was all. Gruffly he cleared his throat.

"I . . . believe I owe you an apology . . . Cousin," he addressed my husband with Sarah's quiet dignity, his acknowledgment, finally, of Draco's relationship to him saying more than mere words ever could.

For a time, I thought Draco would not reply, but then slowly he reached out and shook Esmond's hand.

"So . . . we are quits at last now, are we . . . Cousin?" My husband spoke. " 'Tis best that way, I think. 'Tis all so much water under the bridge now, isn't it?"

"Yes. Yes, it is." Esmond was silent for a minute. Then, swallowing hard, he turned to me. "Maggie . . ." His voice trailed away. He glanced down at the ground, then back up at me. Then he stretched out one hand to smooth back the hair from my face as he had used to do in our childhood, the small, loving gesture speaking for him the words he could not say. "Be happy," he whispered, anguished, and walked rapidly away.

With tears in my eyes, I watched him go, saw him pause and shake Welles's hand, too; and I knew I should not be surprised to hear presently that Sarah and my stepbrother were to wed.

The ebony sky was paling now, fading gradually to grey with the approaching dawn. The rain had stopped; the dragoons and the rest had gone. Now only Draco and I, the misbegotten, remained, perched upon the rocks indelibly stained with the blood of a thousand poor, lost souls. The mist was beginning to lift; the wind blew gently, rippling the tall grass and heather upon the commons. There was no sound save for the breaking of the ocean upon the shingle and against the rugged cliffs, and, from above, the sweet, aching cry of a lone gull as it rose to circle slowly against the sky.

"Why did you come, Maggie?" Draco asked in the hush. "When you thought me a murderer, why did you risk your life to bring me warning?"

For a moment, I was still, gazing at the wild moors and the rough sea that were so much a part of me, and of my husband, too. The spindrift kissed my lips; the brine tasted of salt, like tears.

"Because I love you," I breathed. "I have always loved you. I know that now." I glanced at the shingle beneath my feet, then looked up at him, my heart breaking because I had never told him before. "Oh, Draco, have I left it too late?"

For a long time, he did not answer, and I died a hundred deaths, trembling with the chill of the spring dawn and the winter in my heart. Then he spoke, and a faint, joyous hope stirred, hesitant as a young maid, in my breast.

"I would like to think not, Maggie," he admitted. Then he smiled at me slowly, crookedly, his dear, familiar grin. "What do you say, my girl? Shall we try it again?"

"Yes. Oh, yes. I'd like that very much," I said.

And the sun streaked, rose gold, across the far horizon as together we began the long ride home.